about that fling

about that fling

TAWNA FENSKE

Montlake
Romance

Published by Montlake Romance, Seattle

www.apub.com

Amazon, the Amazon logo, and Montlake Romance are trademarks of Amazon.com, Inc., or its affiliates.

ISBN-13: 9781503944268
ISBN-10: 1503944263

Cover design by Shasti O'Leary-Soudant / SOS CREATIVE LLC

Printed in the United States of America

For anyone who's survived a divorce or bad breakup and come out on the other end bruised and weary, but smarter, tougher, more self-aware, and above all, hopeful.

Chapter One

Jenna McArthur wrapped her lips in a tight "O" around the slender shaft, sliding it back along her tongue as she gently began to suck.

She drew back with a sigh, choking a little on a mouthful of Diet Coke as she reread the note she'd pulled from her lunch bag.

Visualize your inner sex goddess today, sweetheart!
Love, Aunt Gertie

Jenna slid the little neon pink card into the small pocket on the back of her iPhone case and toed off her high heels beneath the desk.

I gave it my best shot, Gert, Jenna mused as she unpacked the rest of her insulated lunch tote. *Performing fellatio on a soft drink may not have been the best starting point.*

She pulled out a menagerie of glass containers with bright plastic lids, followed by a napkin edged with hand-stitched lace.

"God bless you, Aunt Gertie," Jenna said aloud, eyeing her aunt's

Tawna Fenske

homemade fettuccine in red pepper cream sauce, garlic rosemary focaccia, fresh strawberries hand-dipped in chocolate—

"Jenna, I'm so glad I caught you."

She looked up to see the public relations director hovering in the doorway. Marie clasped her hands at her waist the way she did when trying to avoid biting her nails or punching someone in the face.

So much for my peaceful lunch, Jenna thought as she set down her fork. "Marie, what can I help you with?"

"Have you seen the headlines?" Marie stepped into the room and glanced behind her as though expecting a swarm of rabid journalists armed with sharp pencils and sharper machetes. She pushed the door shut and seated herself at the edge of the chair in front of Jenna's desk.

"I haven't touched the newspaper yet today," Jenna said. "I've been in meetings all morning. What's up?" She made a discreet attempt to shove her feet back in her shoes but only managed to wedge the left one awkwardly on her right foot. Marie didn't seem to notice.

"The landfill discovered a bunch of medical waste. Dirty gauze, bloody surgical tubing, that sort of thing."

Jenna glanced at her container of fettuccine tangled in a sea of luscious red sauce and pushed it aside. "The medical waste is ours?"

Marie nodded. "The Belmont Health System logo was all over everything."

"We have procedures in place for medical waste disposal. What the hell is going on?"

"Off the record?"

"Marie, I'm the Chief Relations Officer, not a reporter. My job isn't to broadcast our problems, it's to fix them."

Or to sweep them under the rug like I always do, she thought grimly.

2

"Right." Marie bit her lip and leaned closer. "Well, rumor has it some vigilante members of the nurses' union are doing it on purpose. You know, to get a bunch of scandalous headlines in the paper so the public pays attention to what's going on with the contract negotiations."

Jenna felt her temples start to throb. "Find out if it's true. In the meantime, tell any reporters we're reviewing the purchase of an on-site unit for medical waste incineration. It would save up to sixty thousand a year and improve efficiency by forty-three percent."

"Really?" Marie stood up and smoothed her skirt. "Okay, I'm on it."

"And find out who the hell is trying to make us look bad," Jenna called as Marie marched out the door.

Alone with her lunch again, Jenna reached for the Caesar salad. It was drizzled with her aunt's homemade dressing and dotted with croutons she'd helped Gertie bake the night before. She should probably run down the hall and heat up the focaccia bread, but with her luck—

"Jenna, I'm glad I caught you."

She sighed and set down the salad. "Jon, what can I do for you?"

The CEO folded himself into the same chair Marie had just vacated and thumped his briefcase down on Jenna's desk. He popped it open and pulled out a sheaf of paperwork, giving Jenna a clear view of the risqué-looking paperback beneath it.

Panty Dropper by G.G. Buckingham.

Jenna grimaced and forced her attention back to the CEO.

"It looks like the nurses are getting serious about striking," he said, waving the papers at her. "We have to avoid this."

"We have to avoid the ugly verbal battles around the bargaining table," she said, trying not to let her gaze drop to the dog-eared novel in the briefcase. "That's not helping."

"I wouldn't call it 'ugly,' exactly. Let's not take things out of context."

"Brett Lombard told you to shove the proposal up your ass, and you retorted that his mama got there first. In what context would that be a form of respectful discourse?"

The CEO frowned. "Fine, it wasn't our best moment of communication. Moving on—" he paused, flipping through the paperwork. "We've had complaints from the cafeteria staff about some of our purchasing decisions. Take organic produce, for instance. Apparently five percent of domestically grown romaine lettuce carries salmonella and shigella."

"Okay," Jenna said, frowning down at her salad. "So we'll have them buy produce from another vendor."

"The union is pointing to this as an indication of unsafe practices and unsanitary working conditions. They say if we don't negotiate different contracts for—"

A knock at the door snapped Jenna's attention to the front of her office. She looked up to see her elderly aunt peering into the room.

"Oh, dear," Aunt Gertie said, reaching up to smooth her cotton-white perm. "I'm so sorry to interrupt, sweetie. I thought you'd be on your lunch break."

The CEO stood up and beamed. "Gertrude. So good to see you again. How's the hip?"

"Wonderful, Jon, thank you for asking."

"I know those medical bills were a challenge. If there's anything I can do—"

"Oh, that's so sweet of you," Gert interrupted, reaching out to pat the CEO's arm. "But don't you worry. I found a way to manage and everything's just wonderful. I actually just finished my physical therapy and stopped by to ask Jenna a question, but I'll skedaddle and let you finish your meeting."

"Nonsense," the CEO said. "I shouldn't be interrupting her lunch anyway. We can finish another time."

He reached for his briefcase, and Jenna watched as Aunt Gertie's gaze fell to the cover of the novel. Gert's eyebrows lifted, and Jenna felt her stomach clench as a satisfied little smile crossed Aunt Gertie's face.

The CEO saw it, too, and offered up an awkward chuckle. "Yeah, I know. The wife stuck it in there this morning and told me I should read it. Apparently it's a big runaway summer hit."

"Erotic romance is certainly popular these days," Gertie said, nodding pleasantly. "Are you enjoying it?"

"As a matter of fact, I am."

"Delightful!" Gertie said, folding her hands together and flashing a cherubic smile. "Give Sharon my regards, will you?"

"Absolutely." The CEO shoved the papers back in his briefcase, and Jenna felt a flood of relief. He tucked the briefcase under one arm and turned back to her. "I'll catch up with you later. By the way, have you met the new HR manager?"

"No, not yet," Jenna said. "I didn't even realize you'd made the final hiring decision."

"I'll introduce you next week. She's bringing in a mediator to work with the bargaining team. One of those woo-woo types specializing in positive communication and labor relations. There's a meeting Monday."

"I'll have Sally add it to my calendar."

Jon nodded, then turned and sauntered from the room. Jenna smiled at Gertie and gestured to the empty chair. "Have a seat."

"I don't want to bother you, sweetie. I was just in the neighborhood."

"Trust me, you're the most welcome sight I've had all day. Well, next to your fennel root tart," she added, popping the lid off another Tupperware container. "This looks incredible."

"I made the crust from scratch last night."

"It looks fabulous. Thank you so much for lunch, Aunt Gertie."

"My pleasure, dear."

"So what did you need to ask me?"

Gertie reached into her handbag and pulled out a little notepad with daisies on the cover. "I was working on my grocery list while I waited for my PT appointment. Do you think you'll be home for dinner?"

"Probably not. I'm meeting Mia at the wine bar. It's my duty to drink her share now that she's pregnant."

"Give her a big hug for me. I've been knitting some booties for her baby."

"She'll love that."

Gertie cleared her throat and glanced down at her notepad. "Tell me, sweetie, do you think 'man root' should be one word or two?"

Jenna pushed aside the fennel root tart and closed her eyes. "Is that your grocery list, Aunt Gertie?"

"Right—yes right, of course. The grocery list."

Jenna pressed two fingers to her temple, wondering how long she could keep up this charade of pretending not to know how Gert managed to pay all those medical bills. "I suppose it depends on the context, but—"

"She devoured his turgid man root like a succulent piece of fruit covered in chocolate—"

"That's an awfully long item for a grocery list," Jenna interrupted, pushing the chocolate-dipped strawberries to the back of her desk. "I think 'man root' should be two words."

"You're sure?"

"Absolutely."

"Okay then." Gertie stood up and tucked the notepad back in her purse. "I have to run. Don't work too hard, sweetie."

"Thanks, Gertie. I love you."

"You too, dear," she said. "Oh, and sweetie? Try to get laid tonight at the wine bar."

Jenna opened her mouth to reply, but Gertie had already bustled out of the room, the soft scent of lavender sachet trailing behind her.

Jenna surveyed the array of containers and tried to find something appealing. Maybe the focaccia bread—

"Jenna, I'm so glad I caught you—we need to talk about contract negotiations."

Suppressing a sigh, Jenna set down her bread and looked up to greet the president of the nurses' union. Remembering Marie's habit, she clasped her hands on her desk, appreciating the decreased risk of turning to strangulation as a solution.

"How can I help you, Brett?"

He yanked off the scrub mask dangling around his neck and shook his head. "I've gotta tell you, things are taking an ugly turn. If this keeps up, our JCAHO scores are going to be in the toilet." He frowned down at the assortment of containers on Jenna's desk and shook his head. "Speaking of toilets, the average desk has four hundred times more bacteria than a public bathroom. You really shouldn't eat lunch in your office."

Jenna glanced at the knife Gertie had packed, wondering how sharp it was. Then she glanced at the neon pink note she'd tucked in the back of her iPhone case.

Looks like I won't be embracing my inner sex goddess anytime soon, Aunt Gertie.

She tried not to feel glum about that as she pushed everything aside and slid her hands to her lap.

"I can promise there's zero risk of me eating anything at my desk. So tell me, Brett, how can I help?"

⌒～∂

Adam Thomas walked into The Corkscrew at seven forty-seven. He knew that because he glanced at his watch at least three times en route to the bar.

"Meeting someone?" the bartender asked, wiping down the mahogany surface with a cloth.

"Good guess," Adam said, laying claim to the lone vacant barstool in the place. "Is it always this packed on a Wednesday night?"

He shrugged. "It's Portland. A wine bar's a hot place to be whether you're having a business meeting or a baby shower. Can I get you a wine list, or do you know what you need?"

"I'm not sure. I just realized I got the time zone wrong and I'm an hour early for my meeting. Maybe I should come back."

"You meeting a woman?"

"What?"

The bartender nodded toward a bistro table in a darkened corner. "That woman over there said she's waiting for someone. Thought she might be who you're meeting."

Adam studied the slender brunette with glossy, shoulder-length hair and amazing legs. She'd kicked her shoes off under the table and was staring down at her phone with a slight frown. A lock of hair fell over her face, and as she reached up to tuck it behind her ear, Adam felt something twist in his gut.

"That her?" the bartender asked.

"It could be."

Hell, he had no idea whether the hiring manager was male or female. Every e-mail message had been signed "Kendall Freemont," and the one phone exchange he'd attempted had given him an automated messaging system with a robotic voice.

It was possible the woman in the bar was Kendall Freemont, but more possible Adam just wanted an excuse to talk to her. He pushed himself off the barstool, legs propelling him in the direction of the mystery woman while his brain remained behind asking if this was a good idea.

"Excuse me, Ms. Freemont?"

The woman looked up and blinked at him with eyes so deeply blue, he forgot his name.

She frowned at him. "I'm sorry?"

"Kendall Freemont," he repeated dumbly, knowing this couldn't possibly be his eight-thirty appointment, but wanting to stay and talk to her anyway.

"Hello, Kendall—I'm Jenna. It's nice to meet you."

Her eyes were friendly and welcoming, not at all the expression of a woman who thought he was there to hit on her, or if she did think that, she didn't seem to mind. She uncrossed and recrossed her legs, and Adam forgot his name again.

"No, Adam," he blurted. "I'm Adam, and I'm meeting Kendall, but I'm an hour early. Actually, I'm not even sure if Kendall is a man or a woman, and I thought you might be her, but you aren't."

It came out sounding more like a question than a statement, and Adam realized he urgently wanted her to be Kendall so he could have an excuse to sit down with her. She smiled, and he felt his fingers clench around the handle of his briefcase.

"Nope, I'm not Kendall, but you're welcome to hang out if you can't find a table." She tucked a little neon pink card into a pocket on the back of her phone case before pushing the phone aside. "Looks like my girlfriend had something come up at the last minute, so I'm just going to finish my Sangiovese and head home. Feel free to park it here if you want to nab my table when I leave."

"Thank you, that's very kind." Adam eased into the seat across from her and immediately felt his crotch vibrate. It took him a moment to realize he had a text message. Pulling the phone out of his pocket, he glanced down.

"This must be the night for people to get stood up," he said. "My appointment just canceled on me. Too bad, I was looking forward to that Sangiovese."

"You're a Sangio fan?"

He shrugged and shoved the phone back in his pocket. "Actually, no. I'm not even entirely sure what Sangiovese is. But I've been on a quest to try new things, so that seemed like a good one to add to my list."

Jenna lifted her glass and signaled a passing waiter. "This particular Sangiovese is a good one to start with. A little spicy, hints of strawberry and cherry, medium tannins. Very drinkable."

"In that case, why don't you order another?" He nodded at her glass, which had only a tablespoon of liquid left in the bottom. Hardly enough to keep her here as long as he hoped to talk to her. "My treat. I've been flying all day and I'm wiped. Besides, we might as well drown our sorrows since we've both been stood up for the evening."

She seemed to hesitate a moment, one finger sliding over the pocket on her phone case. Then she smiled. "Sure, why not?"

He ordered for both of them—two glasses of the Sangiovese she suggested and a cheese plate that sounded like the right thing to go with wine, though what the hell did he know? He'd always been more of a cocktail fan, or at least he was when he'd been married. They'd even bought a liquor cabinet and took turns trying out new recipes. That was back before things had gone to hell, before she'd decided she was done with him and moved on with—

"So you're not from around here?"

Her voice jolted him off the dark path he'd been headed down. He met her eyes, trying not to let his gaze stray to her breasts. "What makes you think I'm not a Portlander?"

"You said you'd just flown into town."

"Actually, I said I'd been flying all day. Maybe I'm a pilot. Or a pterodactyl."

"Excellent point. It's also possible you live here and you're returning home after traveling someplace else, but that's clearly not the case."

Adam tugged at the knot in his tie to loosen it. "Oh? What gives me away as non-native to Portland?"

She grinned and took a sip of wine. "Your tie is too straight, your shirt is too pressed, and you don't appear to have any piercings or tattoos."

"Maybe you're not looking in the right places."

He couldn't believe how blatantly suggestive his words came out, and he almost apologized. But instead of tossing her drink at him, she grinned wider.

"Maybe I'm not," she said, her eyes darting to the bare ring finger on his left hand. "I'll have to do a more thorough examination."

He let his own gaze stray to her ring finger, visibly bare on the stem of her wineglass. He brought his eyes back up to meet hers, and she gave him a knowing smile.

"Now that we've gotten the obligatory ring check out of the way and reassured ourselves we're not sharing drinks with a serial philanderer, tell me about yourself," she said.

Adam leaned back in his chair, not bothering to hide his intrigue. "How do you know I'm not a serial philanderer?"

"No tan line where your ring would be, but there's a tan line on your wrist. I saw it when you checked your watch a second ago."

The waitress returned and set down two glasses of wine, along with a platter heaped with at least a dozen mounds of fancy crackers, crumbly cheeses, and cured meats. He plucked an olive and a handful of crackers, arranging them neatly on the small plate in front of him.

"You're very observant," he said.

"I try."

"Are you a private detective? Clinical psychologist? International terrorist specializing in wine-bar espionage?"

She laughed, a sound so sweet and musical he wanted to break out a book of knock-knock jokes just to hear her laugh again. "International terrorist. I like that. Much more exciting than my real profession." She took a sip of wine and set her glass down. "I think I'm going to claim that as my job for the rest of the evening. Thank you for the idea."

"Glad to aid with a positive career change."

"I'm an international terrorist and espionage expert who invented a patented wiretap that doubles as a wineglass."

"A winetap?"

"I see you've heard of it." She leaned forward in her seat, and Adam caught sight of a flash of black lace down the front of her dress. "So how about you?"

"What about me?"

"What's your fantasy job for the evening?"

"Hmmm. How about a chef?"

She smiled over the rim of her wineglass. "I think you can do better than that. Something sexier."

"Sexier," he repeated. He picked up his own glass, emboldened by the liquid and by the sound of that word coming from those perfect lips. "I'll be a gigolo."

"A gigolo?"

"A high-class gigolo. My client—an esteemed senator from California—was meeting me here this evening for a rendezvous, but she got cold feet when she saw the media camped outside waiting to do a big exposé."

"I hate it when that happens." Jenna reached for a piece of cheese. She chewed thoughtfully for a while, then took another sip of wine. "It's just as well. As a terrorist spy, I would have been forced to report any illicit activity to the government, and the next thing you know, the senator's face would be plastered all over CNN."

"No, not CNN," Adam said, keeping his eyes on her face as he unbuttoned his cuffs and began to roll up his shirtsleeves. "In addition to being a sought-after gigolo, I'm also a billionaire media mogul who owns most of the major news outlets around the world."

"You don't say."

He nodded and picked up his glass again, taking a careful sip of wine as he forced himself to hold a serious expression. "Yep. CNN, NBC, ABC, CBS—they're all mine."

"BS?"

"That one, too. Also all the newspapers and magazines in the world. I write all the articles for most of them. Very tedious work."

"Good job on last month's *Cosmo* cover story on finding your G-spot with a golf club and a pair of stilettos."

"Thanks. I initially planned it for *Sports Illustrated*, but we couldn't get Arnold Palmer to wear the stilettos."

"Maybe for next year's swimsuit issue," she said. "I just turned down the opportunity to pose for the cover, so I know they're looking for someone."

Adam snapped his fingers in mock recognition as his brain flashed on an image of Jenna in a bikini. "That's right! I thought

I recognized you as an international supermodel. I saw your *GQ* cover last month, and I really love that photo spread you did for the *Journal of Mutation Research and Genetic Toxicology*."

"Shh!" she said, bringing a finger to her lips. "It's part of my cover as an international terrorist. Don't tell."

"Your secret's safe with me."

She crossed her legs under the table again, and Adam tried not to stare. The supermodel thing wasn't so off base. God, she had amazing legs. He wondered what her real profession was, then decided he'd rather not know. There was something to be said for the thrill of reinventing oneself. He sipped the last of his wine and signaled the waitress for another.

"This wine is really good," he said. "Fruitier than I was expecting. Seems like something you'd drink with lasagna or spaghetti."

"Good call." She smiled over the rim of her own glass. "The grapes were actually grown in the Chianti region of Italy, and there are a lot of similarities between a good Sangiovese and a good Chianti Classico."

"You also work as a sommelier when you're not spying for the Russians and posing for *Vogue*?"

"No, I own ninety percent of the vineyards in the world. I stomp all the grapes myself."

"No wonder you have such great legs."

She grinned and sipped the last of her wine. The waitress paused at the table to ask if she wanted another glass, and Jenna nodded.

"Just half a glass, though."

"A full glass for me, thank you," Adam said. "I have to catch up."

He turned back to Jenna, who was nibbling a piece of cheese. "Try the prosciutto. It's really good."

"This brie is amazing." She smeared some on a cracker, then looked up at him. "So how about you?"

"I don't know that I'd call myself amazing, but I try."

She laughed and bit into her cracker. "No, I mean when you're not gigolo-ing for politicians and writing *Cosmo* quizzes, what sort of hobbies do you have?"

"Ah, I have a diverse range of talents and interests. I crochet office furniture, train and breed fighting beetles, and make abstract potato art. Maybe you've seen one of my gallery shows?"

"Yes, I think so." She took a sip from her new glass. "I must've run across it in the Ashmolean when I was at Oxford earning my doctorate in aromatherapy."

"Was this before or after you attended ninja training camp?"

"Before the ninja thing, but after I won the Ultimate Fighting Championships by strangling a man with my thighs."

"Good skillset for an international spy."

She reached for a piece of prosciutto and Adam tried not to get distracted by the delicate fingers and the lovely, fine bones in her wrist. Whoever this woman really was, she had beautiful hands. He shifted in his seat and kicked over his briefcase, which landed with a smack on the tile floor.

Jenna looked at it, then back at him. "Good thing you didn't have a bomb in there."

He righted the briefcase with his toe and swirled the wine in his glass. "What makes you think I don't?"

"Secret spy sense. Also, I'm telepathic. I can read your mind."

"Oh yeah?" He took a drink of his wine, surprised to realize he'd nearly drained the glass. He wasn't tipsy—not by a long shot—but he did feel bolder. More daring.

He smiled at Jenna and watched something spark in her eyes.

"Okay, then," he said, holding her gaze as he leaned toward her over the table. "What am I thinking now?"

She paused, looking hesitant. There was something about her posture and the primness of her dress that made him think flirty banter wasn't her usual fare, and he felt his ego do an absurd fist pump at the thought of it.

Seeming to decide something, she ran a finger over the rim of her glass and leaned toward him across the table. "I have to say, I'm a little shocked. Well, shocked and intrigued."

"Oh?"

"Yes, your thoughts are rather . . . *explicit.*"

Adam smiled as something surged from his brain to his lower extremities. "Guilty as charged."

"You are a gigolo, so I suppose it goes with the territory. Still, I wasn't aware your services extended to strange women you'd only just met in a bar."

"I'm an equal-opportunity gigolo."

"I see." Her finger made a slow journey around the rim of the wineglass, circling one way, then the other. Adam felt his mouth begin to water.

"What do you normally charge for your gigolo-ing?" she asked, her tone casual as her eyes slid to her phone again. It was face down, so she wasn't checking messages, and it crossed Adam's mind to ask about the neon pink card she'd tucked there.

But instinct told him to stick with the subject at hand. "First round of gigolo service is on the house. I'm toying with the idea of a buy-one-get-one-free coupon in *Ladies' Home Journal.*"

"Very sensible of you. A gigolo with marketing skills."

"And telepathic powers. Did I mention I can read minds as well?"

She looked up at him through her lashes, her fingertip poised on the rim of her glass. "Oh? So what am I thinking now?"

Adam swallowed, hoping like hell he was reading this right. Hoping he hadn't misjudged this whole flirtation and the signals she seemed to be sending. He lowered his voice and leaned closer. "You're thinking the same damn thing I am."

She nodded and licked her lips. "I'll get my coat."

Chapter Two

The instant his eyes snapped open, Jenna was ready. She twisted the bedsheet in her fingers, steeling herself.

"I don't normally do this," she blurted.

He blinked at her, green eyes registering surprise, then confusion, then approval. She flushed and tugged the sheet up over her breasts, wondering if she should have opened with "good morning."

She licked her lips and tried again, conscious of his liquid gaze, of the pleasant warmth in the thin layer of bedding that separated them.

"I don't normally hook up with strange men I meet in bars, I mean," she said. "I had a couple wild months in college, and two or three flings in my twenties, but since I turned thirty a few years ago, I've been so focused on my career that I've only had time for the occasional monogamous relationship—well, and one broken engagement—but that was two years ago and I've really only ever had one other one-night stand in my whole life, so really, this is foreign territory for me and I'm a little uncomfortable."

He nodded, taking in her blur of words. Or her disheveled hair and makeup. Really, she should have planned better, should have run to the bathroom first and splashed water on her face and brushed her teeth with a fingertip. God, she was so out of practice.

"Hello."

His voice sounded low and husky, and Jenna remembered all over again why she'd fallen into bed with a strange man.

Was it wrong that she kinda wanted to do it again?

"Hi," she replied, feeling absurdly shy. "Hello. Hi there. Howdy."

He smiled again, and her stupid heart did a somersault in her chest. She wanted to feel embarrassed, but instead she just wanted—well, *him*. Again. At least two or three more times.

He sat up in bed, the sheet falling away from his chest to reveal the sculpted muscle and fine dusting of hair she'd had such fun exploring the night before. She remembered how it felt pressed against her breasts and wondered if there was any chance she'd get to enjoy that again.

Adam closed his eyes and yawned, stretching in a way that reminded her of what it felt like to have those muscular arms anchored on either side of her body, pinning her down on a hotel bed as she gasped and writhed beneath him.

He opened his eyes and looked at her. "You're staring."

"Sorry."

He smiled. "Don't be. About anything."

"Right." She swallowed. "Um, the thing is—"

He grabbed her around the waist, pulling her close and silencing whatever excuse she'd been ready to make. She thought he was going to kiss her and her whole body arched with approval—to hell with morning breath—but he stopped short and smiled into her eyes instead.

"How about we skip this part?" he asked.

"Which part is that?" She squirmed against him, then stopped as her hip bumped something hard beneath the covers.

"Not *that* part, though you did spend most of the night becoming intimately familiar with it. I'm also well-acquainted now with your parts, which means we're now downright friendly."

She flushed. "Yes, well—"

"So how about we skip the routine where we pretend we had too much to drink and regret it and wouldn't do again. Because I didn't and I don't and I would. Repeatedly."

She blinked, a little surprised by his words, or maybe it was his body. His hand slid over her hip and she shivered in spite of the warmth. She couldn't find any words, so she nodded. "Are you suggesting we consider this more than just a one-night stand?"

"I'm game if you are," he said. "I enjoyed your company, even before we took our clothes off, and I think you felt the same."

"I did. I do."

He reached up and brushed her hair off her face, his hand large and gentle. "Look, I'm not suggesting we start addressing our wedding invitations over brunch, but I'd like to see you again."

Jenna gasped.

"Brunch!" She threw the covers back, shooting out of bed so fast she sent him sprawling across the mattress. She scrambled around the floor, snatching clothes and shoes from piles that looked like the remnants of a yard sale.

"Wow," he said, his eyes following her around the room. "I've never seen a woman so enthusiastic about mimosas and eggs Benedict."

Jenna yanked on her panties and searched for her bra, wondering if she should shower before doing the walk of shame back home.

"No, it's brunch. I'm meeting my best friend and my aunt to look at wedding photos and baby clothes."

His brow furrowed as Jenna grabbed one of her shoes off a high-backed chair. "Which one of you is getting married and having a baby?"

"Not me, I promise. Have you seen my bra?"

"Over there on the lampshade. Is this the aunt who gave you the note about embracing your inner sex goddess?"

Jenna felt the heat creep into her cheeks as she wriggled into her bra. "I can't believe I showed you that. Yes, of course."

"Mission accomplished. Consider her embraced and ravished."

She smiled and ordered herself not to blush again. "I'll ask for a gold star as soon as I get home."

"So can I see you again?"

"I'm not sure." She found her earrings on the nightstand, along with a glass of lukewarm water she gulped down in two quick swallows. "You're not married, right?"

"Definitely not." Something in his tone made her look up, and she caught a glint of steel in his green eyes.

"Spoken like a man who either has a body in his trunk or an ex-wife in his past."

He smiled, and the steel softened a little. "No on the body, though I can't say it never crossed my mind. The divorce was messy."

"Kids?"

"No. No prison record, either, though I did get a speeding ticket when I was twenty-one." He picked up her dress off the chair by the bed and handed it to her. "So can I see you again?"

She accepted the dress and yanked it over her head, stumbling into her shoes. "I had a really nice time with you," she admitted. "A *really* nice time. Not just the sex."

"Likewise."

"All the articles say it's impossible to have any sort of relationship with someone after you've slept together on a first date."

"Technically, we haven't had any dates."

"Good point."

"We gigolos are known for our persuasive skills and solid reasoning."

She gave up her urge to play it cool and let the smile spread unhindered across her face. "What is it you really do for a living?"

"I'm a counselor."

"As in *attorney*, or as in *shrink*?"

"Yes."

She wasn't sure she understood the joke, or even if it was a joke, but there was one way to find out.

"Okay. We should have a real date."

"How about dinner?"

"I like dinner."

"Then it's settled. Now turn around."

She did as he said, and before she could ask why, he was zipping up the back of her dress. His fingers felt warm on her skin, and she shivered remembering all the things he'd done with those fingers.

She turned back around, not feeling any less naked now that she was fully clothed. "Thank you. For everything, I mean."

"Don't mention it."

She glanced down at the nightstand and noticed a notepad beside the condom wrapper. *Wrappers.* She reached for the pad and a pen beside it. "Here's my number. I've got a jam-packed weekend and I'm pretty tight at work this week, but maybe next Friday?"

He took the paper from her and squeezed her hand. "Next Friday. Following your busy work week spying for the Russians and giving aromatherapy to fashion models."

She nodded, wondering if she should volunteer her real occupation or ask to know something about him besides the fact that he had a killer body and a keen ability to make her laugh and come her brains out in a span of ten minutes.

But his lips found hers, and she forgot all about her questions.

"Until next Friday," he said, kissing her again, "I'll be thinking about you."

Jenna floated all the way home, feeling like a giddy preteen with a secret training bra smuggled under her T-shirt. She hesitated for an instant at the front door, breathing in the fragrance of bacon and homemade potpourri and the heady, comforting scents of home.

It hadn't always felt like that. Not before Aunt Gertie's broken hip and Jenna's broken engagement. Somehow, all the broken pieces had fit themselves together, mended into something that felt more like home than the little bungalow had ever been in the six years Jenna had lived here. As an added bonus, it was only two blocks from Belmont Health System.

Jenna smoothed the front of her dress, then opened the door to a warm cloud of German apple pancakes. She took two steps into the room and tripped over something. Glancing down, she saw a box filled with neat stacks of bookmarks, each one adorned with half-clad bodies and the words *Panty Dropper*.

She grimaced and nudged the box aside with her toe, tucking it discreetly under the bench by the door. Then she looked up to see two pairs of eyes staring at her.

So much for sneaking in undetected.

"Woohoo!" Mia called, her mouth full of pancake. Her friend

tossed her long red hair over one shoulder and grinned. "Look who's doing the walk of shame."

Aunt Gertie beamed and set a crystal bowl of powdered sugar on the table. "Congratulations, dear. I'm so proud of you."

Jenna set her purse down and joined them in the breakfast nook, her cheeks faintly warm with embarrassment. "Jeez, you guys—you'd think I'd earned a promotion at work instead of a notch on my bedpost."

"You get work promotions all the time," Mia said, waving a dismissive hand. "An all-nighter with a strange man, on the other hand—that's a much bigger deal."

"I appreciated your text message last night, dear," Gertie said, patting her hand. "I was glad to know you were safe."

Jenna picked a piece of apple from the edge of Mia's pancake. "My man friend seemed confused that I needed to text my aunt before sleeping with him," she admitted. "Once I explained it was your idea, he was a little more understanding."

"'My aunt told me to bone you,'" Mia said, resting a hand on her baby bump. "That's what every man wants to hear."

Gertie gave a satisfied smile as she peered into the oven. "Glad to be helpful."

"So come on," Mia said, bouncing a little in her seat. "Give it up—not that you didn't already. I want details!"

Jenna sighed and nibbled another piece of apple plucked from the corner of her best friend's pancake. "Can I have ten minutes to shower and change?"

"Okay, but don't wash off that beard burn. It's very becoming."

"Try the cold cream on the counter, dear," Gertie said. "Very soothing for beard burn."

Jenna padded toward the bathroom, trying not to think about her aunt's familiarity with beard burn as she closed the door behind her. She stretched her arms overhead, savoring the pleasant ache of muscles she'd worked overtime the night before. God, had she really done that? It was so unlike her, so rash and impulsive and passionate.

Sean always wished I was more passionate, she thought as she lathered up her hair. *A fling with a stranger probably wasn't what he had in mind.*

Fifteen minutes later, Jenna was scrubbed and dressed in a pair of clean yoga pants with her hair in a ponytail. An apple-flecked pancake sat in front of her and two pairs of eyes drilled her from either side.

"Okay now, spill it," Mia said, forking a piece of pancake into her mouth. "I want details."

"There's not that much to tell," Jenna answered, accepting the lace-edged napkin Gertie offered. "We were both at Corkscrew last night, we both got stood up by the people we were meeting, we both liked Sangiovese—"

"You both like Marc Cohn ballads, long walks on the beach, and kinky sex with strangers?" Mia grinned and grabbed the syrup.

"I didn't say anything about kink," Jenna protested, her brain flickering over the memory of chocolate sauce from the ice cream sundae that room service had brought them sometime around midnight. She cleared her throat and reached for the coffee pot. "It was just a good, old-fashioned fling."

"I'm not sure *old-fashioned* and *fling* belong in the same sentence, dear," Gertie said as she set a fresh German apple pancake in front of her niece. "In my day, women had to feel guilty all the time. It's so nice that things have changed. Now they're free to have casual sex and multiple orgasms and bookshelves full of erotic novels."

Gert's voice had taken on a reverence most women her age reserved for their grandchildren or church services, and Jenna smiled in spite of herself as she picked up a pair of silver tongs and plucked a lemon slice from the plate Gertie offered. She squeezed it over the pancake and set the rind aside before drenching the pancake in syrup. "If it's okay with the two of you, I'd rather be a little old-fashioned and not dish too much detail."

"Seriously?" Mia gaped.

"Seriously. I kinda want to keep things private. I know that's lame, but that's how I feel."

Gertie smiled and patted her hand. "You've always been like that, ever since you were a little girl. Never one to kiss and tell, not even with your friends in high school."

"You've never been one to kiss, period," Mia said. "I've known you almost two years and this is the first time you've even dated."

"It wasn't exactly a date," Jenna pointed out, cutting into her pancake with a knife and fork. "But we're going to have one. Friday, maybe. No sex. Just getting to know each other."

Mia smirked and picked up a piece of bacon. "Sounds like you already got to know each other pretty intimately. At least tell me if he was good."

"He was good." Jenna felt her cheeks grow warm, and she bit into her first piece of pancake. "Okay, better than good. Incredible."

"Come on, was he one of those slow, romantic types, or more of a sexy alpha male?"

"Mia—"

"You can share with us, dear," Gertie said. "Indulge a little old lady."

Jenna tried to muster up a bit of indignation, but all she felt was warm and tingly at the memory of her night with him. "Fine, if you must know. He was definitely an alpha guy. Very dominant and in control."

"No kidding? I never pegged you as the submissive sort," Mia mused. "Not that I fault you one bit. That's always been the sexiest thing about Mark. The whole master-and-commander thing is ridiculously hot."

"Agreed," Gertie said.

"Especially after six years of marriage to a guy who used to bicker with me about whose turn it was to be on top," Mia said, poking at the edge of her pancake. "Suffice it to say, my ex didn't want to be. Too much work." She glanced at Gertie and winced. "Sorry. Overkill with the sex talk?"

"Not at all, dear. Sex talk is my favorite. More bacon?"

Jenna accepted a piece and tried to think of a way to change the subject. Thankfully, Mia obliged.

"I almost forgot," Mia said, dropping her fork and grabbing for her purse. She rifled through it, her mouth still full of bacon as she rummaged through the contents of her oversized tote. "I had some extra wedding photos printed for you, Aunt Gertie. Jenna said you wanted to see them."

"Oh! Just let me wash up. This is so exciting!" Gertie bustled over to the kitchen sink and returned moments later wiping her hands on her apron. She took the envelope from Mia and sat down. She slid the pictures out and began to flip through them, clucking the whole time.

"You two look so in love—oh, would you look at this one? These lavender rosebuds look gorgeous with that red hair of yours!"

"Thanks, they're called sterling silver roses," Mia said. "My mother had them in her wedding bouquet. That's her veil, too."

Gertie beamed and flipped to the next image. "This must be your mom here?"

Mia nodded, and Jenna blinked back an unexpected wash of tears. Her own mother had died in a car accident two months after Jenna's sixteenth birthday, leaving Aunt Gertie to tend to Jenna for her remaining high school years. It was one of many reasons Jenna had been eager to repay the favor by taking Gert in last fall.

As though sensing a shift in Jenna's mood, Gertie met her eyes. Gert's expression didn't change, but she reached beneath the table and touched Jenna's knee. Jenna swallowed and placed her hand on Gertie's. Gert smiled, then turned back to Mia.

"Here's another great one of you and Mark," she said. "This neckline is so flattering on you."

Mia laughed. "Gotta show off the pregnancy boobs while I've got 'em."

"You look beautiful," Jenna said, squelching an unwelcome twist of envy for her friend. She was thrilled for Mia, delighted to see her moving on with her life after a rocky divorce and the loss of a pregnancy just a month after moving to Portland two years ago. It was how the two of them had bonded, as the only unmarried people in a support group for women who'd suffered recent miscarriages.

She reached for Mia's hand and gave it a squeeze, releasing any jealous feelings she might've had.

Gertie gasped. "This photo—this must be the first time he's seeing you in the dress?"

"I know, isn't that amazing?" Mia said. "I've never had anyone look at me that way before. Not ever."

"I wish I could have seen it in person," Gertie sighed.

"You were there in spirit," Mia said, giving the older woman a quick hug. "It was important to Mark and me to keep things small and intimate—just the two of us and immediate family. I'm sure you understand."

"Big weddings are too expensive," Jenna agreed, trying not to think of her own broken engagement, of the two hundred cream-colored invitations buried somewhere in the back of her closet.

Mia nodded in agreement and slid a hand over her impressively large baby bump. "Exactly. It didn't seem right to spend any money on a wedding. Not while I'm still digging myself out of the financial pit of divorce."

Gertie continued flipping through the photos. "I know what you mean. I met with an attorney last week about—well, about a new project I'm working on," she said, glancing at Jenna. "Lawyers are so expensive!"

"Particularly when you're divorcing one," Mia muttered. "Not that I blame him for being bitter. I'm the one who had the affair. I'm the one who screwed up."

Jenna patted her friend's hand and looked over Gertie's shoulder at a picture of Mia and Mark feeding each other cake. They looked so happy, so in love.

"You did *not* screw up," Jenna said, surprising herself with the force of her own insistence. She swallowed back an unexpected memory and focused on Mia. "You have an amazing new husband who adores you and a baby on the way. I know we didn't know each other during your first marriage or when you and Mark began your—" she swallowed back the word *affair,* searching for a term that wouldn't send Mia down a path of self-flagellation and guilt. "—your relationship. But I know you had to be terribly unhappy."

"Unhappiness leads to desperation," Gertie agreed, holding up a photo of Mia glowing and voluptuous in her maternity wedding gown. "But you're happy now. That's what matters."

"That *is* what matters," Jenna echoed and nabbed her best friend's bacon.

"As you'll see in just a few minutes, things have gotten very contentious between the nurses' union and hospital administration," explained

Kendall Freemont—the *real* Kendall Freemont—as she pushed a pile of paperwork to Adam from across her desk Monday morning.

"I understand," Adam said, glancing down at the contract. "Organizations don't usually bring me in when everyone's sitting around the conference table holding hands and singing 'Kumbaya.'"

"Right," Kendall said. "I'm sure you see this sort of thing all the time. This is actually my first time dealing with contract negotiations that have taken such a contentious turn."

"Are you new to Belmont Health System?"

Kendall nodded and folded her hands on the desk. "Not new to human resources, but I've only been with Belmont for two weeks. Before this, I worked in HR for a medical center over in Ashland. We had the occasional employee discipline issues and a layoff here and there, but nothing like this."

Adam nodded and continued flipping through the forms, studying the legal language as carefully as possible for a first pass. "I hear you. Union negotiations can be especially tricky. You're very smart to bring in outside assistance. Sometimes professional mediation can really turn things around. Once people are armed with Compassionate Communication techniques and new skills for conflict resolution, I often find it can turn a bad situation into a workable one."

"Yes, of course," Kendall said, fidgeting with a gold pen on the corner of her desk. "The touchy-feely approach is something we haven't tried yet. I look forward to seeing you work your magic."

Adam laughed and flipped another page. "I wouldn't call it magic, exactly. I'm just giving people the tools they need to communicate in a respectful, constructive fashion."

"As opposed to shouting obscenities at each other and hurling paperclips across the conference table?"

"Right," Adam frowned. "How's the CEO's eye, by the way?"

"Better. He'll be joining us today, of course. Here's an agenda for today's meeting. The list at the bottom has the names and titles of everyone who'll be part of today's discussion."

She slid the piece of paper across the table toward him, and Adam skimmed over it. Ten minutes for introductions, that was good. He'd try to push for twenty, maybe introduce a brief get-to-know-you exercise to help break the ice. He made a note in the margin beside an item about salary cap negotiations. Better to save that conversation for the next meeting, to wait until they'd established a better sense of safety and security.

His eyes dropped to the names of participants. Phil Gallow, the CFO. Adam hadn't met the guy yet, but he'd heard good things. Brett Lombard from the Oregon Nurses Association—he'd spoken with him in a phone conference a couple weeks ago. Mia Dawson from the NICU—he didn't know anything about her. Susan Schrader from—

"Mr. Thomas?"

Adam looked up from the paper and caught the worried look in Kendall's eyes. "Yes?"

"You'll be—um, well, discreet about all this, won't you?"

"Labor negotiations are always confidential."

"Yes. Yes, of course." She fidgeted with her pen. "This organization has had problems in the past with the media."

"Yes, I read about that. The previous CEO's wife was running an escort service on the side?"

Kendall pressed her lips together and nodded once. "Yes. It was before my time at Belmont, and obviously that particular CEO is no longer with the organization."

"But the media hasn't forgotten?"

"Nor have the employees. Their trust in Belmont's leadership team faltered after the incident. As I'm sure you're aware, public perception is vital with a respected organization like Belmont."

"I understand completely," Adam said. "I appreciate your desire to keep things out of the newspaper and off the local airwaves. While I can't control the actions of the bargaining team, I can assure you of my own discretion."

"Good. That's good." Kendall took a deep breath. "I want to apologize again for my failure to make our meeting the other night. Family emergency."

"Not a problem. I totally understand. I hope everything's okay now."

She gave a tight nod, then folded her hands together on the desk. "I—um—I understand you also do other kinds of mediation? Outside the corporate world?"

"That's correct," Adam said, not sure what she was driving at.

"Your website mentioned you do—uh, marriage counseling?"

Adam pushed the meeting agenda aside and gave her his full attention. "Not exactly. I spent ten years as a corporate attorney before going through a rather difficult divorce. It gave me some perspective on my career and my life choices, so I went back to school for a degree in counseling. When I'm not working with companies to improve their labor relations, I'm in private practice as a marital mediator."

"Marital mediator?"

"For couples going through divorce," Adam said. "Or deciding whether to divorce. The idea is to work through the issues in a spirit of cooperation instead of launching costly legal battles. It's surprisingly effective, not to mention much less expensive than a courtroom fight."

Kendall sat nodding, her eyes glittering beneath the fluorescent lights. She didn't say anything, so Adam cleared his throat. "Are you looking for someone to work with in that capacity?"

She looked down at her hands. "Maybe. I'm not sure. I'm sorry, this is very unprofessional of me—"

"Not at all," Adam said. "Bridging the gap between emotional and professional is what I do."

"Yes, that's why we hired you." She stood up and ran her hands down her pencil skirt, smoothing out the wrinkles. "Shall we head over to the conference room?"

Adam studied her for a moment, then stood and stepped around the desk. "If you like, I can put together a list of local practitioners. There are some very good marriage counselors in the Portland area. Let me make some phone calls for you, okay?"

Kendall seemed to hesitate, then nodded. "Thank you. I appreciate that. I also appreciate your discretion. With everything."

"Discretion is my middle name," he said. "Let's go to the conference room."

They walked in silence down the hall and around a corner to a narrow corridor. Kendall paused at a blue door, hand on the knob. She turned back to Adam and offered a small smile.

"You ready for this?"

Adam nodded. "Let's get this party started."

She gave a weak smile, then turned the knob and pushed into the room. Adam was three steps behind her, his eyes scanning the room for familiar faces. He noticed a thin man wearing a blue suit and a dark scowl, and Adam tried to smile at him. The man looked startled, then gave a stiff smile in return.

His gaze moved next to a man and a woman in blue hospital scrubs with arms folded over their chests. Defensive posture, nothing unexpected. Adam smiled at them, too, and they nodded in greeting. A man in khakis beside them offered the first real smile Adam had seen. Bolstered by that, Adam slid his gaze to the corner of the room where two women sat conferring over a stack of paperwork. The brunette had glossy hair that fell over her face, while the redhead had something vaguely familiar about her posture.

About the freckles on her arms and the gold pendant around her neck.

A family heirloom.

She'd worn it eight years ago on their wedding day.

Adam froze. All the blood drained from his head, and he heard it rushing past his ears. His hands went clammy, his mouth felt dry, and he gripped the back of a chair to keep from falling over.

Amelia looked up at him, her expression stunned and blank.

The other woman followed suit, her blue eyes locking with his and flashing shock, then horror.

Those same blue eyes he'd seen flash with pleasure two nights ago.

Adam opened his mouth to speak, then closed it again.

International terrorist.

Supermodel.

Aromatherapy expert.

And a member of the bargaining team I just flew 2,100 miles to assist.

Adam took a shaky breath and stepped forward, hand extended to his ex-wife, brain locked on the woman whose perfume still lingered on his hotel pillow.

Chapter Three

"I don't understand," Amelia said, folding her arms over her chest the instant they were alone together in the hall.

The second his ex-wife had recognized him, she'd asked for a few minutes alone with the mediator, hustling Adam out of the room before Jenna or the rest of the bargaining team could do more than offer bewildered nods.

Now, Amelia stood staring at him with a frustration as familiar to Adam as the hives he got when his mother visited. He clenched his fists, willing himself not to speak until he felt calm.

It could be awhile.

"How the hell could you *not* know I worked here?" she demanded.

"Well gee, Amelia, maybe because I moved on with my life and don't spend a lot of time worrying about what you're doing with yours," he began, then regretted the immature snap in his voice. Christ, she always brought it out in him.

No one can make you behave a certain way, he reminded himself, repeating the words he'd uttered to so many people locked in contentious relations. *You're the only one who controls your response to someone.*

Fuck you, he told himself, but swallowed and tried again. "Look, I had no idea you worked here," he said. "I heard you moved west, but that's all I knew."

"It's my *field*, Adam—hospital administration. Wouldn't you at least check?"

"There are nearly six thousand hospitals in America, Amelia. How the hell could I have known you'd chosen to relocate to one halfway across the country with a brand-new HR manager who just happened to contact me out of the blue?"

"Mia," she said, her voice softer this time. "I go by Mia now. I started using my nickname after I moved to Portland." She sighed. "You're right, what are the odds? Still, you could have asked around."

"Honestly, I never gave you a second thought."

It. Gave it *a second thought.*

That's what he'd meant to say, not to make it personal, and it wasn't true anyway. Hell, he'd wanted it to be, especially in those early months after she'd moved out. He wanted to be the sort of guy who moved on easily, who could dismiss his ex-wife without a second thought, writing her off as a cheater and a liar and a woman who'd cut and run at the first sign of relationship trouble.

But he knew it wasn't as simple as the stories he told himself or told the buddies who goaded him for details over beers at the pub. He didn't want to hate her—not exactly—but he didn't want to deal with her again. Not ever.

But here she was now with her brown eyes brimming with indignation, the freckles across her nose as familiar as the back of his own hand. He didn't love her, but he couldn't muster up the anger to hate her, either.

He cleared his throat. "So you go by Mia now. Mia Dawson?"

Her expression softened again. She nodded. "I got married. Mark and I—" she swallowed. "Yes."

"Congratulations." Adam let his eyes drop to her abdomen, to the evidence that she'd not only changed her stance on taking a man's name, but on having his child.

His child. Not yours.

That shouldn't bother him, either. Hell, he never even wanted kids, and he wasn't some caveman intent on claiming his woman or planting his seed. Still, something gnawed at his gut and made him straighten a little so his knuckles didn't drag on the floor.

"Congratulations on the marriage and on the pregnancy," he said. "Both seem to agree with you. You look lovely."

"Thank you," Amelia—Mia—said, her eyes shimmering a little. Adam watched her throat as she swallowed. "I'm sorry, Adam."

He shook his head, not sure what she was apologizing for this time, but knowing it didn't matter anymore. They'd both said the words so many times, they might as well have been speaking Swahili.

"I'm sorry, too," he said. "Look, I'll give up the contract. I can recommend someone else. It might take a few weeks, but I can explain the conflict of interest and step back quietly."

Mia seemed to consider that, then shook her head. "No. I don't want to be the reason you give up a job."

"It's okay, really—"

"No. I should have done my homework and figured out who the mediator would be. I knew you'd changed careers, but I never even considered it could be you." She shook her head and gave a sad little laugh. "What are the odds?"

"You knew I'd gone into counseling and mediation?" He wasn't sure why that surprised him, but it did.

Mia nodded and bit her lip. "Of course. I kept tabs on you. For a while, anyway. I wanted to make sure you were okay after—well, after everything."

"I'm okay." His voice sounded certain, and he was grateful for that. "I'm great, actually."

Mia gave him a small smile, then shook her head. "Why the hell couldn't you Facebook-stalk me like any other self-respecting ex?"

He allowed himself a faint smile in return and shrugged. "Sorry. Not my style."

"You're right, of course. Tuning in to other people's lives and interests was never really your thing."

He couldn't tell if she meant it as a jab, and a small flare of anger flickered in his lizard brain, that pesky, primitive amygdala that controlled emotional responses. He opened his mouth to retort, then stopped. Not this time. That was the old Adam, the one who clung to resentments and fought back even when there was no battle to be had.

The new Adam was self-aware, dammit. The new Adam listened with empathy and compassion and paid attention to others. Hell, the new Adam did spontaneous things like eating ice cream for dinner and skydiving and having one-night stands.

Okay, so it was just *one* one-night stand, and even that was in question since he was desperate to see her again. *Jenna.* God, what was she thinking right now? He'd seen the look of dread on her face when Mia whisked him from the room, but there'd been no chance to reassure her or even offer an apologetic smile. How the hell had he messed this up so badly?

"Look, it really might be best if I recuse myself here," he said. "Conflict of interest and all that."

Mia shook her head and rested a hand on her belly. "No. Look, I read an article about your work last fall. You're practically famous. You have one of the best success rates of any corporate mediator in the country. This organization is in serious trouble, Adam. They need you."

A stupid flash of pride surged through him, and he tried to remember if Amelia had ever said anything close to "I'm proud of you" in the six years they'd been married.

"Isn't there a policy on fraternization among employees?" he asked. "I thought I read something in the handbook."

"Belmont has strict policies about dating between people who work in the same department, but there are no rules about people who used to be married. Not that I know of, anyway."

"Probably not a situation that comes up a whole lot. Still, I could see this creating a conflict. What if a member of the bargaining unit decides to refuse a contract negotiated by a mediator formerly married to a team member?"

Mia bit her lip. "How about this—we go back in there and lay it out on the table for the team and see how they want to proceed."

"Lay what out, exactly?"

Her cheeks flushed, and she looked down at the floor. "Not all the dirty details, of course—that's not necessary. Besides, Belmont tends to be pretty puritanical when it comes to the conduct of its administrators."

"I see," he said, squelching the flicker of annoyance welling in his chest.

"But we explain the mix-up, the fact that we're a divorced couple who moved on with our lives but that we feel confident we can all proceed here with the utmost professionalism and detachment. I can say that," she said, lifting her eyes to meet his again. "Can you?"

Adam studied her, taking a moment to gauge his own responses to his ex-wife. His pulse felt normal, his palms weren't sweaty, and while he didn't particularly like the idea of dealing with Amelia—with *Mia*—he felt confident about the job. About himself.

About the prospect of working with Jenna.

Christ.

He nodded once, then turned back toward the boardroom. "Let's go."

Jenna slipped between a rack of crotchless panties and a display of leather paddles, her eyes on the DVD shelf up ahead. She just needed to stay focused on the goal, on grabbing the merchandise, plunking down the cash, and getting the hell out of here before anyone saw her.

"Jenna?"

She whirled around. "Adam?" She closed her eyes and shook her head. "What are the odds? Seriously, what the hell are the odds?"

"Relax, I came here to find you."

Jenna opened her eyes and frowned. "That doesn't make it any less creepy. In fact, that makes it a lot more creepy. Creepier. Whatever. Are you stalking me?"

Her voice was a little louder than she meant it to be, and the clerk glanced over a display of giant dildos to regard her with curiosity.

"I'm not stalking you, but I do need to talk to you," he said, lowering his voice. "I tried to call. We didn't get a chance to talk in today's meeting, and I'm assuming from your lack of objection to my contract that you wanted to keep our relationship a secret?"

Jenna grimaced at the word *relationship,* or maybe it was their surroundings. Could there be a more awkward place to have this conversation?

She forced herself to stop gritting her teeth. "Pardon me if I didn't stand up in the meeting and volunteer the fact that I accidentally slept with my best friend's ex-husband, who oh-by-the-way happens to be the corporate mediator hired by my employer."

The clerk glanced over again, and Jenna realized her voice had risen above the whisper she'd been aiming for. She grabbed Adam by the arm and tried to push him toward the door. "You have to leave. How did you find me here, anyway?"

"Your aunt answered your phone when I called."

"Shit, I must have left it at the house. I've told her not to answer it. What did she say?"

"She told me where you'd be." He grinned—that stupid, sexy, boyish grin—and Jenna felt her traitorous heart lurch in her chest. "This is the same aunt who told you to sleep with me?"

"Yes," she snapped. "Also the same aunt who sent me on an errand to a goddamn adult pleasure store. Would you just go? Please?"

She pushed him again, which was a mistake. Her palm remembered the contour of muscle in his arm, the swell of his bicep, and she shuddered a little with the pleasure of touching him. Now he was smiling down at her in earnest.

"Your aunt sends you to a porn store on an errand? Now I've gotta hear this story. Come on, meet me somewhere for a drink. I'll buy you a glass of wine and we'll talk through this like professional adults."

"No! We can't be seen in public together."

He raised an eyebrow. "Fine. We can go back to my hotel."

"Definitely not. I know what happens there."

"What happens there, Jenna?"

His tone was teasing, and she felt her cheeks grow warmer. She didn't answer, mostly because she was afraid she might beg him to do it to her again.

"Look, we need to talk," Adam said. "If you're worried about being seen, I think this is a pretty unlikely place to run into your colleagues."

"We are not having this conversation next to the bondage aisle at a porn store," she hissed.

"You're thinking the vibrator section would be better?"

Jenna bit her lip, then grabbed his arm again. "Come on," she said, tugging him toward the bank of adult arcade booths at the back of the shop. "These things must be made for privacy." She grabbed the door of the booth at the far end and yanked it open with more force than necessary.

"You're seriously dragging me into a porn booth?" he asked, but didn't resist as she tugged him inside and closed the door. She flipped the lock with shaking hands and turned to look at him.

The space was dark and small, and Jenna was afraid to touch the rickety folding chair leaning up against the wall. A television screen shone lifeless on one wall, and the red light overhead made the air look smoky.

"Okay, talk," she whispered.

He shook his head, looking around at the black-painted walls. "I've gotta give you credit. This is private. Weird, but private."

"*Weird* doesn't even begin to describe it."

Someone pounded on the outside of the booth. "If you're going to be in there together, you need to pay to play," the clerk called. "Feed the meter, folks."

"What?" Jenna glanced around, not sure if she was looking for hidden cameras or an escape route. Why on earth had she let Gertie talk her into coming here?

"The movies," Adam said, reaching for her. At least it looked like he was reaching for her. Instead, he slid a dollar bill into a slot behind her right hip and pressed a button. The television screen flickered to life, and Jenna blinked as her eyes adjusted to the blare of light and sound.

"What the—?"

"People come in here to get their rocks off," Adam whispered. "Not to hold professional meetings. Avert your eyes if you need to."

"Good Lord, is that porn or a circus act?"

"Must be some sort of clown fetish channel. Hang on, I'll change it."

Jenna tried to look away, but found she couldn't. She wasn't averse to pornography, but she never realized there was such variety.

"There," Adam said, settling on a video that featured a busty young woman talking to a plumber. He drew his hand back and looked at her, and Jenna felt her breath catch in her throat. God, had she noticed before how green his eyes were?

You noticed. Damn straight you noticed.

She forced herself to swallow. "What did you need to talk about?"

"Oh, I don't know—the weather?" He folded his arms over his chest. "The price of petroleum? European Dadaist painters of the early twentieth century? How about the fact that my ex-wife is your colleague and your employer is now my employer and we need to figure out how to deal with that in a professional manner?"

Jenna fought the urge to flinch. "I honestly had no idea. I swear—"

"I know, I believe you," he said, holding up his hands in mock defense. "It's not like our first meeting was a free exchange of factual information."

"No, we were too busy exchanging other things," she muttered, and felt the corners of her mouth start to lift in spite of her effort to keep her frown in place.

"I'm not complaining, but it does complicate things," he said. "How well do you know Amelia?"

"Amelia?"

"Mia. I guess she goes by Mia now. My ex-wife."

"Very well. We met in a support group a couple years ago and spent a lot of time baring our souls. We're extremely close."

"Support group?"

Jenna swallowed, not wanting to reveal too much of her best friend's personal information. Or her own.

"We know each other well," she repeated. "I've heard plenty of stories about you. Not that I knew it was you."

"Right." She could see his jaw clenching and unclenching, but he didn't say more.

"Sounds like it was a contentious divorce."

"You could say that."

"I know she was unfaithful."

She watched his eyebrows lift, and for an instant, Jenna worried she'd spilled the beans on some long-hidden secret.

But Adam just shook his head. "I'm surprised she mentioned that. I wouldn't think that's something she'd go around telling people."

"She's not proud of it, Adam. She knows she made mistakes, and she owns that. Just as I imagine you own some part of the blame for the marriage going off the rails?"

He was quiet a long time, and Jenna could swear she heard the sound of wheels turning in his head. Or maybe that was the smack of flesh on the screen over her shoulder. She fought the urge to glance at the television as the moaning grew louder.

Adam sighed. "My divorce isn't the biggest issue here. The conflict is that you and I slept together." He raked his fingers through his hair, an oddly endearing gesture. "I'll be honest, I'd hoped to see you again. Not just for sex, but to get to know you."

"I'm sure we'll get to know each other through the mediation process."

44

"That's not what I meant."

"I know." She sighed. "I wanted to get to know you, too, but I don't think that's possible. Belmont has strict policies about dating among co-workers. Even though you're a contractor, we're both members of the bargaining team, which technically makes us part of the same department."

She looked down at her hands, which were clenched so tightly around her purse that her knuckles had gone white. She released them and felt the blood surge into her fingers. She met his eyes again. "Look, rules aside, I'm not comfortable with anyone at work knowing what happened between us," she said. "I take my career seriously, and I'm not willing to risk things getting awkward in the mediation process."

Adam nodded, his expression unreadable. "Fair enough."

She let the words hang there between them a moment as the flicker of writhing bodies filled the small space. Moans of pleasure pulsed in the air, and Jenna desperately wanted it to be a turnoff.

But it wasn't. Or at least *he* wasn't. Adam was standing so close she could smell the grassy scent of his shampoo, could feel the heat radiating from his body. She ordered herself to take a step back, but found herself moving toward him instead.

She took a deep breath and felt it catch in her throat. "I don't want Mia to know."

"About what happened with us?"

She nodded. "It was a one-time thing, so there's really no point in putting a strain on my friendship with her."

He seemed to hesitate, then nodded. "I suppose you're right. She's not the sort to see the humor in the situation."

The words stung for some reason. Something about his familiarity with another woman, the intimacy between two people who'd once been married. She tried again to put some space between herself and Adam, but found her feet rooted in place.

"Right, so we agree?" she said, releasing her death grip on her purse so it dangled freely from her shoulder. "No sense complicating careers or friendships by ever speaking of this again?"

"Agreed."

She tried to read his expression. Was it wistful or just uncomfortable? Should they shake hands, or just say goodbye? Jenna held her breath, not moving.

When he leaned toward her, she felt her whole body dissolve. Her limbs responded without orders from her brain, and she slid her hands behind his neck as she arched up to meet him.

His kiss was hesitant at first. Then there was no hesitation at all as Adam pressed into her, his lips everywhere at once, his hands solid on her hips. She kissed him back, fingers hungry to explore each curve of muscle in his back. She devoured him, surprised at her own aggression, but knowing this was the last time she'd ever do this with him. His tongue found hers, and her hands tunneled though his hair, deepening the kiss.

When she drew back, they were both breathless.

He smiled, hands still on her hips. "What was that for?"

"You leaned down to kiss me."

"I was moving to—"

Someone banged on the wall outside. "Pay to play, you two!" the clerk shouted.

Adam shoved another dollar bill into the slot. Jenna swallowed and finally took a step back. "Right. I should be going."

"Not yet," he said, catching her hand in his before she could make an escape. "Why are you at a porn shop for your aunt?"

"She's elderly and can't drive," Jenna said, cursing her hand for reveling in the warmth of his. "She needed me to pick up a few things for a bridal shower she's attending. Lube, crotchless panties, some sort of whip, and an instructional DVD."

"Wow. That sounds like some bridal shower."

"There's no bridal shower." Jenna shook her head. "It's this little game we play where my elderly aunt pretends she's not a sex goddess who writes wildly popular erotica under a pen name to pay her medical bills."

"What?"

"And I go along with it and pretend she just bakes pies and does crossword puzzles because it's easier than having an awkward conversation."

"You're kidding me."

Jenna shook her head. "Look, it started out innocently enough with my aunt writing a few short stories under a pseudonym, but the whole thing snowballed into this crazy erotica career that's taken off like gangbusters in the last month and I don't know how to handle it and—" she stopped, realizing she'd just revealed more to Adam than she had to anyone, ever. She shook her head. "Never mind. Suffice it to say, my aunt and I don't talk about her writing. It's easier that way."

Adam stared at her, the corners of his mouth ticking up in a smile. "That's an interesting family dynamic you have there."

"You have no idea." She sighed. "Look, it's not just me being a prude. Belmont has certain expectations of its executives. As healthcare providers, they have to be above reproach in all things—even their families."

"But your aunt is writing dirty books, not running a brothel."

Jenna grimaced. "I see you've heard about the old CEO and his wife. For the record, I did my best to do damage control on that one, but there's only so much I can cover up."

"So that's your job," he said. "Covering things up. I wondered what the hell a Chief Relations Officer did."

"I handle all kinds of things, ranging from media relations to personnel issues, but yes—I suppose it all comes down to getting paid to sweep bad things under the rug and blow sunshine up people's butts."

"At least you're honest."

She gave him a smile she knew wouldn't reach her eyes and pushed the door open. "Honest," she repeated, stepping into the daylight. "I'm always honest about the things I can't be honest about."

She turned and walked away, feeling his eyes on her as she vanished out the door.

Chapter Four

"A maternity wedding dress? Honestly, what will they think of next."

Jenna reached under the table and gave Mia's hand a squeeze, not sure whether she meant to comfort her best friend or keep her from lunging across the table to throttle the cousin who sat smirking in a hideous pink hat.

Mia gritted her teeth so hard Jenna could hear the sound. She gave her friend's hand another squeeze and reached for her wineglass.

"This is excellent wine," Jenna offered, hoping to change the subject. "Really, Mia, the whole reception is lovely. This was such a wonderful idea."

Across the table, the cousin snorted. "Wonderful? You think it's wonderful she didn't invite any of her friends and family to the wedding but she has this fancy-schmantzy reception at an expensive hotel so she can still get all the gifts?"

"We asked people not to bring gifts, Harriet," Mia said tightly, her wedding band biting into Jenna's hand as she squeezed back. "It said so right on the invitation. And the rental fee on the reception room was a gift from my employer because we do a lot of business with this hotel."

"Hmph," Harriet said, turning back to the stack of wedding photos in her hand. "The dress is white. You can't wear white if you've been married before, especially not if you wore white for your first wedding. The bouquet you carried for that one, by the way, was—"

"How about we talk about something else?" Mark announced from the head of the table. Mia turned and gave her new husband a wilted smile of appreciation and released her death grip on Jenna's hand.

"Yes, let's," Mia said. "Jenna, how was your date last night?"

Harriet gave a grunt of disapproval and stood up, flouncing off toward the canapé table. Jenna watched her go, wondering how much longer she should wait before making an excuse to go home and change from her party dress into yoga pants.

She turned back to Mia. "Date?"

"Didn't you say you were going to see that guy again?" Mia asked. "The one you met at the wine bar."

"Oh, right." Jenna took a sip of wine, reminding herself not to gulp it. "We decided it wasn't going to work out. Our schedules are too busy and there just wasn't enough chemistry."

"Not enough chemistry?" Mia snorted. "Girl, I saw you the morning after you met him. You were oozing with so much chemistry you could have recited the periodic table of elements backward."

"Not true." Jenna frowned. "Also a little weird. Besides, he lives out of town."

"So? Long distance relationships can work, especially if they make you look like you did that morning. Seriously, Mark, you should have seen her." Mia leaned toward her husband, hand on his arm. "She was practically glowing. I don't know what that guy did to her in bed, but he should probably patent it."

Jenna choked on her wine. "Right, well, all the same, I'm not going to see him again. Mark, how are things at work?"

Mark gave her a sympathetic smile and took the hint. "Things are great, thanks for asking. We just landed a contract to build the new Parks and Recreation building over in Gresham. The steel erection should go through the summer, so I've got my work cut out for me."

Mia grinned at him and picked up a stuffed mushroom cap. "Have I told you how sexy I find it when you talk about your work?" She popped the mushroom into her mouth and snuggled closer. "And also that you can say things like 'steel erection' and not mean anything dirty."

"I might have meant it a little bit dirty."

Mia laughed and turned back to Jenna. "Seriously, what is it about guys who work with their hands for a living? I can't believe it took me 'til my early thirties to discover I'm more turned on by a guy with a tool belt than a guy with a briefcase."

Jenna took another hit of wine and tried not to think about Adam's briefcase as Mark planted a kiss on his wife's forehead. "Come on now, let's give Jenna a break and talk about something else. I take it things are still tense at work for you two?"

Jenna nodded and set her wineglass down. "The new mediator they brought in spent half the week explaining why throwing things wasn't conducive to labor negotiations."

"How'd that go?"

"The CEO didn't take it well at first, but then the mediator asked about the stapler-throwing incident and asked when the CEO is getting his stitches out and—"

"You don't have to call him the mediator, Jenna," Mark said gently. "I know it's Adam. It's okay. Mia and I talked about it. If she's okay with her ex-husband working with the team, I totally support that."

Mia rested a hand on her belly. "A man who's secure—also a turn-on, in case you're wondering."

"I wasn't," Jenna said. "But Mark could stand on his head and juggle flaming rutabagas and you'd be turned on."

"Good point."

Mark shook his head and gave his wife a fond look. "There's nothing to be insecure about. It's water under the bridge, and as long as we talk about it, I don't have any problem with your ex being a part of your work environment."

"Open communication and honesty," Mia said, nudging Jenna with her elbow. "Who knew it was that simple?" She frowned. "It's not awkward for you, is it?"

Jenna swallowed. "Awkward? Why would it be awkward for me?"

"I just don't want anyone on the team to feel weird about having my ex-husband there. I know we lived in Chicago when the divorce happened, so you're really the only one at Belmont who knows the details of how it all went down. How bad things were. Still—"

"It's fine, Mia," Jenna lied. "He seems very—um, very competent."

"He does seem that way, doesn't he?" She fell quiet a moment, looking down at her water glass. "I have to admit, the touchy-feely communication stuff surprised me a little."

"What do you mean?"

"Communication was never his forte. I remember our fifth anniversary when I really wanted him to surprise me with a trip to Hawaii. I spent the whole year talking about it, signing him up for e-mail lists for these resorts on Kauai and buying this cute piggy bank so we could save for it."

Jenna wasn't sure she wanted to hear more, but couldn't stop herself from asking. "What happened?"

"Our anniversary rolled around, and he said he had to work late." Mia swallowed, looking stung instead of playful. "At first I thought he was kidding and that he planned to show up and whisk me away to the airport. But when he came home from the office near midnight and just crawled into bed, I knew it wasn't going to happen."

Jenna bit her lip. "I'm sorry. That must have been awful."

"God, no—I'm sorry." Mia rubbed her palms over her cheeks and shook her head. "Look at me, going on about my divorce when I'm here celebrating my life with this amazing man."

"It's okay, hon," Mark said, planting another kiss along her hairline. "It's your party, you can cry if you want to."

"Cheeseball," she said with fondness, smacking him on the arm. "You want to dance?"

"I'd love to." He pushed back from the table and stood up. "You okay here, Jenna?"

"Actually, I think I'm going to get some fresh air. Maybe call Aunt Gertie to check on her."

"Tell her I wish she could have been here," Mia said as her husband lifted her to her feet. "I hope she feels better."

"She thinks it's just a touch of food poisoning, nothing to worry about. It's also possible she just wanted a few hours alone to get some work done."

"Still, there's a nasty stomach bug going around. You can't be too careful with older folks."

"I'm watching her closely," Jenna said, picking up her wineglass as she stood. It was still half full, so she carried it with her as she moved toward the door of the banquet room. She glanced back over her shoulder to see Mia melting into her husband's arms, her face glowing with happiness. Something twisted in Jenna's gut, and she turned back toward the door.

The instant she stepped into the hall, she breathed a little easier. The Spanx weren't helping, and she considered slipping into the bathroom to remove them. She decided against it and moved toward the hotel lobby. She started in that direction, then spotted a sign beside the stairwell.

Roof.

A much better place for privacy, and there'd be plenty of fresh air up there. She pulled open the door to the stairwell, then bent down and yanked off her high heels. Gripping them in one hand and her wineglass in the other, she trudged up the stairs, her dress riding up her thighs as she counted her way past the third floor, fourth floor, fifth floor, and onward.

She was breathing hard by the time she reached the top. She pushed through the door and into the bright wash of daylight. The sky was milky, but it wasn't raining, and the sun shone oddly bright through the film of clouds above. Late August weather in Portland could be unpredictable, and she'd heard there might be thunderstorms in the forecast.

A gust of wind tugged the hem of her dress as she stepped barefoot onto the warm tar surface of the hotel roof, dropping her shoes at the corner of a giant fan.

A stray piece of paper skittered across her path as the breeze carried the scent of cottonwood trees and food from a street fair in the park below. She took a few steps forward, letting the door fall shut behind her as she reached into her purse for her phone.

She froze when she spotted him. A lone figure sitting cross-legged on a bench beside the ledge. She had to squint at first, her eyes fighting to adjust to the glare of light through filmy clouds, but she would have known that body anywhere. He had a laptop open in front of him, and a half-finished sandwich on a tray off to the side. His dark hair was cut short, but spiked a little in the front like he'd been running his hands through it.

She must have gasped, because he looked up then. He blinked, motionless for what seemed like an eternity, green eyes locked on hers.

"Oh," Jenna said, and spilled wine down the front of her dress.

"I'm not an expert on wine," Adam said, jumping up to hand her a wad of napkins. "But I think the object is to get it into your mouth and not your cleavage."

His hand brushed hers as she took the napkins, and he felt something electric in his knuckles. He was close enough to feel the heat from her arms as she looked down in horror at the bloom of liquid on the front of her dress.

"God, I'm glad I'm drinking Pinot Grigio and not Merlot," she muttered, mopping at the space between her breasts. "Hopefully this won't stain."

Adam watched, noticing the way the tops of her breasts glistened with spilled wine. He felt his brain spin and fought the urge to sit down.

"Here, let me grab the salt," he offered, hurrying back to his lunch tray.

"Now's not the time for margaritas."

"It's always time for margaritas, but that's not what this is for." He snatched the shaker in one hand and turned back to her. "This is how you get wine out of linen. That is linen, right?"

"Right. Ugh, I'm going to be sticky."

"Could you stop touching yourself like that? You're turning me on."

Jenna looked up, her cheeks flushed, her dark hair pulled back in some sort of complicated twist that Adam ached to unravel with his fingers. Instead, he plucked the sodden napkin out of her hand.

"Seriously, stop rubbing it," he said, handing her the saltshaker. "You'll set the stain. Just cover it in this and wait 'til it dries."

"How am I supposed to do that?" She pulled the fabric away from her body, then let it fall back against the curve of her breasts. All the blood remaining in Adam's brain vacated the premises.

"It's not exactly a flat surface," she pointed out.

"I noticed," he said. "I'm grateful."

She rolled her eyes. "Come on, what do I do? Should I just shake some on the stain or what?"

"Here, let me help."

He reached for the saltshaker again, fingers grazing hers as he took it from her. He plucked the fabric away from her chest, trying to be as clinical as possible about the whole operation, but how the hell was he supposed to do that with his finger dipping into the warm hollow between her breasts? He'd managed to stay professional all week at Belmont, not letting his libido surge at the sight of Jenna or his anger surge at the sight of his ex-wife. But now—

"What on earth are you doing up here, anyway?" she asked.

"Working."

"On a Saturday? On a hotel roof?"

"Hotel rooftops are only for midweek work?" He plucked at the damp fabric again, admiring its determination to cling to her breasts. "I think better with a little fresh air, so I followed the signs from my room to the roof."

"When did you change hotels?"

"Two days ago. Hold still, will you?"

He tipped a little salt onto the liquid, rubbing it in with his knuckle. A little more, his finger grazing her breast again. Christ, it was hot up here.

He cleared his throat. "I don't suppose I could convince you to take off the dress?"

"Nice try. Actually, that's not a bad idea. I'll just go back downstairs and do it. Hopefully there's something in the hotel lost and found I could change into." She nodded and stepped away from him. "Thank you for the salt."

She turned and started to walk toward the stairwell, but Adam called out to her. "There's one problem with that."

She pivoted back to look at him. "What's that?"

"You just trapped us up here."

She stopped, hand outstretched toward the doorknob, bare feet lovely on the dirty roof. "What?"

"See that piece of paper?" He nodded toward the sports section pinned against the ledge, one corner fluttering in the breeze. "I'd shoved it into the latch so it wouldn't lock while I was up here. It fell out when you came through the door."

She opened her mouth, then closed it again. "How is that possible?"

"See for yourself."

He waited to see if she'd take his word for it, not surprised when she didn't. She gave the door a hard yank, her body jerking as the latch failed to give.

She turned back to face him, expression accusatory. "Why would a hotel have a door that locks people on the roof without some sort of warning?"

"Security. Besides, there was plenty of warning. Didn't you see the signs?"

"Signs?"

"They were on every landing."

She shook her head, eyes flashing with something that almost looked like sadness. "I'm abysmally bad at noticing the signs. In case you hadn't noticed."

He watched her, trying to grasp the turn they'd just taken in the conversation. "Are we still talking about the stairwell?"

She sighed and stepped away from the door. He thought she was going to walk back toward him, but instead she sank down onto the bench beside what was left of his ham sandwich. He walked over and moved the tray aside, sinking down into the space next to her. When she looked up, her eyes seemed a little wild.

"How the hell did I not know you were Mia's husband?"

Those last two words hit him like a punch to the solar plexus, and he waited for the pang of annoyance to ebb. "*Ex*-husband."

"Still, I knew your name was Adam. That should have tipped me off."

"There are more than 500,000 men named Adam in North America," he pointed out, wondering if it was geeky or impressive for him to know that. "How were you supposed to realize you were knocking boots with the Adam who swapped rings with your best friend?"

She flinched, and Adam regretted the flippancy of his words. It was an engrained habit, this tendency to spout humor or data in uncomfortable situations.

What's making you uncomfortable? The memory of your ex-wife, or the knowledge that you're awkwardly attracted to her best friend?

Both. He'd spent a long time eradicating Mia from his life, or at least eradicating the anger that came with remembering her. But working with her again, and finding himself unable to resist the allure of a woman who'd probably heard all the ugliest stories from his marriage—

He frowned, forcing himself to cut the self-analysis bullshit and stay in the present. The present wasn't so bad, really. The scent of Jenna's perfume was sweet and warm, and there was a spicy hint of fall on the breeze. He leaned back against the ledge, stretching his arms out behind him. One rested a few inches behind Jenna's shoulders, but she didn't seem to notice.

"Look, I have my phone," he said. "This isn't some chick flick where we're trapped on the roof together for hours until I ravish you up against the wall. I can call down to the front desk and have us out of here in five minutes."

Neither of them moved, and for a moment, Adam wondered if she wanted to stay up here with him. The thought almost made him smile, but smiling didn't seem like the right thing to do. Not yet, anyway. When she turned to look at him, her expression had softened.

"Why did you change hotels?" she asked. "This obviously isn't where we—" she paused, glancing away. "Where we *met up* last week."

"Belmont likes to woo consultants with the nice digs up front, but for long-term contractors, this place makes more sense. Better weekly rates, and all the suites on the tenth floor have kitchens."

Jenna sighed and leaned back against his arm, and Adam tried not to revel in the softness of her shoulders. "You know, I knew that about Belmont. About which hotels they use. Also a sign I should have picked up on, right?"

"Don't beat yourself up, Jenna. We both could have been a little more inquisitive about each other's identity." He hesitated, knowing he should probably pull out his phone and dial the front desk, but not wanting to make the move until she did. "Why are you here, anyway? You look like a refugee from a garden party."

She shrugged, studying her hands. When she looked back at him, her expression was guarded. "Mia's wedding reception."

He waited for the words to slice through him the way they might have two years ago. There was a dull ache in his gut, but it might have been the ham sandwich. Too much mustard. Or hell, maybe he was still affected by the thought of his ex-wife with another man. With the man she'd—

"I thought Mia was already married," he said, interrupting his own thoughts.

"They got married in Kauai a few weeks ago—at Mark's parents' place. Private, only immediate family. They're having a reception here to celebrate with the people who couldn't be at the wedding."

Adam nodded, letting the words sink in, feeling nothing. Well, that wasn't entirely true. He felt something, but he wasn't sure he could name what it was.

Some counselor you are.

"That's smart," he said, sticking with the basics. "Having a smaller, more intimate ceremony. I wish we'd done that the first time."

She met his eyes and nodded. "I heard the first wedding was quite a show."

"More than four hundred guests. Most of them friends of Mia's mother. It was a nightmare. We wanted to serve chicken because several people in my family don't eat red meat, but Sally—that's her mother—insisted filet mignon was more high-class."

"So she talked you into it?"

"Worse," Adam said, surprised to feel anger swelling in him after all this time. "Sally called the caterer herself and changed the order the week before the wedding. We never knew until we all sat down to dinner under this big expensive canopy she also ordered without our knowledge."

"I'll bet Mia was livid."

He shrugged, remembering the way his new bride had put her hand on his arm and whispered for him not to make a scene.

"Appearances are important to her," Amelia had murmured, glancing around nervously at her assembled family. *"Let's not make a big deal. Besides, she is paying for it."*

It wasn't the first time Adam had realized the price that came from letting someone else control his financial future, but it was the moment he vowed never to do it again.

He'd busted ass over the years to make sure of it, working extra hours at the law firm to get ahead, to provide for Mia so she'd get out from under her mother's thumb. He remembered how much she'd wanted to go to Hawaii, how he'd scrimped and saved to surprise her with a vacation at Christmas.

He'd had the tickets in his briefcase that day. The day he'd come home early to find her and Mark—

"Is this weird for you?" Jenna asked, jarring him back to the present.

"Is what weird?"

"Knowing I've probably heard every dirty detail about your marriage and divorce," she said. "Women talk, you know. I heard about the time you got busted after she talked you into sex in a hotel pool. I know about your camping trip to the Grand Canyon when you fought the whole time about whether or not to have kids. I know you were there for her when her father died, and that you had a big disagreement about whether to visit your parents in Africa after they joined the Peace Corps."

The string of memories she'd just laid out made him want to punch something. Not a person, of course. A soft pillow, maybe a stuffed animal.

Dude, you're losing it.

He didn't care what Mia had said about him. It was water under the bridge, ancient history.

Only he *did* care. He cared that Jenna knew only one side of the story. One side of him—Mia's version of events, of the marriage gone sour, of the ex-husband she'd chosen to leave.

He shook his head and gave a shrug he hoped conveyed indifference. The wind caught a stray lock of hair that had escaped her updo, and it tickled the back of his hand. "Weird," he repeated, returning to her original question. "Weird is the right word. Not sad, not angry, it's just weird."

She smiled. "That's the clinical term?"

"Exactly." He smiled back, breathing in the soft, floral scent of her perfume. Something like lilacs, maybe, with a hint of lemon. "Years of training as a counselor make me highly qualified to diagnose weirdness."

The light flickered back into her eyes, and Adam felt the mood shift from awkward to playful in the span of two heartbeats.

"I enjoyed watching you work this week," she said. "You might have even made some progress with the team."

"You mean after I disarmed the CEO and suggested the ER manager might want to consider addressing people by name instead of as twatwaffles and ass-hats?"

"That was progress. What was that technique called again?"

"It's based on some of the principles of Imago theory," he said, shifting on the bench so his leg was scant inches from hers. "It's a form of relationship and couples' therapy based on collaboration, understanding, giving, and responsibility."

"Couples' therapy? You're handling a feuding staff like a bunch of pissed-off spouses?"

He grinned, relaxing back into the conversation now. "That's pretty much what they are, right? Minus the sex and the arguments about who farted under the covers."

He felt her shiver beside him and wondered if it was the mention of sex or the breeze. Or maybe the fart joke. Not exactly classy. He should probably call the front desk, just get them out of here and on with their respective lives.

But Jenna settled back against his arm again, and any urge to flee evaporated into the late-summer breeze.

"Tell me more about this couples' therapy stuff," she said. "How's it going to fix our screwed-up team dynamic?"

"Well, next week we'll work on Imago Dialogue."

"Is that a form of dialogue that doesn't involve yelling and throwing things?"

"That's the funny thing about dialogue," he said, fingers brushing the loose strand of hair again. "People think it's two people talking, but it's actually meant to be one person talking and the other listening. We're going to work on listening techniques with the group—something called mirroring—to ensure people are feeling heard."

She nodded, her expression intrigued as she leaned a little closer to him. "Do it to me."

Adam's breath caught in his throat, and he fought the urge to reach for her. "Pardon me?"

"I want to understand how it works," she said, laughing as she turned her whole body to face him, drawing her bare legs up between them on the bench so her knees touched the side of his thigh. "Come on, Imago me."

"I'm not sure Imago is meant to be a verb, though it sounds pleasantly dirty when you say it like that." Adam cleared his throat and wondered if he should remind her they still hadn't dealt with the wine on her dress. He should probably do that, get some more salt on the stain, or call the front desk to—

"Okay, first things first," he said, his gut giving a pleasant twist as she leaned against his arm, the side of her breast grazing his sleeve. "Let's do a little role-play."

"I assume you don't mean the kind where I dress up as a naughty schoolgirl and get called to the principal's office?"

He laughed, wondering if she was channeling her aunt's note again. It seemed like a sex goddess sort of thing to say, not that Adam was complaining. He didn't want to make her self-conscious, so he continued on.

"We'll save the schoolgirl costume for another time. With this sort of role-playing, you'll be the sender and I'll be the receiver. Let's pretend you have something you'd like to express to me. For now, we'll make it an appreciation, though this type of dialogue is also helpful for expressing something that's bothering you."

"An appreciation," she repeated, nodding.

"You start by saying that—*I'd like to express an appreciation.* And you check to make sure this is an okay time for the receiver."

"I'd like to express an appreciation," she parroted, smiling. "Is this a good time for you?"

"I'm available now."

Her nose wrinkled, but she was still smiling. "This feels weird. It's not a normal way of talking."

"It always feels weird at first. The point is that the normal way of talking isn't working—at least, not with the bargaining team—so we're trying something new with a structure we've all agreed on."

"Okay, I'd like to express an appreciation," she said, smiling up at him as her knee pressed against the side of his leg. "I appreciate your eyes. You have great eyes."

He laughed, taken aback. "An appreciation isn't usually meant to be of a physical trait, but thank you."

"No, really—I like the way you make eye contact. You look me right in the eye, always. Like, sometimes I can't tell if you even blink."

Adam nodded, flattered she'd chosen something he'd worked to improve over the years. Eye contact used to make him uncomfortable, especially in the courtroom when he'd argue cases in front of hostile judges or defiant witnesses.

Your lousy eye contact makes you seem untrustworthy, Mia had told him years ago, the irony of the suggestion lost on him until much later. Still, he'd vowed to work on it.

It said something that Jenna had noticed, though he wasn't sure what.

"Okay, so now it's my job to mirror and check for accuracy," he said. "I'd say something like, 'let me see if I've got you—I heard you say you like the way I hold eye contact. Did I get that right?'"

"Yes," she said, the syllable a little breathless tripping from her tongue. "That's right."

"Is there more?" he asked. "That's part of the dialogue—I ask you if there's more, which opens the door for you to share something else. Like maybe how it makes you feel or why eye contact is important to you."

"Okay," she said, "I was engaged once and my fiancé had this habit of looking at his phone all the time, even when I was talking. It drove me batty, made me feel like he didn't care what I had to say. I love that it always feels like I have your undivided attention."

"You do," Adam breathed, losing his place in the conversation. "Okay, now I use the mirroring technique again. I heard you say your fiancé spent a lot of time checking his phone instead of looking at you when you were talking, and that frustrated you and made you feel like he didn't care what you were saying. You appreciate having my undivided attention, and the eye contact lets you know you have it. Is there more?"

"More?"

"The point of the exercise is to continue drawing out what you're trying to express to make sure you know I'm hearing you. This is a good place for you to tell me more about how the eye contact makes you feel."

"God, this is a bizarre way to talk," she said. "Okay, yes, there's more. When you make eye contact, it makes me feel listened to. Understood. Noticed. Appreciated."

Adam nodded, struggling a little to remember his lines. "And this is where I summarize. What I hear you saying is that you like when I hold eye contact because it makes you feel listened to, understood, noticed, and appreciated. Did I get it all?"

"No."

"No?"

She bit her lip, and Adam had the sense she was about to say something a little outside her comfort zone. The thought of it thrilled him, and so did the next words out of her mouth.

"It also makes me feel a little turned on." She smiled. "If I'm being honest."

Adam swallowed, fighting to keep his head in the game. "Honesty is good." His voice cracked on the last syllable, and Jenna smiled and leaned closer.

"I picture you undressing me with your eyes, and it makes me want to take my clothes off."

"Okay," Adam breathed, aching to claim her mouth with his. "Now it's my job to validate you by saying something like, 'what you say makes sense, and I understand that feeling listened to, understood, noticed, and appreciated is important to you.'"

"And turned on," she repeated, emboldened now. "Don't forget that."

"I couldn't possibly."

Her face was inches away now, a cue Adam couldn't possibly miss even if he wanted to.

"So what comes next?" she murmured.

"In the Imago Dialogue?"

"Sure."

"Um—something about empathy or accuracy-checking or some shit like that. Dammit, Jenna."

His mouth was on hers in an instant, kissing her hard despite the buzz in the back of his brain that told him it was a bad idea to let his libido make decisions for the rest of him. Why was that again?

His fingers tangled in her hair and she gave a soft moan against his mouth and he felt his brain dissolve. His hand slid down the side of her neck, tracing the soft, warm hollow as he moved down to the curve of her shoulder. His palm grazed the top of her breast and she whimpered against him.

Jenna moved up onto her knees, her whole body leaning into the kiss. She caressed the back of his neck and he realized absurdly he was still gripping the saltshaker. He couldn't think of a good way to put it down. Couldn't think of anything, really, except how good it felt to kiss her like this, in spite of everything in him that said it was a bad choice.

Real love is a decision, not a feeling.

The words buzzed in the back of his brain, and he tried to remember which part of his training they'd come from or why they'd chosen that moment to resurface in his mind.

Don't think. Just feel.

Something clicked behind them and in the distance he heard a gasp.

"Jenna? What the hell?"

Chapter Five

Jenna jumped at the sound of Mia's voice, her teeth clacking against Adam's as she jerked back.

"Ouch."

From the corner of her eye, Jenna saw him raise a hand to his lower lip, but she was already on her feet and blinking against the glare as her best friend strode toward them in the sunlight.

Jenna swallowed and folded her hands in front of her. "Mia! What a surprise."

She hoped her voice didn't sound as guilty as it did in her head. What had Mia seen? It was possible the rooftop glare provided enough cover, but equally possible they were busted.

What the hell were you thinking?

Mia smiled and stepped around a fluttering page of newspaper with a hand shielding her eyes. "I thought that was you," she said, dropping her hand from her brow to rest it on her pregnancy bump instead. "Didn't realize that was Adam sitting there. God, the glare up here is awful. Why the hell would they paint a roof silver?"

Behind her, Adam rose to his feet. "The aluminum particles have reflective properties designed to resist ultraviolet rays and keep the building cool, plus the material is used to fill small cracks and extend the lifespan of a flat roof."

Both Jenna and Mia turned to blink at him. His lower lip looked swollen, and Jenna wondered whether to blame the kiss or the dental collision. She ached to reach out and touch the spot with her fingertip, but instead she edged closer to Mia.

"Right," Mia said, nodding at her ex. "I forgot your fondness for useless trivia."

"It wasn't that useless, since it answered your question," he pointed out.

Jenna took a step closer to Mia, not sure who she wanted to shield from the tension she felt rising between the two exes.

"Anyway," Mia said, "I needed to get away from those beasts I share DNA with. What are you two up to?"

Jenna swallowed, hoping the guilt didn't show on her face. "I came up here to get some air and found Adam working. He startled me and I spilled wine on myself, so he was helping me get the stain out."

"Oh—that's why you were sitting like that?"

"Salt," Adam announced, holding the shaker out like some sort of talisman. "Works magic on wine stains. Learned it from that book."

A grin broke over Mia's face, and she pushed a shock of red hair off her forehead. "God, that's right—*101 Ways to Clean Everything*! The most romantic wedding gift ever, courtesy of my mother. What ever happened to that, anyway?"

"I got it," Adam said, his tone flat and unreadable. "Remember? I got all the cookbooks and how-to manuals, you got the small kitchen appliances and silverware."

"Right, right. Except the knife set from your Nana because she bought it on that trip to Germany. How's she doing anyway?"

"She's had a rough year," Adam said, running his fingers through his hair. "She's nearing the final stages with the Alzheimer's. She doesn't remember anyone in the family most of the time, not even Gramps."

"Oh, Adam—I'm so sorry. Tell everyone I said hello?"

Jenna looked down at her bare feet, suddenly feeling like an outsider instead of like the woman who'd helped Mia shop for nursing bras the day before.

Or like the woman who swapped spit with Adam five minutes ago.

God, what had she been thinking? Guilt surged through her like a hot rush of poison, and she swallowed hard to keep it from drowning her. No matter how long ago Mia had divorced Adam, this still felt like a betrayal. The fact that Mia wasn't freaking out must have meant she hadn't seen the kiss, or if she had, the rooftop glare had been sufficient to disguise groping as innocent stain removal.

Seeming to remember the third party present at their discussion about custody of the toaster, Adam and Mia turned back to her.

"Good thing you were drinking white wine," Mia said, eyeing the front of her dress. "At least you look more like an inkblot test than a knife-fight victim."

Jenna nodded, wondering if her friend suspected anything. "I'll have to see if my dry cleaner can save it."

"You're lucky Adam was here with his geeky knowledge of fabric cleaning," Mia said, linking her arm through Jenna's. "Come on, I've got three bags of clothes in my trunk I meant to haul to Goodwill before the reception. None of it fits me anymore, but there's bound to be something you can change into in the meantime. There were a ton of really cute dresses in there—even that yellow silk one you always loved that just made me look like a big banana."

Jenna let Mia tow her away, trying not to look back at Adam. They'd almost made it to the stairs when Jenna gasped.

"The door!" She closed her eyes, overwhelmed by the prospect of being stuck on a roof for even five more minutes with her secret fling, his ex-wife, and her own best friend—no matter that two of those people were one and the same. Christ, could this be any weirder?

"The door," Jenna repeated, frantic now. "The door locked behind you. We're all stuck up here and—"

"Relax, girl," Mia said, giving her arm a squeeze in the crook of her elbow. "I used my wedding program to prop the latch open. We're fine. Come on, let's get out of here."

Relief flooded Jenna's limbs as she let Mia drag her away. She could feel Adam's eyes on them, and wondered if this was as weird for him as it was for her. She glanced over her shoulder and saw him watching them with an unreadable expression.

"Thank you for the salt," she called.

"You're welcome," he replied evenly, shaker still clutched in his hand. "Call me anytime you need cleaning tips."

Jenna nodded, her gut clenching with guilt. For the kiss, or for the fact that they'd worked together to cover it up? She couldn't say for sure.

⌒～

Jenna dropped her keys in the little dish by the front door, smiling at the freshly crocheted doily beneath it. Gertie wasn't good at sitting idle, not even when she was sick.

"Aunt Gertie?" she called, then kicked herself. What if the old woman was sleeping?

But Gertie's voice called back from the bathroom at the other end of the hall. "Just a second, sweetie. Oh, dear—this stomach bug doesn't seem to want to let go of me, I'm afraid."

"I stopped at the store and got some ginger ale and soda crackers on the way home. Why don't you get back into bed and I'll bring them to you, okay?"

"That would be lovely, dear. Thank you."

Jenna toed off her shoes and padded into the kitchen with her shopping bag, glancing at the dining room table where Gertie's laptop sat open and glowing. No screensaver, which meant Gert hadn't been away long.

Something on the screen caught her eye, and Jenna blinked at it, then angled closer, feeling like a horrible snoop, but curious just the same.

New York Times Bestseller!!!!!!!!!!

That was the subject line on an e-mail chain that had started earlier in the week. Jenna glanced toward the silent hallway that led toward Gert's room, then back at the laptop. She took a step closer, peering at the screen.

At the top of the message was a screenshot of what Jenna could only presume was the week's *New York Times* Bestseller list. A familiar name was in slot number three.

G.G. Buckingham.

Gert's pen name. Not that they'd ever discussed it. It wasn't that Gert kept things a secret. Honestly, she'd probably be thrilled to chat about it.

It was that Jenna didn't want to know. She wanted to keep pretending, to stick to their tacit agreement never to speak of Gert's crazy life penning tales of lust and passion and illicit trysts.

It had never mattered before. Gert got to earn extra income to help pay her medical bills, Jenna got to pretend Gert sat here all day crocheting doilies and baking pies.

Jenna shook her head, torn between pride in her aunt's achievement and confusion about what it all meant. She looked back at the e-mail. Beneath the screenshot, there was a typed message.

Gertrude,

Congratulations again! As I said on the phone, we need to schedule a call to discuss what this means for the future of your writing career. How's next Monday for you?

It was signed *Michelle*. Gert's agent, another secret Jenna knew only from the monthly royalty checks that showed up in the mailbox. Gert pretended they were from Publishers Clearing House sweepstakes, and Jenna played along because it was easier that way.

It was stupid, really, but what choice did she have? Even when the ex-CEO had claimed not to know about his wife's escort service, he still went down with the ship when the story broke. With negotiations as tense as they were at Belmont, Jenna couldn't afford to have Gert's secret get out.

A toilet flushed at the end of the hall, and Jenna jerked upright. She turned and placed her shopping bag on the counter, then began pulling out her purchases. A box of crackers, a pack of chamomile tea, a six-pack of chilled ginger ale, and one of the gossip magazines Gert enjoyed reading. Jenna reached into the cupboard above her for a plate and a glass, torn between guilt for snooping, pride in her aunt's achievement, and a sadness she couldn't quite place.

She couldn't congratulate Gert, right? They didn't talk about it, so a pat on the back wasn't the right thing. Still, it seemed like an occasion she should mark somehow.

She heard Gertie's slippered feet shuffling down the hall, and turned to see her aunt moving into the kitchen. Jenna placed a handful of soda crackers on a china plate and turned to face her aunt.

"Aunt Gertie, I told you to get in bed and I'd bring these to you. You should be resting."

"I know, dear, but I couldn't wait to hear about Mia's reception. Were there a lot of people? What did she wear? Did she have flowers and cake?"

Jenna looked down at the pink and white flowered lei Mia had looped over her head as she left the reception. She pulled it off and placed it gently around Gert's neck, straightening it over her housecoat. Then she bent to plant a kiss on her aunt's weathered cheek.

"You look beautiful," she murmured, surprised at how deeply she meant it. "You and mom always looked amazing in pink."

Gertie smiled, fingering the flowers. "Your mom was always the head turner. Remember that pink dress she wore at your sweet sixteen?"

Jenna nodded, her eyes prickling with the memory. "She looked like an angel."

"And she got up and gave that beautiful toast about working hard to achieve your dreams."

"And you wore a red dress with those stiletto heels I would have killed for. And you slipped me that secret sip of champagne—"

Jenna stopped, her throat clenching tight. She swallowed hard, torn between a sad ache for her mother and an overwhelming pride in her aunt. Gert blinked, her eyes the same shade of blue Jenna remembered in her mother, in her grandma, in every woman on their side of the family.

Jenna swallowed again. "Ginger ale would be better for your stomach," she said softly. "But there's one of those mini-bottles of champagne in the back of the fridge. We could save it for later, or—"

"No," Gert said, smiling. "Let's share it now. I feel like celebrating."

"Me, too," Jenna said, and bent down to wrap Gertie in another hug.

⌒ ↄ

Two hours later, Jenna sat at the dining room table with her own laptop and a glass of Chianti. Mia had insisted she take a whole bottle home—*"I can't drink it anyway, so it's your job as my friend to polish it off"*—so Jenna was doing her best to be a good friend.

Gertie had dozed off after half a glass of champagne and a full hour of hearing every detail of Mia's wedding reception. She'd sat with rapt attention through the stories of canapés and Mia's rude cousins, but she'd really perked up when Jenna got to the part about being stuck on the roof.

"It's a good thing the young man was there with the know-how to tackle that wine stain," Gert had said, her eyes fixed on Jenna's.

Jenna had nodded, hoping Gert didn't see the heat creeping into her cheeks. "Good thing."

"Do you want me to take a look at the dress? Salt only goes so far, after all."

"I already dropped it off at the cleaners. Why don't you get some rest, okay?"

"I'm just too excited to rest." Gert beamed, then seemed to remember something as she fingered the lei around her neck. "About Mia's reception. I'm excited about Mia's reception, of course."

"I know," Jenna said, resting a hand on Gert's arm. "I'm excited, too."

It was the closest they'd come to talking about Gert's literary achievement.

Now, as Jenna sat looking at her laptop screen, she wished she'd been able to properly congratulate her aunt. She'd known the

75

bestseller thing was a big deal, but until she started researching, she hadn't realized how big. Not only did it likely mean some bigger royalty checks for G.G. Buckingham, it was a feather in Gert's proverbial author cap. Something that meant she was more than just a little old lady tapping out flowery romance novels in her spare time.

Not that Gert's novels were flowery. True, Jenna had never read one, but she suspected G.G. Buckingham's *Panty Dropper* series ran closer to *50 Shades of Grey* than *Pride and Prejudice*.

Well, maybe she'd send Gert some flowers. Anonymously, of course. She could spring for a gift certificate to Massage Envy and convince Gert it was a bonus she got from work that she wouldn't have time to use. That was something, right?

Jenna clicked off the *New York Times* page and scrolled over to her Facebook icon, hungry for a little mindless browsing.

She took a sip of wine and clicked "Like" on a video about a kleptomaniac cat. She moved her cursor down the page, rolling her eyes over a distant cousin's latest political rant. A few slots down, one of Mia's sisters had posted shots from the reception, several of which made Mia look like a red-eyed walrus. Intentional, no doubt, but at least Facebook-phobic Mia wasn't likely to see them.

Jenna scrolled a little further, smiling at a puppy meme, then at a photo posted by an old college friend honeymooning in Belize. Wasn't that where Mia and Adam had honeymooned? She thought she remembered a story Mia told about Adam getting belligerent with a street vendor who tried to overcharge them.

"Honestly, it was only five dollars," Mia had told her with a sigh. "It probably meant more to the guy than it did to us. That should have been a warning sign right there, if my new husband wanted to bicker about pocket change instead of gaze at the sunset with me."

Jenna frowned and kept scrolling, not wanting to go too far down that path. How weird was it that she knew details about her lover's honeymoon with another woman? Details he probably never imagined she knew?

He's not your lover, and it's none of your business.

Right. How well did she even know him, anyway? She frowned, then clicked her mouse in the search window. She hesitated. Then typed his name.

Adam Thomas.

A shiver snaked up her arms, and Jenna wasn't sure if it was guilt or intrigue. But really, what was the harm in a little Facebook stalking?

It took her a few tries to find the right one. Adam Thomas in Germany had an unfortunate overbite and a BMW he liked to pose beside while wearing a red leather jacket. Adam Thomas in Iowa appeared to be in the middle of gender reassignment surgery.

Finally, she found him. Adam Thomas from Chicago. No mutual friends, of course. Though Mia had a Facebook account, she rarely checked it, and had obviously unfriended her ex years ago. Or was it the other way around? What was the Facebook etiquette with divorce, anyway? Did you unfriend each other instantly, or only if the split was contentious? Did you divvy up friends the way you divvied up furniture and silverware, or did everyone try to keep up the pretense of staying chummy instead of picking sides?

Oddly enough, she hadn't needed to deal with that when she and Sean had split up. Though her ex-fiancé lived life with his smart-phone glued to his palm, he'd avoided Facebook like the plague.

"Social media is a waste of time," he'd declared, barely glancing up from his game of Angry Birds to key in the stock trade he needed to complete during a romantic brunch.

God, she didn't miss that.

Jenna studied Adam Thomas's Facebook page, a rush of intrigue making her skin prickle. She clicked the file for his photos, surprised his privacy settings allowed it. Jenna kept hers locked down tight.

No one could see anything unless she'd specifically friended them, not even her photos. But Adam Thomas was practically an open book. True, there were probably things she couldn't see without being his Facebook friend, but she was surprised at how much was wide-open for perusal by a total stranger.

You slept with the man. You're hardly a total stranger.

She took another sip of wine, feeling like a stalker as she scrolled through his photos. There was a shot of him in a suit at a conference. Not something he'd posted himself, so someone else must've tagged him. Another more personal shot of him fly-fishing. Another image from that series showed him shirtless on a riverbank, and Jenna shivered, remembering the feel of that chest beneath her fingertips, the smooth plane of his abdomen, and the springiness of his chest hair under her palms.

Stop it, she ordered herself. *Get off this page and go click on some cat videos.*

But she didn't stop. She kept scrolling, hoarding tidbits of information the way a squirrel gathers nuts to stash in a tree. Adam enjoyed cooking. Had Mia ever mentioned that? She'd complained her ex hadn't helped much around the house, but this Adam had an entire folder of photos featuring meals he'd learned to make in a cooking class the previous spring. He'd also done a triathlon the summer before, and Jenna squirmed a little at the sight of that physique showcased in a neoprene wetsuit. Damn, the man looked fine.

She kept scrolling, smiling at the HeartMath quote he'd posted several weeks ago about the importance of not living your life for someone else. It was one of her favorites. Jenna took the last sip of wine and set down her empty glass, eyes still glued to the screen.

"Jenna?"

She jumped, feeling like a schoolgirl caught reading a dirty book under the covers. Then she remembered Aunt Gert wrote dirtier books than anything she'd ever smuggled beneath the bedsheets.

"You need something, Gertie?" she called, scrambling up from the table with a hasty glance back at a photo of Adam holding a friend's new baby.

"If it's not too much trouble, sweetheart, could you bring me my crochet basket from the living room? I left it right next to the davenport."

"Sure thing. Sit tight."

She reached over to put the laptop in sleep mode, but knocked her empty wineglass onto the keyboard instead. She righted the glass and hurried to the living room where she snatched up Gert's basket of yarn and crochet needles. She hustled down the hall and rounded the corner into Gert's room.

"Here you go, Aunt Gertie. Can I get you anything else? Chamomile tea? Another pillow?"

"I'm fine, dear, really. A little weak, but I'm feeling much better."

"Want to watch another *Sex and the City* marathon on Netflix?"

"Maybe later, dear," Gert said, burrowing her spindly fingers into a sea of blue and green yarn. "Right now I'd love to work on those baby hats for the hospital birthing center. I promised them two more next week."

Jenna brushed a shock of white hair off Aunt Gertie's forehead, checking the old woman's temperature just to be safe. No fever, but she did look a little flushed. "I'm sure they'd understand if you were a little behind, Gert. You need your rest."

"I've been resting all day. It's just food poisoning, sweetheart, I'm fine. I promise I'll stop if I feel too tired."

"Okay," Jenna said, dropping a kiss on the old woman's head. "Yell if you need anything."

She turned and headed back down the hall, reminding herself to check on her aunt again in a few minutes. It wouldn't do to have Gert nod off with a crochet needle in her hand and poke herself in the eye.

Dropping into her seat at the kitchen table, Jenna stroked a fingertip over the trackpad on her laptop. The screen flickered to life, revealing a pop-up message.

Friend request sent.

"What?"

She fumbled for the keyboard, panic making a rocky lump in her throat. She stroked the trackpad again, frantic now. She was still on Adam Thomas's Facebook page.

"Holy hell!"

"What's that, dear?"

"Nothing, Gertie. Everything's fine."

Shit, shit, shit. Would he receive an instant notification of the friend request, or could she make it go away before he noticed? What if Mia checked Facebook to see if anyone posted wedding photos and saw Jenna had friended her ex? Was that how Facebook worked? What the hell determined the things that showed up in newsfeeds? Jenna tried to recall details from a social media workshop given by the hospital's marketing director, but she honestly couldn't remember.

She mouse-clicked frantically around the page until she found what she was looking for.

Cancel friend request.

She clicked the words, then clicked to confirm. There, that should work. Jenna bit her lip. Wait, would Adam get a notification that she'd rescinded her friend request? Would other people see that in their timeline?

Dammit. Dammit, dammit, *dammit.*

If she'd already friended him in the first place, maybe the damage was done. Unfriending him might make things worse. Besides, she could see his full profile if she friended him, right?

She clicked the button again.

Friend request sent.

Shit, no. That was stupid. He had to accept the friend request first, didn't he? Why hadn't Jenna paid more attention to how Facebook worked?

She hovered her cursor over the *Cancel friend request* command, casting a furious glance at her damn empty wineglass. That was the problem, really. An empty wineglass was at the root of most of her mistakes so far with Adam. Or maybe a full wineglass. Hell, maybe she should swear off wine altogether.

Cancel friend request.

Dammit, she hadn't meant to hit the button. Or hell, maybe she had. Adam would probably know, what with all his Freudian training and knowledge of the inner-workings of the subconscious.

She thought about what Aunt Gertie would do in this situation. Or what about a woman determined to embrace her inner sex goddess? Jenna bit her lip.

Friend request sent.

Dammit. She should just cancel the request, wash out her wineglass, and go to bed. Or maybe she should fill up the kitchen sink and drown herself in it.

An alert dinged on her laptop, and a little dialogue bubble popped up on the bottom right side of her screen.

Adam Thomas: Made up your mind yet?

Chapter Six

Adam stared at the dialogue bubble for a few beats, wondering what Jenna was up to. He'd been mindlessly browsing Facebook for funny memes and photos of a buddy's Yosemite climbing trip when the notification popped up that he had a friend request from Jenna.

Okay, that wasn't entirely true.

The friend notification thing was true, but he hadn't just been looking at quotes and pictures. He'd started out that way, but he'd found himself drawn by the temptation to steal a glance at his ex-wife's page. He didn't do it often. Hell, the last time was probably two years ago, and he'd clicked away feeling dirty and a little nauseated the instant her profile photo flashed up on his screen.

Besides, it wasn't like she posted more than a few times a year. No point going there, not even out of morbid curiosity.

But something drew him to Mia's page tonight. Maybe it was the forced proximity of working together, or the knowledge she'd gotten married and pregnant, though not necessarily in that order. Before he knew it, he was sitting there in his boxer shorts in a dark hotel room, skimming his ex's Facebook page like some kind of creeper.

He hadn't been Facebook friends with her for years, though he honestly couldn't recall who'd pulled the unfriend trigger first. Maybe he had, the same day he'd changed his status from "married" to "single."

Even so, he could see a few photos on her page, and several scattered posts other people had left on her wall.

Those were the ones that left a funny feeling in his gut.

"I heard the news from Jamie. Congrats, babe! Wishing you all the happiness in the world!"

That was a message for Mia from the wife of one of Adam's old college buddies. Apparently she and Mia had remained Facebook friends. And why wouldn't they? It's not like a judge signed divorce papers and instantly reassigned all Facebook friends to their rightful owners. Besides, it was obvious neither woman spent much time on Facebook. Mia probably hadn't seen the message at all.

"So happy for you! You deserve the best!"

Those words came from one of Mia's high school classmates. She'd been a bridesmaid when Adam and Mia wed, clad in a frilly lavender dress and clutching a bouquet of daisies.

Adam stared at the words again, his fingers twitchy on the edge of his hotel pillow. *You deserve the best.*

Was she suggesting that's not what Mia got the first time?

"Dude," he said out loud, shaking his head at his own stupidity. "You're being a dumbass. It's got nothing to do with you."

True enough. See, this was why cyber-stalking an ex was an idiotic idea. Lesson learned. Again.

He was just about to shut down Facebook entirely when the friend notification popped up. He had half a second of panic thinking it was Mia—that she'd figured out somehow he was snooping on her page.

He clicked on the little head and shoulders icon with a twinge of dread.

Friend request: Jenna McArthur.

A shiver of excitement ran through him, followed by a moment of confusion.

Really? That seemed odd. Jenna had been adamant about keeping their personal involvement a secret. Or hell, killing their personal involvement altogether. She was the one who insisted things needed to stay professional between them, right?

Then again, she was the one who kissed him in the porn booth. And on the roof. Kissed him hard and deep and with a passion that contradicted her insistence there was nothing between them but a professional tie.

Like hell, Adam thought, and hovered his cursor over the window showing Jenna's friend request.

Confirm?

What did it mean that she'd sent him a friend request? Was it an olive branch of some sort, or a mistake?

"You're a fucking idiot," he told himself. "What is this, an after-school special on social media relationships?"

He clicked the damn icon.

Sorry, this request is no longer valid.

Adam frowned at the monitor. What the hell? He typed her name into the search window and spent a few moments locating the right Jenna McArthur. Her profile was locked down tight. He could see her name and profile picture, but everything was privacy protected to the max.

That figured.

He was ready to shut down again when another notification popped up. He clicked the icon.

Friend request: Jenna McArthur.

What the hell?

He clicked the *Confirm* button to accept.

Sorry, this request is no longer valid.

Adam shook his head, not sure whether to be amused or annoyed. It was possible she'd been hacked, or that someone else was messing around on her computer.

He watched as the friend request icon lit up again and clicked *Confirm* as fast as he could.

Friendship established, he clicked the icon to send her a direct message.

Have you made up your mind yet?

He wasn't sure if she'd see the message or if it would get routed into an invisible folder. That might be the case if she'd already unfriended him. What were the Facebook rules there?

He waited a few minutes, wondering whether he'd spooked her or if she hadn't seen the message at all. Maybe this was some sort of weird computer glitch. Maybe it was a trick.

Maybe he'd been watching too much television.

He watched the little pop-up window, feeling disturbingly like a preteen girl passing notes in class and wondering if her crush would reply or not.

The little ellipsis popped up in the dialogue bubble, indicating she was typing a reply. A prickle of anticipation traveled up Adam's arms, and he sat waiting, watching the screen. And waiting. And waiting some more.

Christ, was she writing an essay?

Jenna McArthur: Sorry about that. My wineglass fell on the keyboard.

Adam stared at her message, more curious than he'd been a few minutes ago.

Adam Thomas: Repeatedly? On the same key?

Jenna McArthur: Apparently I should switch from stemware to sippy cups.

He smiled, appreciating the wisecrack even if she hadn't addressed the question. He hesitated a moment, then typed a reply.

Adam Thomas: Did you get the stain out of the dress? Incidentally, this is the same message Bill Clinton would have sent Monica Lewinsky if Facebook had been around in 1996.

He wondered if he'd made her laugh, and hoped he hadn't crossed some line in the sand. Seconds later, he had her reply.

Jenna McArthur: Unlike Ms. Lewinsky, I had the good sense to visit the drycleaner on my way home. If our Facebook accounts are ever subpoenaed, this exchange will look highly incriminating.

Adam Thomas: You spies are always thinking ahead. Shall I come over with a blowtorch so we can destroy our laptops together?

Jenna McArthur: Won't matter. Everything lives in infamy in cyberspace. Maybe you can dismantle the Internet. Was Internet hacking one of your specialized gigolo skills?

He smiled. Hesitated. Put his hands on the keyboard again.

Adam Thomas: Well, if we're busted anyway, let's make the most of it. What are you wearing?

The pause dragged out, and Adam kicked himself for going there. The ellipsis popped up to indicate she was typing a response, and Adam braced himself to be shut down.

Jenna McArthur: Very funny. Did you just try to sext me?

Adam Thomas: Is it still called sexting when it's a Facebook PM?

Jenna McArthur: Does it still count when you use a phone sex pickup line in a typed message?

Adam Thomas: I'll consult my official guide to social media sex. Please hold.

He was contemplating his next message when a reply popped up.

Jenna McArthur: Since you asked, I'm wearing your ex-wife's dress. Because clearly, this whole thing wasn't creepy enough.

Adam winced. He wasn't sure how to respond to that. Cracking a joke about his ex-wife's hygiene would be tasteless, not to mention making Jenna feel defensive of her friend. Playing it cool might be the right approach, but that wasn't really Adam's style.

He settled for honesty.

Adam Thomas: Er, sorry about that?

Jenna McArthur: Don't be. It's not your fault that I'm sitting here wondering if you've ever removed this garment from my best friend. Hey, I was wrong! This can get creepier.

She'd ended the message with a smiley, but Adam grimaced anyway. Was she upset? He didn't think so, but it was so damn hard to read someone's tone in writing. This is why normal people dated in person. Normal people who weren't hiding their connection from ex-wives and professional colleagues.

Adam was still considering his reply when her next message popped up.

Jenna McArthur: Problem solved. I took off the dress.

Holy shit.

Well, that was one way to do it. Was she joking or serious? He honestly couldn't tell.

Adam Thomas: So you're sitting there in your underwear?

Jenna McArthur: What makes you think I'm wearing underwear?

Okay, she was definitely being flirty. She'd mentioned an empty wineglass, so maybe that was it. Or maybe the elusive aunt had given her another pep talk. Whatever the case, he couldn't stop his brain from forming a vivid picture. Had she really taken off the dress? Was she sitting in bed like him, stripped down to nothing? Or was she parked at a desk in a home office still fully clad and laughing at her own joke?

Adam Thomas: So now we're both in our underwear and I'm in bed. Didn't we pledge not to end up here again?

Jenna McArthur: POIDH.

Adam Thomas: What?

Jenna McArthur: Clearly, you're not hip to the cybersex lingo, Mr. Thomas.

Adam Thomas: Clearly, hip people don't use words like hip *and* lingo.

Jenna McArthur: LOL! POIDH = Pics or It Didn't Happen.

Adam laughed out loud. She was definitely flirting, no question about it. If he didn't have written evidence, he might never have believed it. He thought about brushing off the request, but what the hell? Photos of average-looking thirty-something guys in boxer shorts weren't exactly scandalous viral Internet content.

He clicked on Photo Booth, then fired off a couple shots. One turned out blurry, but one wasn't a half-bad image of him sitting shirtless in blue plaid boxers with his reading glasses slightly askew. He clicked the button to attach the image, then waited.

Jenna McArthur: HOLY SHIT!!!!!

Adam frowned, not sure how to read that response. He didn't have to wait long.

Jenna McArthur: Christ, I was kidding, but oh my God. How is it possible for someone to look that hot lounging in bed on a random Saturday night?

Adam smiled. At least she wasn't annoyed, or worse, offended. He decided to push his luck.

Adam Thomas: Your turn.

Jenna McArthur: No way. I'm a woman. I know better than to send sexy photos to strange men on the Internet. Besides, I wasn't kidding about wearing your ex-wife's dress, but I was kidding about taking it off. Still wearing the damn thing. Does that weird you out?

He hesitated, sensing a distinct shift from flirtation to something much more serious. He went for honesty again.

Adam Thomas: You mean does it weird me out that you swap clothing with my ex-wife, or does it weird me out that you're still fully dressed? Yes to the first question. No to the second.

Jenna McArthur: It's a yellow silk sheath dress with an asymmetrical hemline and contrast stitching beneath the bust. Familiar?

Adam frowned. Was she asking if she was wearing a garment he'd ever removed from his ex? He wasn't sure if this was a joke or not, but it definitely wasn't flirtation. He could understand why the whole thing might feel odd to her. It wasn't jealousy, precisely, but something else. It was one thing to know a partner had lovers before you. It was quite another to don her clothing.

Adam Thomas: I understood "yellow," "dress," and "bust." Beyond that, you've lost me in the fashion nuances.

Jenna McArthur: You'd make a terrible cross-dresser.

Adam Thomas: I'll mark that off my list of professional ambitions.

He stared at the screen a moment, not sure whether to keep the conversation going in this direction or to try to shift things back to humorous flirtation. What did she want?

Jenna McArthur: I'm sorry about this afternoon. About kissing you on the roof.

Adam Thomas: You can kiss me on the veranda anytime. Though maybe the lips would be better.

Jenna McArthur: LOL. The Three Amigos, right?

Adam Thomas: Yep. And don't worry about it. The kiss was perfectly tolerable. Maybe a little less tongue than I might have liked, but I'm not in a position to be picky.

Jenna McArthur: Thanks. I'm not sure why I keep doing that.

Adam Thomas: Kissing me or stopping?

Jenna McArthur: Yes.

Adam Thomas: Kissing me = Because I'm irresistible. Stopping = Beats me.

Jenna McArthur: Maybe because we're working together and you used to be married to my best friend?

Adam Thomas: Oh, yeah. Details.

Jenna McArthur: She's my best friend, Adam. I can't betray that.

He frowned, fingers hesitating over the keys.

Adam Thomas: Understood.

That wasn't entirely true, but this wasn't the forum to delve into it. He hesitated with his fingers on the keys, trying to think of some way to avoid letting go of this connection with her.

Adam Thomas: Okay then, what's a platonic topic? Baseball? Books? Pizza?

Jenna McArthur: I hate baseball, I love spy novels, and I will fight to the death if anyone challenges my assertion that Rigatelli's makes the best pizza in Portland. Maybe in the universe.

Adam Thomas: Rigatelli's?

Jenna McArthur: It's a few blocks from your hotel. You should check it out. Friday nights they have karaoke.

Adam Thomas: You do karaoke?

Jenna McArthur: No way. But it's fun to watch.

Adam thought about making a voyeurism joke, but decided they'd moved beyond the sexy flirting. He tried not to feel sad about that.

Jenna McArthur: I'd better go check on my aunt. It's been good chatting with you. Goodnight, Adam.

Adam Thomas: Goodnight, Jenna.

Jenna McArthur: Oh, and I'm rescinding that last friend request. Sorry for the confusion.

Adam Thomas: Probably best. See you Monday?

Jenna McArthur: xoxoxo

He stared for a moment at the cyber hugs and kisses. They seemed like a deviation from the business-formal writing he'd come to expect from her. Had she done it on a whim, or carefully counted each *x* and *o*?

He tried to remember which one stood for hugs and which represented kisses. Either way, they weren't the same as the real thing. Not by a long shot. But they were all he was likely to get from her.

He knew why, and it all came down to the other thing he'd written that wasn't entirely true.

Because he remembered that goddamn yellow dress. Mia had bought it the summer before they split, and she'd worn it during a weekend getaway to the Jersey Shore. A failed, last-ditch attempt to rekindle the marriage.

The vacation and the dress had been no match for the problems between them.

Adam shut down his Internet browser, trying not to picture the dress on Jenna. On the floor of his hotel room.

He closed his laptop and put it on the nightstand, a funny lump in the pit of his stomach.

⁓

"We're going to kick off this morning's mediation session with an icebreaker exercise."

Adam surveyed the assembled group, noticing a few annoyed expressions and several staff members who didn't look fully awake.

He kept his eyes away from the corner of the room where Mia and Jenna had seated themselves next to the refreshment table. He had to appreciate both their resourcefulness and their position out of his immediate line of sight.

"Let's start things off with a very basic question," Adam continued, shrugging off his suit jacket and draping it over the podium someone had set there like he was some sort of stuffy inspirational speaker. He moved around it to sit on the edge of an empty table in the front row, his eyes scanning the room to make sure he had everyone's attention.

"Toilet paper." He paused there, watching a few eyebrows raise and a few sleepy expressions flicker to alert curiosity. "Over or under? Those of you who prefer over, I'd like you to go to that side of the room." He gestured to the right, keeping his eyes off Mia and Jenna. "Those who prefer under, please gather over there. I'll give you a moment to get settled."

He watched as members of the bargaining team swiveled their gazes around the room. There were a few suspicious looks, and Adam had to stifle a laugh at the notion that high-level executives might think a discussion of toilet paper could lead to a strategic gain in contract negotiations.

At least one person looked embarrassed, and several more still looked sleepy. But most looked intrigued, even a little amused.

He dared a glance at Jenna, and saw her look around, a little self-conscious at first. Then she strode to the opposite side of the room, joining the ranks of the "under" crowd.

His ex-wife stayed put on the "over" side of the room, and Adam tried not to give too much thought to the argument they'd had the first year of their marriage when she'd steadfastly insisted on the opposite configuration in their bathroom. Not particularly set in his ways at the time, Adam had been fine with giving in.

He turned his thoughts away from Mia and Jenna and focused back on the group.

"Okay then," he said, pleased to see everyone had picked a side. "Obviously most of you have a pretty solid opinion about the proper positioning of toilet paper. Let's take a moment to discuss why that is. Who'd like to give me a reason for your preference?"

He let the silence stretch for a few beats. He'd call on someone if no one stepped up, but someone always did. Even with something as innocuous as ass wiping, people couldn't resist the urge to share and defend their opinions.

"It just rolls off easier," the board president said at last, crossing her arms over her chest. "When the toilet paper comes over the top of the roll, you can see where it's coming from and it flows better."

"Thank you, Nancy," Adam said, nodding in encouragement. "Great input. Now how about someone on the other side of the room?"

Brett Lombard, the president of the nurses' union, was already shaking his head. "Actually, I find it rolls better coming from underneath. Plus it tears easier when you can press it against the wall."

There were a couple scowls from the other camp, but most people were observing with expressions that ran the gamut from amusement to embarrassment to thoughtful intrigue.

"It's harder for my cat to get to when it rolls from underneath," shared the CFO. "One time when I had it rolling over the top, Maggie spun the whole roll into a giant pile on the floor and then took a nap on it."

A few people laughed, lightening the mood a bit, and Adam said a silent thank you to Phil Gallow for bringing pets into the equation. That was always a good equalizer with a crowd like this.

"My mom taught me to always roll it over the top." Adam turned to look at Susan Schrader, the other union rep who'd ended up on the same side of the room as the CEO. The fact that neither had thrown a punch yet seemed like progress.

Susan rubbed her hands together and continued. "She and my dad used to fight about it, actually, and he said she should be thankful that he changed the roll at all."

"My parents were the same way," the CEO said, looking surprised to be bonding with his sworn enemy over bath tissue. "My mom liked to fold the end of the paper into a little fan when we had company coming."

"I just think it looks tidier."

Adam recognized Jenna's voice without having to turn, but his eyes slid to the "under" side of the room anyway. Jenna shrugged, her cheeks faintly pink as she touched the pendant at the center of her throat. "When it rolls from underneath, it's more hidden. It looks neater that way."

He nodded, trying not to read too much into Jenna's fondness for keeping things tidy and hidden. He heard his ex-wife laugh across the room, and he forced himself to turn to her with the same impassive expression he'd given everyone else.

"In my house, we count our blessings if the toilet paper makes it onto the dispenser at all," Mia said. "Preteen girls don't always have the best recall when it comes to household chores. Honestly, do they think there's a magical fountain of toilet paper that just appears on the roll?"

"I hear you, sister," called a woman Adam recognized as a physician who'd been asked to join the bargaining team on the medical side. "Try living with three teenage boys."

There were some titters of agreement from other parents in the room, and Adam nodded along with them. He'd forgotten Mark had a daughter from a previous marriage, which would make Mia a stepmother now. The uncharitable side of his brain flashed on an image of the wicked stepmother from Cinderella, but most of him hoped the kid was doing okay. That *Mia* was doing okay.

A movement on the "under" side of the room caught his eye as the Chief Clinical Officer stood and made his way to the other side of the room. Adam watched him go, pleased at the unexpected acknowledgment of the validity of arguments from the opposite side.

"Changing your mind about your preferences, Doug?" Adam called. "That's not an uncommon response to hearing the thought processes from the opposite side of an issue, no matter how small it may seem. Great to see you illustrating that so clearly."

"Nah, I misunderstood the question when you asked," he said, looking a little sheepish as he tugged his necktie and took a spot on the "over" side of the room. "Thought you were talking about wiping methods, not how the roll should spin."

A few people snort-laughed at that, and Adam saw Jenna cover her mouth to hide a smile. Adam grinned and gave the CCO a mock salute. "Doug, in three years of doing this exercise, I can't say I've ever had someone say that."

"I fancy myself a trendsetter," the man said, grinning back as he tugged off his tie. Another good sign, Adam thought, glancing around the room again to see a number of others loosening up.

"We can always use more outside-the-box thinkers when it comes to negotiations," Adam agreed.

He cleared his throat and went back to addressing the whole room. "Okay, so obviously everyone has reasons for feeling the way they do about toilet paper distribution. Can we all agree on that?"

There were a few nods around the room. A board member whose name slipped Adam's memory raised her hand a little timidly. "I never really thought about why I did it that way. I just always have."

"I might have to try that trick going under." Adam turned to see Susan Schrader looking at the other side of the room with an odd mix of surprise and respect. "My cat does the same thing with the toilet paper."

"Works great," the CFO said, looking a whole lot friendlier than he'd been ten minutes ago. "We also got one of those scratching posts to put in the corner of the bathroom and that seems to help."

"I'll give that a try. Thanks for the tip."

Adam smiled, always pleased when someone created the perfect segue. "That's the way it is with a lot of opinions we hold," he said. "Sometimes there's a lot of thought and research that goes into them, and sometimes it's just the way we've always done things. Either way, we all have valid reasons for making the choices we make."

He picked up the glass of water he'd nabbed at the start of the session and took a drink, holding the pause until he set the glass down again. "As I'm sure you've guessed, this isn't just about toilet paper."

A few folks nodded, several looking decidedly less bored or hostile than they had at the start of the session.

"What I'm hoping right now is that you're all taking a moment to reflect on the idea that each person in this room has a valid reason for wanting things the way he or she wants them," Adam said, letting his gaze travel from one team member to the next as he held eye contact for at least three seconds. "Obviously we can't all have things precisely the way we like in every situation, but we need to keep in mind that everyone's opinion has merit and value."

He let his words hang there in the air for a moment as he continued making eye contact with everyone. The CEO looked thoughtful, which Adam hoped was a good sign. Mia looked amused, and maybe a little bewildered. Adam wondered what that was about, but didn't dwell on it as he shifted his gaze to Jenna.

When his eyes found hers, Adam felt his pulse kick up. He fought the urge to look away, letting himself linger for a few beats while the room buzzed around him and everything else melted away. His heart was pounding, and he felt certain everyone could see his palms growing damp, hear his pulse thrumming in his head. He watched Jenna's chest rise as she took a steadying breath. She held his eyes, not looking away, not even blinking.

At last, Adam shook off the trance. He let his gaze slide to the CFO, then the board president, and all the rest of the faces that watched him with rapt attention. Not one of them gave an indication of having noticed his connection with Jenna. Had he imagined the intensity of it, or just the duration?

You didn't imagine a damn thing.

"Okay, then," Adam said, as his heart rate slid back to normal. "Let's get started on the first discussion item on the agenda."

He grabbed a stack of folders from behind the podium and began to pass them out, significantly less excited to talk about wage caps than toilet paper. His hand brushed Jenna's as he handed her a packet, and he watched a flush spread over her cheeks.

"Thank you," she murmured.

"My pleasure," he said, wishing that were true in every sense of the phrase.

Jenna walked out of the conference room with Mia at her side, conscious of Adam's eyes on her. She dared a glance at him, hoping that was the right thing to do to maintain the pretense of being platonic colleagues unacquainted with each other's genitals.

A smile played at the edges of his mouth, and he gave her a nod of acknowledgment before turning his attention to the CEO. Mia was talking to someone else now, so Jenna seized the opportunity to stare openly at Adam for a few more seconds. His expression was engaged and lively, and his hair was endearingly rumpled. He'd rolled up his shirtsleeves, and Jenna felt the heat creep into her cheeks again at the sight of his bare arms.

She remembered those forearms anchored on either side of her shoulders, the weight of his body pinning her to the bed as he held her eyes with his.

"So you're still coming over after work?"

Jenna blinked and turned her attention back to Mia. "Absolutely."

"I'm so glad," Mia said, stopping outside the conference room door to lean against the wall. "I'm dying for a girls' night in." She smoothed a hand over her belly and closed her eyes for a moment, looking more tired than Jenna had seen her in weeks.

"You sure you're up for company?"

"Definitely." Mia opened her eyes again and smiled. "I've been looking forward to it all weekend."

"What can I bring?"

"I have everything for nachos, and I'll pick up some margarita mix on the way home. Virgin for me, of course, but Mark grabbed tequila last night in case you want it."

Jenna nodded and tried not to glance at the door. Adam was bound to come strolling out any moment, and part of her wanted to scurry off so she wouldn't have to deal with the awkwardness of making conversation.

But part of her just wanted another glimpse of him. Just one quick look at those green eyes flashing with amusement and empathy and a sexy heat she wondered if anyone else recognized. Ridiculous, that's what this was. She'd just spent the last five hours staring at the man, for crying out loud. Did she really need another fix?

She swallowed and forced her attention back to Mia. "Want me to bring a salad tonight?"

"Nah, I don't feel like being healthy. I just want to put on my PJs, watch trashy TV, and enjoy some girl talk. Are you almost done for the day?"

"I wish. I've got a two-hour meeting with the Cancer Center team about some personnel issues, and then I have to run home and check on Gertie to make sure she's doing okay."

"She's feeling better now?"

"Right as rain, but I want to check on her to be sure. How about I swing by around six?"

"Perfect. See you in a few."

Jenna hustled away, breathing a sigh of relief she'd avoided running into Adam, even as she cast a glance over her shoulder hoping for one last glimpse.

The hallway was empty.

God, she must have looked at that shirtless photo of him at least a hundred times last night. It was stupid how thoroughly entranced she was by an image of a man wearing nothing but a pair of boxers and eyeglasses.

Not just any man, her conscience reminded her. *If it were that simple, you'd be Googling "shirtless men with glasses" instead of staring at a photo of the guy who made your toes curl.*

Jenna powered through the next few hours, soothing bruised egos and trying to mend fences for one of the most dysfunctional teams in the hospital system. By the time she slid her key into the lock of her front door, she was ready to take Mia's pajama request seriously.

She opened the door, surprised to find the house silent. "Aunt Gertie?"

No reply. She moved down the hall toward Gert's room, hating that her brain automatically went to the worst-case scenario. Gert not breathing. Gert unconscious in the bathtub.

As she rounded the corner to her aunt's room, Jenna's gut flooded with relief. The old woman was sound asleep, her chest rising and falling as one hand rested on the laptop folded shut on the bed beside her. Jenna watched her breathing for a few beats, moved by the faint smile etched into the creases of the older woman's face. She looked peaceful and serene, with her white halo of hair feathered out across her pale yellow pillowcase.

Jenna turned and moved back toward the kitchen, setting her handbag by the door so she wouldn't forget anything when she left for Mia's house. In the middle of the table was a note anchored by the salt and pepper shakers. The neon pink stationary was adorned with Gertie's flawless cursive.

Jenna,
I had a busy day today, so I'm taking a little nap. I know you're having girls' night with Mia, but I made a big pot of soup for my book club luncheon today. There's plenty left if you want some. Please take a couple slices of cherry pie to Mia. I saved some just for her. Love you!

Jenna smiled, and glanced back down the hall, pleased Gertie had formed such a busy social life in Portland. Did her book club even know they had a bestselling author in their midst? Jenna touched the note, wondering how Gert's call had gone with her agent.

She turned away and busied herself slicing pie and tucking it into a Tupperware container. By the time she arrived at Mia's place, it was two minutes after six. She'd just raised her hand to knock when the door flew open.

"Hey, Jenna! Great to see you again. You can head on in if you want." Mark beamed in greeting, then turned and leaned back into the house. "Hey, Mia—Jenna's here. Come on, Katie—we're gonna be late."

Jenna stepped aside as a mousy-looking preteen slid past her with a nod of acknowledgment. Katie shrugged her backpack higher onto her shoulders and moved into step behind her father. "Hey, Jenna. Good to see you. Gotta go."

"Hey, kiddo," Jenna said, shifting her Tupperware to the other hand as she leaned down to give Katie a one-armed hug. "You're getting so tall. You're headed back to your mom's?"

"Parent-teacher conferences. It's pretty lame they make the kids come."

"It's a good chance to be accountable for your academic life," Mark said, resting a hand on his daughter's shoulder as they headed down the front steps. He smiled again at Jenna. "Not sure what she's worried about anyway—she's got straight *A*s this term."

"Way to go, girl," Jenna said, waving to them as they reached the car. "Have fun."

"Good luck!" Mia called, and Jenna turned to see her friend standing in the doorway with a wistful expression. She waved as her husband and stepdaughter slid into the car. "I'm proud of you, Katie-cakes."

"Thanks," Katie said, smiling faintly as she closed the car door and clicked her seatbelt over her small frame.

Jenna stood there watching, her eyes on the car, her shoulder brushing Mia's. She waited until the car drove out of sight to turn back to her friend.

"Don't you usually go to those parent-teacher things with Mark?"

"First one I've missed in two years," Mia said, stepping aside to wave Jenna into the house. "But Ellen called last night to say she's uncomfortable having me there."

"Mark's ex gets a say in whether you attend school conferences?"

Mia shrugged. "Mark scrambled to see if we could arrange separate conferences for us and for her, but it was too last-minute. I didn't want to make a big deal about it and risk embarrassing Katie, so I said I'd sit this one out."

Jenna rolled her eyes. "You'd think she'd be happy that you want to be involved in her daughter's life. That you're a supportive stepmom."

"You'd think." Mia shrugged. "I don't know. They'd been divorced for two years before Mark ever met me, but I think she always hoped they'd get back together."

"Katie or Ellen?"

"I meant Ellen, but maybe Katie, too. Not that she's ever been anything but sweet to me. She's a great kid," Mia smiled and pushed the front door shut, giving Jenna a flash of the new sapphire-dotted wedding band tucked up against her engagement ring. Mia had the ring custom-made, adorned with Katie's birthstone as a nod to her stepdaughter's place in her life and marriage.

Jenna looked back at Mia's face, which was still a little wistful. "She *is* a great kid, but I'm sensing a *but* there."

Mia shook her head. "It's nothing. Come on, let's get going on the nachos."

Jenna caught her friend's arm and gave it a gentle squeeze to keep her from fleeing. "It's not nothing. You seem upset. What's up?"

"I'm sure it's just pregnancy hormones. I'm fine."

Jenna shook her head, seeing more in her friend's eyes than the glitter of hormone-induced tears. "Come on, if you can't vent to me, who can you vent to?"

Mia let out a long breath, and the fatigued look Jenna had noticed earlier was back in her face. "I can't vent, that's the thing. Do you know what Nancy Jensen said to me after the meeting today?" Mia swallowed and shook her head, looking up at the ceiling like she was trying to keep tears from falling. "She said 'I hope your stepdaughter doesn't know you say disparaging things about her. It can be very detrimental to the stepfamily relationship.'"

"Disparaging? What the hell was she talking about?"

"The thing about the toilet paper."

Jenna blinked. "Are you kidding me? The board president is critiquing your parenting now? That wasn't disparaging. That was a mom joking around about the challenges of raising a preteen."

"That's just it, though. I'm a stepparent." Mia rubbed her hands down her face then turned toward the kitchen. Jenna followed, hating the despair in her friend's voice. "There are different rules for stepmothers, apparently. Someone forgot to give me the rule book, but I know we're not allowed to joke about parenting challenges. When bio parents do it, they're bonding. When stepparents do it, we're whining. Or worse, we're maligning kids who don't truly belong to us. Not really."

"That's ridiculous." Jenna shook her head. They'd reached the kitchen, and she leaned against the counter beside Mia. "I'm sorry, Mia. I think you're a great stepmom. And you're going to be a great biological mother, too."

"Thank you." Mia managed a small smile. "I'm sorry, I don't know what's gotten into me. I had a rough morning when Katie kissed her dad goodbye and thanked him for packing her lunch and buying her the cool new socks she was wearing, and I just stood there like an idiot biting back the urge to tell her those were things *I* did. Me. I stayed up late making the damn sandwich with her favorite pastrami and I picked out the socks because I remembered how much she loves pigs." Mia shook her head. "I didn't say anything, of course. I know she didn't mean anything by it. She's the most polite kid on the planet, and I know she just wanted to thank someone, so she thanked her dad."

"Did Mark say anything?"

"He started to, but I stopped him. I don't want to become one of those families where dad's always ordering the kid to say thank you to the stepmom and the kid ends up feeling guilted into it. It wasn't worth it. Like I said, I'm just being hormonal."

"Still, I'm sorry." Jenna leaned in and gave her a squeeze, breathing in the familiar apricot scent of Mia's shampoo. "It can't be easy."

"I'll get through it," Mia said, offering a small smile as she drew back. "Just a few more weeks and the hormones should settle down." Mia leaned back against the counter, resting her hand over her belly. Her eyes held Jenna's for a long time, and Jenna felt something shift between them. "I've been thinking about you, hon. It'll be two years this Friday, won't it?"

Jenna nodded, fighting the surge of emotion that threatened to choke off her airway. "You're probably the only person in the world who'd remember."

"It was the day after my mom's birthday, so that's probably why. But really, every woman who's had a miscarriage has the date permanently etched into her brain." She squeezed Jenna's hand. "It helps to have a friend help carry the memory."

Jenna nodded and blinked hard to hold back the threat of tears. "Come on. Let's drown our sorrows in nachos and bad television."

"Deal!" Mia spun around and grabbed a bottle of margarita mix from the fridge. Nudging the refrigerator closed with her hip, she bent down and pulled the blender out of a cupboard at her knees. She set it on the counter and turned back to the freezer for ice. "Want me to add tequila to yours?"

"Nah, I'll go virgin in a show of solidarity."

Mia laughed and began scooping handfuls of ice into the blender. "Virgin. Right. Speaking of, any word from your mystery guy?"

Jenna forced herself to swallow, keeping her expression as neutral as possible as she moved past Mia to grab a big brick of cheddar from the fridge. "I told you that's over. It was just a one-time thing."

Mia shook her head, looking stern. "You don't just walk away from sex that makes you glow like the way you were that morning. I got a contact high just sitting next to you."

"The glow doesn't last forever." Jenna thunked the cheese down on the counter, deliberately choosing a workspace with her back to Mia so she wouldn't have to meet her friend's eyes. "I'll keep dating, don't worry. Just not that guy."

"Suit yourself. I still think that one had potential."

"Well, I don't," Jenna said, hoping she didn't sound like a petulant toddler. She began to strip the plastic wrapper off the cheese, trying to keep her tone light. "So aside from the snippy comment from Nancy, how do you think the mediation thing is going?"

There was a long silence from Mia, and for a moment, Jenna feared she'd given herself away. Stupid. How obvious to make such an abrupt transition from talk of her one-night stand to a review of Adam's mediation session?

She glanced over her shoulder, relieved to see she wasn't the cause of Mia's distraction. "Damn blender," Mia muttered, flipping the switch. "I swear, I should have let Adam take this one and just bought a new one when we split. I think this is left over from his college days." She wiggled the cord and punched a button, and the blender finally whirred to life. She turned back to Jenna, brushing a handful of red hair from her face. "I'm sorry, what did you just ask?"

"Uh, the mediation. How do you think it went?"

"I thought it was productive," Mia said, jiggling the blender as ice crunched between the blades. "Enlightening. We made a lot of progress, I think. Gotta give props to my ex for that one."

"Oh?"

Mia blew the hair off her forehead and turned back to the blender. "I guess I should say props to Adam. That man talking about open communication and the value of expressing your feelings sure as hell isn't the guy I was married to."

Jenna reached into the cupboard above her head and pulled out the cheese grater, fighting to keep her voice detached and disinterested. "Really? Seems odd someone would have changed that much."

Mia shrugged and flipped off the blender. "I suppose it's different when it's a marriage instead of a corporate negotiation, huh? Instead of colleagues with opposing views, you fall into the role of the shrewish, nagging harpy who's never satisfied, or the humorless, detached bastard with a selfish streak."

Jenna nodded and began to grate the cheese, trying to wrap her brain around the idea of Adam as humorless or detached or selfish. The same guy she'd flirted with over phony careers and wine? The same guy who'd taught her communication strategies on a hotel roof? The same guy who'd slid down her body and driven her crazy with his fingers and tongue and—

"You want the big one?"

"What?" Jenna whirled around to see Mia with two margarita glasses and a bemused expression.

"The big glass." Mia smirked. "What did you think I meant?"

"The glasses, of course. I'll take the green one."

She laughed and began to pour, while Jenna put down the cheese grater and reached for the tomatoes. "Well, hopefully Adam's techniques are successful," Jenna said. "Seems like some of the rumbling is dying down about a nursing strike. That's a step in the right direction."

"True. I just hope the whole thing goes quickly. Having Adam around is just too weird."

Jenna bit her lip. "How so?"

"Would you want to work with *your* ex?"

"Good point."

Mia sighed. "I don't know, I guess I just got comfortable thinking that part of my life was behind me. We moved 2,100 miles away, I got a new job, I started using my nickname professionally, Mark and I got married instead of being this scandalous, adulterous couple. I felt like I had a fresh start, you know?"

Jenna nodded and sliced into a tomato. "At least you only have to see Adam a few times a week."

"True. And at least he'll be gone as soon as this negotiation is over."

"Amen." Jenna swallowed back the pang of melancholy threatening to throb its way up from her chest. Part of her wanted to confess everything, to break down this stupid wall she'd built between herself and Mia.

Most of her wanted to put up a fresh coat of plaster and hope to God it held so everyone could stay safe and warm and happy.

"So what are we watching tonight, anyway?"

"I think we've got three episodes of *The Bachelor* on TiVo," Mia said, handing her a glass.

"Three? We only missed one week."

"Yeah, but I'm pretty sure yesterday's was a double episode. Hang on a sec, let me look it up." She started down the hallway, then turned. "Shit, I left my laptop at work."

"Use mine," Jenna said, nodding toward the briefcase she'd dropped at the edge of the counter. "I forgot to dump it out of my bag when I ran home. I think I've even got that celebrity gossip site bookmarked if you just open my browser."

"Cool, thanks. You don't have to chop all those, Jenna. I didn't invite you over to slave away in my kitchen."

"It's not a problem. Put your feet up and point to where you put the onions."

"Bottom crisper drawer. I got the green ones you like."

"Perfect." Jenna pried open the fridge and pulled out the bottom drawer while Mia flipped open the laptop and hit a few keystrokes. As Jenna set the onions on the counter, she heard a gasp from her friend.

She looked up to see Mia's eyes glued to the screen. She wore a look of horrified fascination that sent Jenna's stomach plunging to her knees.

"Oh my God, Jenna. What the hell is this?"

Chapter Seven

Jenna's heart lodged thick in her throat as Mia stared unblinkingly at the computer screen. Had she seen the shirtless photo of Adam? The Facebook exchange from last night?

When Mia lifted her eyes to Jenna's, her expression was unreadable.

"Wh-what's what?" Jenna stammered.

"This article about bestselling author G.G. Buckingham and her *Panty Dropper* series. That's Aunt Gertie, right?"

"Right," Jenna said, sagging against the counter in relief. "I mean, no one else knows that, and I haven't talked to her about the bestseller thing, but—"

"This article says someone's outed the author—that they've discovered her secret identity."

"Wait, what?"

Mia looked back at the screen and began to read. "'According to an anonymous source, the reclusive G.G. Buckingham is actually an elderly man living in rural Canada. Calls to Buckingham's agent went unanswered, but if reports turn out to be true, this could be a juicy twist in the summer's runaway bestseller about kinky sex and secret liaisons.'"

"Oh, God." Jenna set the knife down on the counter, but missed. It skittered across the floor, nearly skewering her foot, but she barely noticed. "Where did you see that?"

"It's trending on this gossip site I just pulled up, but there are links to other articles. The cat's not exactly out of the bag, but it's clawing at the edges." She looked up at Jenna and frowned. "Are you okay? You don't look so hot."

"I'm fine, I'm just—does it say anything else?"

"It says the author photo on her book jacket is some model in Australia, and that the bio is totally fabricated. How'd they pull that off?"

"I don't know," Jenna whispered. "I think her agent and editor handled all the details of the pseudonym. They created the whole G. G. persona to be the author, and they seemed like they knew what they were doing."

"If it makes you feel any better, it sounds like they haven't actually pinpointed who G.G. Buckingham is yet. Do you think Gert knows?"

Jenna shook her head, thinking. "Maybe not. Maybe the whole thing will blow over. They think she lives in rural Canada? And that she's a man?"

"That's what the article says."

"So they're on the wrong track." Jenna unclenched her fist and bent down to retrieve the dropped knife, her hand shakier than it had been five minutes ago.

"I don't know, Jenna. If people want to figure it out, it might not take them very long. Should we tell her?"

"No!" Her voice came out more snappish than she intended, and she pressed her palms against the counter to keep them from shaking. "I don't want to worry her unnecessarily."

"You think she'd care that much?"

"Privacy is very important to Gert."

"Huh." Mia didn't say anything, but the look on her face was skeptical.

Privacy is very important to me, Jenna thought, then bit her lip. *And my career.*

"Why don't we just sit on this for now?" Jenna said. "I'll put out some feelers with Gert, maybe try to get a sense of what she knows. She's got a great agent. If Gert doesn't want to be found, I'm sure Michelle can do something to throw them off track."

"And what if she wants to be found?" Mia tapped a fingernail against the screen. "This article is trending, which means a lot of people are seeing it. The book is selling like hotcakes. Maybe a scandal like this is exactly what Gert wants."

"I don't think so," Jenna said turning back to the block of cheese in front of her. She took a deep breath and said a small prayer she was right.

Jenna's week crawled by in a shimmery haze of avoidance. She avoided Adam's eyes in the mediation sessions, and avoided the temptation to stalk him on Facebook.

She avoided Mia's teasing about her love life and the jumbled thoughts of how Mia might react if she found out about the fling with Adam.

She avoided talking to Gert about her books or the risk to her anonymity, though she did manage a conversation with Gert's agent.

Jenna tracked down Michelle's number from the caller ID on their landline, and she plugged it into her iPhone with a pang of guilt. True, she'd spoken to Gert's agent a few times over the years, making idle chitchat when Gert was slow getting to the phone.

But she'd never gone out of her way to call Michelle. Never gone behind her aunt's back to discuss her career. Michelle was guarded at first, but she warmed up when Jenna asked about the article threatening to out G.G. Buckingham.

"I saw it on one of those gossip sites," Michelle said, giving an indignant snort. "An elderly man in Canada? Please."

"Still, they're not too far off. What if they find her?"

"I've got it under control. I'm meeting with a PR firm tomorrow. Tell Gertrude not to worry about it."

"I don't think she is," Jenna said, biting her lip. "The thing is, I'm not sure she knows, and she was sick last week—"

"Gertrude is sick?"

"Well, not on her deathbed or anything. Just a touch of food poisoning, but she's an old woman. Her health is frail, and I don't want anything to upset her."

"I hear you." Michelle fell silent a moment, thinking. "Listen, I'll do my best to keep the speculation going without letting them actually track her down. A little mystery is good for book sales."

"I can imagine. I've been watching her sales rankings online."

"Great, right? You don't think Gertrude has noticed?"

"No. She said something this morning about not being online all week."

"She does that when she's on deadline. Doesn't like the distraction."

"Good," Jenna said. "That's good. I don't want her distracted, either."

"I'll definitely need to talk this over with Gertrude if the blood-hounds sniff any closer."

"Got it," Jenna said. "I'll, um—I'll try to keep her calm."

"Calm, hell—just keep her writing. She's been ignoring me all week while she works on the next book in the series. I hope it's going well?"

"I'm sure it is," Jenna said, feeling a little guilty about the conversation. She didn't talk to Gert about her writing career, so was it wrong to talk to her agent? "She's been very focused the last week. We've hardly had time to talk, what with me working late and Gertie holed up in her room with her laptop."

"That's what I like to hear," Michelle said, and disconnected the call.

By Friday evening, Jenna was jumping out of her skin. She'd only been home an hour, but she'd already changed into jeans and a comfy sweater. She glanced at the clock, dismayed to see it was only six fifteen. Why hadn't she made plans with friends or done something to keep herself occupied?

She wandered down the hall, poking her head in to see what Aunt Gertrude was up to. The old woman was fluffing her hair in front of the mirror, her cheeks flushed and rosy. She looked up and smiled.

"Hello, dear. Good day at work?"

"Long day."

"Oh? How are the negotiations going?"

Jenna shrugged. "I can't really talk about it, but it's okay. It's just tough balancing my regular workload on top of the stuff with the bargaining team, you know?"

"I can imagine. You've been putting in some late hours this week."

Jenna shrugged. "At least it's Friday. Any chance you want to order pizza and watch a movie?"

"I'd love to, dear, but I have a date." Gertie fastened a clip-on earring to her lobe and eyed Jenna up and down. "Speaking of dating, isn't it time you got out there?"

"I've been out there. I'm just not sure I'm ready for a relationship right now, and anyway—"

"Sweetie, it's been two years since you broke off the engagement. Besides, who said anything about a relationship?" She patted Jenna's hand and gave her a kindly smile. "I just want you to have some sex."

Jenna felt the heat creep into her cheeks. "I did. A little over a week ago, remember?"

"Please, dear. A woman needs more than one little fling."

Tell me about it, Jenna thought, but she was saved from answering by the ring of the doorbell.

"Good night, dear!" Gert called as she headed toward the door and flung it open to greet her new gentleman friend. A tall, dark-haired man stood on the porch looking fit and handsome and at least ten years younger than Gertie. Gert tossed a sly look over her shoulder, winking at Jenna. "Don't wait up."

"I won't," Jenna murmured, her voice echoing in the suddenly silent living room.

It was too quiet. The grandfather clock Gertie brought with her when she'd moved in made a rhythmic ticking in the corner, and the whoosh of cars on the street outside reminded her that other people were out enjoying their Friday evening. Dammit, now what?

"Pizza," Jenna said aloud just to break the silence.

She could order in, but something urged her to get out of the house.

She knew what that *something* was.

Two years ago today . . .

Jenna shivered and wrapped her arms around herself. How would her life be different now if it hadn't happened? Would she have married Sean? Would she be happy to stay home on a Friday night chasing a baby who would have started walking by now?

Jenna shook her head, shaking off the dark thoughts, too. Admittedly, nostalgia wasn't the only thing drawing her to Rigatelli's. Hadn't she told Adam about the amazing pizza and Friday karaoke? It was only a few blocks from his hotel. Maybe he'd be there.

All the more reason not to go there tonight.

She grabbed her purse and strode out the door, not even sure where she was headed. The next thing she knew, she was standing in front of the counter at Rigatelli's, definitely not waiting for Adam. The smell of pepperoni was heavy in the air, and Jenna breathed in the scent of bubbling cheese and wood-smoked nostalgia.

"Jenna? Is that you?"

She blinked, then blinked again. Sean? He was striding toward her, looking as surprised as she probably did. His dark hair was neatly combed, his shoulders still broad and muscular beneath a polo shirt she knew was one of at least two dozen in his closet.

Her ex-fiancé hadn't changed much in the year since she'd last seen him, or in the two years since she'd broken off the engagement. That was disappointing. It might have been better if he'd gained fifty pounds or sprouted another chin.

That's not nice, she chided herself, trying to remember some of the touchy-feely things Adam had been teaching them in mediation this past week.

"Sean," she said, running a hand over her hair. "What are you doing here?"

"Uh, getting pizza?" He said it with a smile to take the edge off, but Jenna still felt idiotic. "I assume you're doing the same?"

"Yeah. I hadn't been here since—well, for a long time. I just thought—"

"I know," he said, reaching out to touch her hand. "Two years ago today, right? We must've been thinking the same thing."

Jenna gaped at him, a little dumbfounded he'd remembered the date at all. He must have read her thoughts, because he offered a sad little smile. "Don't look so shocked, Jenna. It was a big deal to me, too. Come on. Want to split a pizza?"

She tried to think of a good reason not to share a meal with her ex-fiancé at their old haunt on this cheerless two-year milestone, but all she could come up with was, "Um."

Sean nodded, taking that as concession, so he took her hand as well. Jenna let him lead her to a booth near the back, far away from the karaoke stage. She was numb enough that she almost didn't notice it was the same booth they'd been sitting at when they had their first date five years ago.

"You want the usual?" he asked, and Jenna nodded, figuring it was easier than trying to remember complex words like *pepperoni* and *olive*.

She glanced toward the bar. "Split a half carafe of their house red?"

"Coming right up."

She started to open her wallet, but he waved her off and headed for the counter. Okay then. She put her wallet away and tried to calm her nerves. She wasn't nervous about seeing him again, at least not that way. She didn't still love him. She wasn't even sure she liked him all that much, but she was surprised to realize the resentments had cooled and the sadness had ebbed, leaving behind something that felt like—

Like what, exactly? Numbness? A sense that she should be feeling something—anything—but really she just wanted to paste a smile in place and plow through the awkwardness as quickly as possible.

Was this what closure felt like?

"Here you go," Sean said, dropping into the chair next to her and handing her a glass of red wine. "Pizza will be up in a few. So how have you been, Jenna?"

"Good," she said, taking a tentative sip. "Aunt Gertie is healthy and happy. Work's going great."

"Work," he said, nodding as he pulled his iPhone out of his pocket and set it on the table beside his own glass. "That's great. You're still at the hospital?"

"Yes. Did I hear you changed to a different accounting firm?"

"Yeah, I'm with Grover and Frank now. It's really great. They've got an office right on the river."

Jenna watched as his fingers slid over the power button on his phone. His eyes were still on hers, but she could tell his brain was already wandering through his in-box.

"Must be nice working that close to home," she said.

"Actually, I moved. I'm over in Lake Oswego now. The commute is a bitch, but I love the new house. The views are great."

"Great," she said, doing a mental head-slap at the fact that two educated people couldn't seem to come up with a better adjective than *great*. "I'm very happy for you."

His phone vibrated, and she watched his gaze flick away to read the message. He moved his eyes back to hers an instant later, doing a perfect impression of a man connected to the conversation. "You still living in the old place and walking to work all the time?"

"Yes. I love having a little bit of fresh air and exercise at the beginning and end of each day."

"Uh-huh." His eyes flicked back to the screen, though he left the phone flat on the table, tucked behind his wineglass. At least he was trying to be discreet about it. At least she no longer cared, no longer felt the urge to reach across the table and grab his cell phone so she could beat him over the head with it. His inability to carry on a conversation without checking his goddamn phone every ten seconds was no longer her concern.

Was it someone else's? She tried to decide if she cared. She didn't, at least not in the sense that it bothered her if some other woman was now sharing his bed, his life, his dreams.

He tapped a couple words on the phone, and Jenna had to admit it still grated on her nerves. She took a deep breath, remembering the tip Adam had offered in mediation about breathing before speaking. She did it a few more times for good measure.

"So you like the new job?"

"What's that?" He looked up at her, his hand still poised on the phone.

"Your job. You like the new place you're working?"

"Yes, definitely. Much more challenging. The pay's better, too."

His phone buzzed with the sound of an incoming text message, and Sean looked down at it. He nodded absently, then reached for the device and began typing out a message with his thumbs.

Jenna took another sip of wine and glanced around the restaurant. Was it only a couple years ago this had been their old stomping ground? Funny how much her life had changed since she'd been Sean's fiancée, since they'd been planning a future together and—

"Will you excuse me a sec?" he asked, interrupting her thoughts. "I just need to check on the pizza."

He needed to make a phone call, she guessed, but Jenna just nodded and watched him walk away. She looked at her watch and wondered how long she had to make polite conversation with him before she could safely go home and put on her pajamas and watch trashy TV. An hour? Forty-five minutes?

She slid off her chair, catching Sean's eye and gesturing to the far corner of the restaurant to let him know she was going to the bathroom. He was fiddling with his phone, but he gave her a thumbs-up as she moved through the crowd, picking her way past bistro tables strewn with beer mugs and half-eaten pizzas.

As she neared the restrooms, she took one last glance at Sean. He had his phone pressed to his ear, and was making a hurry-up gesture with his hand. Jenna suppressed an eye roll, shaking her head as she pivoted fast and marched around the corner.

"Ooof!"

She crashed into a wall with a fleeting thought of who changed the layout of the restaurant. Belatedly, she realized it wasn't a wall at all. Not one made of bricks or wood, anyway.

She put her hands out to catch herself, pressing her palms against the chest she'd spent too much time staring at in a photograph lately. She looked up into those green eyes and lost her breath.

"Hello, Jenna."

If thinking about Jenna on a random Friday evening was enough to conjure her up and have her fall into his arms, Adam figured he should probably spend more time imagining himself winning the lottery.

It wasn't random, dumbass. You came here hoping you'd run into her.

Not literally, though. "Whoa there," he said, catching her by the shoulders and setting her upright. Mistake. A surge of electricity fizzed through his fingers and up his arms, leaving him eager to touch more of her. All of her.

"Adam," she gasped, looking flustered. She stared at her own hands, looking like she was trying desperately to figure out how they'd ended up pressed against his chest. Adam didn't care, he just wanted them to stay there.

Instead she pried her hands away and took a step back. "What are you doing here?"

"Well, I was planning to take a leak, then order a pizza. Pretty much the normal things you do when you're walking to the bathroom at a pizza parlor."

"No, I mean *here*—I mean—never mind."

"You told me Rigatelli's was the best. I wanted to check it out for myself."

"Right. The karaoke doesn't start for another hour."

"I didn't come for the karaoke."

He let the words hang there for a moment, wondering if she'd read into that or just assume he meant the pizza. He wasn't sure himself.

She glanced over her shoulder at a table in the corner where a dark-haired guy with the build of an NFL linebacker sat hunched over a table, fiddling with his phone. Adam studied the guy for a moment, then looked at Jenna.

"Ah, I get it. You're on a date. Don't worry, Jenna. I'm not planning to make a scene. Well, not unless you want me to."

"No, it's not that. Not a date, that is." She blew out a breath and glanced over her shoulder again. "It's just my ex-fiancé. We sort of ran into each other, and it's kind of a significant date in our history, so it sorta morphed into dinner together." She shrugged and gave a look like she wanted the ground to swallow her up. Or maybe Adam was reading too much into it. "Anyway, the whole thing feels really awkward, you know?"

Adam nodded, oddly relieved to discover she could relate to the sort of ex weirdness he'd been dealing with all week. "Ah, the joys of unexpected fraternization with an ex. Is there anything more awkward?"

Jenna gave a funny sort of half smile and looked thoughtful. "How about singing along with Vanilla Ice and realizing your car windows are down?"

"Good point. Or how about when a waiter tells you to have a good meal and you reply, 'You, too!'"

She was smiling for real now, and he watched her shoulders relax. He ached to touch them again, but settled for shoving his hands in his pockets.

"What about pushing a door and then realizing it says 'pull' in big red letters?" she offered.

"Having a coughing fit in the middle of a meeting when you choke on your tea?"

"Watching a movie with your elderly aunt and discovering there's a really graphic sex scene."

"Ha! How about answering a question you think a stranger just asked you and then it turns out he's just talking on his Bluetooth?"

"Awkward," she agreed. "Been there, done that. Once with a woman having a conversation on the other side of the bathroom stall. I kept answering questions she was asking, thinking 'this is kind of weird, but maybe she's just friendly.' She finally put the call on hold and told me to cut it out."

Adam laughed and leaned against the wall, really enjoying himself now. "That's a good one. Definitely ex-fraternization level of awkwardness. How about splashing your crotch at a drinking fountain and feeling compelled to explain to everyone that you didn't really pee yourself?"

"Oooh, good one. What about smiling at someone who's checking you out in a bar, and then realizing they're looking at the person behind you?"

"I've done that a time or two," he admitted. "Once I was on the opposite end of it though, and a girl standing near the one I was making eyes at thought I was flirting with her. She came over to my table and introduced herself."

"What did you do?"

He shrugged. "Bought her a drink, talked to her for an hour, and walked her home. I didn't want to hurt her feelings."

"Geez, you really are a standup guy."

"Or a wuss. I suppose it's all about perspective. Okay, how about saying goodbye to someone you've been talking to and then realizing you're walking the same direction?"

"Yeah, definitely awkward." Jenna seemed to hesitate a moment, then leaned back against the wall beside him, their shoulders touching companionably. "How about when a car stops to let you cross the street and you start jogging to be polite, but then realize you're giving him a jiggle show?"

Adam laughed and did his best not to look at her chest. "You win. I don't think I've ever given anyone a jiggle show. Not that there's anything wrong with that."

She smiled and took a deep breath before glancing back toward the dining room. Toward the linebacker. When she turned to Adam again, the smile had faded a little. "Thanks, Adam. I needed that. I should probably get back."

"Don't you have to pee?"

"Not really. I just needed an excuse to get up and walk around."

"Fair enough. Also, for the record, if I could rewind and strike that last question from the record, I'd do it. In the future, I'll do a better job of making conversation that doesn't involve inquiring about someone's bathroom habits."

She smiled again, but it wasn't reaching her eyes anymore. They'd flickered again to the table in the corner, and Adam wondered whether she was eager to get back to the guy or eager to end this conversation.

"I should probably let you go," he said. "If the ex awkwardness gets to you, you can always pull the fire alarm."

"I'll try to remember that." Jenna sighed and ran her hands over her hair. "It's okay, really. He's a good guy, and probably exactly who I ought to be hanging out with tonight."

Something in her tone made Adam lose the urge to joke. "How do you mean?"

"Nothing. Forget it. It's been nice talking to you, Adam."

"Likewise," he said, stepping aside to let her pass. She stood there for a moment with her hands at her sides, looking a little lost. When she moved, it was in the direction of the bathroom.

"I guess I'll go after all."

"Good plan," he said.

He turned and walked into the men's room before any other idiotic utterances could pass his lips. He took care of business quickly, then washed his hands while looking in the mirror and giving himself a silent pep talk about not lusting after women he had no business pursuing. She'd made it clear that wasn't in the cards for them. There was no point giving it any further thought.

He left the men's room and headed for the front counter, happy to discover the pizza he'd ordered was ready to go. If he'd had it delivered instead of walking four blocks from his hotel, he never would have seen Jenna. He tried to decide if that was a good thing.

The pizza box was warm and fragrant and bigger than it had any right to be, considering he was a guy who planned to eat it alone in front of the television in his hotel room on a Friday night. He tucked it against his chest and headed for the door, but he couldn't resist the urge to look back at the corner table.

Jenna had rejoined her ex. Whatever they were talking about looked intimate, and their heads were bent close together. Even from this distance, Adam saw something tender and wistful in her eyes. When the guy reached out and put his hand on Jenna's, she didn't pull away.

Adam hadn't realized he'd stopped walking until someone bumped him from behind. Even then, he stood frozen in place. Something twisted in his gut, and he stood there transfixed, his eyes on Jenna and the man she'd once planned to spend the rest of her life with. How long ago was it?

She must have felt his eyes on her then, and she looked up. She didn't seem startled at all to see Adam watching her. She blinked slowly, then looked down at her hand. The other man's palm still covered it, and she seemed to hesitate a moment. Then she drew her other hand up and placed it on top of his.

A hand sandwich, Adam thought absurdly, then turned away. He stepped out into the rainy Portland evening, wishing like hell he'd had the pizza delivered.

An hour later, Adam sat shirtless in his boxer shorts on sheets too clean to be truly comfortable. He'd polished off his pizza and felt a little sick. He was pretty sure it was just the pepperoni, but who was he kidding? The image of Jenna with that other guy kept flashing through his brain, which was stupid. He had no right to be jealous. No right to judge her for reconnecting with a man she'd loved enough to agree to marry at one point.

The idea of getting back together with Mia seemed ridiculous to him now, but there'd been a time he would have considered it. Could he blame Jenna for doing the same with her ex?

He picked up the remote and began flipping through channels, trying to get the image of her out of his mind. QVC was selling some sort of kebab maker that caught Adam's interest for at least twenty minutes. One of the *Rocky* movies—was it IV or V?—flickered on the next channel. He flipped the remote button again, feeling irritated. Did MTV even play music anymore?

Adam sighed and set the remote down. None of it was any match for the image of Jenna's eyes meeting his from across the room, the sight of her fingers entwined with someone else's.

He needed to get the fuck over it; that was obvious. There was at least another month left in his contract with Belmont, maybe longer, but he could at least do a better job of keeping her out of his field of vision. Out of his thoughts.

Grabbing the remote, he flipped off the television, then picked up his laptop. He opened up the folder containing all his materials for the Belmont negotiations. The screen lit up with an Excel spreadsheet he'd been working on earlier, and he reached for his glasses. Shoving them onto his nose, he began making notes in the file. He'd have to remember to talk with Human Resources about some changes in the dental plan, and he needed to crunch a few numbers on some proposed changes to the ETO system. That was going to be a contentious discussion, especially with the folks from the nurses' union.

He made a note to talk with the CEO about the legal ramifications of—

What the hell was he doing?

He frowned, staring down at the spreadsheet. Working late on a Friday night? This is what the old Adam Thomas would do. He'd stay up late crunching numbers and planning strategies instead of doing something fun or engaging. Instead of going home to his wife.

Okay, so there was no wife now. He was glad about that, but it didn't mean he had free license to behave like a workaholic jerk.

Closing out the file, he clicked to his Internet browser. He ignored the Facebook icon, not giving in to the ridiculous urge to look up Jenna or her linebacker boyfriend. He hesitated a moment, then scrolled to his favorite travel website and began browsing.

How long had it been since he'd taken a vacation? Hawaii would be nice this time of year, or maybe somewhere in the Caribbean. He thought about tropical drinks and warm, sandy beaches. About palm trees swaying in the breeze and calypso music lilting across the bay. About Jenna in a bikini and—

No. Focus, dammit.

Maybe a vacation was exactly what he needed. Something to reset his clock, give him some new perspective on life. Maybe he could take up scuba diving or bird watching.

A knock sounded at the door, bursting in on his thoughts. He frowned down at his watch. Who the hell would stop by at eight on a Friday evening? No one even knew he was here.

He rolled out of bed, not bothering to pull on a shirt or pants. Anyone bold enough to knock on a stranger's hotel room door after dark on a Friday evening could damn well deal with the sight of him in Batman boxers.

Adam pulled the door open and froze. Jenna stood there in the hallway, her hair matted and rain soaked, her hands clenched in front of her. Her mascara was streaked from rain or from tears, and she looked ready to break in two.

"Jenna?"

"I'm sorry," she said, and launched herself into his arms.

Chapter Eight

Adam staggered backward, surprised by the force with which Jenna hurled herself at him. He felt his arms go around her without any thought to whether it was a good idea, what she was even doing here.

"Jenna? Are you okay?"

"Mmmphwalawonwugoo," she murmured against his chest, and it felt so good to have her cradled there that he didn't really give a damn whether he understood a word she was saying. She was soggy and cold and the best damn thing he'd ever felt in his life.

He held her for a moment longer, not sure whether to close the door to offer some privacy, or stand here holding her until she decided to tell him what the hell was going on. He should probably put on some clothes, but somehow it was the last thing he wanted to do.

"What are you sorry for, Jenna?" he asked, and felt her stir in his arms. "Did something happen?"

She shook her head and drew back, and Adam felt the absence of her warm breath on his chest. "I tried to make myself feel something for Sean," she said. "He held my hand, and I let him, and it felt so good to have someone touching me that way and when he asked me to come back to his place I started thinking about how good it would feel to—"

She broke off there, scrubbing at her eyes in a way that made the mascara streaks look like war paint. Her gaze drifted from his face down to his chest and seemed to freeze there. He waited, not sure what etiquette called for. He should definitely get dressed.

"Hang on, let me grab a shirt."

"No!" She put a hand out to touch his chest, a gesture that seemed to startle them both. "I mean, don't do it on my account."

"Okay." He ran his hands through his hair and tried to remember what they'd been talking about. "So you slept with your ex and now you feel even more awkward about the whole thing?"

"No! I didn't sleep with him." She took a shaky breath and met his eyes again. "I said I thought about it, but I couldn't. I just *couldn't.* And the next thing I knew I was bawling and blabbering to him about how I needed to come find you and apologize, so that's what I'm doing now. Apologizing."

He frowned, not sure he was following her line of thought. "For what?"

"For blowing you off. For not introducing you to Sean or inviting you to join us for dinner. For holding hands with my goddamn ex."

"You don't owe me an apology for any of that, Jenna. You were reconnecting with someone you cared about. You and I aren't dating. Hell, we're pretending not to even know each other that well. You're free to sleep with your ex anytime you want."

Those last words came out stilted, and they tasted bad on his tongue. He felt relieved when she shook her head.

"That's just it, I don't want to sleep with him. *Fuck!*" She raked her hands through her hair, making weird wet rows around her face that gave her a beautifully crazed appearance. "I want to sleep with you, but obviously that's not possible, and the whole thing made me think about how I'd feel if you slept with *your* ex—I mean, forget the fact that she's married to someone else—"

"Seems fair, since she managed to forget it when she was married to me."

Adam could have kicked himself for the bitterness in his own tone, but Jenna just shook her head.

"I thought about how I'd feel if you slept with an ex. Or anyone, really. I didn't like it, Adam. I didn't like it at all."

He nodded, not sure what he was supposed to say, but pretty sure he was underdressed for any sort of serious conversation. For that matter, Jenna wasn't very well attired either, and she was dripping puddles of rainwater on the floor beside his door. She shivered, and Adam felt goose bumps prickle his own skin. A breeze drifted through the open door, so Adam pushed it shut, hopeful it wouldn't make her feel trapped.

"Look, first things first. You're soaked to the bone." He fingered a damp strand of her hair, knowing he shouldn't go any further with touching her. Not yet. Not while she was this upset. "What did you do, go for a swim in the Willamette?"

"No," she said. "I just started walking, not really going anywhere, and then I got caught in the rain and I realized I was standing right in front of your hotel. I started feeling guilty, but I couldn't decide whether to come up or not, so I ended up standing out there a lot longer than I meant to."

"How did you find my room anyway?"

She shrugged. "You said you had a suite with a kitchen, and all of those are on the tenth floor. From there, I just started knocking. I'm pretty sure the guy in the room next door thinks I'm a hooker."

"A hooker with a bad sense of direction and a habit of forgetting to take her clothes off before showering. Come on. Let's find you something dry to put on."

She shot a nervous glance around the room, seeming to realize for the first time that she'd landed herself in a room alone with him and a bed. She stood motionless for a moment, then stepped forward, hands at her sides. "Thanks."

"No problem," he said, moving to the bureau beside the bed. He pulled open the drawer where he'd stuffed his gym clothes, thankful she'd caught him just a couple days after he'd done laundry. He grabbed a pair of workout pants and a sweatshirt, along with a thick pair of socks. He handed them to her and shivered as his fingers brushed her frigid knuckles. "Here, try these. Bathroom's right over—"

Jenna yanked her sweater over her head, and Adam lost track of whatever the hell he'd been about to say. She wore a pink bra made sheer by the rain, and he couldn't tear his eyes away as she reached between her shoulder blades to unhook it.

"—or you can just change right here."

She smiled and gave a small shrug. "It's not like you haven't seen it before," she said, turning her back to him as the bra dropped to the floor. "I'm sure my aunt would say this is what a sex goddess would do."

"Absolutely," he agreed, too transfixed to come up with anything smarter than that.

She pulled the sweatshirt over her head, making Adam dizzy with the thought of those lovely bare breasts pressing against the soft fleece of his favorite college sweatshirt. "Besides," she said, "it seems fair considering you're standing there wearing nothing but your boxers."

"Very team spirited of you."

"Thanks. I've been working with a mediator on my team-building skills."

She toed off her clogs and reached for the button on her jeans. Adam hesitated, wondering if she wanted him to watch. Hell, he'd pointed out the bathroom, so she had privacy if she needed it. He gave up wrestling with the etiquette and just stared openly, transfixed by the sight of her peeling her wet jeans down those pale, flawless legs. He stood mesmerized as she hooked her thumbs in the waistband of her panties.

"You're staring."

"You want me to stop?"

"No. I figure I owe you. For the photo the other night. And for answering the door looking exactly like you did in the picture."

He laughed. "In case you wondered if I had my team of Photoshop experts airbrush the shot before I sent it to you?"

She shook her head and wriggled out of her panties. His sweatshirt hung to midthigh on her, which prevented the whole thing from being a strip show. This was hotter somehow. Less staged, more intimate.

"You definitely don't need any airbrushing," she said.

"Neither do you."

Jenna pulled the sweats on, rolling them a few times at the waist so she wouldn't trip on the cuffs. She pulled the socks on, then ran her fingers through her hair. Adam shook off the haze of the last few minutes to turn toward the bathroom. He grabbed her a clean towel, and while he was there, spotted another pair of workout pants on the floor. Tugging them on over his boxers, he returned to the room and handed her the towel.

"Thank you," she said.

"No, thank you. Definitely the highlight of my week."

She grinned. "Leave your shirt off and I'll be able to say the same."

He watched as she began scrubbing the towel over her head. She wandered over to sit on the edge of the bed, and Adam stood there, not sure what his next move should be. Did he join her? Give her space?

The hell with wondering. If he'd learned nothing else as a counselor, it was the benefit of direct communication.

"What are we doing here, Jenna?"

She pulled the towel away from her face and sighed. "Trying to remember why it's a bad idea to sleep together?"

He smiled, pleased she didn't try to play games or pretend she didn't understand the question. "It feels different when we're behind closed doors, doesn't it?"

She nodded, and Adam made his way over to the foot of the bed. He sat down beside her, enjoying the warmth of her shoulder brushing his arm. His bare foot touched her sock-covered one, and the intimacy of it made something inside him twist into a big, glowing knot. He hesitated, then put his hand on her knee. It felt comfortable there, the curve of her kneecap fitting perfectly into his palm.

He turned to look at her and felt his heart lodge in his throat. She'd wiped off most of the mascara, so her face was bare and lovely. Her eyes met his, and he tried to remember if he'd ever seen such a deep shade of blue anywhere else. What was the word for it? Azure? Cobalt? Cerulean? Where was the fucking Crayola box when he needed it?

"You're staring again." Her voice was breathy and soft, and he knew she was thinking the same damn thing he was. He ached to kiss her. Every atom in his body screamed with the need to slide his fingers into her damp hair, to tip her chin up so their mouths fit together and their knees bumped on the edge of the bed.

"If I kiss you right now, we know where this will end up." His voice didn't sound like his voice, but that seemed okay somehow.

Jenna nodded. "I know."

"So it seems we have two choices here. Option one, I put your wet clothes in a bag, shake your hand, and send you on your way home." He swallowed, wondering how it was possible to feel this warm with only half his clothes on. "Option two, we undo all this fine work we've just put into donning clothing and I take you in my arms and kiss you until neither of us can breathe. The gentleman in me says the latter isn't a good idea, since you're a little upset."

"I'm not upset. Not anymore."

"Okay," Adam said. "Which do you choose?"

She was silent a moment, her eyes dark and needy. He waited, not wanting to rush her, knowing whatever they decided would change everything. Jenna licked her lips, and Adam nearly groaned with desire.

"I choose option three," she whispered.

"Option three?"

"Option three. You kiss me once. Only once, and with both of us remaining upright and fully clothed."

"Okay."

"Then we agree that even if we can't make love, we seem to be drawn to each other for some reason. So maybe we should just explore that friendship and connection in the most platonic, unromantic way we can think of."

"Unromantic?" Adam raised an eyebrow. "What did you have in mind?"

"I'm not sure. Shoveling dog doo for my neighbor?"

"That's certainly unromantic, though it might be a little late for that. You and I might get a ride in a squad car if your neighbor spotted two strangers roaming his backyard in the dark with shovels."

"Okay then." She frowned in concentration. "How about algebra?"

"I just closed out a spreadsheet, so that's too much like work. We could watch a documentary on bizarre medical procedures."

"What about a robust discussion of Marxist philosophies of dialectical materialism?"

"Now you're just getting me hot again."

"I know!" Jenna jumped up so fast she nearly knocked Adam backward on the bed. "Let's shoot guns!"

"Guns?"

"Yes. That's unromantic."

"Absolutely, but it's also illegal. At least in the city limits. Or were you planning to rob a liquor store? I think that's an entirely different level of illegal."

"No, not like that," she said, bouncing excitedly in the wool socks. "At a shooting range. Come on, it'll be fun."

Adam glanced at the bedside clock. "It's eight thirty on a Friday night. Where are you going to find a shooting range that's open?"

"Oh, please—it's Portland, Oregon. The weirdness capital of the world. You can wander out at midnight and get a bacon-wrapped donut, take your dog into a bar, and see a parade of naked cyclists all on the same block. I'm positive we can find an open shooting range. Actually, I think it might be ladies' night at Guns-a-Go-Go."

"In case it escaped your attention, I'm not a lady."

"Trust me, it didn't escape my attention." She shot a pointed look at his crotch before smiling up at him. "You're still allowed, you just have to pay a little extra for your ammo. Have you ever been to a shooting range?"

"No," he said, a little surprised to realize they were even having this discussion. "Not really my idea of a great date."

"Exactly! That's why it's perfect." She clapped her hands together, looking so giddy with excitement that Adam had to laugh.

"Okay, fine. A shooting range. Aren't you forgetting one thing?"

"What's that?"

"The kiss. The one we're exchanging just to get it out of the way in hopes it'll be awful and we'll have the closure we need to move forward with our platonic friendship."

"Right." She planted herself back on the edge of the bed and nodded. She made an exaggerated production of sidling up beside him, pretending to brace herself for something unappealing. "Okay, I'm ready. Pucker up."

She closed her eyes and made an absurd kissy face he knew was supposed to crack him up. But honest to God, he'd never wanted her more than he did in that moment.

He slid his hand into her hair, tangling his fingers into the damp strands and pulling her close. Jenna opened her eyes, and a startled "oh" passed her lips an instant before his mouth found hers. Then he was kissing her hard and deep and wet.

She moaned and arched against him, changing course as quickly as she'd changed into his sweatpants. He curved his palm around the nape of her neck, angling him against her so he could deepen the kiss. He felt breathless and dizzy and so desperate to keep kissing her that he would have given his left testicle to never have to leave this room.

When he finally drew back, Jenna looked as mind-wacked as he did. He took a shaky breath and sat back on the bed.

"Was that awful enough for you?" he murmured. "Bad enough to call it closure?"

She took a shaky breath and slowly shook her head. "Not even close."

Walking out of that hotel room without tearing her clothes off was one of the hardest things Jenna had ever done.

The fact that Adam was right behind her helped some, but all she really wanted to do was launch herself back onto that flawless white duvet and beg him to make love to her.

Instead, she turned her attention to their plans to blow some paper targets to smithereens. "Why don't we swing by my house first so I can change clothes?" she suggested, bouncing up off the bed and away from the temptation of Adam. "My aunt isn't home tonight, so we'll be able to slip out without anyone asking questions."

"What about the risk of seeing someone we know at the shooting range?"

She shrugged. "I don't have any friends who shoot. Mia hates guns, and I can't imagine anyone else from hospital administration who'd want to spend Friday night with a .45 slimline Glock. I think we're safe. Worst-case scenario, we'd tell them it's a precursor to some team-building workshop you're doing with us next week."

He raised one eyebrow. "I'll be introducing the principles of Nonviolent Communication."

"I take it that doesn't involve handguns?"

"Not usually, but we can adapt."

"Okay then," Jenna said, feeling oddly chilled by the shift to a work-related conversation. It was probably the splash of cold water her libido needed, but still. It was a helpful reminder why she had no business taking her clothes off in front of Adam. Or kissing him in a way that left every nerve in her body shrieking with desire.

"This is good," she said. "We're working together. Keeping things professional."

Adam gave her an odd look, but nodded. "Let's get your car."

They reached the shooting range a little after nine thirty, with Adam looking curious, if a little uncertain. She tucked her keys in her purse and laid a hand on his arm.

"You've really never fired a gun before?" she asked.

"Not even a BB gun."

"You're not opposed to them, are you? I just do it for target practice, and I've taken a couple classes on self-defense. I don't even own a gun of my own. We don't have to do this if you're anti-gun or something."

"No, I'm fine. Besides, it's all part of my post-divorce resolution."

"Your post-divorce resolution involves handguns?"

"No, my post-divorce resolution involves a pledge to try new things. Things I never did in my ex-life."

Jenna blinked, then she realized he'd said ex-life, not ex-*wife*. Funny how similar the two things were. Even so, she felt a pang of betrayal for her best friend. Would Mia be hurt to know Jenna was here firing pistols with Mia's ex? Between the pregnancy and work drama and the challenges with Mark and Katie, Jenna knew damn well Mia was having a rough time. It wasn't kind to rock the boat.

But hell, it wasn't like Mia had peed on Adam to mark him like a fire hydrant. Had she ever actually said, 'Don't date my ex?'"

She never explicitly asked me not to light her house on fire, either, but I can safely assume that's a given.

"Come on," Jenna said, pulling Adam through the front door before her train of thought could get any weirder. "We check in first at the front counter to rent guns and reserve a lane. Handguns okay?"

"As opposed to what?"

"Rifles. Grenade launchers." She grinned, enjoying the novelty of being with him in a non-work setting with all their clothes on. "I'm kidding about the grenade launchers, but there is an outdoor rifle range. Can't you hear it?"

"That's rifle fire? I figured someone was playing with firecrackers."

"You really are a novice."

"Guilty as charged." He looked around and lowered his voice. "I shouldn't say that out loud, huh? They probably won't give me a gun if I'm a felon."

Jenna laughed and towed him toward the counter, unsurprised to see a line of women waiting their turn while the group at the head of the line debated the merits of a standard Ruger versus a Smith & Wesson. She watched Adam taking it all in, his green eyes studying the cases of ammo behind the counter, the posters for shooting classes and handgun safety.

There was something thrilling about being here with him. About the idea of introducing him to something new, something he'd never tried with anyone else.

You're renting a handgun, not testing out a new sex position.

She shook off her annoying inner voice and studied him some more. His eyes were bright and curious, and his jaw was pebbled with stubble. He'd donned an old T-shirt and jeans that looked so soft she wanted to rub her cheek on his thigh. She looked back at his face, amused to see he was still surveying the lobby.

The instant his expression froze, Jenna felt her heart clench. All the color drained from his face, and Jenna felt her mouth go dry.

"What is it? Adam? What's wrong?"

He opened his mouth to reply just as a female voice echoed over the crowd. "Adam Thomas? Is that you?"

Jenna turned to see a petite blonde woman making her way toward them. Their eyes locked, and the woman blinked in surprise. "Jenna? What brings you here? Are the two of you together?"

"Ellen."

Jenna uttered the word at the same time Adam did, and some immature part of her wanted to call "jinx" and laugh about the whole thing.

But most of her wondered why Adam was so affected by the sight of Mark's ex-wife.

"Hello, Ellen," Adam said. "I didn't realize you'd moved to Portland."

"Well, when Mark relocated with—with *her*—it just made sense to do the same. I can work from anywhere, and it was important for Katie to have a relationship with her father, even if he does make piss-poor decisions in life." She frowned and looked at Jenna. "Sorry, Jenna. I didn't mean that the way it sounded. I know Mia is your friend."

"It's okay," Jenna murmured, even though it wasn't. She'd only met Ellen twice before, both times when she'd been at Mia's house and Ellen had shown up to retrieve Katie. She hadn't been pleasant.

With the tension radiating off the woman like sonic waves, Jenna wasn't feeling too pleasant herself.

"So what brings you here?" Ellen asked, looking from Adam to Jenna and back again, a hint of amused suspicion on her face.

"I'm in town doing some mediation work at the medical center where Jenna works," Adam supplied, finding his words first. "Jenna's part of the bargaining group, so we're preparing some team-building exercises in advance of next week's session."

"Nonviolent Communication," Jenna supplied, feeling stupid and out of place uttering the words. "With handguns."

"Right," Ellen said, frowning. "I'm not familiar with that method."

Adam cleared his throat. "So what brings you here, Ellen?"

"Oh, just came out for girls' night. I took up target shooting as a hobby last year, so this helps me unwind. Blow off a little steam, you know?"

"Absolutely," Jenna said, remembering how frustrated Mia had been when she'd learned about Ellen's new hobby.

"She keeps guns in the house with Katie," Mia had said, raking her fingers through her bright red hair. "Guns! With a twelve-year-old sleeping down the hall."

Thinking of Mia filled Jenna with a lukewarm mix of fondness and guilt, and she forced herself to turn her attention back to the conversation at hand.

"So, it's been good seeing you," Adam said. His tone was almost normal now, but Jenna could see the tension in his jaw. "Take care, Ellen."

Ellen blinked, visibly surprised by the dismissal. "Of course. I hope you're doing well, Adam. All things considered."

"It's water under the bridge," he answered. "Let bygones be bygones. Forgive and forget and all that."

He was spewing clichés like some sort of broken motivational tape, so Jenna mustered up the most genuine smile she could, and made her best effort to save him from whatever was troubling him. "It's great running into you, Ellen. I saw Katie the other day. She's growing into such a smart, beautiful young woman. You must be so proud."

Ellen's eyes narrowed, and Jenna wondered where she'd misspoken. Was it the reminder that Katie had Mia in her life? Another female role model who was nothing at all like Ellen herself?

"Right," Ellen said, nodding sharply before turning away. "Have a nice night, you two."

"Shoot hard," Adam called. "Or shoot well. Or—" He shook his head and lowered his voice. "Whatever the fuck you wish someone at a shooting range."

Jenna watched as Ellen vanished into the crowd. When she was certain the woman was out of earshot, she turned back to Adam.

"What the hell was that?"

"What do you mean?" His expression was less guarded now, but he hadn't unclenched his jaw.

"You acted like you were being forced to make conversation with a serial killer."

"Not a serial killer. Maybe someone convicted of chronic jay-walking or a few instances of petty theft."

"What?"

"It was a metaphor." He sighed and took a step forward with the line. "There's some history there."

"Besides the fact that she used to be married to the guy who stole your wife?"

He flinched at the words, and Jenna instantly regretted them. She opened her mouth to apologize, but he'd already moved on.

"It's more complicated than that."

"How do you mean? Mark and Ellen had been divorced for a while when he and Mia had their—" she stopped, cleared her throat of the word *affair*. "When Mark and Mia got together. Mia told me Ellen and Mark divorced more than a year before that." She paused as it occurred to her she only knew Mia's version of the story. "Right?"

Adam shrugged. "Sort of. Mark and Ellen split up, but they were working on patching things up. Dating again, trying to see if they could make it work. For their daughter's sake, and because there was a lot of history there. Then Mia came along and derailed things."

Something flared in Jenna. Defensiveness for her friend, and maybe a touch of annoyance at being in this situation in the first place. "According to Ellen." Jenna wasn't sure if she meant it as a question or a statement, and she saw Adam's brow's lift ever so slightly.

"You don't believe it?" he asked. "That Mia would knowingly wreck someone else's relationship?"

"No, that's not what I meant. I mean, obviously I know about what happened with your marriage. She was up front with me from day one. She takes full responsibility for the affair, Adam."

"Okay," he said. It sounded like agreement, but his jaw was still clenched tight.

"I'm just saying, I think she would have told me if the affair broke up two marriages instead of one. That's all."

"Does it matter?"

"Maybe," she said, not sure why it did. The line moved forward and Jenna shuffled along with it, only dimly aware of the hum of female voices around her and the distant crack of gunfire. "Is it possible Mark never told Mia he and Ellen were trying to patch things up?"

"Anything's possible. Is anyone ever the villain in their own version of a story?"

"What do you mean?"

"Just that when someone has an affair—" his face twisted a little on that word, and Jenna longed to reach for his hand, but she stayed still. "When someone has an affair, that person can always find a way to justify it in their mind. In their explanations to other people. Even if they admit later on that it wasn't the right choice, deep down, they can tell the story in a way that convinces you it was a reasonable choice."

"So what's the alternative?" she asked, surprised by the prickliness in her own voice. "You want her to wear a scarlet letter? To don a hair shirt and spend the rest of her life hiding in a cave doing penance? People make mistakes, Adam. It happens all the time, and they can't be expected to spend the rest of eternity being punished for it."

Adam shook his head and took a deep breath. "Look, I don't want to argue about this. I'm sorry. This is a tender subject for me, and yeah, I'll admit it—it bothers me sometimes to know you've only heard Mia's side of the story."

"Is there a side you want me to hear?"

"No. I'm not interested in an endless game of *he said, she said.*" He shook his head again and took another step forward with the line. "I just want you to consider the possibility that things are more complicated than it might seem. It's not a simple case of, 'her husband neglected her, so she had an affair,' nor is it a cut-and-dried instance of 'his evil wife cheated and broke his heart.' Both stories are completely true and completely false, and we can't pick just one to believe."

"Okay," Jenna said, glancing up to see they'd almost reached the front of the line. Ellen was nowhere to be seen, which was a bigger relief than it should have been. Jenna took a few calming breaths and tried to steer the conversation onto slightly safer ground. "How did you know Mark's ex-wife, anyway? Did you join a support group of thwarted exes or something like that?"

"Something like that," Adam said, and took a step to the front of the line. "I slept with her."

Chapter Nine

Adam followed Jenna to their assigned lane, keeping a wary distance. Her shoulders were rigid and her pace was so brisk he practically had to jog to keep up.

When they reached the last lane on the end, she spun to face him with an expression that was all business. "Are you right-handed or left?"

"Right."

"Is that comfortable in your hand?"

"Yes," Adam answered, weighing the gun in his palm as he watched Jenna's face for any sign of what she was really thinking. "Heavier than I expected, but yes."

"You've got your ear protection?"

"Yes."

Adam waited for the next question, pretty sure none of the questions were what she really wanted to ask him. They'd marched through the business of flashing their IDs and choosing their weapons and finding their position, all without any further comment from Jenna about his history with Ellen.

They had ten more minutes until the range was hot—a term he'd learned just five minutes ago—but Jenna's body language was downright chilly. He could see the tension in her shoulders, but she kept her focus on the box of ammo she was tearing open with more force than it probably required.

"Jenna?"

"Yeah?" She didn't look up.

"Do you want me to explain? To tell you more about what happened between Ellen and me?"

She shrugged and looked up. "Is it any of my business?" Her tone was softer than her words, but Adam could see something flashing in her eyes.

"It seems like something's bothering you, and it started right before we got our guns. Either you're uncomfortable with what I told you about Ellen, or you're more upset than I realized that all the Glocks were rented."

Jenna sighed and closed her eyes, letting the box of ammo rest on the narrow counter beside her. When she opened her eyes, she looked conflicted. "It's never going to be simple between us, is it?"

"Couldn't you say that about any relationship?"

"Sure, any relationship where one partner has bumped uglies with half the people the other person knows."

"You're giving me more credit than I deserve for sexual prowess. For the record, it was two times and it was almost three years ago."

She sighed and set the box of ammo down on the counter. They had some measure of privacy here in the little lane that separated them from the other shooters, but it was still a public place. He could hear gunfire in the distance from the outdoor rifle range, but things were eerily quiet in the space around them.

145

"It's fine, Adam. We both have a history. I'm just not used to the men I date having this much history with the women I know. I'm okay. It's really none of my business, is it?"

He could tell she wanted to ask more, but something held her back. Pride? Embarrassment? Uncertainty about whether she really wanted to open this can of worms?

Adam went ahead and opened it for her. "I was pretty devastated when I found out my wife was sleeping with someone else. At first I tried to fix it. I asked her to give me three months of intensive marriage counseling to see if we could repair the marriage."

Jenna glanced away, fingering one of the pistols. She'd chosen two different guns for them, suggesting they could trade back and forth to give him a feel for firing both a .32 and a .22. He wasn't entirely sure what that meant, but he'd nodded anyway.

She picked up the one the clerk had called a Kel-Tec, turning it over in her hand without comment. "Did Mia agree? To the counseling, I mean."

"At first. We went for two weeks, but it became obvious she'd already made up her mind. That's often the way it works with marriage counseling. It's usually about saying hello or saying goodbye. For us, there was no hope of starting over. No chance of hello. So after a couple weeks, we threw in the towel and said goodbye."

He watched her throat move as she swallowed. A blast of gunfire sounded somewhere outside, but she didn't jump. "I'm sorry."

"Don't be. I'm fine now, but I was in a pretty dark place then. That's where I was when Ellen found me."

"She reached out to you?"

Adam nodded and set his own weapon on the counter beside the box of ammo. It wasn't loaded, but the damn thing still gave him the willies. Even so, he felt ridiculous holding it in the midst of a conversation like this.

"After Mark told her their reconciliation wasn't going to work, Ellen wanted to know why. After he told her about Mia, Ellen tracked her down. Said she wanted to meet 'the other woman.' Eventually, that led Ellen to me."

Jenna was fiddling with a button that moved the target, making the paper outline of a head and shoulders zoom back and forth absurdly. She didn't seem to realize she was doing it, so Adam said nothing.

"So you met Ellen."

He nodded and watched the paper man bob back and forth, the head and shoulders waving like a bizarre white flag. "She thought we could support each other, maybe work together to bring our spouses back."

Jenna met his eyes again. "And you thought having sex with each other might do that?"

He choked back a laugh. "No. Not at first. But when we realized our efforts were futile, we turned to each other for comfort. I knew it was stupid even before I did it. But people don't always make the smartest decisions when they're grieving."

She snorted. "Tell me about it."

Something in her tone told him there was a story there, but now didn't seem like the time to push. "You can relate?"

"Who can't?" She picked up the box of ammo and began loading bullets into the clip, a gesture Adam took as an end to that line of questioning. "Sorry, I didn't mean to interrupt," she said. "This is fascinating, in a way. I mean, I've heard of this before. Of the spouses who get cheated on finding their way into each other's beds and arms. Isn't it some sort of psychological phenomenon or something?"

"I don't think there's an actual syndrome, if that's what you mean. I think there was a country singer who married her best friend's ex after the friend stole her husband."

"Shania Twain, right—I remember that."

Adam raised an eyebrow. "Are gun fanatics required to be country music fans?"

"Are head shrinkers required to be patronizing assholes?"

"Touché," he agreed, glad she was smiling when she said it. "Anyway, it's easy to fall prey to that sort of fantasy. That maybe all the bad stuff happened for a reason, and now we can live happily ever after with the right person who just magically appeared out of the ashes of the affair."

She nodded and flipped the lever on the gun to make it so it wouldn't fire. At least that's what Adam hoped it was. He had no idea what any of the parts were called, so he settled for watching her hands move over the intricate pieces of metal and wood. The clerk had called this one a .22 Mark III Hunter with a fluted five-inch barrel, and Adam had flinched at the word *Mark*.

Then he'd felt stupid for doing it, and forced himself to choose that gun just to prove he wasn't bothered by it. That his ego could handle using a firearm that shared a name with the guy his wife had left him for. Christ, did the echoes of ex-lives ever get quieter, or was it just a matter of learning to ignore the noise?

Jenna picked up the other weapon and slid the clip into it, and it occurred to him this was the weirdest setting he'd ever had for a heart-to-heart discussion about relationships.

"So things didn't work out with you and Ellen?" she asked.

"Not even close. Like I said, it only happened a couple times. It wasn't long after that she moved away, so we really never talked about it after that."

He waited for more questions, for a reaction that would tell him how she was feeling. She had every right to be weirded out by this. How often did a woman get together with a guy and discover she's surrounded by females who've shared his bed or his heart or some combination of the two?

Still, they both had histories. She'd said it herself. Wasn't this what modern dating was like most of the time?

She slid the clip into the other gun, seeming to decide something. When she met his eyes again, there was an odd sense of calm there.

"Come on," she said, adjusting her earphones before fitting the gun into her palm. "Let's blow the shit out of something."

It was close to midnight by the time Jenna pulled the car to the curb outside Adam's hotel and turned to face him. He watched her in the dim glow of the streetlight, a fresh pang of longing sliding over the current of adrenaline still pulsing under the surface of his skin.

"That was hands-down the best unromantic non-date I've ever had," he said. "Maybe we should give the Marxist discussion a try next time."

She laughed, leaning back against the headrest to reveal the smooth column of her throat, and Adam ached to kiss her there.

"You did great for your first time," she said, and for a moment, Adam was still hung up on the kissing thing. "Once you got the hang of it, your aim was pretty good."

"Thanks. If this mediation thing doesn't work out, I can always fall back on joining a gang."

He unhooked his seatbelt and turned so his whole body was angled toward her. "Seriously, Jenna. I had a really great time with you."

"Me, too. Spending time with you is just—"

She didn't finish the sentence, but she didn't have to. She was smiling, albeit a little wistfully, but that was enough.

Adam sighed and reached out to lay a hand on her knee. "I know when we first hooked up, we thought it was just a quick fling. When we realized it couldn't be more than that, I figured it was no big deal. There are other fish in the sea and all that. But every minute I spend with you—"

He stopped there, not sure what he meant to say. Not sure what he could say that wouldn't make this whole thing harder.

"I know," she said, swallowing. And he felt certain she did know. For some reason, words seemed to be failing both of them now. Perhaps it was the late hour, or maybe it was that there was too much they *could* say.

"We won't be working together forever," he said, reaching up to brush a lock of hair off her cheek. He left his hand there, and she leaned into it like a cat craving the touch.

Her cheek felt smooth under his palm, and for a moment they just sat there connected by only the lightest feather of contact.

"My contract with Belmont will end in a month or two," he said. "After that, we wouldn't have to worry about the professional side of things. About your employer claiming it's a conflict of interest or anything like that."

He waited for her protest, but it wasn't the one he expected.

"You live in Chicago," she said. "That's a long ways away."

"I travel all over the country for my work. It doesn't matter that much what city I call my home base."

"What are you saying?"

He swallowed, not sure if he'd gone too far or presumed too much. He was probably supposed to be cagier, but dammit, he liked her. He liked her enough to consider what a future with Jenna might look like. Was she on the same page?

"I have family in Seattle," he said. "I've considered relocating before, just to be closer to them. I'm just saying that if things got serious between the two of us, I could see myself moving to the Pacific Northwest. Hypothetically, I mean."

She sighed and closed her eyes, still leaning into his touch. Adam curved his palm to cup the side of her face, then slowly traced the line of her jaw and the satiny skin of her throat.

For a moment, she didn't say anything. Just leaned into his touch, breathing in and out and mingling their breath behind the fogged-up windows of her car.

When she opened her eyes, they glittered beneath the streetlights. He could see the doubt in her expression before she uttered a single word. "We might not be working together forever, but you'll always be my best friend's ex-husband. There's no getting around that, is there?"

"No," he said slowly. "That won't ever change. But maybe your feelings about it will?"

She sighed and shook her head. "It's like you said earlier, Adam—things are always more complicated than that."

"How do you mean?"

"It's not just *my* feelings I'm worried about."

He nodded. There was no arguing with that, even though he wanted to. Even though part of him raged with the urge to yell that he gave up caring about his ex-wife's feelings the second he signed the divorce papers.

But most of him knew that wasn't true. As much as he hated it, as much as he no longer cared for her that way, the ghost of her silent judgment would always be hanging over him. Every career choice he made, every romantic entanglement he entered, it would forever be filtered through a fleeting question of what Mia might think. He hoped it might fade with time or a new relationship, but a whisper of it would probably always echo in his mind.

It wasn't the same hesitation Jenna had, but it was still there.

"Understood," he said at last, even though that wasn't entirely true. "Good night, Jenna."

He leaned in to kiss her, and there was something more gentle about it this time. A breath of longing and sadness about what could never happen between them.

When they drew apart, her eyes glittered brighter than before. "Goodbye," she whispered.

On Sunday morning, Jenna set the table with Aunt Gertie's good china.

"I'm so glad this is becoming a tradition," Gertie said, stirring a big pot of gravy on the stove. "What time did you say Mia would be here?"

"A few minutes after nine," Jenna said, smoothing the corner of a blue and white checked placemat before she set the plate down. "Mark had something to do for work, so Mia had to take Katie to her mom's house."

Jenna folded a napkin with a more severe crease than it needed, wondering if Mia would stop and chat with Ellen. She knew the relationship wasn't great between the two women, but Mia always tried. What if Ellen mentioned seeing Jenna and Adam together? Would Mia buy the cover story about team-building prep, or should she come up with something else?

The fact that she was giving so much thought to hiding something from her best friend sent a fresh wave of guilt surging through her, and she gripped the counter to hold herself steady. God, maybe she should just tell Mia everything. It had to be better than lying, didn't it?

"Everything okay, dear?"

Jenna turned to her aunt. "Sure, why?"

"You just seem distracted. Is there anything you want to talk about?"

The fact that I'm falling for my best friend's ex-husband? The fact that you're a bestselling erotica author and I'm afraid the scandal could cause labor negotiations to blow up in my face? The fact that I slept with the mediator my employer is counting on to bail us out of the worst personnel disaster in the company's history?

"Nope, nothing," she said, and turned to place a fork neatly beside Gert's spot at the table.

The doorbell rang, and Jenna set the last piece of silverware atop her own placemat. She smoothed her hair as she crossed the living room, feeling oddly self-conscious as she opened the door to greet her best friend.

"Hey, chica," Jenna said, leaning in for an air-kiss. "How are things going?"

Mia's hair was rumpled and her cheeks seemed flushed from something besides the glow of pregnancy. She sighed and walked into the house, her steps heavy and slow. She set her purse on the table by the door and moved toward the kitchen clutching a bright blue bowl filled with fruit salad. Jenna fell into step beside her, trying to read her best friend's mood.

"Gawd, what a morning," Mia said, setting the bowl on the table. She turned to lean against the kitchen counter near the spot where Aunt Gertie was setting a baking sheet lined with biscuits. "I walked Katie up to the door with a bunch of extra tomatoes from our garden. She's been gobbling them up all weekend, and I thought Ellen might like to have some, you know?"

Jenna bit her lip. "You talked to Ellen?"

"No. She didn't even come to the door. Not even when Katie called after her and said I wanted to say hello. She just yelled from the back of the house for Katie to give back the tomatoes and say her goodbyes."

Any relief Jenna might have felt over the near miss was replaced by a sense of sadness for her friend. "I'm sorry, Mia. I know how hard you've been trying."

"It's okay." She pasted on a smile and pushed away from the counter, reaching over to hug Aunt Gertie. "Everything smells delicious. What can I help with? Need me to stir the gravy or put the biscuits in a basket or something?"

"Sit down, sweetheart," Gert said, waving her toward a chair. "Goodness, you look like you're about to burst."

Mia seemed ready to argue, but she cast a look down at her ankles. "Thanks, you're right. I swear, I'm running out of shoes that can fit. Why the hell didn't anyone tell me about all the swelling?" She dropped heavily into a chair. "Thanks, you two. I'm so happy to be here right now."

"Are you okay, dear?" Gertie frowned as she began piling the biscuits into a wooden bowl lined with a crisp gingham cloth. "You look a little worn out. Is something bothering you besides the run-in with Katie's mom?"

Mia picked up a grape that had fallen from the fruit salad bowl and rolled it around between her fingers. "It's been a rough weekend."

Jenna grabbed the biscuit bowl and tucked the cloth around the edges, covering everything carefully before carrying it to the table. "What's going on?"

"It's Mark. Things have been—strained lately."

"How do you mean?"

"We're having trouble with boundaries," Mia said, setting the grape down and fiddling with the tines on her fork. "I don't think it's unreasonable to put limits on how often Ellen calls, or at least on how often he answers the phone."

Gert frowned and began ladling the gravy into a bowl. "Are they talking about Katie?"

"That's just it—I'd totally understand if they needed to talk about grades or soccer camp or dentist appointments or even how Katie is doing with friends. Believe me, I get it. I married a guy with a kid, and I know that will always be a priority."

Gertie started to carry the gravy to the table, but Jenna headed her off and picked up the bowl. She set it down in front of Mia, then turned to grab a spoon for Mia's fruit salad. "So what's different about these calls?" Jenna asked.

"Mark answers them all the time," Mia said. "Even if we're on a date. Even if we're in the middle of family movie night or being intimate."

Gert's eyes went wide as she lowered herself into the seat beside Mia. "He talks to his ex-wife during sex?"

"Well, not during sex. I mean the sex stops so he can answer the phone. He's not pumping away while they chat about curfews and college plans."

Jenna grimaced as she shoved a serving spoon into the fruit bowl, then took a seat between Mia and Gert. "Have you talked with him about how it bothers you?"

"I tried." Mia bit her lip and reached out to take a biscuit. "He said he feels guilty."

"Guilty?" Jenna watched her friend's face, remembering Adam's words. Had more than one marriage been wrecked by the affair? Did it matter at this point? It's not like Mia owed her a detailed explanation or justification for her every action.

"About not being married to Katie's mother anymore," Mia said. "About breaking up the family when he chose to leave. About a lot of things, I guess. 'Daddy guilt.' That's what one of the books I read called it."

Jenna grabbed a biscuit for herself and split it open, breathing the doughy fragrance of buttermilk. "How long had they been divorced when you and Mark got together?"

Mia bit her lip as she opened her own biscuit. "They'd been divorced a year or so. I know Ellen hoped they'd get back together, but Mark wasn't interested."

Gert pushed the bowl of gravy across the table, nudging the ladle toward Mia. "These things are always hard. It doesn't really matter who did what to whom on which timeline. The point is that you're all where you are right now, and you have to find a way to work together to move forward."

Jenna nodded and watched as Mia slathered her biscuit with gravy. She passed the bowl along to Gert, while Jenna loaded her plate with fruit.

"You're right, of course," Mia said. "But sometimes I try to think about it from Ellen's perspective. How would I feel if someone just moved in and took over my husband and my life?"

Gert helped herself to a biscuit. "Has your ex-husband remarried?"

Jenna gripped her glass of orange juice, but didn't raise it to her lips. The guilt felt like a lead weight pressing down on her chest, smothering her with its bulk.

"No," Mia said with a shrug. "Honestly, I don't know how I'd feel about it if he did. I know that's horrible and selfish and petty and stupid, especially since I was the one who left."

Gert patted Mia's hand, oblivious to the fact that her niece had grown tense enough to generate electrical currents. "You're entitled to your feelings, dear."

Mia shook her head. "It's not that I'm possessive of him. Adam, I mean. That's not it at all. It's that I wanted so badly for so long for him to make these changes for me. To stop working late hours, to do a better job communicating with me, to try new things and be more spontaneous. So what does it say if he's willing to do all that for someone else, but not me?"

Jenna took a big gulp of orange juice and hoped no one noticed her hands were shaking. She set the glass down and tried to think of something innocuous to say.

Gert beat her to the punch. "Maybe it's not about you," she said. "Maybe someone has to want to change for themselves."

"You're right, of course." Mia sighed and took a bite of biscuit. "I can know that rationally, but it still doesn't make it any easier to sit with the feelings." She shook her head and gave a funny little laugh. "Listen to me, I sound like our marriage counselor."

"You're seeing a marriage counselor?" Jenna asked. "I didn't realize things had gotten to that point."

"I know, lame, right? We've only been married a couple weeks and we're already in counseling." She shrugged and took another bite of biscuit. "I guess it's more of a preemptive thing. We've both been through counseling in the past when it was way too late to do any good. We're trying to get a handle on problems now before things escalate."

Jenna nodded, thinking about what Adam told her about marriage counseling being about saying hello or saying goodbye. She hoped for Mia's sake they were saying hello.

"I ran into Sean the other night," Jenna blurted, hoping the subject change wasn't too abrupt. "Speaking of exes."

"Wow, it's been a while, huh?" Mia took a sip of orange juice. "How was it?"

"Weird. Awkward. But it felt good to catch up."

Mia nodded, eyeing her closely, and Jenna felt a flicker of fear she could see right through her. "You didn't sleep with him, did you?" Mia asked. "There's something a little glowy about you this morning."

"Glowy?" Jenna swallowed and shook her head. "No. Definitely not. Though I guess the thought crossed my mind."

"No kidding? What stopped you?"

Jenna shrugged, already regretting her choice in subject change. "I just wasn't feeling it."

Gert nodded knowingly beside her. "Sean certainly must have been feeling something. He's already called the home phone twice this morning."

Jenna bit her lip. "Thanks for telling him I wasn't here."

"My pleasure, dear. You're entitled to your feelings."

"Or lack of feelings, as the case may be," Mia said, stabbing another bite of biscuit. A blob of gravy dripped from her fork, and Mia jumped back in her chair.

"Dammit," she said, plucking at the front of her shirt. "Would you look at that? I got gravy on my shirt. I swear these pregnancy boobs have screwed up my whole sense of where my body stops and starts."

Jenna reached for the saltshaker. "Try this?"

Mia laughed and shook her head. "That's just for wine, not grease. Though I'm glad to see my ex managed to teach you something."

Jenna felt her face grow warm, and she set the shaker down. Gert stood up. "Let me grab the stain stick for you, dear."

"Sit down, Aunt Gertie," Mia said, lurching out of her chair. "You've done enough already. You've been on your feet all morning fixing this amazing breakfast. Just tell me where to find it and I'll grab the stain stick."

"Let me," Jenna said, but Mia was already halfway down the hall.

"It's in the laundry room in the basket next to the dryer," Gertie called. "Just bring it back out here and I'll help you work it into the stain."

Mia disappeared around the corner, and Jenna turned to Aunt Gertie with a grimace. "You think she's doing okay?"

Gertie shook her head. "Pregnancy hormones can really take a toll on a woman. I can't say for myself, but I remember when your mother was pregnant with you, those last few months were especially hard."

Jenna swallowed and tried not to let her brain go there. She'd never told Gert about her own miscarriage. About the reason she and Sean had split up or how everything fell apart—

"Hey, ladies?"

Mia's voice echoed from the other end of the house, breaking Jenna's train of thought. "Can't find the stain stick?" Jenna called back, rising to her feet to aid her friend.

"No, it's not that. Just wondering where this sweatshirt came from."

"Sweatshirt?" Jenna called back, her arms prickling with an unease she couldn't explain.

"Cornell University Law School. Not the most common school in the world."

"Oh?"

"Yeah, and it's kinda weird. That's my ex-husband's alma mater."

Jenna closed her eyes and wished for the ground to swallow her up.

Chapter Ten

Jenna's eyes were still closed when she heard her Aunt Gertie's voice across the table.

"Cornell University Law School, you say?" Gert called out to Mia. Jenna opened her eyes to see Gert watching her with interest. "That must be Arthur's sweatshirt."

Mia trudged back into the room, a Tide stain stick clutched in one hand and an expression that was more curious than suspicious. Jenna willed herself to breathe.

"Who's Arthur?" Mia asked as she dropped back into her chair and popped the top off the stain remover.

"Arthur is my new gentleman friend. He stayed over one night last week, so he must have left that behind."

"He graduated from Cornell?"

"Why yes, I believe he did. Practiced family law for quite a few years down in the Bay Area before he retired. He dabbles in a bit of elder law now and then over at the Senior Center. Another biscuit, dear?"

Jenna blinked and reached out to take the wooden bowl her aunt had nudged toward her. When Gert caught her eye, she gave a wink so faint, Jenna was sure she'd imagined it.

She knew she should feel relieved, but the guilt pressed heavily into her chest. She split open a biscuit and reached for her orange juice.

What Mia doesn't know won't hurt her, she told herself.

It just might, her conscience argued back.

Jenna gulped down the last of her juice, her stomach roiling. She felt like the worst friend on the face of the planet. She probably was.

Beside her, Mia chattered on.

"I'm glad you're seeing someone, Aunt Gertie," Mia said as she finished rubbing the stain stick over her shirt and recapped the pen. "Love is a wonderful thing at any age."

"Pish, who said anything about love?" Gert grinned and pushed the gravy toward Jenna. "I'm just after the sex."

Two hours later, Jenna was up to her elbows in soapy water, washing the last of the breakfast dishes.

She still hadn't managed to wash Gert's mental picture from her mind. As if conjured by dirty thoughts, Aunt Gertie strolled into the kitchen and fluffed her hair.

"Did you have a good nap, Aunt Gertie?"

"Lovely, dear. Thank you so much for taking care of those. My energy level just isn't what it used to be these days, I'm afraid."

"You made an entire breakfast from scratch. I'd say your energy is pretty good for seventy-eight." Jenna pulled the last plate from the suds and began to rinse, her brain trolling for the best way to ask her question. "Aunt Gertie?"

"Yes, sweetheart?"

"I was here all week. You didn't have an overnight guest."

"No? Hmm, perhaps my memory isn't what it used to be, either."

Jenna set the plate aside and turned to face her aunt. "There's no beau who went to Cornell Law School, is there?"

Aunt Gertie smiled and picked up a dish towel. "Of course not, dear. Arthur was a proctologist who went to Oregon State—an ass-man from OSU, as he likes to say."

"Right," Jenna said, turning back to the sink. "So why did you cover for me?"

"You looked like you needed it. Like there's something you weren't quite ready to talk about with the group, or at least not with Mia."

Jenna fell silent a moment, digesting her aunt's words. How much did Aunt Gertie know? How much could Jenna still hide? Her mind was still racing when Gert spoke again.

"You know, dear, Mia loves you very much."

Jenna kept her eyes on the water, feeling it sluice warm over her hands as she rinsed another plate. "I know that. She's a very loyal friend."

"Hmm, yes, loyalty is important. So are other things, too."

"Like what?" Jenna's voice was barely a whisper, and she was gripping the china so hard she feared she might break it.

"Like the ability to be honest with one another. To care for each other even when one friend does something the other might not like very much."

Jenna nodded, not sure how to respond. Part of her ached to tell Gertie the whole story, to break down and confess everything, to ask her aunt what she should do.

But part of her wanted to keep the secret locked up tight. To protect Mia. To protect herself.

"All I'm saying is that Mia would want you to be happy," Gertie said. "Even if that happiness comes with elements that might make her a little uncomfortable."

Jenna turned to face her aunt. "How do you know?"

"About you and Adam, or about the fact that Mia will forgive you?"

The words hit her like a punch to the gut, and all she could do was nod.

"Intuition, dear," Gert said. "And a fondness for stories about love and longing and human relationships."

Jenna looked down at the plate in her hand, thinking about her aunt's books. "We aren't just talking about Adam and me now, are we?"

Gert reached out and patted her hand. "We're talking about whatever you're comfortable talking about, dear. And if you're not comfortable," she shrugged, withdrawing her hand, "well then, we'll continue to pretend nothing's going on. Is that what you'd like?"

Jenna kept her eyes on the plate. This was her chance. The opportunity to have everything out in the open. Gert's writing career and the possibility of worldwide exposure. Her feelings for Adam and her fears about what that might mean for Mia. The fling that could cost her professional reputation, even if they waited until Adam's contract ended. Everyone would remember. Everyone would know.

She reached up to turn off the taps, then handed the plate to her aunt. "Let's keep pretending for now."

Gertie nodded. "Okay then. But sooner or later, you're going to have to confront things."

"All right," Jenna murmured, burying her hands in a dish towel. "Not now, though. Just—not yet."

⌒‿♂

"Can you please state, for the record, whether this is or is not your genitalia?"

Kendall Freemont pushed the photograph forward across the table in the HR conference room while Jenna sat beside her, doing her best to keep a straight face.

It wasn't easy. The task was complicated by the fact that Adam sat directly across from her, and beside him was the man who'd been caught taking one of the least impressive dick pics Jenna had ever seen.

Brett Lombard looked like a mouse caught in a trap and thinking of chewing off its own foot. Considering the image on the paper in front of him, the mouse analogy wasn't so far off.

"I'm going to repeat the question, Mr. Lombard," Kendall said, pushing her glasses up the bridge of her nose. "I don't think I need to remind you, you're the president of the nurses' union. You have a professional responsibility to answer honestly. Is this, or is this not, your genitalia?"

Adam cleared his throat and turned to Brett. "As the contractor hired to assist this organization with labor negotiations, I'd advise you to tell your employer anything they ask." He leaned closer to Brett, glancing once at Kendall. "However, if I were your attorney, I'd advise you not to answer that question."

Brett frowned. "Aren't you both of those things?"

"I'm not technically *your* attorney," Adam said. "I was trying to help you out."

164

"This is pointless," Kendall said, throwing up her hands. "We know you sent the photo to your colleague using the company e-mail system with a subject line that read, 'check out my junk.' The message got stuck in our filters."

Which is not where he'd hoped the object in question might be stuck, Jenna mused, trying hard not to glance at the picture again. She stole a look at Adam instead, then realized her mistake. He looked confident and professional with an air of genuine compassion, which was sexy as hell. Christ, this is exactly why companies had policies about co-workers dating each other. One longing look across the boardroom and the next thing you know, you're spread-eagled on the conference table.

Jenna pushed that image out of her mind and arranged her face into something she hoped might pass for professional composure. Adam was doing a much better job of it than she was. Then again, she could see the telltale crinkle around his eyes that meant he was on the brink of losing it.

Yet another reason companies don't like colleagues to date. You know entirely too much about what the other person is thinking.

Jenna took a deep breath and tore her thoughts and her eyes away from Adam. Instead, she regarded Brett with her most serious expression.

"Ordinarily, you'd be dismissed outright for an offense like this," she said. "Belmont Health System takes sexual harassment very seriously. We'd usually handle this situation as a personnel issue through HR, and there'd be no need for Mr. Thomas or me to even be party to this discussion."

Brett looked down at his dick pic, seemingly lost in thought for a moment. Jenna did her best to avert her eyes, though it was hard. Not the penis—it was actually quite flaccid. Honestly, what was the point in sending a dick pic if it looked like a half-filled water balloon?

Focus, dammit, she commanded herself, tearing her eyes from the photo. Brett did the same, then frowned at her. "Why *are* you here?"

"Because in case it escaped your notice, this organization is in the midst of one of the most contentious labor battles in its history," Jenna said, smacking her hand on the table. She meant to underscore the seriousness of her statement, but instead she sent the dick pic flying across the table.

It drifted into Adam's lap, where he stared at it a moment as though analyzing the appropriate next move. Kendall stared, too, clearly unsure what HR protocol called for in this situation.

At last, Adam picked up the photo by one corner and set it gingerly in front of Brett. "Your penis, sir. If, in fact, it is your penis."

Brett nodded. "Thank you."

Jenna sighed. "Brett, you are a key member of the bargaining team, which means you've become a high-profile individual as far as the local media is concerned."

She saw his eyes widen at that, and his Adam's apple bobbed as he looked back at the photo. "The newspaper doesn't have this, right?"

"We've been able to keep it quiet. For now." She let the words hang there for a moment. The threat wasn't real—there was no way in hell she'd ever let that happen—but she didn't need Brett to know that. What she needed was to have him nervous enough never to pull this kind of shit again. At least not until negotiations were over.

"I believe what Jenna is saying," Adam said, glancing at her, "is that we're here to offer you a second chance."

She watched Brett's frown deepen, and she wondered if he was thinking about retaking the photo. She couldn't blame the guy. The lighting was all wrong, and the shadow under his balls made it look like he had a strange growth. Honestly, why had Kendall printed the thing at this size? It was practically a poster, though not one she could imagine hanging above her bed.

"A second chance?" Brett swallowed. "Like—I'm not getting fired?"

Adam cleared his throat. "Here's the deal, Brett. We need to get through these negotiations fairly, legally, and with all parties bringing their viewpoints and experience to the table. As the president of this organization's bargaining unit for nursing staff, we need you to be part of this."

"Preferably with your pants on," Jenna added, folding her arms over her chest.

Kendall pressed her palms against a thick file on the table in front of her. "We've already spoken with Susan Schrader, the intended recipient of your—uh—"

"Artistic imagery," Jenna supplied, willing herself not to look at the photo. Or at Adam. Or—Christ, was there any place safe to look?

"Susan does not intend to press charges," Kendall continued. "Apparently the message, while not solicited, was not rebuffed."

"Though not using the company's e-mail system," Adam clarified.

"Or her stapler," Jenna said, daring a glance at the photo again. "Though she did feel it was an artistic touch to position it like that."

They all stared for a moment at the photograph, at the stapler that bore a strategically placed nameplate that read, 'property of Susan Schrader.' Jenna tried to imagine the straight-laced nursing manager bouncing in her chair as she opened the message. It was a mental picture she could do without, so she turned her attention back to Brett.

"Do you have any questions for us?" she asked. "Or anything to add?"

"Thank you," Brett said, nodding at the photo with a sense of pride Jenna thought was sorely misplaced. But it wasn't her place to say so.

It was her job to make sure this story didn't get out. To keep a lid on things so the local media didn't turn this into a circus and distract the organization from helping patients and doing good work in the community. That's why they were all here, dammit. For the patients. Not for bureaucratic bullshit or climbing corporate ladders or earning money or any of those other things.

At the heart of this, that's what it all came down to. That's why she did this job.

She was feeling good about her little pep talk until she glanced at the photo again. Good Lord, had the man never heard of manscaping? At least a little trim here and there, or some general tidying around his—

"So I'm going to do my best to make this go away," Jenna said. "The potential scandal, not your penis."

Adam nodded. "Belmont Health System frowns upon castration as a motivational tool. Clinical studies have shown positive reinforcement is a much more effective form of inspiring employee performance."

He choked a little on the word *performance,* and Jenna had to look away so she didn't lose it completely. She stood up, deciding it was time to call a halt to the meeting before things took a turn for the worse.

"Brett, I hope you're able to use this as a learning tool."

"A valuable tool, yes," Adam agreed, getting to his feet as well. Jenna avoided his eyes.

Kendall stood as well, though she looked a little uncertain. She glanced from Jenna to Adam, then back at Brett. "Mr. Lombard, I have some paperwork I'd like you to fill out. This will become a part of your permanent personnel record, which is a confidential document. It will, however, be made available to your supervisor, which could have an impact on your career in the event that you decide to change departments."

"I understand," he said, joining the rest of them on their feet. "Is, uh—is the photo going in my file?"

"A detailed account of the incident will be recorded in your file, and we'll make a note of the fact that you're treading dangerously close to the company's policy about fraternization among co-workers," Kendall replied. "Since you and Ms. Schrader work in different departments, you're not technically breaking company policy, though the fact that you're members of the same union and bargaining team complicates the matter."

"But the photo? What happens to that?"

"The photograph will be destroyed. Both the file and the printout."

"I see," he said, looking down at the image. "I understand."

"If you'll meet me in my office, we can take care of that paperwork."

Brett nodded as Kendall reached across the table and snatched the photo. She folded it in two, creasing it sharply down the middle. Brett looked a little forlorn, but he turned and walked out of the room. Kendall watched the door close, then turned to Adam and Jenna.

"Thank you for being a part of the discussion."

"I appreciate you including us," Jenna said. "Your instincts were spot on. This is the sort of scandal that could derail the whole negotiation process."

"My thoughts exactly," Kendall agreed. "The last thing this organization needs right now is bad PR with the community or the staff. Even a small scandal like this could make everything implode."

Jenna nodded, swallowing hard. The words hung there between them like bubbles, and she fought the urge to reach out and pop them. She thought of her secret liaisons with Adam, of Gertie's book.

Adam stood up and pushed in his chair. "You know, at some point, this organization is going to need to review some of its more antiquated policies."

Kendall blinked at him. "Are you suggesting employees should have free rein to use company e-mail to send photos of their genitalia?"

"Of course not. But the policy manual hasn't been updated for six years, back when the old CEO was still here. From what I've learned in my short time with Belmont, the company culture has shifted significantly since then."

Jenna stood up, not sure where Adam was headed with this. Was he talking about the fraternization policy, or puritanical views in general? Either way, she couldn't risk Kendall catching on.

"This is certainly a valuable discussion," Jenna said, straightening her chair with a little more force than she intended. "Perhaps we should table it until we've gotten through some of the meatier topics we're covering in the negotiations?"

Kendall nodded. "Agreed. Now if you'll excuse me, I need to get back to Mr. Lombard."

She hustled out the door, the poster-sized dick pic still gripped in her hand. The instant the door closed behind her, Adam turned to look at Jenna. "There's a photo worth adding to the family album."

Jenna groaned and shook her head. "Good Lord, this is not what we need right now. Scandal on the bargaining team? Dick pics and co-workers bumping uglies? The newspaper would have a heyday with this."

Adam regarded her curiously for a moment. "But you're making sure they don't."

"That's right. That's my job."

"You're very good at it."

"I know."

Neither of them said anything else right away. Jenna glanced around the room, wondering if they were being watched or recorded. She doubted it—was that even legal?—but she couldn't be too careful. She could never be too careful.

"Well," she said, meeting Adam's eyes at last. "Thank you for being here. I think it helped give Brett a better sense of how this whole thing fits with the big picture."

"Big picture," Adam repeated. "Could Kendall have printed that thing any larger?"

Jenna snort-laughed. "I couldn't look away."

"If she was trying to make a point, I think she succeeded."

"You mean like keep your pants zipped at Belmont or else?"

"Something like that," Adam said, his eyes softening a little as he looked into hers. "We'll have to use that in the company mission statement when we work on that next week."

"Along with 'thou shalt not use company e-mail to transmit porn.'" Jenna felt her phone buzz and glanced at it, expecting an alert about her next meeting. Instead, she saw a text message from Sean wishing her a good afternoon.

"Bad news?"

She glanced up at Adam. "What?"

"You looked at your phone and scowled. Just making sure it wasn't bad news on the Belmont negotiation front."

"No, it's not. I mean—it's a personal message."

"Oh?"

Jenna couldn't tell from his inflection if it was a question or a statement, and his expression was perfectly neutral. She knew she didn't owe him an explanation, but found herself babbling one anyway.

"It's Sean. My ex. He invited me to some charity event next month and I told him I'd consider it. Purely professional."

Adam quirked an eyebrow. "A professional date?"

"It's not a date. Not exactly. Several Belmont administrators sit on the board of directors for the charity and—"

"Jenna, it's none of my business. You don't have to explain yourself to me."

She nodded, then looked away. "I haven't agreed to go. I'm thinking about it. Thinking about a lot of things, really."

"Me, too."

Something about the softness in his voice made her meet his eyes again, and she felt her stomach twist into a tight, fizzy knot. The backs of her knees began to tingle, and she touched a hand to a chair to steady herself.

It was ridiculous. She'd fielded half a dozen calls from Sean since they'd run into each other, and the ones she hadn't ignored had left her feeling flat and unaffected. How was it possible mere eye contact with Adam could make every atom in her body flicker like twinkle lights?

She looked away, letting her gaze fall to her watch. "I have to get to a meeting over in the ER. I'll see you in the next mediation session?"

"I promise to wear pants and leave my porn at home."

"Good plan," she said, giving him one last look. "It's a pleasure working with you."

"Likewise."

She turned away, the formality of it all making her jaw ache.

The next morning, Adam made it a point to greet every member of the bargaining team—including Brett Lombard—with a smile and a handshake.

His ex-wife's grasp was cool and familiar, and she pulled away quickly as though fearful he hadn't washed his hand after using the bathroom. Jenna was up next, and Adam held her gaze as he closed his palm around hers.

"Jenna. Good to see you."

"You, too," she said, and hurried past, leaving Adam with his fingers tingling.

As soon as everyone had filed in, he returned to his spot at the front of the room. "We're going to start the next segment of the mediation with some training in Nonviolent Communication strategies."

He took a seat on the table in front of the podium. As usual, it was vacant, with none of the bargaining team willing to occupy the front row. "Is anyone here familiar with NVC principles?" He scanned the room, making a point to meet every set of eyes.

Okay, maybe not Jenna's. Or his ex-wife's. And Brett Lombard looked away the instant Adam's eyes caught his. Still, twelve out of fifteen wasn't bad.

No one raised a hand, so Adam hopped off the table and picked up a pile of handouts. He split the stack in half, handing one pile to Nancy Jensen in the far corner of the room. Nancy took one and passed it behind her while Adam made his way to the opposite side of the room. Halfway there, he realized Jenna occupied the far corner. He tried not to let his hand brush hers as he handed the stack to her. She looked up at him and flushed, but her gaze slipped away quickly.

Adam turned and retreated to the front of the room. "NVC, Nonviolent Communication, is also known as Compassionate Communication. It's a way of taking a conversation out of a framework of judgment and blame. Can anyone take a guess what sort of response you generally get when you communicate with someone using judgment and blame?"

The silence stretched out for a few beats, but Adam waited. "Defensiveness?"

Adam nodded at Susan Schrader, trying not to imagine her admiring the photo of Brett's junk. "That's right. Anything else?"

"A punch in the crotch."

Adam wasn't sure who said it, but a few titters of laughter cropped up around the room, so he smiled. "That's right. Also known as a counterattack, either literal or figurative. So instead of prompting that sort of response, we want to learn to speak and hear from the heart to create harmony and understanding. We learn to express feelings and universal needs, as opposed to judgments."

In the right corner of the room, the CEO yawned. Adam stifled the urge to clock the guy in the head. It was always the ones who needed it the most who tuned out first.

"Jon, would you help me out with a little demonstration?"

The CEO looked up, his brow creasing in an expression Adam had come to recognize as the reluctance of a man who would rather be asked to stick a hot fork in his eye and twist.

"Absolutely," Jon said. "Always happy to participate in anything that can help facilitate this valuable process."

Bullshit, Adam thought, which was precisely the judgmental language he needed the group to avoid.

He slid back onto the table with his feet on a chair, bracing his arms across his knees. "Okay, let's start off with a personal example, shall we? Tell us about something in your home life that routinely causes friction between you and another member of your household. It can be anything."

The CEO frowned, clearly trying to decide how much personal information he wished to reveal. Adam half expected him to report that his life was devoid of personal conflict, so he was surprised when Jon spoke again.

"My wife is a neat freak," he said. "Always straightening pillows and snapping at me if I leave a bowl on the kitchen counter. We've been married twenty-seven years, but we keep having the same fight over and over."

Adam nodded, intrigued by this human side of the man who, just last week, had called members of the nurses' union "whiny little crybabies."

"Most couples have fights like that," Adam agreed, trying not to let his eyes stray to his ex-wife. In his peripheral vision, he saw her shift in her seat. Discomfort, probably, though Adam couldn't say if it was the pregnancy or the fact that the subject hit too close to home. How many times had they had their same arguments until they could have tape-recorded their lines and just played them at each other?

You're always working late. It's like you don't want to spend time with me.

My job is very challenging, and I don't need the added stress of you micromanaging how I spend my—

Adam cleared his throat and wiped away the memory of those bitter arguments.

"Okay," he said, slapping his palms on his knees to focus his attention on the CEO. "Let's do a quick demonstration of how the argument usually unfolds. Would you like to play yourself or your wife?"

Jon scowled, clearly displeased at the thought that he might empathize with Mrs. Conway to that degree. "I'll be me."

"And I'll be Mrs. Conway."

"Archibald," Jon grunted. "Sharon Archibald. She kept her maiden name."

"A woman's prerogative," Adam supplied, trying to sound more positive about it than Jon had. "Okay then, I'm Ms. Archibald. Ready?" Adam cleared his throat, and raised the inflection of his voice just a little. "Jon, you left the bread out on the counter again. You know I hate that, and it's so disrespectful when I have to pick up after you."

"She doesn't allow bread in the house. Gluten intolerant."

"Okay then, milk."

"Dairy free."

"Work with me here, Jon," Adam said, trying not to let his exasperation show. "What's a food item we'd find in the Conway-Archibald residence that might occasionally be left on the counter?"

"Squash."

"As in zucchini?"

"Yes. I say it can be left on the counter; Sharon says it goes in the crisper."

"Good, that's good." Adam cleared his throat and tried his Sharon Archibald voice again. "Jon, I keep telling you the zucchini goes in the crisper drawer, not on the counter. I feel like you never listen to me, and it's so disrespectful when you leave things lying around the house that I have to pick up."

Jon scowled. "Stop nagging me. I just worked a twelve-hour day while you sat around fluffing the pillows in the living room. You want to talk about disrespectful, I—"

"Good," Adam said, cutting him off before he could take it too far. There was a blue vein starting to bulge on the CEO's forehead, and Adam was beginning to wonder if he'd picked the wrong guy for this exercise.

"What you just demonstrated so well for the audience," Adam began, careful to stroke the guy's ego, "is the sort of defensiveness that results from using judgmental language. Nice work, Jon."

Jon nodded, and Adam looked around the room. "Can anyone here identify the parts of what *I* said that were especially judgmental?"

He looked around, curious to see who'd been paying attention.

Jenna was watching with an uneasy sort of alertness. Beside her, Mia was biting her lip and scribbling notes on a spiral notepad with a blue cover.

"Disrespectful," Jenna said, surprising him. Then again, it was probably good for her to speak up. It would look suspicious if the two of them avoided each other altogether.

"Good. Exactly. *Disrespectful* is definitely a judgment word. Anything else?"

"Nagging." Nancy Jensen crossed her arms crossed over her chest. "I hate that word. Men use it all the time when they want to degrade a woman or dismiss whatever she's saying as petty and annoying."

"Hey," called Brett Lombard, scowling. "No generalizations about how men always do this or always do that."

"Good, this is good," Adam said, scrambling to divert the conversation back to the example. "You guys are doing an excellent job of modeling the sort of language we don't want to be using."

Several members of the group frowned at the backhanded compliment, but no one argued.

"As I was saying," Adam continued, "there were a number of examples of judgmental language in the dialogue Jon and I just had. One example is something you may not have picked up on because it sounded very much like I was trying to be sensitive and express an emotion. Did anyone catch that?"

He surveyed the room, wondering who'd picked up on it. On the far side of the room, his ex-wife tapped her pen three times on her notepad. A familiar gesture, one Adam remembered well. She had a thought, and was wrestling with whether to voice it. When she looked up, her eyes met his, and Adam forced himself not to look away.

"You said 'I feel like you never listen to me.'" She glanced down at her notes as though confirming she'd gotten the words right, then looked back at him and nodded. "*Never* is a very inflammatory word."

"Exactly," he said, his voice hitching a little on the second syllable. "And that's only part of what makes the sentence so judgmental. Can you pick up on anything else?"

She hesitated, tapping her pen again. "I'm not sure."

Adam swallowed. How many times in their marriage had she uttered that phrase? Never, not that he could remember. She'd always been so goddamn certain about everything, sure he was working too many hours and not being spontaneous enough, sure he should be listening better instead of—

"It's the word 'like,'" he said. "It's a tricky one. On the surface, it sounds as though I'm trying to express a feeling, right? The sentence began with 'I feel like,' so it's gotta be an emotion, right?"

She shook her head, but didn't say anything. There was something in her expression that suggested she was dangerously close to tears, and Adam had no earthly idea what he'd done to provoke that. So much for being a perceptive professional mediator.

"Generally speaking," he said, softening his voice a little. "If the word 'like' follows the words 'I feel,' you're expressing a judgment, not a feeling. For instance, 'I feel like you're being unprofessional,' or 'I feel like you aren't hearing me'—those are judgments, not genuine feelings."

Mia nodded, then looked down at her notebook again. She began to jot something in earnest. She was taking this whole process very seriously. Part of him wanted to be flattered. Hell, had Mia ever hung on his every word before?

Part of him just wanted to be pissed that the answer was *no*.

Adam took a breath. He needed to move on. "The worksheet I handed out at the start of this exercise has a list of universal feelings," he said. "These are internal sensations without reference to thoughts or interpretations. They can range from embarrassment to uneasiness to suspicion to helplessness, and they are feelings everyone can relate to. Every single one of us."

Every eye in the room was watching him now, and for the first time in days, Adam felt sure he was getting somewhere with the group. He held up his copy of the sheet and pointed to the list at the top. "Up here we have a list of universal human needs. I want you to study these without reference to specific people, actions, or things."

He gave the group a moment to look at the sheet. He stole a glance at Jenna and saw her frowning down at the page. She had a furrow between her brows that Adam wanted to stroke with the pad of his thumb, caressing the worry away. He forced himself to look away, turning his attention back to the CEO.

"Okay then. Jon, could I get you to walk through that example with me again?"

"Sure. Yes, absolutely."

"This time, I'd like us to use language that expresses feelings and needs. I'll start by being Ms. Archibald again." He looked down at the sheet, though he pretty much had it memorized. He hadn't always known how to work through conflict like this, but it had become second nature to him now. How would it have changed his marriage if he'd found the tool seven or eight years ago?

He folded his arms across his knees and cued up his Sharon Archibald voice again. "Jon, I'm feeling anxious and overwhelmed and a little helpless."

"Okay," the CEO said, looking leery, but he didn't interrupt.

Adam continued, treading carefully. "When it comes to the household, I have a real need for order and harmony. It's what helps me feel safe in our home."

He heard someone on the opposite side of the room mutter "cheesy," but everyone else was paying attention. Even the CEO sat blinking at him in surprise.

"Did you catch how I expressed both feelings and needs?"

Jon nodded, saying nothing.

"Now it's your turn," Adam said, skipping the part where Jon needed to repeat everything back to make sure he got it. It was clear from his expression that he did. "Tell me how you feel and what you need. Use the sheet, it'll help."

Jon nodded and looked down at the page. When he looked up, his scowl was gone. "I feel exhausted. I work long days, and I come home and just want to relax, but instead I feel like—" He stopped there, grimacing at his own use of the word "like." Adam could have kissed him, but instead he let him keep going. Jon trailed a finger over the page, looking for the right words on the list. "I feel discouraged. I want to do a good job, and I just need acceptance and trust and maybe a little space."

The room was silent. Adam let the silence hang like that for a few beats. The first voice to break it was one he knew well.

"Wow."

He looked over at Mia. Her mouth was open, and her pen was dangling from the tips of her fingers. Adam turned back to Jon and nodded.

"Perfect. Absolutely perfect."

The CEO beamed. "Thank you."

"It's powerful stuff, isn't it? When you share feelings instead of judgments, it compels people to relate to you."

"And hearing what someone needs instead of a list of complaints—it's kind of empowering?"

Adam looked at the nursing manager who'd spoken and gave her a quick nod. "Exactly. And empowered is a much better way to feel than attacked and helpless. Not a bad shift, with just a few changes in wording, wouldn't you say?"

Several heads nodded. A few people looked uncertain, but nearly everyone in the room was looking at the list with renewed interest.

"Okay then," Adam said, standing up and beginning a stroll around the room. "I'd like you all to pair up with someone else in the room and practice running through scenarios until you feel comfortable with this format. For now, stick with personal examples—no talk of company business until we're all sure we've got the hang of the tool. Any questions?"

"Yes." Adam turned to see Nancy Jensen smiling. "Will you come home with me?" she asked. "I'd love to have you teach my husband and me to relate to each other like this."

Adam laughed and ran his hand through his hair. "I can certainly recommend a number of excellent resources for Compassionate Communication training. There are plenty of NVC specialists in Portland."

"Are you single?" Adam looked to the corner of the room where Susan Schrader was smiling at her own joke. "It's hard for me to imagine someone with communication skills like this wouldn't be snapped up pretty quickly."

It took every ounce of strength he had not to look to the other corner of the room. "You'd be surprised."

Later that week, Adam was standing in the produce aisle staring at a limp-looking cauliflower. His hotel suite had a kitchenette, which should be all the motivation he needed to whip up home-cooked meals every evening when he finished his workday at Belmont.

But between working late and feeling out of sorts living in a hotel, he hadn't managed to assemble anything more complicated than a veggie omelet one morning last week.

He had the skills to do it. The cooking class he'd taken last spring had seen to that, and he'd gotten pretty good at making impressive meals from scratch since he and Mia had split up. What was his problem now?

"Salmon chowder," he decided, setting the cauliflower down and snatching up a few large carrots. He turned around to add potatoes and onions to his basket, trying to remember the rest of the recipe he'd learned in his last cooking class.

That's when he spotted her. An elderly woman teetering on the second row of shelving, scaling the display like a monkey as she stretched up to reach something on a high shelf.

"Ma'am, stop!" Adam called, dropping his basket and hurrying over. "Let me help you, please. I don't want you to get hurt."

The woman turned and blinked at him. There was something familiar about her startlingly blue eyes, but Adam pushed the thought aside as she started to wobble. He got there just in time as the woman toppled backward, falling into his arms. She was surprisingly light, and he half expected her to smack him with her purse and accuse him of molesting her as he set her back on solid ground.

"My, my," she said, fluffing her hair. "I haven't had a man sweep me off my feet like that for some time. You're a regular romance novel hero, aren't you?"

Adam stepped back, a little surprised by her sass. "Nope, just a man who doesn't want to see a lady get hurt. Climbing on store shelves is a pretty much a recipe for a lawsuit."

"Do you work for the store?"

"No, but I practiced law for a number of years. You fall and break your neck here, that could turn into an ugly legal situation for everyone involved."

The woman's face lit up, and she gazed at him with renewed interest. "A lawyer? That's wonderful!"

Adam laughed. "I don't hear that very often. Usually people make jokes about how many lawyers it takes to screw in a lightbulb."

"Oh, but I've been needing some qualified legal counsel. The lawyer I met with a few weeks ago turns out to know almost nothing about literary contracts, and I've got a situation I could use help with. I don't suppose you're for hire?"

"No, ma'am. I'm not really taking on any new clients right now."

Adam glanced up at the top shelf and realized for the first time that it held an assortment of sex lubes and prophylactics. What the hell had she been reaching for?

"I don't necessarily need to hire you," she said, brushing her snowy-white hair from her face. "Just ask you a few questions, that's all. Do you know much about publishing law?"

"I actually specialized in literary contracts my first couple years out of law school, but like I said, I'm not really practicing anymore. My license isn't even active right now. I'd be happy to refer you to someone who could help."

"Oh, dear, I was hoping for something a little more informal. Like maybe a casual conversation over a homemade dinner. Pot roast and roasted root veggies and green salad and homemade apple pie?"

Adam's mouth started to water, and he urged himself not to be tempted. Something seemed off here, but he wasn't sure what it was. Something besides the fact that this little old lady was inviting a strange man back to her home.

"Ma'am, how do you know I'm not a serial killer?"

"How do you know *I'm* not one?"

"Good point."

She touched his elbow. "It's your T-shirt, dear. Cornell University Law. You seem like an educated man, and serial killers don't buy things like fresh carrots and potatoes."

"That is some of the oddest logic I've ever heard in my life." He smiled so she wouldn't take offense.

"Well, besides that, I've taken self-defense training, and I live with my niece, who's an excellent shot. Please, dear—won't you come to dinner?"

"You mean right now?"

She nodded, looking earnest. "I put the roast in the Crock-Pot earlier this morning."

"But I don't even know your name."

"Gigi," she said, smiling up at him. "Gigi Buckingham."

"Adam Thomas," he said, sticking his hand out for her to shake.

She beamed up at him with a look that told him he was still missing something here.

Even so, he turned and followed her out of the store.

"So let me get this straight," Adam said, taking a sip of the chamomile tea Gigi had poured him in a delicate blue china cup. "You're concerned about having your pseudonym compromised and you want to keep your identity from being exposed, or you're looking for the smartest way to capitalize on the fact that those things are about to happen?"

Gigi smiled and set a small plate of cookies in front of him. They looked homemade, and she'd lined the plate with a lacy white doily. The smell of pot roast hung fragrant in the air, mingled with the scent of potpourri scattered in crystal bowls around the living room. A basket of yarn and needles completed the picture of domestic bliss, but it was a contrast to the laptop sitting beside it.

She'd opened the Amazon page for one of her books, and a book cover emblazoned with two mostly nude figures twisted together in a pose that made Adam's thighs ache.

He looked away, trying to focus on the woman who'd kicked off this whole conversation by offering him tips for cooking a moist pot roast. He felt a twinge of sadness as he thought about his grandmother. How long since he'd seen her? His sister had moved to Seattle six years ago, securing a spot for Nana at one of the nation's top Alzheimer care units. Adam had been to visit plenty in the early years, but once Nana forgot who he was, the visits had been less frequent. It had been at least three months. He needed to get up there, especially now that he was here on the West Coast. He could make a weekend of it, drive up to see Shelly and Nana and Gramps.

"The thing is, I'm not opposed to making the most of my career," Gigi said, and Adam drew his attention back to the woman offering him a gingersnap. "My first book has been more successful than I ever imagined, and there are two more coming."

"The *Panty Dropper* series, I've heard of it," Adam said, not sure if it was okay to admit that. "So what I'm hearing you say is that you don't really mind if your pseudonym is compromised. That you're okay with people knowing who you are?"

"I don't mind so much. It's just that—"

The front door burst open, and Adam turned to face the gust of wind blowing in from outside. The cookie he'd been nibbling dropped from his fingers, bouncing off his knee and onto Gigi's spotless rug.

"Jenna?"

She stood there blinking as her purse fell to the ground with a thud. "Adam?" She blinked harder as though hoping he might vanish if she just waited long enough. "What the hell are you doing here?"

It dawned on him what had been niggling at the back of his brain since he first spotted Gigi in the store. He looked from the old woman to Jenna and back again, confirming they shared the same eyes, the same forehead. Jesus Christ, how had he missed it?

You're a regular pro at missing all the signs.

"Your aunt," he said, running a hand down his face. "Gigi is your aunt? The one you mentioned in the porn store? The one who told you embrace your inner sex goddess?"

Jenna closed her eyes and shook her head slowly. "For crying out loud, Aunt Gertie—what are you trying to pull here?"

"Hello, dear," the old woman said, standing up and straightening the lace edge of her apron. "Did you have a nice day at work?"

Jenna opened her eyes again and Adam watched her chest rise and fall as she took several deep breaths. The door was still open behind her, and Adam wondered if she was considering fleeing.

"I can explain," he said, even though he couldn't. He managed to stand up though, figuring he shouldn't be the only one seated at this point. "Your aunt invited me back here for legal advice and pot roast, and—"

"My aunt invited you here because she knew exactly who you were," Jenna said, folding her arms over her chest as she regarded her aunt. "What did you do, Aunt Gertie? Stalk him?"

Gigi—or should he call her Gertie?—shrugged and gave a *who, me?* kind of smile. "Really, dear, I don't see what the big deal is. I follow him on Twitter, and saw he was shopping at Whole Foods just down the street."

Adam blinked. "Wow, this just got kinda creepy."

"*Just?*" Jenna repeated. "As in it wasn't already creepy enough to find out I slept with my best friend's husband?"

"Ex-husband, dear," Gertie offered helpfully. "They've been divorced almost three years, from what I understand."

"Aunt Gertie—"

Adam held up his hands, trying to divert their attention before things escalated too far. "I'm sorry, do you need me to leave you two alone for a minute? It seems like you might have some things to work out, and I really should be going—"

"Stay!" Gertie grabbed his shoulder and shoved him back down onto the couch with enough force to knock the rest of the cookies off the plate. He started to pick them up, but kept his eyes on Jenna.

She sighed and kicked the front door shut. "I can't believe you, Aunt Gertie."

"Well I wanted to meet him, and besides—he knows something about publishing law."

"Publishing law?"

"Yes. I've made a decision, dear. I'm going to go ahead and let them out me."

"Out you?"

"I want everyone to know that the author of *Panty Dropper* is a little old lady." She clapped her hands together, looking terrifyingly gleeful. "Can you imagine the publicity? It'll be quite the scandal."

She seemed delighted at the prospect, but Jenna looked a little sick. When she spoke, her voice was barely a whisper.

"I thought we agreed we were going to keep things quiet for now. Keep the secrets a secret and all that."

Gert shook her head. "That's what you agreed, dear. I'm tired of hiding everything. I want to take credit for my books. I worked hard, and I deserve my time in the spotlight. Me, not just some faceless pen name."

Adam watched as the panic in Jenna's eyes gave way to tears. "I know you've worked hard, Aunt Gertie. And I'm proud of you. It's just that my career—" she swallowed. "I've worked so hard to build a professional reputation."

The quaver in her voice seemed to move Gertie forward. In a few strides, she was at Jenna's side with an arm around her niece's shoulders.

"We have different last names, dear. It isn't like people will make the connection right away. Adam certainly didn't. And even if they did, you and I are completely different people."

Jenna choked a little on a laugh. "I'll say."

"Your colleagues can't possibly judge everyone based on their insane relatives, can they? But really, that's a moot point. I'll be careful, I promise."

"What is it you're wanting to do?"

"Book tours. Television engagements." Gert flung her arms out to the sides, her eyes twinkling with exhilaration. "All the publicity things my agent offered to set up for me if I'm willing. If only Regis were still on the air."

Jenna swallowed again, and Adam could see her working to control her breathing. He had to give her credit—she was trying. It wasn't exactly comfortable, but she was trying.

"And that's what you want?"

"It is," Gertie said. "I've been talking with Adam here about some of the legal implications, but really, I've already made up my mind. I'm ready to move forward with the next stage in my career."

Jenna nodded and bit her lip. "Okay." She took another breath, and seemed steadier when she spoke again. "I want you to be happy. I guess I can get used to the idea."

"I'll be careful, dear. I promise. And I'll do my best to make sure this doesn't turn into another scandal like the thing with the old CEO's wife and the hookers."

Jenna winced. "Okay. That's all I can ask. I love you, Aunt Gertie."

"You too, sweetheart."

The two women embraced, and Adam stood quietly in front of the sofa. It was a beautiful moment, and it felt nice to be able to witness it. Aunt Gertie looked small and fragile in Jenna's arms, while Jenna looked lovely and warm and fine boned. The scent of home cooking and cinnamon and orange peel gave the whole room a homey feel, and it felt like he was standing on the fringes of a Norman Rockwell painting.

The mood evaporated with the blare of Justin Timberlake's "Sexy Back" blaring from Jenna's purse. Adam clenched his hands behind his back, trying not to be annoyed. It used to be Mia's favorite song. She'd dragged him out to a club one night, determined to draw him out of his shell, to get him to try something new, to cut loose and be spontaneous for a change.

It'll be fun, I just want to dance and have a good time . . .

"Hey, Mia, what's up?"

Adam blinked. As he refocused on the present, he saw Jenna with her phone pressed against her ear.

"Right now?" The panic was back in Jenna's eyes again, and this time she looked ready to bolt. "You're already on your way here?"

Adam gritted his teeth. For a moment there, he'd felt hope. Jenna seemed to be letting go of the idea that other people were judging her. He'd felt a flicker of hope that maybe—just maybe—it meant something for them.

But as Jenna cut her eyes to him, he saw how very wrong he'd been. They stayed frozen like that for a moment, staring at each other across the expanse of the living room. Gert stood silent, as if waiting to see what would happen. Jenna held the phone to her ear, gripping it so hard her knuckles had gone white.

Adam stood up. "I'll grab my coat," he said, and slipped past her out the door.

Chapter Eleven

Jenna felt like hell.

It wasn't just the memory of Adam's expression as he'd moved past her out the door, his eyes flashing with the knowledge of being thrown over for his ex-wife.

That was bad enough. But the sight of Mia sobbing at the kitchen table was like a splintered Popsicle stick through her spleen.

"I feel like such a failure," Mia sniffled, dabbing at her eyes with a tissue she'd already shredded to ribbons. "I had such high hopes for the counseling stuff, you know? But maybe I'm just not cut out for relationships."

Gertie tucked a plate of pot roast in front of her and petted her hair. "There there, dear. I'll just leave you two alone to talk—"

"No, stay!" Mia caught the old woman's hand in hers and gave a watery smile. "You're like a mother to me, Gertie. A nonjudgmental mother who doesn't berate me for my life choices or make me feel financially beholden to her."

Gertie squeezed Mia's hand and smiled. "You're a dear. I wish I could stay, but I have a phone interview in ten minutes and I need to get ready. I know you and Jenna have a lot to talk about, so I'll leave you to it."

Jenna tried not to wince as Gertie gave her a pointed look, then drifted out of the room. Mia blew her nose again, blessedly oblivious to Gertie's prodding. Jenna reached out and touched her friend's arm.

"So you tried the Nonviolent Communication stuff with Mark?"

Mia sniffled again. "I tried to. Honestly, I probably did it wrong. I took home the worksheet and everything, but he just got mad. Said we should be able to talk to each other like normal people without needing a flowchart and printouts from my ex-husband."

"You think that's what it was all about? That Adam's the one who presented the tool?"

"Maybe. I don't think so. Honestly, things have been bubbling up for a while now. Way before the wedding. Before we got pregnant, even." She grabbed a tissue and mopped at her eyes again. "Why am I so bad at this?"

"Bad at what?"

"At relationships. If you'd asked me three or four years ago, I would have told you I was just married to the wrong guy. Now—I don't know. Maybe I'm the wrong guy."

"Don't say that." Jenna squeezed her hand. "You're a great guy. You're smart and funny and beautiful and one of the kindest people I know."

Mia sniffed again and crumpled the tissue in her hand. "You're so sweet. I'm sorry I've been such an awful friend lately. I feel like it's become all Mia all the time between us."

Jenna felt a pang of guilt in her gut, but she pushed it aside and rubbed her friend's arm. "Hey, you've been there for me plenty of times when I needed you. That's what friends are for."

"Maybe. I feel like I've been so needy lately. It's just—" She stopped, seeming to consider her words. "Do you think I made a mistake leaving Adam for Mark?"

All the blood drained from Jenna's head. She felt dizzy and a little sick as she balled her hand in her lap under the table. "What?"

"I don't mean I want him back. Adam, that is. I guess what I'm asking—" She shook her head. "Hell, I don't know what I'm asking."

"Try!" The word came out more harshly than Jenna expected, and Mia leaned back a little in her seat. Jenna softened her voice and tried again. "I mean, tell me what you're thinking. I want to understand."

Mia sighed. "I guess when I chose to leave my marriage, I felt like I was doing it for the right reasons. The relationship was broken, and there was no way to fix it. But learning all these new communication tools, and now seeing how hard things are with Mark . . . I don't know, I guess I'm wondering if I didn't try hard enough with Adam."

Jenna swallowed, trying to keep her throat from closing up. "You want Adam back?"

"No! That's not it at all. But it's like art history."

"What?"

Mia looked down at her hands as she spread her fingers out on the table. "When I was in college, I took a bunch of art history classes. I needed credits for arts and culture, and the classes fit around all the courses I needed to get my nursing degree." She took a shaky breath and kept going. "I went to most of the classes, and I memorized big chunks of the textbook so I could ace the tests. But I didn't really appreciate it. I didn't sit back and enjoy the pictures or learn the stories behind the paintings. I didn't really absorb the way the art made me feel because I was so busy memorizing so I could pass the class. Do you know what I mean?"

"Yes," Jenna said, her voice barely a whisper. "I think I do."

Mia gave a small smile, seeming pleased to be understood. "So it's not that I want to go back and take art history again. Not really. I guess I just wish I'd done it differently the first time. Spent less time taking notes and more time looking at the pictures. Done less cramming for tests and more standing in art galleries just admiring the paintings."

Jenna swallowed, wishing she knew the right thing to say here. Wishing there were some magical guidebook she could consult. "No one gets relationships right on the first try. We probably never get it right, when it all comes down to it. All we can do is take the lessons we've learned and keep moving forward."

Mia nodded and buried her hands in her lap. She studied them for a moment, then met Jenna's eyes.

"Have you ever wanted a do-over in a relationship?"

Jenna bit her lip, too unsure to speak. "I—I don't know."

"With Sean, for instance. You said you had dinner with him last Friday night. How did it feel to be back together like that?"

"Weird," Jenna admitted. "Familiar. Easy. Sometimes comfortable, sometimes really, really awkward."

"Yeah. I know that feeling." Mia rubbed a thumb over a line in the table. Her nails were chipped and chewed down to nubs, and Jenna felt an ache in her gut. "Do you think there's any chance you'll get back together with him?"

"With Sean?" Jenna looked up at the ceiling. Honestly, the answer was no. But hell, maybe Mia had a point. Maybe she'd given up too easily, or hadn't had the right tools, or—

"He's been calling," Jenna said. "Once last night, and again this afternoon. He says he wants to talk some more. That's it, just talk."

"You think he means more?"

Jenna nodded. "I think so."

"So maybe this is your chance to get it right this time. To not make the same mistakes again."

"Maybe so," Jenna said, closing her eyes.

But it wasn't Sean's face she saw in her mind. And when she thought of regrets, that relationship was the furthest thing from her mind.

Adam glanced at his watch as the elevator doors opened onto the tenth floor of his hotel. It was after eight, so he really should think about getting dinner. He'd left Jenna's place in such a hurry that he'd barely heard Aunt Gertie chasing him down the driveway, urging him to come back so she could fix him a Tupperware container of pot roast and mashed potatoes.

"I'm fine," he'd insisted, smiling down at the old woman. "I'll just grab something in the hospital cafeteria. I need to go back there anyway."

"But I promised you a home-cooked meal."

"And I promised you free legal advice. If we both break our promise, we cancel each other out, right?"

He'd been trying for a lighthearted tone, but Gertie had just looked at him with sadness. "I'm sorry, Adam."

He wasn't sure exactly what she felt sorry for, but he shook his head anyway. "Don't worry about it."

He probably should have gone right back to the grocery store after that, but he couldn't resist the siren call of work. He'd returned to the hospital and spent several hours sifting through documentation. Though the talk of a nursing strike had quieted down, the tension still bubbled hot beneath the surface. One of the union reps had started passing out protest stickers for staff to wear on their name badges, and the landfill had turned up more illegal waste. Intentional, someone suggested, though Jenna had done a good job keeping it out of the press.

She's damn good at her job. Damn good at covering things up so everyone can go about their business like nothing ever happened.

Adam sighed as he stepped into the hotel hallway and started toward his room. He couldn't fault her for it. He'd known from the start who she was. Well, maybe not from the very start. But even now, knowing everything, he wanted her still.

He also wanted that damn pot roast. Hell, he could still smell it. He probably should have taken Aunt Gertie up on her offer. Maybe that takeout place down the street would have pot roast, or maybe he could grab a TV dinner with some half-decent mashed potatoes, or maybe—

Maybe Jenna will be sitting in front of your door with a giant bag of leftovers.

He blinked twice, making sure he wasn't imagining things. She must've heard his footsteps, because she turned then and hit him with the full force of those bright blue eyes.

He watched as she stood up in seeming slow motion, unfolding herself from a tangle of limbs and disheveled hair. She held up a white canvas bag, the cartoon dog on the front of it looking cheerfully out of place in the dim hallway. Her face broke into a half smile, half grimace that made Adam feel like someone had slugged him in the gut.

He stood frozen, still far enough away that he could run if he wanted to. Still far enough she had to raise her voice to call out to him.

"I don't want to say I'm sorry, because I feel like I'm forming a bad habit here," she called. "Of showing up at your doorstep all weepy and remorseful and trying to apologize for the way I've acted around you in front of other people."

Somehow, Adam found a way to make his legs work. He took a few steps toward her, then several more until he was standing close enough to feel the warmth of her body.

"It's okay," he said, breathing in the scent of Jenna and the pot roast, not sure which he craved more.

"It's not okay." She shook her head, letting the bag drop to her side. "I've been thinking."

He glanced at the bag. "Would you think better at a table with that food on plates in front of us?"

She laughed. "Hungry, are you?"

"I didn't realize how hungry until you showed up."

Her laughter faded to a sad little smile, and she looked at him oddly for a moment. "Funny how that works."

"Are we talking about something besides pot roast?"

"Come on," she said, gesturing to his door. "We can talk about pot roast and regrets and everything else once we get inside."

"Deal." Adam moved past her and slid his key card into the slot, his arm brushing the side of her breast as he twisted the knob and pushed open the door. He felt her close behind him as he moved into the room, but he didn't turn around. Part of him feared he'd scare her away. Part of him feared he'd give in to temptation and say to *hell with it all,* throwing her back onto the bed and making love to her again the way he'd been dying to for weeks.

He headed for the kitchenette and pulled open a cupboard. He kept his back to her as he gathered plates and silverware. "Did you bring that apple pie?"

"Two slices. Want me to put it in the toaster oven to warm up while we eat?"

"That would be perfect."

Adam grabbed a few napkins left over from his pizza run last

Friday. Christ, was that less than a week ago? His time at Belmont was flying by.

Jenna twisted a knob on the toaster oven and turned away, moving toward the small dining table near the window. He'd left the curtains open, and Portland's city lights spread out below like a sheet of black felt sprinkled with glitter.

"So I've been thinking," Jenna said again. He turned to look at her and watched her move his pile of books and spreadsheets to an empty chair. "About my Aunt Gertie."

"Oh?" Adam carried the plates to the table, his hand brushing hers as she began to unpack the canvas bag of food.

"About the look on her face when she told me how hard she'd worked. How badly she wants this."

"She does seem passionate about it."

"I know. And I feel bad that I've been holding her back. That I'm the reason she writes under a pen name and hasn't claimed any of the fame she's worked so hard to earn. She loves what she's been writing."

"I could see that," he said slowly, not sure where she was headed with all this. "Your aunt seems like a very passionate woman."

"She is. And even though I'm scared about what's going to happen, I'm excited for her, too. I'm proud of her for going after what she wants."

He set the plates on opposite sides of the table, anchoring napkins beside each one with a knife and fork. He watched Jenna's hands as she unpacked the food, pulling out glass containers of pot roast and mashed potatoes and roasted veggies. His mouth was watering so much he feared he might drool on the floor.

"What do you want, Adam?"

He blinked. "The pot roast."

She smiled and handed him the container. "I meant out of life. Your career, your relationships, your place in this world."

"That's a pretty heavy discussion to have on an empty stomach." He filled his plate with mashed potatoes, piling it with two slabs of pot roast and dousing the whole thing with gravy while he thought fondly of Aunt Gertie and of the niece who'd brought him this feast.

He grabbed half the roasted veggies, then took his seat and picked up his fork. "I guess I want happiness. Stability. Some career milestones to be proud of, people around me who make me laugh, and the ability to go to bed each night and think, 'I made a difference for someone.'"

He forked up a bite of pot roast and chewed as Jenna stood watching him, not taking her seat yet. She nodded, her fingers lightly touching the corner of the table, seeming to hesitate there on the edge. "I want all that, too," she said. "And also, I want you."

Adam choked on his pot roast. Jenna reached over and tried to whack him a few times on the back, but he waved her off. He stood up and made a beeline for the kitchenette where he leaned over the tap and guzzled at least twelve gallons of water before stopping to fill two glasses. He made his way back to the table as Jenna watched him, her expression somewhere between amusement and uncertainty.

He set one glass in front of each plate and took his seat. Picking up his fork, he cut off a piece of meat and chewed thoughtfully, spearing up some veggies as he watched Jenna's eyes flit from the table to the bed and back again.

"I want you, too," he said. "Very much. Sadly, we can't do anything about it."

"I've been thinking about that," she said. "But I've also been thinking about my aunt. About the look on her face when she talks about her writing. About the passion she feels when she does something she's really good at. I'm good at my job, Adam, but it's not the same thing. I want the other kind of passion."

"The sweaty kind?"

"Right. I mean, something like that. I want the kind of passion I felt with you."

Adam swallowed his next bite, not sure what else to do. He speared another bite of potatoes, then another, before he took a sip of water and washed it all down.

"I remember," he said. "Our little fling was pretty phenomenal in the grand scheme of flings."

"I know!" She smacked the table with her hand, something he'd started to recognize as her trademark when she felt strongly about something. He was used to seeing it at work, but seeing it here with the knowledge that he had something to do with rousing her to this state—

Adam took another bite of pot roast and ordered himself to think rationally. "So what are you suggesting?"

"I don't know, exactly. I just know I want that feeling again."

"You're propositioning me?"

She stayed poised at the edge of the table, twisting a napkin in her hands. "I'm not sure. All I know is that I loved the way I felt when I was with you. Alive. Inspired. Amazing."

He swallowed and picked up his water again, not sure whether to lunge for her or let her keep fumbling her way through this awkward seduction attempt. "Are you always this analytical when it comes to passion?"

"I don't know. It's kinda new for me."

"You don't say."

"Look, I've had only one other one-night stand my whole life, Adam. Obviously the fling thing isn't my forte."

"Maybe we're meant to be something besides a fling."

"Maybe." She bit her lip. "Or maybe we just need another go at it. I want to feel that again. The desire, the heat, the energy. Seeing that kind of emotion on my aunt's face—I want that, Adam. I really, really want that."

"Here's a seduction tip for you," he said, cutting a final bite of meat and chewing it slowly. "Maybe stop talking about your aunt. It's throwing me off my stride."

She gave him a funny half smile. "Okay. There's also Mia—"

"No ex-wife talk, either. And maybe put a kibosh on the seduction attempts until the guy you're seducing is done with dinner."

"So does that mean you're considering it?"

He set his fork down and rested his hands on the table. "Honey, I've been considering it every moment of every day since I first walked into that wine bar and saw you sitting there with your shoes kicked off and your hair in your face."

Her eyes flashed with a heat he remembered from their night together, and he suddenly wanted her so badly he ached with it. He wasn't hungry anymore. Not for food, anyway.

He shoved his plate aside and reached for her. It wasn't hard, since she hadn't bothered to sit down yet. She gave a little gasp of surprise, then came willingly into his arms. He pulled her onto his lap, loving the way her body melted against his like she'd done this a thousand times before. Maybe she had, but never like this. Never the way it was between the two of them. He felt sure of it.

She slid her legs around his thighs, her body tight and hot against his. There were too damn many clothes between them, but he didn't want to pause long enough to remedy that. All he could think about was kissing her, feeling her mouth against his, her breasts warm and heavy in his palms as he slid his hands beneath her sweater.

"Jenna," he murmured. "Bed."

"Yes." She slid off his lap, wobbling a little as she found her feet. He caught her hand and stood up, pulling her to the other side of the room where the white duvet was spread open and waiting. He caught her around the waist and pulled her to him again, falling backward onto the mattress with Jenna on top of him.

The exquisite weight of her body left him breathless, all curves and softness and a dense heat that enveloped him as he drew her down to claim her mouth again. She moaned and twined her fingers in his hair. He could feel the heat between her legs as she ground against him, the seams of their jeans making him mindless with their incessant friction.

He rolled against her, flipping her so she was on her back. Her hair spread wild and tangled on the pillow, and her eyes held a question he didn't want to answer right then.

"You're beautiful," he whispered, and pulled her sweater over her head.

Jenna smiled and reached for the button on his jeans. Their clothes seemed to fly off with no prompting at all, a shoe here, a belt there, a random jumble of cotton and leather and satin sailing through cinnamon-tinged air. Adam gave a brief thought to the apple pie warming in the toaster oven, and decided he didn't care about any of it. Let the goddamn kitchen burn. He just wanted her.

Somewhere in the haze of his brain, he had the good sense to fumble for the condom he'd stashed in the nightstand two weeks ago. It had been a fleeting thought, a far-flung hope that Jenna might come back to him again.

But he'd never imagined it like this. She was hungry and wild and burning with an urgent heat he'd never seen in her before. In any woman.

She arched beneath him as he slid into her, and he watched her eyes go wide.

"Adam."

She gasped his name like it was the only one she'd ever said before. The only one that mattered.

In that moment, he felt sure it was.

⟶

Afterward, they lay sweaty and satiated in a tangled mass of sheets and limbs. Jenna turned to look at him, admiring the stubbled line of his jaw, the faint dusting of curls on his chest. He was beautiful, if that was the right adjective to use for a man.

Adam rolled toward her and propped himself on one arm. He slid a possessive hand over her hip and planted a kiss on her forehead. "Planning your escape strategy?"

"What?"

"Just wondering if you're going to freak out like last time and run from the room like you're being pursued by a herd of rabid lemurs."

She smiled and shook her head. "Last time was different. I was late for breakfast with your ex-wife. Not that I knew at the time she was your ex-wife. Not that—"

He slid a hand from her hip to her bottom and gave a light squeeze, forcing Jenna to abandon that train of thought.

"Stop that," he said. "No talk of exes right now. No regrets. No what-ifs. No fretting about what's going to happen or what happened before or what might have happened in some alternate universe if we'd met in third grade and shared an ice cream cone and lived happily ever after. Just be here in this moment. Savor the afterglow for a minute."

"I'd be savoring it more if I had apple pie." She grinned and vaulted out of bed. She walked slowly toward the kitchenette, trying not to think about whether her thighs jiggled or if it was unseemly to eat dessert naked in bed with a man she'd only known a few weeks.

She pulled open the toaster oven, relieved to see the pie hadn't burned to a crisp. It felt like they'd made love for hours, but the practical side of her felt relieved that was only how it worked in romance novels. In real life, it was just enough time to warm a couple pieces of pie.

"You're thinking again," Adam said behind her.

"What?"

"Your shoulders get tense when you're thinking."

She smiled as she shoveled the pie onto two plates, then grabbed a pair of forks and returned to the bed. She tried not to bounce as she sat down beside him, dragging a pillow over so she could prop her plate on something besides Adam's bare chest.

Now there's a thought . . .

He rolled over and grabbed the second plate, picking up his fork and giving her bare knee a soft poke before using it to stab into his pie.

Jenna laughed and wriggled away, forking up a piece of her own pie. "I was thinking, you're right." She took a bite of pie. "This was amazing, obviously."

"The pie or the sex?"

"Yes," she said, and smiled around her next bite. "I know the timing isn't right. Maybe not until your contract is over and things settle down with Mia's life and—"

"What's wrong with Mia's life?"

"Nothing," she said, feeling a pang of disloyalty. It wasn't her place to tell Adam anything was going on in Mia's marriage, even though part of her wondered how he'd take it. Would he feel vindicated? Sad? Smug? Disappointed? She honestly couldn't guess.

"The pregnancy hormones have been tough for her," Jenna said, which wasn't untrue at all. "Anyway, it won't be long before the contract is over and the baby is here, and maybe, just maybe—"

A buzz from the vicinity of Adam's pants made her lose her train of thought. His jeans were a tangled mess on the floor, but even from this distance, she could see the back pocket appeared to be vibrating.

"Do you need to get that?"

He shook his head. "Whoever it is can wait."

Jenna nodded as the phone went silent and the pocket stopped vibrating. She waited a moment, remembering what Mia said about boundaries and Mark leaping out of bed to answer his ex-wife's calls.

She took another bite of pie and chewed before speaking again. "Like I was saying. Maybe in a month or so after things start to settle, we could see where this goes. Maybe we could go away together, just the two of us. A chance to reset, maybe connect outside the sphere of work and exes and—"

The phone buzzed again. Adam took another bite of pie, but Jenna shifted uncomfortably, shooting another look at his pants. "Are you sure you don't need to get that? The person's awfully persistent."

"I'm giving you my undivided attention."

"I know, and I appreciate that." She bit her lip, thinking of Sean. Had she ever had his undivided attention? The phone went silent, and Jenna started to relax. She opened her mouth to speak again, but the phone started buzzing.

"Please get it," she said. "What I'm saying can wait."

He raised an eyebrow. "You're sure?"

She nodded. "Positive. If you don't answer it, *I'm* going to sit here fretting about it and I'll never remember what I was trying to say anyway."

He smiled and rolled over, stretching to reach the jeans. "Anyone ever tell you that you worry too much?"

"All the time," Jenna said, watching the smooth lines of his torso as he grabbed the phone and drew back, his abs contracting as he sat up.

She watched as his expression went from relaxed amusement to something else entirely. The color seemed to drain from his face, and Jenna swallowed hard as he studied the readout on the screen, then hit a button.

"Shelly? What is it, what's wrong?"

Jenna set her fork down, the apple pie all but forgotten. Who was Shelly? Was it any of her business? She should probably leave the room and give him some privacy. Maybe she could wash the plates or put some clothes on or—

"How long does the doctor think she has?"

Jenna froze and looked back at Adam. His face was pale and tense, and his fist was clenched in the sheet. She stared at that hand, thinking how gentle, how capable it had felt sliding over her body just moments ago.

"I'll be there tomorrow," he said. His eyes slid to Jenna's, and she knew something was about to change between them. "I won't be coming alone."

Chapter Twelve

"Are you sure about this?"

Jenna shoved her hands in the back pockets of her jeans while Adam tossed his suitcase into the trunk of her car. He looked up at her and smiled, and every unsure part of her suddenly felt a whole lot more certain. And turned on. But mostly certain.

"Positive," he said. "You said, and I quote, 'maybe we could go away together, just the two of us.'"

"Right. I was thinking more like a romantic weekend."

"Visiting my dying grandmother isn't your idea of romance?"

Jenna bit her lip. "I'm sorry, Adam. I'm just so sorry. I don't know what I'd do if something happened to Aunt Gertie."

"It isn't quite the same," he said. "Nana hasn't been herself for years. We've been in the final stages of Alzheimer's for a while now. My sister Shelly—she and I have been saying our goodbyes to her for five years. In some ways, this is a formality."

"Still, I'm sorry you didn't get a better goodbye. Maybe if you'd been able to get up to Seattle sooner—"

"Shhh," he said, nudging the trunk shut and turning to press his lips against hers. It was probably more about halting the flow of nervous words than a passionate gesture, but it still felt good.

He drew back and smoothed her hair back from her face. "Let's not make this about what-ifs. I want you with me this weekend, Jenna. I *need* you with me. I need some light and laughter and joy in a situation that might be pretty grim. Can you do that for me?"

She nodded, then handed him her keys. "Yes. Would you mind driving? Seattle traffic makes me nervous."

"You're sure you don't want to take my rental car?"

"I'm sure. I told Mia and Gertie I'm going to Seattle to spend the three-day weekend with some old friends. They'd think it was weird if I didn't take my car."

"And I think it's weird you're calling me an old friend when we've been acquainted a few weeks." He smiled and moved around to the driver's side. "It's okay. We've got a three-hour drive to get acquainted better."

Jenna turned and opened the passenger door, trying not to feel giddy at the prospect of six whole round-trip hours in a car alone with Adam. Truth be told, that was the part of the journey Jenna looked forward to the most. She was nervous about meeting Adam's family, about tagging along for something that should be a solemn occasion.

But there was something about joining him for a trip like this that made things between them seem more real.

"I want my sister to meet you," he said, sliding into the driver's seat as Jenna buckled herself in beside him. "After I got divorced, Shelly got protective. Swore she never liked Mia anyway, which is never very useful to know after the fact. From the moment I started dating again, Shelly's been suspicious of any woman I went out with more than once."

Jenna regarded him warily from the passenger seat. "So the fact that your sister hates my best friend and judges all the women you date is supposed to make me feel better *how*?"

He grinned. "She's going to love you. You're the first woman since before I got married who's meeting Shelly in person, so that's significant. When I told her you were coming, she knew right away what it meant."

"Which is what?"

"That we're more than just a fling. That things are getting serious."

Jenna bit her lip and tried not to grin like some goofy idiot. "Is she going to sit me down for a stern discussion of my intentions with you?"

Adam laughed. "Shelly doesn't do stern. She does wedgies and dirty jokes, often within ten minutes of meeting someone. You can relax."

"Well, still. If she hated Mia—"

"You're nothing like Mia," he said. "Shelly will notice that right off the bat and adore you."

Jenna kicked off her clogs and tucked one foot beneath her on the seat, not sure whether to feel defensive or pleased about that. She settled for saying nothing, nestling back into the passenger seat as Adam steered the car onto the I5 on-ramp headed north toward Seattle. It was just after five thirty on Friday evening, less than an hour after the bargaining team had broken from a long negotiation session to grudgingly wish each other a good Labor Day weekend.

Three whole days. That's what she had alone with Adam, after telling everyone she was going away to visit a group of old college roommates for the weekend. Mia had seemed delighted.

"I'll stay at your place to watch after Gertie," Mia had insisted. "She needs someone to drive her to that meeting with the TV people, and I need a break from being home with Mark."

"Things still aren't going well?"

Mia had shrugged and trailed a finger over one of the roses in a vase at the center of her dining room table. "We're both trying. He brought me flowers last night. I made his favorite bourbon pecan chicken for dinner. We tried the Compassionate Communication thing again last night, and it wasn't so bad."

"Sounds like progress."

"I hope so. Maybe we've just had too much drama in the last couple years. Between moving to Portland and planning a wedding and the pregnancy and everything—" She shrugged. "Maybe we just need a little break."

"For the weekend, you mean?"

"Just the weekend," Mia had said, kissing her on the cheek. "Have a good trip, sweetie."

Jenna had nodded and smiled and tried not to feel too guilty about the whole thing. Was it wrong to let her best friend babysit her aging aunt while Jenna flitted off to Seattle to make nice with Mia's ex-husband's family? The whole thing sounded like a soap opera.

You're not exactly going to Seattle for a party, she argued to her guilty conscience, and her conscience had to admit she had a point.

She looked over at Adam. The last remnants of sunlight glinted through the windshield, making flashes of cinnamon in his hair. He wore his glasses, which sparked glints of green and gold in his eyes. He'd changed from his suit into jeans and a faded T-shirt with the logo from a brewery in New Hampshire, and she wondered when he'd gotten it and who he'd been with.

He must have felt her eyes on him, because he glanced over and smiled. "What are you looking at?"

"You." She stretched her legs out, feeling oddly relaxed for someone en route to a death vigil. "You're lovely to look at."

He laughed and turned his attention back to the road. "Thanks."

"Tell me something about your grandmother before she got sick."

Adam signaled left and passed a semi, then merged back into the middle lane. He looked relaxed behind the wheel, at ease. One hand rested on the edge of the passenger seat, the tips of his fingers grazing her knee. Jenna liked seeing it there.

"My grandma was always a survivor," he said. "She had triple bypass surgery in her sixties and breast cancer in her seventies."

"Wow, that's a lot. She sounds tough."

"She was. *Is.* After the double mastectomy, she said she didn't want to bother with reconstructive surgery or implants. Said she was proud of her scars, and thought one of them looked like a jack-o'-lantern."

"Sounds like a spirited woman."

He nodded, his eyes still on the road. "I went to visit her one afternoon around Halloween, and she disappeared into the bathroom. When she came out, she'd drawn a full jack-o'-lantern face in eyeliner over one of the mastectomy scars."

Jenna laughed, trying to picture the old woman in her mind. It wasn't hard. "That sounds like something Gertie would do."

"Your aunt reminds me a lot of Nana. My grandfather had to stop her from showing it off to trick-or-treaters at the door."

Still smiling, Jenna angled a little in her seat, letting her bare forearm brush the tips of Adam's fingers. They were warm and felt so natural trailing over the bones in her wrists. "Tell me another story."

He slid his palm over her knee and rubbed it thoughtfully. "She never could stand to see anyone mistreated. One time my grandfather was having the riot act read to him by a woman who got mad at him for leaving his cane propped up against his chair. Nana was in the bathroom at the time, but she came back just in time to hear the woman yelling at him for being careless. She called him a crotchety, clueless old man who didn't care if people tripped over his stupid cane and broke their necks."

"What did your grandmother do?"

"She stood there for a second, assessing what was going on. Gramps is hard of hearing, though he tries to play along like he knows what people are saying, but as the woman was yelling all these nasty things at him, he just nodded and smiled and said how nice the weather was that day."

"The weather?"

"That just made the woman mad, so she tried to grab his cane."

"Jesus. So then what happened?"

"Nana just cleared her throat and said, 'excuse me.' As soon as Gramps's tormentor turned around, Nana decked her."

"What?" Jenna laughed, picturing a little old woman smugly sucking a bruised knuckle. "She hit her?"

"Yep. She was aiming for her jaw, but just got her shoulder. Still, it was a good punch. She grabbed the cane back and told the woman not to touch any member of her family ever again. Guess it worked. No one ever messed with Gramps—or with Nana—after that."

Still laughing, Jenna shook her head. "I'd have loved to see that."

"I'll have to show you the video sometime."

"There's video?"

"Yeah. It was at my wedding. Actually, Gramps's tormentor was Mia's mom."

Jenna blinked. "Seriously?"

Adam nodded, while Jenna's mind reeled. She'd heard this story before, but from a completely different viewpoint. She could hear Mia laughing a little sadly over cocktails one night not long after they'd become fast friends.

I'm divorced, yes. Probably should have known the marriage was doomed when one of his relatives punched my mom at the wedding, and I realized it was the first time all day he'd stopped complaining about how much everything cost and actually smiled.

Jenna must have fallen quiet for a few beats too long, because Adam shot her an inquisitive look. "What's on your mind?"

Jenna looked out the window, considering. "Do you think there's any chance Mia regrets leaving you?"

Adam didn't respond right away. He also didn't ask what prompted the question, which surprised her. She studied the side of his face, enjoying the way his eye color changed in the flash of oncoming headlights.

"Do I think she regrets the affair? Sure, in hindsight I think she realized it wasn't the most graceful way to exit a failing marriage."

"No, I don't mean that, exactly," Jenna said. "I guess I meant—I don't know, do you ever think she wants you back?"

Something dark flickered in his eyes, but it might have been the headlights again. The sun had dropped low behind the coastal range to the west, casting dark shadows on the interstate. "Why would you ask that?"

"I don't know. Just wondering, I guess. Is it harder to be the person who leaves or the person who's left?"

"That's a question I've thought about myself." He turned and looked at her as if assessing something. Jenna waited, hands folded in her lap.

"I've never told anyone this before," he said.

"What?"

"About six months after she moved out, Amelia's car broke down. She was in a seedy neighborhood on the south side of Chicago. It was late at night and her tire blew out."

"That must have been terrifying."

"She called me. Mark was out of town, and the place she got stuck wasn't too far from my office. It was late at night, but she knew I'd still be working."

"She couldn't have called a tow truck?"

"She could have, but she didn't."

Jenna tucked her other leg up under her, feeling chilled even though Adam had switched the heat on a minute ago. "What did you do?"

"I went to get her, of course. It was nearly midnight, and I was scrambling on a case I had to present the next morning, but I didn't want her to get hurt. So I went." He took a breath, and Jenna waited, not sure she wanted to hear the rest of the story.

"Did something happen?"

She tried to keep her voice from shaking, but must not have succeeded. Adam glanced over, then shook his head. "Nothing like that. Not like you're thinking. But I can't say it wasn't on her mind."

"How do you mean?"

"I let her wait in my car while I changed the tire. After I finished, I got back in and told her she was good to go. That's when she broke down crying. She kept saying how sorry she was, how she felt scared and confused and that she missed me."

Jenna gripped the armrest, hating the image of Mia in tears almost as much as she hated the thought of Adam sitting solid and strong beside his ex-wife with his arm around the back of her seat, trying to comfort her.

"Was it the first time she'd apologized for—for what happened?"

"God, no. She'd apologized so many times at that point that I'd stopped hearing the words. But this was the first time I'd seen any sign she genuinely regretted it. That if she had a do-over, she'd have done things differently."

"She wanted you back?"

He nodded tightly, just once. "She said she did. Right then, I think she believed it. I told her no. I gave her a Kleenex and sent her on her way. Called later to make sure she got home safely."

"Did you ever talk about it again?"

"Yeah. A week later, I got an e-mail from her. It was all business-like, mostly talking about divorce papers and court dates. Toward the end, she apologized for her 'moment of weakness.' That's what she called it. Said she hadn't meant anything by it and could we please forget the whole thing happened."

"And did you?"

"Not exactly, but I'd mostly pushed it out of my mind until now." He cleared his throat. "The thing is, I believed her. She really didn't mean it. She didn't want me back. But the fact that I screwed up her narrative—well, that threw her for a loop."

"Her narrative?"

Adam seemed to hesitate a moment, his eyes on the horizon. Or maybe he was just watching traffic. It was surprisingly thick for a Friday evening with stars pricking the black sky and a soft spatter of rain on the windshield.

"When you make a decision to leave someone, you tell yourself a story," he said. "You convince yourself you have no choice, or the relationship is doomed, or the person or the situation is so awful that this is the only thing you can possibly do. Maybe it's true, but you believe the story with all your heart. You have to believe it if you want the courage to leave."

Jenna nodded. How many times had Mia said that? *I had to leave, I was dying inside.*

How many times had she said it herself? *I couldn't marry Sean. Not after everything, I couldn't spend the rest of my life with him.*

"So you messed up her narrative by coming to her rescue," Jenna said. "By leaving work to be there for her when she needed you."

He nodded. "Something I hadn't always done. I can admit that."

"Sometimes, kindness is the worst thing," she said. "Especially if it unravels your entire justification for something you've done. Something you might not be very proud of in the first place."

He looked at her. "Very true." He glanced back at the road, quiet again. "How about we talk about something else? Something more uplifting."

Jenna untucked her feet, lowering them to the floor. She let her left hand drift so it was touching his now, fingers twining with fingers.

"More uplifting than your dying grandmother and your painful divorce?"

He smiled, his eyes flicking to hers. "Sure. Like the Holocaust."

"How about dead puppies?"

"The black plague?"

"Euthanasia?"

He lifted his hand, folding his palm over hers. He slid them both to her knee, the heel of his hand rubbing her knuckles like the space behind a cat's ears.

"That's what I love about you, Jenna. You always know how to make me smile."

She smiled in response, almost a required reaction to the word *smile*. Or maybe the word *love*. It was getting difficult to tell.

Early the next morning, Adam drove from their Seattle hotel to his sister's house in Ballard. Shelly had tried to convince them to stay over the night before, but he'd insisted he didn't want to bother her by arriving late.

It wasn't the whole truth.

In reality, he wanted more time alone with Jenna. He'd made sure to book a hotel room with two beds, not wanting to presume anything.

But Jenna had taken one look at the setup, tossed her suitcase on the bed closest to the door, and turned to smile at him. "Looks like we've got a place to store our bags." She'd grinned wider, then pulled her sweater off over her head and reached for the button on her jeans. He stood there blinking at her in the rosy light of the hotel room, utterly transfixed by the creaminess of her skin, the static that made her hair float like a halo around her head.

He was absolutely certain he'd never seen anything so beautiful.

Adam shook his head and hit the blinker, bringing himself back to the present. Probably not a good idea to show up with a hard-on for his first visit with his sister in three months.

He turned onto the narrow avenue where Shelly had lived for the last five years, counting off houses and hoping he'd remember which place was hers. He'd been there plenty of times, but he usually came straight from the airport from some nearby city where he'd been contracted to do mediation.

He glanced over at Jenna, who was smoothing her hair with her hands. Reaching over, he rested a hand on her knee. "You'll do great."

She gave him a weak smile and nodded. "I hope so."

"Just be yourself."

"Yeah, but which self? The professional self who stoically holds it together in business meetings about illicit penis pictures, or the self who gets giddy on wine at girls' night?"

Adam grinned and pulled into his sister's driveway. "You weren't that stoic."

"My stoic self is insulted you think so. My girls' night self admits you're probably right."

He turned off the ignition and leaned over to plant a quick kiss on her mouth. The temptation to make it a longer kiss surged like a wave, but he resisted. "Just be whichever self feels right in the moment. Maybe not the one who did that swirly thing with her tongue last night, though."

"I'll keep that in mind," she said, and reached for the door handle.

Shelly was waiting on the doorstep before they even got all the way up the walk. Her brown curls frizzed in the Seattle drizzle, and she was barefoot and slender in jeans and a bright blue tank top. Spotting Adam, she hurled herself at him, engulfing him in a hug that smelled like sunshine and the floral perfume their mother used to wear.

"Hey, doofus! Long time, no see." She squeezed him hard, then released him. "Now get out of my way. I need to meet the new woman in your life."

He turned to see Jenna extending a polite hand, but Shelly pulled her into a hug.

"No need for the handshake bullshit," she said, squeezing Jenna so tightly Adam heard her spine crack. "We're a hugging family."

Adam stepped aside to give them space, while Jenna laughed and hugged back with equal fierceness. "I've heard so much about you."

"I've heard almost nothing about you," Shelly replied, giving Jenna another squeeze before drawing back to glare at Adam. "My brother's communication skills leave something to be desired. We message each other a dozen times a day over Words with Friends, but I have no idea what you do for work or for fun or even what your last name is."

He watched Jenna's shoulders relax, and she met Shelly's grin with one of her own. "Full name Jenna McArthur, and I'm the Chief Relations Officer for Belmont Health System. For fun, I read spy novels, practice target shooting, and drink copious amounts of good wine. Here."

She reached into her handbag and pulled out a bottle of something with a lot of Italian words on the label. She handed it to his sister with a reverence other women might reserve for religious artifacts. "My favorite Chianti from Italy. I hope you like it."

"Oh, I like it," Shelly said, reaching out to take the wine. She looked over at Adam and gave him a smile that made something swell warmly in his chest. "I like it very, very much."

She turned and walked into the house, waving them to follow. "Bathroom's down that hall if you need it. Want to drive together to Nana and Gramps's place?"

"That sounds good," Adam said, resting his hand in the middle of Jenna's back as he guided her into the living room. "Would you mind if we headed over right away? I'd like to get there as soon as visiting hours start."

"I'll just grab my keys," Shelly called. "Jenna can ride up front with me."

"What, you don't want some brother-sister bonding time?"

"Nope. We're already bonded, jerk. I spent my entire childhood with you pulling my pigtails and stealing my candy and fighting with me about who took longer showers." Shelly grinned as she led them out to her bright orange MINI Cooper. "I already know your annoying ass. Now I need to get to know Jenna better."

"I promise I will neither pull your hair nor hog the shower," Jenna replied, settling into the passenger seat of Shelly's car. "No promises about the candy though."

The two women chatted all the way to the west side of Seattle, and by the time they reached the assisted living facility, it was clear they'd become fast friends. Adam watched from the backseat, feeling equal parts relief and nostalgia. It had never been like this with

Mia and Shelly, not even before the affair. There had always been something stiff in their interactions. Something guarded and even a little competitive, though he could never figure out which of them set that tone. No matter how many courses he took in counseling and human behavior, there was no accounting for chemistry.

He'd wondered sometimes how Mia and Jenna had become so close after only two years of friendship. Now, seeing how quickly his sister connected with her, he didn't wonder anymore. Jenna was easy to love quickly and fiercely.

Love.

He'd said the word to her yesterday in the car, and watched her eyes widen.

That's what I love about you, he'd told her, and he meant it. But he meant more than that, and he wondered if she knew.

"Here we are," Shelly said, pulling into a parking spot. "How much did Adam tell you about what to expect?"

"I know your grandmother is in the last stages of Alzheimer's, and that your grandfather barely leaves her side," Jenna said. "Not even when the nurses come to tend to her."

Shelly nodded and reached for the door handle. "There's a good chance Nana won't wake up at all. She's been sleeping a lot lately, and honestly, that's better. Before this, she went through a real combative stage."

"Does she recognize you?"

Shelly shook her head, and Adam watched her features pinch with sadness. "Not usually. Not anymore. When she's lucid these days, she doesn't even seem to know who Gramps is, though she does perk up a little when he sits by her bed and plays Beatles songs on his guitar."

Adam swallowed hard and pushed the passenger seat forward, clambering over it to emerge from his sister's clown car into the drizzly morning air. They filed through the front door together, stopping to sign in at the front desk. Shelly signed first, then Jenna. Adam looked at her signature, feeling an odd swell of pride when he saw she'd written "lady friend" in the relationship field.

Shelly led the way down a corridor bathed in fluorescent light and the cloying pine scent of cleaner. She stopped in a doorway at the end of the hall and knocked loudly before trooping in.

"Hi, Gramps! Look who's here to see you!"

Noticing Jenna's hesitation, Adam stepped past her and into the cramped little room. He watched Gramps's eyes go wide with surprise, then delight. As the old man struggled to get to his feet, Adam hurried to his side.

"Don't get up, I can hug you right where you are."

He wrapped his arms around Gramps, surprised at how bony he felt. He wore a faded Chicago Cubs sweatshirt Adam remembered buying him for Christmas ten years ago. His pants were baggy enough to fall off his hips if he stood up, so it was probably best to keep the old man sitting. Drawing back, Adam glanced at the hospital bed where Nana lay. She seemed peaceful enough, though her face was creased in a frown.

"Good to see you, son," Gramps said, and Adam turned back to see Shelly smothering him in a hug. "Shells said you were bringing someone with you?"

"I did," Adam said, waving Jenna into the room. She took a few timid steps forward to stand beside him, and Adam felt his heart twist with affection for every damn person in this tiny room.

"Gramps, meet Jenna," he said. "Jenna, meet Gramps and Nana, also known as Floyd and Edie."

Jenna smiled and took a step toward Gramps. She seemed to hesitate, and he saw her rub her palm against her thigh, readying herself to offer a handshake. Instead, she stooped down and wrapped her arms around the old man's bony shoulders.

"It's a pleasure to meet you, sir."

"Call me Gramps, everyone does. Even the nurses and doctors."

"Gramps," she said, trying out the word as she drew back from the hug and stood upright again. "I see you're a Cubs fan? My grandfather took me to see them play at Wrigley years ago."

"Wrinkly ears?" He scrubbed his hands down his face, frowning. "Sure, I've got wrinkly ears, wrinkly cheeks, wrinkly jowls. That's what happens when you get old."

Jenna blinked, her mouth dropping open in horror. "No—I—Wrigley Field. Um, baseball? Adam told me in the car you're a fan of the game."

The old man grinned. "Oh yeah? What else did he tell you about me?"

"He said you worked as a lumberjack for forty years and that you're very good with your hands." She smiled, warming up a bit. "He also said you love dogs—that you had some really great ones when Adam and Shelly were growing up." She pointed to a framed photo on the end table beside him. "That must be Shaggy on the grass next to you in that photo?"

Gramps raised a bushy eyebrow. "Saggy ass? Well, missy, you're getting a little personal now. An old man can't help it if things start to droop a little bit here and there as he gets older. 'Course Edie never had any complaints in that department."

Adam stifled a laugh and turned away, leaving them to get acquainted. He edged over to his grandmother's bedside. She looked small and pale, as though she might blow away if he sneezed on her. Not that sneezing on old people was ever a good idea. He'd done enough jobs in healthcare to know that.

His brain was drifting to absurdity, so he reached out and squeezed Nana's hand. It felt bony and frail, and there was no sign of recognition from her at all.

"Hey, Nana—it's me, Adam."

No response. He stroked his finger over the back of her hand, tracing the knuckles and thin bones. Did she even know he was here? The nurses had warned him she'd been unresponsive all week, but still. He'd hoped for some sign.

Behind him, Jenna was still trying to connect with Gramps. "I've always wanted a dog myself, but we had cats growing up. A big Maine Coon named Sugarbear and a sweet little black-and-white tuxedo kitty we called Spot."

"Bald spot?" Gramps ran a hand over his shiny scalp. "Yeah, well, that runs in the family, too. You wait and see, Adam here will be dropping clumps of hair left and right when he gets to be my age."

"No, I—"

"Jenna is Adam's girlfriend, Gramps," Shelly said. "Don't you think he did better this time around?"

At that, Adam turned to face them, not sure if he was more interested in Gramps's reaction or Jenna's. He saw his grandfather grin widely, and Jenna followed suit, looking a little nervous.

"Sure am happy to have you here," Gramps said, leaving it open whether he meant Jenna or Adam or the whole family. He looked past Jenna to Adam and nodded. "You have her eyes, you know. Edie's. She sure was proud of what you made of yourself, boy."

"Thank you," Adam said, swallowing back the lump in his throat. "That means a lot."

Gramps swiveled his gaze back to Jenna's and grinned. "You sticking around for lunch, girlie? Corned beef and mashed potatoes. 'Course it's not as good as what Edie used to make. Boy, she was one helluva good cook in her day."

Jenna gave Adam a nervous smile, then turned back to Gramps. "Yes, that's what Adam said. He told me about the little diner she used to own. How people would come from miles and miles just to have a slice of pie at Edie's."

"ED?" Gramps frowned. "Well, now you're getting *real* personal, missy. A man's erectile dysfunction is his own business, and they got those little blue pills now that can—"

"Okay, Gramps, cut it out." Shelly was snort-laughing in the corner, wiping tears from her eyes.

Jenna gave her a perplexed look before turning to Adam. "I'm so sorry," she whispered. "You told me he was hard of hearing, but I had no idea—"

"What'd you say about my hard-on?"

Adam choked on a laugh of his own, his hand gently squeezing Nana's. "Gramps hears just fine, Jenna."

"What?"

"He got hearing aids a few years ago, so now he hears better than I do. He's yanking your chain."

Jenna blinked, then turned back to Gramps. "Is that true?"

"I'm not allowed to yank anything around here," Gramps said, grinning wider now. "Nurse came by just last week and smacked it out of my hand when I was sittin' there in the common area enjoying a little adult television. If they don't want us to watch the Playboy channel, they shouldn't have it out there."

"They didn't have the Playboy channel, Gramps," Shelly said, still dabbing at her eyes. "Not until you figured out how to hook it up illegally." She nudged Jenna with her elbow. "In addition to his hearing being perfect, his mind is still sharp as a tack."

"He teased us mercilessly when we were kids," Adam said, watching as Jenna's shoulders started to relax. "If it's any comfort to you, he only screws around this way with people he likes."

Jenna shook her head and turned back to Gramps, a smile spreading slowly across her face. A look of fondness had replaced the horrified expression she'd worn moments ago, and Adam gave her hand a squeeze.

"Jeez, you had me worried," Jenna said. "I think I see now where your grandson gets his sense of humor."

Gramps grunted. "Well if he's good in the sack, he gets that from me, too. If he's lousy, blame his father."

Jenna laughed and leaned back in her chair, turning to beam at Adam. "I think I like this family."

"Yeah?" he said. "I think I can speak for all of us when I say it likes you, too."

Nana's fingers twitched against his palm, so faintly Adam knew he might have imagined it. He looked down and saw her expression hadn't changed. Her face was still serene and creased with age, and her hand still felt limp in his.

But her fingers twitched again, this time curling faintly against his, and he knew he hadn't imagined it. Across the room, Jenna and Gramps and Shelly sat laughing as the tiniest ghost of a smile played across Nana's lips. Then her hand went limp again, the rhythm of her breathing making the blankets rise and fall in a soothing tempo.

It was enough.

Later that evening, Jenna leaned back against Shelly's sofa, comforted by the feel of Adam's arm around her shoulders. It felt natural there, like it had always belonged.

"Here you go," Shelly said, rounding the corner of the kitchen and handing her a stemless wineglass. "It's a cab from a winery just a few miles from here. Very juicy, though it probably needs to open up a bit more."

"Mmm, it's delicious," Jenna said, taking a sip. "Thanks again for dinner. It was amazing."

"Don't mention it. It was the least I could do after subjecting you to that bland crap at Nana and Gramps's place."

"I didn't mind at all," Jenna said, taking another sip. "Your grandfather is quite the character. Made me miss my own grandpa."

Shelly smiled. "We're lucky we've had both our grandparents this long. Most of my friends lost theirs in middle school and high school."

Adam slid his arm around Jenna's shoulder and craned his neck to look at his sister. "So what did the doctor say on the phone?"

"Nothing new. He said it could be a few weeks, could be a few hours. Usually at the point where the patient stops eating and drinking, it doesn't take long."

"Yeah, but this is Nana we're talking about," Adam said. "She's probably got a little more fighting spirit than the average ninety-year-old."

"Could be," Shelly said, dropping into a tufted leather chair beside the television. "Then again, she might be ready to quit fighting and rest for a change."

Jenna slid her hand to Adam's knee and gave a small squeeze she hoped he took as comforting rather than lecherous. Then again, he might find lechery comforting. Now that she'd met Gramps, she wouldn't be surprised.

She turned to Shelly, who was making fast work of her own glass of wine. "Do you have any videos of your grandmother? I'd love to see what she was like before she got sick."

"That's a great idea," Shelly said, thunking her wineglass onto the end table and dropping to her knees in front of a large chest fringed with copper rivets. "I've got a bunch of old VHS tapes here. I swear, I'm the last person on earth who hasn't converted them all to DVD."

"Luckily, you're also a packrat," Adam said, plucking Jenna's wineglass from her fingers and taking a sip. "You're also the only person on earth who still has a VHS player."

Shelly grinned and shoved a tape into the player, while Jenna leaned back against Adam's arm, feeling warm and safe and stupidly happy. "You like the wine?" she asked.

"I do," he murmured. "It's different from what you've been introducing me to lately—Sangiovese and Chianti?"

Jenna nodded, surprised he noticed. "The cab is really juicy—a little higher in tannins. Chianti and Sangiovese tend to be a little closer to medium bodied, and the earthy ones are my favorite. Kinda like the one we had with dinner."

"Juicy versus earthy," he repeated, taking another thoughtful sip of the cab. "Yeah, I think I see what you mean."

"You sure you don't want your own glass?"

"Nope, I don't want the wine," he said, planting a kiss along her hairline as he handed the glass back to her. "I just wanted a chance to put my lips someplace yours had been."

"In that case," she whispered, "you should work on your contortionist skills."

He laughed and kissed her forehead this time, pulling her tighter against him so she could feel the ridges of his abs against the base of her ribcage. Funny how aware she was of every spot where their bodies touched, all the little ways they connected. She felt like she belonged here. Like they'd always been together, connected by breath and bone and skin.

"This should be a good one," Shelly said, sitting back on her heels and hitting a button on the VHS. "It's from that family reunion six or seven years ago. Remember that?"

226

"Yeah," Adam said, nuzzling Jenna's hair. "Nana wore a red dress that Gramps said made her look like a tart."

"He meant it as a compliment, I'm sure," Jenna said, watching as the video flickered to life on the screen and a scattering of relatives appeared, joking and laughing as they juggled paper plates and bottles of beer.

"There's Uncle Martin," he said, nodding toward the screen. "Ten bucks says he's already wasted."

"No bet," Shelly said, getting to her feet. "He was wasted before he got there. Speaking of which, I'm going to grab the wine bottle so we don't have to get up again. You sure you don't want your own glass, Adam?"

"I'm good," Adam said, pulling Jenna closer.

She snuggled against him and took a slow sip of her wine as Shelly moved toward the kitchen. Jenna kept her eyes fixed on the screen, watching Adam's relatives smiling and singing and tossing a Frisbee. "Who's the woman in the white shorts?"

"That's my cousin, Ginny. She's a brain surgeon out in Vermont. We don't see her much. That guy over there in the Hawaiian shirt is my dad. That was just before he and mom joined the Peace Corps."

"You must miss them a lot."

"I do, but I know they love what they're doing. They're happy."

Jenna nodded, transfixed by the sight of Adam's dad throwing his head back and laughing the same way Adam did sometimes. The scene swiveled left, landing on a woman in a brown peasant skirt who waved at the camera, then stuck her tongue out and crossed her eyes. They were the same as Adam's eyes, the same speckled green Jenna had come to know so well in the last few weeks. She nestled deeper against his chest, savoring the feel of his fingers stroking her hair.

The camera swung right, landing on a couple locked in a passionate embrace beneath an oak tree. The man dipped his hand into the curve of the woman's back, pulling her tight against his body just like Adam did when he kissed.

Jenna blinked. It *was* Adam. And the woman arching her body against his was Mia, her long red hair trailing down her back as she twined her fingers around his neck, her wedding ring glinting in the sun.

"Oh," Jenna breathed, staring at the screen.

Behind her, Adam tensed. The hand that had been stroking her leg stopped in mid-caress, his fingers frozen on her knee. "Shit. Hey, Shel? Where's the remote?"

"What? Oh." Shelly scrambled from the edge of the kitchen, dropping to her knees in front of the television. She fished around on the floor, fumbling with a silver controller.

"Dammit, wrong one."

Jenna couldn't look away. She wanted to—God, she wanted to—but there was something pulling her eyes to the screen like magnets. She couldn't blink. She couldn't breathe. All she could do was stare at the young couple kissing, so passionate, so young, so in love.

"So disgusting," Shelly said, dropping the silver remote and picking up a black one. She aimed it at the television and hit a button. The image lurched into fast-forward, and Jenna watched the blurry figures moving at warp speed as Mia realized they were being filmed and turned laughing toward the camera, waving them away. The image shifted to another scene, a set of school-aged kids chasing each other with squirt guns. Shelly took her hand off the button and the image slowed to normal speed.

"Sorry about that," Shelly said, giving Jenna a sympathetic look. "That's the kind of shit you can't unsee, huh?"

"It's fine," Jenna said, blinking at last.

"I'm so sorry," Adam murmured into her hair. "We were newlyweds there. I didn't realize—"

"Don't be silly," Jenna said, taking a sip of her wine and trying not to notice the way the glass shook in her hand. "It's not like it never occurred to me you might have kissed someone else before me. I have a past, you have a past, we all have a past."

"Yeah, but how often does Adam have to watch videos of you polishing some guy's tonsils with your tongue?" Shelly set the remote down as the camera settled on an image of Gramps passing a soda to a younger, healthier-looking Nana. Jenna watched, feeling numb as Gramps glanced around, then reached around his wife to give her backside a firm squeeze. Nana laughed and swatted him away, looking rosy and vivacious and not the least bit eager for him to stop.

Jenna took another sip of wine, her eyes fixed on the television. Had Nana been diagnosed yet at this point? Did she know what lay ahead for them?

She blinked back the tears, pretty sure Gramps and Nana were to blame.

Back in their hotel room that night, Jenna took a long time getting ready for bed. She scrubbed her face with the soft, white washcloth from the rack, hoping to soothe away any traces of puffiness around her eyes.

She was being ridiculous. It wasn't like she'd never considered the possibility Adam and Mia had an intimate and loving relationship at some point. They'd gotten married, had a honeymoon, and stayed married for five years. People didn't do that without some serious affection between them.

It also wasn't like she herself hadn't been intimate with anyone else. She'd loved her fair share of men, exchanging kisses and family stories and promises neither of them ended up keeping. Hell, she'd been engaged. She'd even conceived a baby with another man, for crying out loud.

But there was something different about witnessing someone else's affection in living color. Something about knowing the trill of Mia's laugh, the softness of Adam's lips.

"Jenna? Everything okay in there?"

She nodded at her reflection in the bathroom mirror, then felt silly. "Coming."

"That's unfortunate," he called from the other side of the door. "I kinda hoped you'd wait for me."

Her mouth twisted into a half smile, and she turned away from the mirror to open the door. She walked out to find Adam sitting on the side of the bed.

"Hey," he said softly. "Want to talk?"

"About?"

"Oh, I don't know—world religion? Recipes for corn bread? Child-rearing techniques of the early nineteenth century?" He held out his hand, and Jenna found herself reaching for it before she'd even made up her mind to join him. "Come on, Jenna. I think we're past the point in this relationship where either of us can fool the other into thinking things are peachy keen when they're not. I know that video upset you. I'm sorry you had to see that."

She sighed and sat down beside him, her knee bumping against his through the terrycloth of her hotel robe. He wore nothing but boxer shorts, and the urge to touch his chest almost overwhelmed her urge to talk this through.

Almost.

"It's stupid," she said. "It's not jealousy I'm feeling, exactly. I don't know what it is."

"Want me to get out one of my NVC worksheets with a list of emotion-related words you can pick from?"

She laughed and shook her head. "No, that's okay. Tell me this, though—if you saw a video of me making out with my ex-fiancé, do you think it would upset you?"

He seemed to consider it a moment, then nodded. "Probably a little."

"A little? Okay, how about a sex video?"

He frowned at that. "Okay, a lot."

She smiled and edged closer, feeling something inside her start to thaw as Adam folded an arm around her. "That's the thing about modern dating. Back before the age of technology, all you had to go on were your own mental pictures of how things were in your lover's last relationship. A man could picture his new girlfriend's ex with a tiny penis or a receding hairline, and it would automatically make it so."

Adam nodded and pulled her closer to his side. "And you could imagine my ex-wife as some horrible shrew I never really loved, due in part to her grating personality and preponderance of warts." He planted a kiss on her temple, and Jenna felt herself start to melt. "Doesn't work out so well when the shrew is your best friend."

"Or when there's video evidence to the contrary."

She snuggled under his arm, content to just settle there with her feelings, whatever the hell they were. She might not be able to name them, exactly, but there was something reassuring about discussing them with a guy who acknowledged they were there.

"So about that sex tape," he said, kissing her neck this time instead of her temple. He planted another kiss behind her ear, his breath warm and soft against her skin, and Jenna shivered despite the heat of the room. "Was that just an example, or is there really an illicit video floating around out there?"

"Oh, it's not floating," Jenna said, closing her eyes as Adam kissed his way down her throat and pushed aside her robe, baring her shoulder. "It's in a box under my bed, along with two hundred unsent wedding invitations and a bunch of sex toys that wouldn't be appropriate to use with other partners, but I'm not sure what to do with them. Seriously, is there a recycling center for adult artifacts left over from past relationships?"

"Mmm," Adam murmured, peeling her robe further off her shoulder and baring the tops of her breasts. "Are you trying to make me jealous?"

"Not really. Are you trying to make me forget?"

"Absolutely. Is it working?"

"Without a doubt," she breathed, and pulled them both back onto the bed.

The call came at 5:00 a.m.

Jenna heard the faint buzz of Adam's cell phone on the night-stand, and she tried to roll over. She found herself pinned beneath the weight of his arm and the heft of his bare leg.

"Adam? Wake up, Adam, it's your phone."

"Hmm?"

"Your phone. I think it's ringing."

She watched his eyes blink open, saw him roll and reach for the phone, knowing with a heavy feeling in her gut what the call was about before he even answered.

"Yes?"

He was silent a moment, and Jenna reached out to wrap his fingers with hers.

"So she went peacefully? Of course. No, I understand. That's what we'd hoped for, I guess."

Jenna sat up, pulling the sheet around her breasts as she wrapped her arms around Adam and just held him. He leaned against her, his bare shoulder chilly, but solid.

"And Gramps agreed to that? No, I think it's best. I appreciate you doing that, Shel. Okay then. We'll be there."

Adam disconnected the call and sat quiet for a moment.

"She's gone?" Jenna whispered, already knowing the answer.

"Yeah. Shelly has Gramps at her place. She invited us to come for breakfast. We can go now, or we can stop by the assisted living facility to say our goodbyes."

"What do you want to do?"

He sighed. "You know, I feel at peace with it. Like I already said my goodbyes this afternoon. Or years ago, really. Is that wrong?"

"Not at all. There's nothing that says you need to look at a dead person to have closure." She winced. "I'm sorry, did that sound insensitive?"

Adam offered a small smile and moved in her arms, turning to face her in the dim glow of the hotel's clock radio. "No more insensitive than if I tell you I'm looking forward to my sister's bacon. Come on. Let's get dressed."

They showered together with the lights out. Jenna meant to keep a respectful distance, to stay stoic and supportive and reverent. But Adam reached for her in the dark, his hands slick and searching. She slid willingly into his arms, crying out as he drove into her beneath the hot spray of the shower.

They got to Shelly's house a little after sunrise. True to Adam's word, she had a platter of the best-looking bacon Jenna had ever seen. Shelly's eyes were red-rimmed, but she smiled as they walked into the kitchen.

"I'm so sorry," Jenna said, wrapping Adam's sister in her arms.

"I'm glad you could be here," Shelly murmured, hugging back with her hands smothered in oven mitts. "Adam might act tough, but he's an emotional guy. I know he's glad to have you with him this weekend."

"I'm glad to be here. Is Gramps sleeping?"

"Yeah, he drifted off a few minutes ago in the guest room. I'm not going to wake him. We can save the food for when he wakes up."

Jenna nodded and stepped back, letting Adam take her place in his sister's embrace. She watched as the two siblings clung together, murmuring words of support and love and memories.

"I'm just going to run to the bathroom," Jenna murmured, knowing they didn't hear her. She turned and walked down the hall, patting the back pocket of her jeans as she felt her cell phone vibrate.

She closed the door behind her and pulled the phone out. A chill snaked up her arms as she read the words of Mia's text message.

Emergency with Aunt Gertie. Please call right away.

Chapter Thirteen

Jenna dialed the phone with trembling fingers, Mia's words imprinted on her brain in bright, neon letters.

Emergency with Aunt Gertie. Please call right away.

"Mia, hello? What is it, what's wrong, is Aunt Gertie alive?"

On the other end of the line, Mia gave a surprised gasp. "Alive? Of course she's alive. You don't really think I'd use a text message to tell you your aunt kicked the bucket?"

"No, of course not." Jenna let her body sag, sliding down the wall until her palms pressed into the cold tiles of Shelly's bathroom floor. "I'm sorry. I must just have funerals on the brain or something."

"That's some girls' weekend you're having there."

Jenna winced as the sour taste of guilt surged up the back of her throat. Did Mia suspect anything?

"Anyway, sorry to scare you," Mia said. "There is an emergency, though. You know that screen test Gert asked me to drive her to?"

"Yes. It was for some little cable TV program that broadcasts in Nebraska or something, right?"

"Wrong. Well, that's what Gert told us, anyway. Turns out it's a much bigger deal."

"How much bigger?"

"Remember that time we went to that male strip club and we saw the one guy with the modest marble sack dancing next to the guy who looked like he'd shoved a salami in there?"

"Um—"

"That much bigger. Like, enormously bigger."

"Mia, what is it?"

"*Good Morning America.* They loved the interview she did with the local station, and they want more. They offered to fly her to New York to tape an in-studio piece that will air later this week."

"Oh, Jesus." Jenna dropped her head into her hands, feeling her temples start to pound. "What did you tell her?"

"I told her I needed to call you. Not that she needs your permission, but it seems like something the two of you might want to talk about if she's going to put herself on-air in front of five million viewers."

"Oh, God."

"She didn't commit yet. She said she wanted to talk to her lawyer first anyway, which I told her was a very good idea. Jenna? Are you still there?"

"I'm here." She bit her lip. "How much do you think the hospital administration would freak out about this?"

Mia was quiet a moment. "That's what you're worried about?"

"Kinda."

"Hell, I thought you were worried about her personal safety or privacy or something."

"That would make me a better person, wouldn't it?"

Mia laughed. "I think you're fine, hon. I mean I know you and Gertie have this weird thing going where you pretend she doesn't write really filthy, amazing smut—which I've enjoyed very much, by the way."

"You and half the women in America."

"That's not a bad thing. I know the two of you do your damnedest to avoid discussing the fact that she's this mega-bestselling erotica author, but I think you might be overestimating how much anyone else cares. No offense."

"None taken." Jenna bit her lip. "You weren't at Belmont when the shit hit the fan with the old CEO. You didn't see how bad things got, how much it affected the staff's trust in leadership. It tainted the way the whole community saw the hospital system."

"Honey, you're missing a key difference here."

"What's that?"

"Running an escort service is illegal. Last time I checked, writing smutty books wasn't. Not in this country, anyway."

Jenna sighed. "Still, things are rocky with the negotiations right now. I don't want to muddy the waters."

"Sometimes getting a little dirty isn't the worst thing. You should try it sometime."

A fresh wave of guilt knocked Jenna backward, and she glanced at the door. Had Adam and Shelly noticed how long she'd been gone? She was keeping her voice low, but still. For some reason, she didn't want them to hear this. To know she was huddled in the bathroom whispering with Adam's ex-wife like they were exchanging covert spy secrets.

"Sweetie, can I say something?" Mia asked.

Jenna drew her attention back to the conversation. "Have you ever needed my permission?"

"Not really. I was just being respectful. I just think you spend too much time worrying what other people will think of you. Just live your life the way you want to live it and don't get so hung up on everyone else."

The words felt like little daggers between her ribs, and she glanced at the bathroom door again.

Okay then, Mia—I'm sitting on your ex-sister-in-law's bathroom floor in the midst of a weekend spent bonding with your former in-laws while alternately consoling your ex-husband and fucking his brains out.

"Jenna? You still there?"

"I'm here."

"Just think about it, okay? Maybe it's time you quit worrying so much about everyone else."

"Okay," she breathed, not sure she trusted herself to say anything more. "How are things going for you? Is Mark missing you madly while you keep Gert company?"

"Yeah, I guess so. I cooked dinner for Gertie last night, and I invited Mark and Katie to stop by afterward. I made Katie's favorite peach cobbler, so I thought she might enjoy it, you know?"

"Sure, she's always loved that. So what happened?"

Mia sighed. "Katie said she's decided to go gluten free because her mom told her it's healthier. She wouldn't eat the cobbler, and then Mark got a text from Ellen asking him to come to the car dealership right away because she was buying a new car and needed him to sign off on the old one she was trading in. His name was still on the title."

"It couldn't wait?"

"Apparently not." Mia sighed again. "I'm trying, Jenna. I'm trying so hard it hurts sometimes."

"I know you are, honey. Maybe you need to try less. Invest less so you aren't so disappointed all the time?"

Mia laughed. "Listen to us. You need to care less what other people think, and I need to care less what other people do. Maybe there's a twelve-step program for us. Think Adam could recommend something?"

"I—I imagine so," Jenna said, the guilt welling up in her again. "Look, I'd better go. Can you tell Gertie to wait until I get home to make any decisions on the TV show?"

"Will do. You're coming home tomorrow afternoon?"

"That's the plan. You've got a birthing class at three?"

"Yeah, my last one. Mark and I are going out to dinner afterward. Your favorite restaurant—Gerlake? It was the first place we ate together when I came out here to interview for the job."

"Sounds romantic."

"I hope so. It's hard to feel romantic when you're thirty-eight weeks pregnant and threatened by your husband's relationship with his ex-wife, but I'm doing my best."

"That's all anyone can ask, right?"

"Right. If you're home before I leave for birthing class, maybe we can have coffee? Fucking decaf, of course."

"Deal. Thanks again for all your help, Mia. I really owe you."

"Don't mention it, babe. Have fun with your old roommates."

"I will," Jenna said, swallowing back a new surge of guilt.

On Monday afternoon, Adam pulled Jenna's car up beside his rental car in the parking garage at his hotel. He turned in the driver's seat and looked at her. God, he could never get tired of doing that.

"Thank you for going with me this weekend, Jenna," he said. "I couldn't have done it without you."

"I was honored to be part of it," she said, brushing the hair from her eyes. "Your family is amazing."

"I know they'd love to see you next month for the memorial service. A lot of the East Coast relatives will be making the trip. Maybe if things keep going like they are between us—"

He stopped, recognizing the alarm in her eyes. "What?"

"Nothing." She bit her lip. "It's just that we're back to reality now, right? Back in Portland, back to real life."

"Right," he said, not entirely sure what she was saying.

She touched his hand, the warmth of her fingers a marked contrast to the chill of her words. "We're still working together, Adam. For several more weeks, possibly months. As far as I know, this is still against company policy."

"Of course. Maybe in a few weeks."

"Maybe," she agreed, not meeting his eyes. "I should go. Mia has a birthing class at three, and I told her I'd try to get there before she leaves so we can have a cup of coffee and catch up."

"Tell her hi for me."

"Uh—"

He grimaced. "Sorry, force of habit. Kinda like when you called me Sean in bed last night."

Her eyes went wide, and he watched the color rise in her cheeks. "I did not!"

He laughed and squeezed her hand. "Did too. Right at the moment you arched your back and—"

She grabbed the back of his head and pressed her lips to his, cutting off the stream of words and most of his oxygen flow. He didn't care. He'd only been joking with her, and if he could get a kiss out of the deal, all the better.

Jenna drew back and smiled. "Shut the fuck up, Adam."

"I love you."

She blinked, fingers still twined in his hair. "What?"

"I said I love you. My segue could use a little work, but it's true."

Jenna bit her lip. "I don't know what to say."

He shrugged, trying not to feel too disappointed. "You could admit you're fond of me, maybe compliment my driving or my ass."

"You know all that's true," she said, waving a dismissive hand. "And I love you, too. But—"

"You do?"

"You're ignoring my but."

"I would never ignore your butt."

"Come on, Adam. Be serious for one second. We can't get serious here."

"What?"

"You know what I mean."

"I'm not sure I do."

She sighed, her fingers still twined with his. "We can't get serious in a relationship. Not now, anyway. Not with my job on the line and my best friend's emotions so wonky right now."

"I get the job thing, I really do. But what makes you think Mia would even care?"

"I just do."

"Have you asked her?"

Jenna shrugged and looked away. "I've broached the subject. Not of me dating you, but of you getting serious with anyone at all."

"And?"

"Look, the timing is just lousy. Her hormones are all topsy-turvy and her marriage is shaky and I just—"

"Her marriage is shaky?"

Jenna frowned down at her hands. "I didn't mean to say that."

"But you said it," he said, curling a finger beneath her chin and forcing her to look at him. "Why didn't you want me to know?"

"Because I didn't want you to feel glad about it." Her eyes flashed with a different sort of passion than what he'd seen there all weekend. "I didn't want to see *I told her so* in your eyes. I didn't want to see even one tiny shred of delight that my best friend is having a hard time. She's my *best friend*, Adam—it's bad enough I'm betraying her by sleeping with you, but I couldn't stand the thought of anyone taking pleasure in her struggles."

Adam gritted his teeth. "Jenna, I'd never derive happiness from anyone else's unhappiness. I hope you'd know that about me."

"This is different. This is the woman who left you flat for someone she thought was better. You can't honestly tell me you wouldn't feel at least a tiny twinge of satisfaction if it turned out she didn't live happily ever after with her new life and marriage."

"I can," he said, trying to keep his breathing even. "I can absolutely say that."

She smiled, then leaned forward and planted another kiss on his lips.

"We can talk about this later," she said. "For now, I need to get home. Thank you for the amazing weekend. I told your sister I'd call her tonight, but if you talk to her first, can you give her my regards?"

"I will."

"I'm sorry about Nana, Adam. She was an amazing woman."

"I'm glad you got to meet her. It wasn't much, but—"

"It was everything," she said, squeezing his hand. "You have no idea how much it meant to me."

Adam nodded, feeling a lump welling up in his throat. "I'm glad. It meant a lot to me, too."

She gave him a sad little smile, then unbuckled her seatbelt and opened the door. He watched her swing her legs out of the car, watched as she shut the door and strode away.

He might have actually kept driving if she hadn't walked around to the driver's side and opened the door. He looked up at her, confused for a moment, and a little dazzled by the sight of her, silhouetted by golden sunlight streaming in through the side of the parking garage.

"Um, my car?"

"Right," he said, getting out. "I'll just grab my bag from the trunk. Thanks again, Jenna."

She nodded as he popped the trunk and collected his suitcase, taking great pains to close the trunk softly and without force. He walked around to the front of the car where she stood beside the open driver's side door.

"Drive safely," he said. "I'll see you at work Tuesday."

"Okay," Jenna said, then leaned up to kiss him softly on the lips. It was probably meant to be just a peck, but she seemed to dissolve against him, her mouth opening to his as he pulled her into his embrace and their bodies melted together. The smell of car exhaust mingled with the scent of her perfume, and her hair was the silkiest thing his fingers had ever explored.

She drew back with a sigh. "Goodbye, Adam."

"I love you."

"I love you, too."

His mouth was still tingling as she drove away, and he watched her taillights blink and fade and trail around the corner of the parking garage. He watched until her car drove out of sight, until the scent of her shampoo faded from his fingers, until he lost the urge to kick himself in the head.

The last one was the toughest. Because what she'd said was true.

As much as he hated it, as much as he wished it weren't so, a tiny, awful part of him felt smug at the thought of Mia's marriage in trouble.

He gritted his teeth, hating himself, loving Jenna, and wondering what the hell that left him with.

$\sim$

An hour later, Jenna was saying goodbye to Mia at the door. "You're sure you don't want me to come with you to your birthing class?"

"That's okay," Mia said, slinging her purse onto her shoulder. "Mark said there's still a small chance he might make it. Not a big one, but it could happen."

Her expression was so hopeful it scrunched Jenna's heart up into a tiny, painful knot. "I know he hated having to cancel," Jenna said. "Maybe he can still make dinner?"

"Maybe," Mia said shrugging. "The reservation's kinda early, so that doesn't leave a lot of time."

"I'm sure he'll do his best," Jenna said. "And if he doesn't make it, I know he'll wish he was there instead of repairing his ex-wife's roof."

Mia winced. "It sounds awful like that. The hole is right over Katie's bed and it's been raining like crazy. They can't get a repairman out there on a holiday weekend, and Mark knows how to fix things."

"Absolutely," Jenna said, leaning forward to give Mia a hug. "Call me if you change your mind about the birthing class. I can be there in ten minutes. That's the benefit of living this close to the hospital."

"Thanks, sweetie. You're a great friend."

Jenna nodded and tried not to cringe. "You, too."

She closed the door behind her, feeling lousy and wistful and guilty all over again. Part of her wanted to celebrate the fact that Adam said he loved her. That she'd said it back. She was still glowing from the amazing weekend they'd had together.

But what the hell kind of friend could revel in her own happiness when her closest pal's marriage was teetering on shaky ground?

"Did Mia make it out okay?" Gertie called, padding into the living room.

"She just left. Thanks for giving us a few minutes alone. She's going through some rough stuff right now, and she needed someone to talk to."

"I totally understand. She's been here all weekend keeping an old lady company. We had a nice time together, but I know when a woman needs her best girlfriend."

Jenna sighed and sank into the overstuffed loveseat by the door. "I feel like an awful friend. And an awful niece, come to think of it."

Gert sat down beside her, patting her knee. "Why's that, sweetheart?"

"You know how I told you I was going to Seattle to see some old college roommates?"

"I assumed that was just a cover story for a romantic weekend with Adam."

Jenna blinked. "What? How did you—"

"For one thing, you don't have any college roommates in Seattle. For another, I overheard you on the phone with him the night before you left. My hearing's better than you think it is, sweetheart."

Jenna buried her face in her hands, thinking of Gramps's hearing and Shelly's cooking and the whole tangled-up mess of love and lies and loss. "God, I'm so sorry, Gert. I didn't want you to have to lie to Mia. I thought it would be better if I told you both the same story."

"It's fine, dear. I realize you're feeling very secretive with this relationship. I know I tried to draw you out before by bringing Adam to the house, but now that I see how reluctant you are—" She gave Jenna a squeeze, forcing her to look up. "I guess I'm willing to go along with that."

"Thank you. For everything, Gertie. Really."

"Not a problem. How was your weekend?"

"Incredible. Heartbreaking. Earth-shattering."

"Sounds like a good title for a romance novel."

Jenna sighed and sank deeper into the loveseat. "I just had one of the most amazing weekends of my life with a man I know used to be the light of Mia's life. Once upon a time, they were crazy in love. Now I'm finding happiness with that same man, and here's Mia struggling and trying to hold her new marriage together. It doesn't seem fair."

"Life's not fair, honey. I don't think Mia would trade places with you. Not even now."

Jenna sighed and leaned against her aunt's shoulder, more comforted than she expected by the feel of Gert's arm curving around her shoulders. "I suppose not, but it might hurt Mia to see it anyway. Especially under the circumstances."

"Maybe. Or maybe she's stronger than you give her credit for."

"I guess." Jenna turned a bit so she was looking at her aunt. "I'm just not ready to tell her yet. I can't risk hurting her like that. Maybe after the baby comes and Adam's contract is up with the hospital—"

"You don't think that might make it worse in the long run? If Mia finds out you were seeing him in secret?"

"She doesn't have to know. We've been careful. Besides, a lot can happen in a few weeks. I just—I don't think it's the right time."

Gert looked at her and nodded. "Fair enough. I can respect that."

"Thank you." Jenna squeezed her aunt's hand. "So do you want to talk about this TV appearance?"

Gert smiled. Jenna could tell she was trying not to, but she practically glowed with it. "*Good Morning America*. Can you imagine?"

"I can. You're famous, Aunt Gertie. I'm proud of you."

"I know it's big, and I know everyone you work with would probably see it, but I just thought—"

Ding-dong!

Jenna frowned at the door. "Who do you suppose that is?"

"Could be Mia. She forgot her overnight bag. That's what I came out here to tell you. It's over there in the corner."

Jenna stood up and grabbed the bag, reminding herself to get back on track with this conversation the second Mia scurried off to her birthing class.

But when she flung the door open, it wasn't Mia standing on the threshold.

"Adam? What are you doing here?" Her traitorous heart leapt at the sight of him, thudding in her chest and trying to crawl its way up her throat.

"My laptop," he said, shuffling a little on the front porch. "I'm sorry, I forgot it in your backseat. I wouldn't have come, except that I need it and you mentioned Mia had a class at three. I figured the coast was clear, especially since her car isn't here."

"Sure, no problem," Jenna said, feeling a little bad about the fact that the man she loved was forced to act like a secret agent. She glanced at her watch, relieved to see it was after three and Mia would be safely in her birthing class. "I haven't unpacked the car yet, but it's in the garage. You can come through the house to grab it."

"Thanks."

She waved him through the door, pointing toward the kitchen. "Garage door is right over there next to the kitchen."

"I'll be quick," he said, dipping his head a little as he stepped into the living room. "Gertrude—or should I say Gigi? Lovely to see you."

"Lovely to see you, too, dear. And please, just call me Gertie."

"Gertie, you're looking ravishing as ever. I'll just grab my laptop and be on my way."

"Oh, please—stay!" Gert jumped up and followed him to the kitchen, trailing behind as he headed for the garage door. "I feel like

I owe you a cup of tea at least. You missed out on the pot roast the other night."

"I didn't miss out," Adam said, shooting a look at Jenna that left her blushing to the tips of her hair.

"Right," Jenna said, hurrying to the kitchen. "I'll get the tea going. I left the car unlocked."

"Thanks," he said, scooting by her on his way to the garage. His elbow brushed her breast as he moved past, and Jenna felt faint all over again. She watched the door close behind him, wondering how it was possible to crave him this much after a weekend of having him every time she wanted.

"Wow."

She turned to see Aunt Gertie studying her with frank interest.

"What?"

"You've got it bad," Gertie said, leaning against the counter with a Cheshire cat smile. "I've never seen you look at a man like that before. I didn't realize things had gotten this serious between you. That must have been some weekend."

Jenna thought about demurring, but her smile broke through. "It was," she said. "It was incredible. His family was amazing, and we talked for hours and hours about everything."

"From the way you're glowing, I'm guessing you did more than talk."

She laughed and shot a glance toward the garage door. "I guess you could say that." She lowered her voice. "He told me he loves me."

"Really?"

"And I said it back. I know this is fast, and I know we've only had a few weeks together, but—"

"You don't have to justify anything to me, sweetheart," Gertie said, squeezing her hand. "Sometimes the chemistry is just there."

"You're telling me."

Gertie smiled. "So you're keeping things quiet for now?"

"For now." Jenna bit her lip. "There are rules against colleagues dating at Belmont, and then there's the other complication of Mia and—"

Ding-dong!

Jenna frowned at the front door. "Now what?"

"Probably Jehovah's Witnesses. I made the mistake of giving them some cookies last week, and now they keep coming back."

Jenna glanced at her watch. It was only ten past three, so it couldn't be Mia yet. Her birthing class was a full hour long. Jenna reached for the knob, ready to announce that her soul was beyond salvation and no, she wouldn't like a copy of their special magazine.

But as she yanked open the door, a cold gust of wind hit her in the face.

So did the full force of what was about to happen.

"Mia."

"I'm so sorry," Mia said, wiping a smear of rain from her cheek. "I just couldn't do it. I know it's my last birthing class and this probably makes me a terrible mother. But I got halfway there and just couldn't stand the thought of going in there alone without my husband when—Adam?"

Jenna turned slowly, knowing before she did that she'd see him standing behind her, looking as perplexed as his ex-wife did.

She held her breath as she watched the wave of emotion wash over his face, from recognition to anger to guilt all in the blink of an eye.

"Mia."

Chapter Fourteen

Adam stood staring at his ex-wife for what seemed like an eternity. He stole a look at his watch, not sure if he was checking the timeframe for eternity or to confirm that Mia wasn't supposed to be here.

"It's after three," he said stupidly, not sure what the hell else to say.

Mia frowned from the doorstep. "Is that your impression of a cuckoo clock? If so, I'll just wait here while you crow three times and then go back in your little hut."

He watched Jenna look from Mia to him and then back again. She cleared her throat, clearly not any better at coming up with a lie on short notice than he was. He should probably feel glad about that, but right now gladness didn't fill his heart.

"Mia," Jenna said. "I wasn't expecting you. I—please, come in."

Adam stepped back, trying desperately to think of an excuse for being in Jenna's house. Something about a personnel issue at

Belmont, or maybe an urgent need for her best banana bread recipe, or perhaps—

"There you are!"

He turned around and closed his mouth—grateful no words had emerged from it yet—and saw Gertie marching into the living room. She beamed at him and held out her hand. "Adam, can we please get to work now? I have a meeting in an hour, and I really want to review those contracts. You have everything on your laptop?"

He blinked at her, then looked down at the computer case gripped in his hand. "Yes—I—where would you like to set up?"

"Let's head to the office and give these girls some privacy. Mia, dear—so good to see you again."

"Gertie," Mia said, her expression dubious. "How do you know my ex-husband?"

"Oh, it's such a funny story. I had a little trouble at the grocery store last week, and Adam here came to my rescue. We got to talking and I learned he's an attorney with some expertise in literary contracts."

Mia frowned and turned to Adam. "I thought you didn't practice law anymore. And you said there wasn't enough money in literary contracts."

"I don't. There isn't. I mean, Gertrude needed someone to look over her contracts, and she offered to pay me in home-cooked meals, so what could I do?"

He smiled at her, hoping some shred of latent charm in him might still stir some softness in her heart. Mia studied him a moment, assessing. She'd always been the better liar between the two of them, or maybe she just paid more attention. Mia knew how to read people, how to tell when someone was uncomfortable or disingenuous. He hated that about her, but he also admired it.

Christ, no wonder Jenna couldn't stand lying to her.

"Come on, Mia," Jenna said, putting an arm around her friend. "I just put the kettle on. I'll make us some tea. You want some of Gertie's chocolate chip cookies, or do you need to save room for that fancy dinner?"

Mia shot Adam a look he couldn't read. She bit her lip and turned back to Jenna. "There won't be any fancy dinner. Actually, would you like to be my date?"

"What? Where's Mark?"

"Still working on the roof at Ellen's place. Apparently it's taking longer than he expected."

"God, I'm sorry."

Mia shrugged. "You love Gerlake, right? And I already have a reservation. Come on, my treat."

"Mia, I shouldn't—" She shot a look at Adam, then turned back to Mia. "When are you going?"

"Right now. It's an early reservation, so we've got plenty of time to make it."

"Yes. Okay, why not? Can you give me a second to change into something a little nicer?"

"Yeah, I'll just sit for a minute and rest my ankles." Mia moved toward the sofa, giving Adam a wide berth.

"Oh! Let me grab those special foot lotions we tried out yesterday," Gertie said, bustling off down the hall. "You said that peppermint one was helping a bit?"

"Thanks, Gertie." Mia dropped heavily onto the sofa, looking exhausted and a little sad. Adam glanced around, surprised to realize he was alone with his ex-wife for the first time in ages. Her eyes were closed, which gave him a chance to study her. She had lines on her face that hadn't been there before. Brackets around her mouth that could have been laugh lines or frown lines. Either way, did he have anything to do with them?

She took a heavy breath and opened her eyes, looking more exhausted now than she had before she'd closed them. Adam felt another pang of sympathy, which made him all the more angry with himself for his twinge of smugness in the car with Jenna. What kind of dick felt even the slightest hint of jubilation over someone else's misfortune? He wasn't sure what she was going through exactly, but it was clear all wasn't right in Mia's world.

"You okay?" he asked.

He hadn't meant to butt in, and it was clear from the way her eyes flashed that she didn't welcome the intrusion. The flicker of hurt in her face was something Adam wished like hell wasn't so familiar.

"I'm just great, Adam, thanks for asking."

Her sarcasm was so heavy that her words thudded like rocks onto the living room floor. He knew he should leave, but he wasn't sure whether to go looking for Gertie to keep up the ruse of legal consultation, or just get the hell out of here.

"Sorry your feet hurt," he tried. "I'm sure if you ask Mark to rub them for you, he'd be happy to oblige."

He hadn't meant it to sound snarky, or hell, maybe he had. Sometimes it was such a goddamn ingrained habit. The spark of anger in her eyes told him that's exactly how she took it.

"Fuck you, Adam."

He reeled back. "Hey. What the hell was that for?"

"You know exactly what it was for, you smug ass. You show up here with your woo-woo words and perfect communication skills and everyone thinks you're some sort of expert on compassion and human relationships. That's bullshit, and you know it."

He blinked. "I don't—"

"I'll tell you what you don't," she snapped, sitting up straighter with her green eyes flashing. "You don't get to waltz back into my circle of relationships and be the wonderful, perfect man who cooks his own meals and posts heartfelt quotes about trust. You don't get to be this exciting, carefree guy who does pro bono work for little old ladies and volunteers for charity instead of working 'til midnight every night. Most of all, you don't get to waltz around now pretending you give a shit how I'm feeling when you spent five years of our marriage barely noticing I existed."

"Well, Mia." Adam swallowed, reeling from her words. "Don't hold back. Why don't you tell me how you really feel?"

"Don't patronize me. You gave up the license to do that the second you signed the divorce papers."

Adam shook his head, not sure what stunned him more. The depth of her anger? The fact that her words revealed she'd been Facebook stalking him? The thought that she saw him as smug and callous?

Or the faint possibility she might be right.

"I'm sorry, Mia," he said, wanting to take the high road. Wanting to get out before things turned uglier. "I'm sorry for everything."

"It doesn't matter. You've gone and made yourself a much better life, and you can tell all the women you date how you narrowly escaped your cheating bitch of a wife. Congratulations, Adam—you sure showed me."

He shook his head, tamping down the urge to rage back at her. "You think this is somehow *my* fault? You're unhappy now, and I'm the one to blame?"

"I think it's pretty fucking convenient you embark on this mission of self-improvement now instead of when we were married. It's like some sort of, 'fuck you, Mia.'"

"I see," he said tightly, trying not to take the bait. "Despite what you seem to believe, my happiness has nothing to do with you."

She glared at him as she gripped the arm of the sofa in fingers that had gone terrifyingly white. "You're right. It never did. And you made damn sure mine had nothing to do with you, either."

He opened his mouth to reply, but he stopped himself as Jenna bustled into the room wearing a black wraparound dress that showed off her curves. Her hair was pinned up and she wore black boots with spikey heels and a spritz of perfume that made him dizzy. He wanted to gather her up in his arms and kiss her until they were both horizontal.

"You look—" he stopped himself, swallowing back the compliment and taking a step away from her, "—like you're in a hurry. I won't keep you ladies. If you'll excuse me, I'm going to get to my meeting with Gertrude."

"The office is down there," Jenna said, frowning as she caught sight of his face. She glanced at Mia and he watched her frown deepen. "Is everything okay here? Did I miss something?"

Adam looked at his ex-wife. He saw all the anger, all the disappointment, all the resentment flashing in her eyes. How was it possible after three years to still feel responsible for that?

"Everything's fine," he said, turning to walk away.

The host at Gerlake sniffed when Mia told him there'd been a change in plans.

"The reservation is under the name Mark Dawson," he said, looking down his nose at Jenna and Mia. "Do you mean to tell me Mr. Dawson will not be joining you this evening?"

"That's correct," Mia said, her voice shaking a little. Jenna reached over and squeezed her hand.

"You realize that dinnertime reservations at Gerlake fill up months in advance—particularly on a holiday weekend," he said, flipping a page in the reservation book. "I'm going to need to see some identification."

"Oh, for crying out loud," Jenna said, stepping forward. "Is there really a rash of people impersonating diners with reservations? I can see our table over there. It's the one with the sterling silver roses on it, right? They're Mia's favorite. She had them at the wedding."

Mia gave her a smile of gratitude and pulled out her phone, flipping quickly to the photo album. She thrust the phone in the host's face. "That's right. See? Right here. There's me, there's Mark Dawson, and there are the damn sterling silver roses. Just like the ones on the table. Do you want me to text my husband, or can we just sit down now, because my feet are killing me."

"Hmmph," the host said, and turned his back on them. "Follow me."

They trudged through the restaurant to the flower-adorned table by the window. Jenna pulled out Mia's chair, then sat down across the table from her. A waiter appeared beside them wearing a starched white shirt and the same disdainful expression their host had worn.

"I understand there's been a change in the reservation?"

Jenna sighed. "The reservation is for two people. There are two of us here. Is that a problem?"

The waiter frowned, shooting Jenna a look like she'd just piddled on the floor. "Gerlake prefers to reserve this particular table for special occasions. If you're not celebrating a milestone of some sort, we'd prefer to find you a more suitable table. There's a lovely spot right over there next to the kitchen—"

"Thank you, but that won't be necessary," Jenna said, placing her hand on Mia's. "My wife and I are celebrating the impending birth of our baby. Now if you'll give us a moment to look over the menu, we'd be grateful." She flicked her hand at the disgruntled-looking waiter. "Run along now."

The man harrumphed and turned on his heel, leaving Mia giggling behind her hand.

"I'm your wife now?"

"Why the hell not?" Jenna said, reaching over to grab a pitcher of ice water from a nearby server's station. She filled Mia's glass first, then her own. "It's legal in Oregon, and we get along better than most spouses. I'm totally going to expect you to put out."

"You'll have to buy me the lobster then."

"Deal. The flowers are beautiful, by the way. That was nice of Mark to have them waiting for you."

"He didn't."

"What?"

Mia sighed and fingered a petal. "I ordered them. I wanted to make things romantic."

"You did," Jenna said, squeezing her hand again. "As your wife, I appreciate it."

"Thanks."

"So," Jenna said, clearing her throat. "What the hell was going on back at the house? I feel like I walked in on something between you and your ex."

Mia set down her menu. "Was it that obvious? Adam and I were having a few words."

"A few words? If I'd been ten seconds slower in coming out there, I think I might have tripped over severed limbs."

"It wasn't that bad." She closed her eyes for a moment, then shook her head before opening them. "That's a lie. It was exactly that bad. I don't know what got into me."

"You're stressed, for one thing. You're hugely pregnant, your workplace is in turmoil, and your husband just pulled a no-show."

"Is this supposed to be cheering me up?"

Jenna winced. "Sorry."

"No, it's okay. I was bitchy to Adam, and he didn't deserve it. I'll e-mail him an apology as soon as I get home. It's just—I get so angry sometimes."

The waiter reappeared at their table and discreetly cleared his throat. "Congratulations, ma'am and—um, ma'am. So you're celebrating the impending arrival of your baby?"

"That's right," Jenna said, and reached across the table to take Mia's hand again. "My wife is due in two weeks."

"It's kind of our last big date before the baby comes," Mia added. "If she plays her cards right, she'll totally get lucky."

"Or *you* might," Jenna said, smiling up at the waiter. "The server at our anniversary dinner wasn't planning to be a sperm donor, but look how that turned out."

"I, uh—"

"So I think we're ready to order an appetizer," Mia said, offering up the first real smile Jenna had seen from her all evening. "Do you still have those bacon-wrapped apricots?"

"Absolutely, ma'am."

"I'll have an order of those."

"Make that two, please," Jenna said. "And a bottle of your house champagne. You know how pregnant lesbians are. Can't get enough of the bubbles."

"Er, right. Yes, of course. Uh, will there be anything else?"

"Mineral water," Mia said, smiling in earnest now. "Extra bubbles, if you can manage it."

"Of course. Right away."

The waiter hustled away, and Jenna turned her attention back to Mia. "So you were saying about Mark?" The name *Adam* had been on the tip of her tongue, but she resisted the urge to make this all about him.

"Right, yes." Mia sighed. "Look, I get that he can't make it to every birthing class, but this was the last one, and we'd made such a big deal about it. It wouldn't be so bad if he was caught up in traffic or having gall bladder surgery or visiting some sick relative, you know? But fixing the roof on his ex-wife's house?"

"You said yourself it was all about Katie. About needing to fix the roof over Katie's bed."

"Right, right—I know." She picked up a piece of bread, but didn't take a bite. She just flipped it around in her fingers, fiddling with it like a worry stone. "It's just—well, there's a guest room at Ellen's place. How hard would it be to move Katie's things for a couple nights and call a repairman after the holiday weekend?"

"Maybe it's a guy thing? He wants to be the rescuer. That can be a pretty strong male instinct." She picked up her own piece of bread, trying not to think about the story Adam had shared in the car. The one about Mia desperate and alone on the side of the road asking Adam for another chance.

The waiter appeared again with a disgruntled look on his face, and Jenna felt a fresh wave of urgency to protect Mia. For crying out loud, all the woman wanted was a nice dinner in her final weeks of pregnancy. She didn't need snotty waiters or absent husbands or—

Or a best friend sleeping with her ex.

Jenna bit her lip as the waiter shot Mia a look of disdain and set two champagne flutes on the table, then began to uncork the bottle.

"Thank you, but we only need one glass," Jenna said, picking hers up by the stem.

"Ah, you were joking about the mother-to-be sipping champagne?"

"No, she loves the stuff," Jenna said, squeezing Mia's knee under the table and earning herself another smile from her friend. "She just prefers to drink it straight from the bottle."

"Uh—pardon?"

"It gets to the baby faster that way," Mia said, resting a hand on her belly. "You do anything you can to jumpstart the labor."

"Not here, though." Jenna offered a reassuring smile to the perplexed-looking waiter. "You know what they say—most laboring mothers poop on the delivery table. We want to avoid that in your fine dining establishment, if at all possible."

"Er, yes. Yes, of course. Would you excuse me?"

"Of course." Jenna turned back to Mia as the waiter hustled away. "Think he's going to get us a free appetizer?"

"I think he's going to get a police officer. You know, sometimes I'm amazed to realize you're the same person who can lead a board meeting of a dozen C-suite executives without cracking a smile."

"He deserved it. He was being a dick."

"Can't argue with that."

Jenna picked up her glass of champagne, which the waiter had thoughtfully poured before fleeing. "So back to your conversation with Adam." She took a sip of her drink, hoping she wasn't being too obvious with her subject change. "It sounded like a pretty heated conversation."

"Yeah, I guess it was." Mia sighed. "I think I was just surprised to see him there. Being there with you and Gertie is kinda my safe place, and it was jarring to have him invading the space. It's one thing to have him in my workplace, but in my best friend's house—"

"I'm sorry," Jenna said, swallowing back the guilt with a bit of champagne. "I didn't realize you were struggling so much working with him."

"It's not a huge deal. It's just—seeing him again brings up a lot of stuff, you know?"

"What kind of stuff?"

"Memories about how bad things got between us. Between his emotional abandonment and my angry disappointment, we never gave that marriage a fighting chance." Mia shook her head and reached for the mineral water, giving the cap a sharp twist. "I don't know. Is it bad to say I'll be glad when he's gone? When this whole Belmont thing is over and he goes back to Chicago."

Jenna swallowed, suddenly aware of how warm it was in the dining area. "You don't think you could get used to having him around?"

Mia quirked an eyebrow at her. "You mean if he signed on for a long-term contract or something? I don't think that's a possibility. Adam always loved Chicago. Wouldn't even think of leaving, not even when I talked about wanting to move to Oregon or when his sister tried to get him to check out job prospects in Seattle."

"I see," she said, hoping like hell Mia couldn't see the way her face was flaming. Thank God for candlelight.

And thank God for the waiter, who returned to their table looking a bit like a man marching down death row. He glanced at his watch, as though he had someplace more important to be.

"Have you had time to look at the menu?"

"We haven't," Mia said, taking a sip of her mineral water. "Maybe you could tell us about some of your specials?"

"Very well. This evening we have a filet of sea bass prepared with a creamy vanilla coriander sauce—"

"Mmm, no creamy sauces," Jenna said, shaking her head. "Ever since we saw that childbirth video about mucus plugs, we've been shying away from those."

"The cream sauces, not the mucus plugs," Mia offered. "Mine's still fully intact."

"For now," Jenna agreed, looking back at the waiter to see his face had turned an interesting shade of green. "What else do you have?"

"Er, there's a twelve-ounce filet mignon in a rich balsamic glaze served with smashed garlic potatoes and herb-roasted root vegetables."

"No knives," Jenna said, reaching over to touch Mia's hand. "Knowing what we know about episiotomies, well—you can imagine the visual."

"Right. How about I give you another minute or two to study the menu?"

"Good idea," Jenna said, and watched him scurry away.

"That was fun."

"He's totally going to spit in our food."

Mia giggled, then shoved her menu aside. "Would you hate me if I wanted to scrap the fancy dinner and go to Rigatelli's for pizza instead?"

"Are you sure?"

"Yeah. I know you love Gerlake, but right now it's giving me the creeps."

"I don't blame you a bit. We can go anyplace you want."

"I can have him box up the apricots to take home to Mark. He won't mind a little waiter spit as long as it comes with bacon. Besides, I'm craving sausage and pepperoni."

"Never get between a pregnant woman and whatever she's craving." Jenna fished into her purse and pulled out enough cash to cover the drinks and appetizers, waving Mia off when she tried to plunk down her credit card.

"If I pay, you still have to put out," Jenna said, prompting another smile from Mia.

They swung by Mia's house en route to Rigatelli's, stopping to put the apricots in the fridge and confirm that Mark hadn't made it home yet. By the time they reached the pizza joint and placed their order, it was almost eight.

"Thanks, Jenna," Mia said, taking a sip of root beer as she wriggled her shoes off under the table, her bare toes bumping Jenna's shins companionably. "God, I can't tell you how relieved I'll be when I can finally have a glass of wine again. Or a beer. There's something about IPA and pepperoni, you know?"

"I know. That's why I'm having root beer in a show of solidarity."

"That would be sweet if you didn't also have a glass of red wine."

"Hey, they've got a really good house Sangiovese. I couldn't resist. Want another breadstick?"

"Yes, please. Think we should call Gertie and see if she wants to join us? I feel like having people around me right now. Kinda like an impromptu party."

"The fact that you consider my elderly aunt a party either says something about your idea of fun or hers."

"Probably both," Mia said, pulling out her phone and setting it on the table. She glanced at the screen and smiled. "Mark sent me a text message with xoxo typed about three million times."

"That's sweet. He seems like he's trying."

"I know, he is." Mia sighed. "I should try harder, too."

"Text him a cleavage shot."

Mia giggled. "Good idea." She glanced around, then picked up the phone and aimed the camera down the front of her V-neck top. "Gotta make good use of these pregnancy boobs while I can."

"Carpe diem," Jenna said, biting into a breadstick. "Or carpe pectoris? Seize the boobs."

"Amen," Mia said, and fired off a text message. "I'll send one to Gertie, too. A message, not a boob shot."

"Glad you clarified."

"I'll see what she's up to. If she's free, we can send a cab to go get her."

Jenna took another bite of breadstick and chewed, losing herself in the cheesy goodness of yeasty dough and garlic. She was so absorbed in the flavors that she almost didn't hear the familiar voice calling her name.

"Jenna? We have to stop meeting like this."

She turned to see Sean approaching their table with a surprised smile on his face. His shirtsleeves were rolled to the elbows, showing off forearms Jenna had to admit were pretty impressive, though the ever-present smartphone was gripped in his right hand.

"Sean," Jenna said, swallowing her bite of breadstick. "I didn't realize you spent so much time here."

"I don't. Haven't been back since the last time you and I ate here."

"You've met Mia Dawson, right?"

"Sure, yeah—at that barbecue about six months after you and I—uh, separated."

Mia nodded. "Good memory."

"Good to see you again, Mia. Wow, you're looking—vibrant."

Mia laughed and sipped her root beer. "It's okay, Sean. You can say 'pregnant.' Or 'huge.' If the shoe fits, I might as well wear it."

"Or kick it off under the table in a crowded restaurant," Jenna added.

Sean rested a hand on the edge of the table. "Sorry, I just know it's a bad idea to ever assume a woman is expecting unless she's shared the news."

"That's sweet," Mia said. "But when it's obvious she's on the brink of giving birth at the dinner table, I'd say you're safe to go ahead and make the assumption."

"Well, congratulations." Sean gestured toward the front counter. "I hope you two got your order in already. They just told me I'm looking at a two-hour wait. I should know better than to come here on a holiday weekend to fight the dinner crowd."

"Here, have a breadstick," Mia said, thrusting one at him. "We ordered way too many." She looked at Jenna with an unspoken question, both about the breadstick and the empty chair at their table.

"Please, help yourself," Jenna said, nudging the whole basket at him and nodding at Mia. Her ex-fiancé wasn't what Jenna considered a party, but Mia had said she wanted people around her. If nothing else, Sean was nice to look at, and Mia seemed like she could use the visual distraction.

Mia smiled, reading Jenna's nonverbal affirmation. "Sean, do you want to join us for pizza? Assuming Jenna's okay with it. We were hungry when we placed the order, so we may or may not have ordered enough for a small developing nation. I feel like having company right now, so you'll do nicely."

Jenna nodded in agreement, so Sean pulled out the empty chair. "In that case, I accept." He looked at Jenna. "You sure you're okay with this?"

"Absolutely. The more, the merrier."

She watched as Sean eased into the chair and set his phone on the table. He poked at the screen a few times in case the world had ended in the two minutes since he last checked it. He frowned, poked at the screen a few more times, smiled, then poked some more.

Jenna looked at Mia and rolled her eyes, but Mia just smiled and shrugged.

"So, Jenna," Sean said, turning his attention back to the real live humans at the table. "You still seeing that guy?"

Mia cocked her head and gave Jenna an apprising look. "What guy?"

"The guy she hustled out of here to meet up with last time we were here. Said she owed him an apology for something."

Beneath the table, Jenna gave Mia's shin a light tap. At least, she thought it was Mia.

Sean frowned. "Why'd you just kick me?"

"I didn't—I—you want some ranch dip?"

"No thank you," Sean said, looking down at the breadsticks. "I'll stick with the marinara. So you're not seeing anyone right now?"

Seeming to sense Jenna's need for rescue, Mia jumped in. "Oh, that guy. Yeah, he's hot." Mia bit into her breadstick. "How about you, Sean? You seeing anyone?"

"Nope, no one special. Gotta admit, it's crossed my mind a time or two that Jenna and I could get back together."

Jenna bit down on a breadstick, chomping off a bite that was much bigger than she could handle. She chewed hard, wondering if choking to death might be preferable to this conversation. "Uh, that's sweet, Sean. I don't think that's going to happen, though. There's something a little uncomfortable about reconnecting with an ex, you know?"

"Tell me about it," Mia muttered, dunking her breadstick in the marinara. "I've been working with mine, and I've gotta tell you, it's awkward as hell."

Sean laughed. "More awkward than having pizza with one?"

"I'll defer to Jenna to answer that. You know in hindsight, I should have taken him up on his offer to turn down the contract."

Jenna gulped down the last of her root beer, and wished for a meteor to fall on the table and end this conversation.

The meteor came in the form of two extra-large pizzas.

"One sausage and pepperoni with olives, one veggie-licious with prosciutto?"

"Right here," Jenna said, gathering up a pile of napkins to make room on their table. She shot the server a grateful look, wondering if she'd ever been so happy at the sight of a pizza.

"Need any parmesan or hot pepper?"

"Both, please."

Mia reached up to take the stack of plates the waitress offered under the assumption the massive quantity of cheese and meat was intended to feed at least a dozen people instead of a pregnant newlywed, her guilt-ridden friend, and the friend's unsuspecting ex.

"God, this looks amazing," Sean said. "You're sure you don't mind if I join you?"

"Does it look like there's going to be any shortage of food here?" Mia reached for a slice. "If you want, you can share your pizza with us whenever it gets here. Might as well enjoy this one while it's hot."

"Thanks, ladies." Sean frowned. "Hey, isn't that your Aunt Gertie?"

Jenna jerked her head up and blinked. It did indeed look like Gertie, weaving her way through the crowd with her white hair rustling in the breeze from the overhead fans. She seemed to be scanning the room for someone, or maybe an empty table. There were none in sight.

Jenna looked back at Mia. "I thought you just texted to ask what she was up to."

"I did," she said, glancing at her phone. "She never responded. I didn't even tell her where we were."

Sean stood up. "Want me to wave her down?"

"Yeah, she looks a little lost."

He stood—all six feet three inches of him—and waved his arms in the air. "Gertrude? Aunt Gertie! Over here!"

Gertie turned and blinked, then smiled. She began weaving her way toward them, threading past tables packed with families and frat boys devouring fragrant masses of meat and cheese. Jenna watched her aunt's progress, not sure why she felt a faint sense of unease.

"Hello, sweetheart!" Gertie said, fluffing her hair as she arrived at the edge of their table. "What a surprise seeing you here! I thought the two of you went to Gerlake."

"Change of plans," Mia said, biting off a piece of pizza and fanning her mouth. "Pull up a chair and join us. We ordered plenty."

Sean jumped up, vacating his seat. "Here, take mine. I see an extra one right over there."

"Can you grab the other one, too?" Gert asked. "I have a date joining me."

"Coming right up."

She smiled at Sean and patted his arm. "It's good to see you again, sweetheart."

"You, too, Aunt Gertie."

He hustled to an adjacent table and hurried back toting two chairs. Mia and Jenna moved over, making room for Gertie and her date in the space between Jenna and Sean. With everyone seated, Sean sat back down and picked up his phone. Jenna picked up her wine and took a tentative sip, not wanting to overindulge with this much potential for awkward tension at the table.

"I can't wait to meet your gentleman friend, Gertie," Mia said, swallowing her bite of pizza. "Is this the guy who went to Cornell?"

"Oh—well yes, he did, but it's not Arthur. My date is Adam."

Mia blinked. "What?"

"Adam." Gertie frowned, glancing at Jenna. "Oh, dear, I'm sorry. We can find a different table if this is going to be a problem."

"No, it's okay," Mia said, reaching for her root beer. "If Jenna can handle eating pizza with her ex, I can do the same."

Jenna bit her lip and looked at Sean, who appeared to be engrossed in either a stock trade or a game of Angry Birds. It was tough to tell.

"You're sure it's okay?" Gert asked, looking from Mia to Jenna and back again. "I could try finding another table, though I don't see anything free. I told Adam I'd find us a place by the time he parked the car."

"I'm a big girl, Gertie," Mia said. "Besides, I feel like I owe Adam an apology for some things I said earlier. This is my opportunity to make nice."

"In that case, we accept the invitation," Gertie said. "I'm going to run over to the bar to order some drinks. Any idea what Adam likes?"

Mia shrugged. "He's not very experimental. Probably a Bud Light or something."

Jenna took another sip of her wine and pushed it aside, wishing the waitress would bring a glass of water. Sean was smiling and nodding, pretending to follow the conversation while his thumbs fluttered over the screen. Jenna cut her eyes to Mia, who was watching Sean with a bemused expression.

"Isn't this what you said the whole relationship was like?" Mia murmured under her breath.

"Pretty much," Jenna murmured back.

"I see some things never change."

"Sure they do. Isn't that an iPhone 6? They didn't have those when we broke up."

"You're right, I stand corrected."

Jenna leaned closer, not that there was much risk of Sean overhearing or lifting his gaze from the phone. "Which is worse," she whispered. "The ex who changes everything about himself after you split, or the one who doesn't change a damn thing?"

"I'll get back to you on that one." Mia reached for another piece of pizza.

Gertie returned to the table and set down two mugs of beer. "I hope one of these is what Adam likes."

"I'm sure it'll be fine," Mia said.

Jenna bit her lip and glanced toward the front of the restaurant. As if on cue, Adam appeared in the doorway, his dark hair tousled and windblown. His shirtsleeves were rolled up, too, but seeing his forearms made Jenna shiver in a way Sean's didn't. Adam was scanning the room, and Jenna sat breathless as his gaze moved from table to table, looking for Gertie.

The instant his eyes locked with Jenna's, she felt a surge of static. He felt it, too, she could see by the way he stepped back, then moved toward her in slow motion, wading through a sea of bodies and noise and clatter.

"Ladies," he said, nodding at Jenna, then Mia. "This is a surprise."

"Adam." Jenna took a deep breath, half of her wishing the ground would swallow her up, while the other half fought the urge to throw herself into his arms. "Uh, good to see you again."

Sean glanced up from his phone, then stood and extended a hand. "Hey, I'm Sean. You're Gertie's boyfriend?"

Mia rolled her eyes. "I think you missed part of the conversation, phone boy."

"What?" Sean frowned and studied Adam. "Hey, you look familiar. Have we met before?"

Adam gripped the back of a chair, clearly undecided about whether to sit down. Jenna couldn't blame him.

"I don't think so. I'm from Chicago, just here on business."

Jenna could tell he was deliberately standing a few feet away from her, but she could feel the tension radiating from him anyway. She glanced at Mia, who gave a helpless shrug, then looked down at her own phone vibrating on the table. She smiled, which Jenna took as a good sign. Mark must have replied favorably to the cleavage shot.

"Aunt Gertie grabbed you a drink," Jenna said, nodding toward the center of the table where all the glasses had been shoved to make room for the pizza.

"Thank you so much," he said, reaching for Jenna's wineglass before she had a chance to say anything. "Mmm, Sangiovese? This is excellent."

"Um, actually, that's yours." Jenna pointed to one of the mugs of beer. "But you're welcome to finish off my Sangiovese. I'm done drinking for now."

Mia glanced up from her phone, regarding her ex with a curious look. "Since when do you like wine?"

"I've been branching out," he said, pushing the glass back toward Jenna. "Sorry about that. Here—I don't want to take your drink."

"Please, take it. I'm done. I'm sure Gertie or Sean would love the beer."

Sean nodded, distracted, his eyes on Adam again. "Chicago, huh? I don't know, I never forget a face. Did you go to school out here?"

Adam picked up the wineglass again and shook his head. "Nope, Cornell University Law School. Maybe I have one of those familiar faces?"

"Huh," Sean said, clearly still puzzling it out.

"Have the other beer, dear," Gertie said, nudging a mug toward Sean. Jenna shot her a grateful look, hoping the amber suds were enough to distract her ex from interrogating Adam. Across the table,

Mia glanced down at her phone again and smiled. At least someone was connecting well with a loved one.

Adam turned back to Jenna. "I thought the two of you went to some fancy restaurant downtown?"

"We did, but we changed our minds."

"A woman's prerogative," Mia murmured, tapping out a message on her phone.

"So I hear," he said lightly. "Sorry, I would have gone someplace else if I'd known. Gertie wanted pizza, so I just thought—"

"Cornell University Law School," Sean said, sticking with the basics of macho posturing and career comparisons. "So you're an attorney?"

Adam turned and gave Sean a polite nod. "I'm in corporate mediation now. I work on contract with organizations experiencing turmoil."

"Ah, let me guess—Belmont? That must be how you know Mia and Jenna."

"That's how he knows Jenna," Mia said, looking annoyed. "He knows me because we once shared a last name and a bank account."

"Actually, you never took my name," Adam said, shrugging. "Not that there's anything wrong with that."

"I was speaking figuratively," Mia said. "It seemed better than suggesting we shared bodily fluids."

"Good point," Adam said, taking another sip of wine.

"I know!" Sean snapped his fingers. "The bathroom."

Everyone turned to look at him. "It's over there," Adam said, pointing to the far corner.

"No, I mean that's where I know you from. You were talking with Jenna last time we were here. I wouldn't have noticed, but she was gone a long time." He cocked his head to the side, considering. "Wait, that's who you had to run off and meet that night?"

Jenna felt all the blood drain from her head. She gripped her root beer glass, swallowing hard. "What? No, we just ran into each other. We'd been working together and stopped to say hello and—"

"Hey, it's no big deal," Sean said good-naturedly, returning his attention to his phone. "Just trying to figure out why he looked so familiar."

"Glad we could piece it together for you," Adam said, not looking particularly glad. Not that it mattered. With the mystery solved, Sean's attention was already back on his phone.

"Wait, how come you never mentioned this?"

Jenna cut her eyes across the table. Mia was frowning, her own phone gripped in her hand.

"What?" Jenna said, palms feeling sweaty all of a sudden. "I told you I came here for pizza that night—August fifteenth—you know?"

She waited for Mia to get sidetracked, to recognize the date and abandon her line of questioning. But Mia shook her head.

"I'm not talking about the whole running-into-your-ex-on-the-anniversary-of-the-miscarriage thing, though I do think—"

"Miscarriage?" Adam frowned.

Sean looked up from his phone, apparently sensing he'd missed something major. "What?"

"Nothing." Jenna said, digging her nails into her palms. "Go back to your game."

Jenna felt Adam's eyes drilling into her like lasers. She swallowed hard, her gaze still locked on Mia's disapproving one. She opened her mouth to explain, but Mia shook her head and held up her phone.

"I'm not talking about that. Mark just texted. He said Ellen wanted me to ask you whether you liked the .32 Kel-Tec you were firing with or the .22 Ruger Mark III Hunter Adam had." She looked from Jenna to Adam, then back again. "What's going on here?"

Jenna swallowed again, wishing like hell she hadn't emptied her root beer or given her wine to Adam. The last bite of pizza had formed a sticky lump in the back of her throat, or maybe that was a thick wad of guilt. On the table, Jenna's phone buzzed. She shoved it away, trying to keep her focus on coming up with an explanation that might appease everyone.

"Jenna?" Adam asked. She looked at him, her heart twisting when she saw the stricken look on his face.

"I—"

"Sweetheart?"

Jenna cut her eyes to Gertie, who was studying Jenna's phone with frank interest. Jenna felt a flood of relief, certain Gertie had a rescue strategy. She'd get her out of this, away from Mia's accusing gaze and Adam's bewilderment and Sean's clueless oblivion.

"Yes, Aunt Gertie?"

"Why is my agent calling you?"

Jenna's mouth went dry. "I, uh—I'm not sure."

"You've spoken with her recently?"

"She called the house sometime last week, but—"

"You've obviously been in contact beyond that," Gertie said, nudging the phone toward her. "You've got her name and number programed into your phone."

Gert's expression was more curious than angry, but Jenna's palms were slick now with fear and dread and guilt. She opened her mouth to speak, but realized she didn't have any words at all. Not for anyone. She looked from Sean to Mia to Gert to Adam, all of them staring at her with some mix of confusion and anger and betrayal.

Jenna stood up, legs shaking as she knocked her empty root beer glass over. She had to get out of here. She had to leave now, before everything came crashing down around her. If she could just rewind, take back all the lies and half-truths and cover stories that weren't covering anything at all anymore.

Everyone at the table was staring, some confused, some angry, some hurt. "I'm sorry," she said, righting her empty glass, only to knock it over again. "I didn't know—I just—excuse me."

She turned and ran from the restaurant.

Chapter Fifteen

"Jenna, wait!"

Adam was breathing hard by the time he caught up to her on a street corner less than a block from the restaurant. He watched her hesitate, then turn to see him chasing her down, determined to—what, exactly?

He didn't know.

She froze, rooted in place, coiled with an energy that said she was on the brink of running again. "Adam, stop."

He halted beside her, breathless and caught somewhere between hurt and frustration. "What are you doing?"

Her eyes flashed in the hazy light of a street lamp, and she looked like she wanted to be anyplace but here with him. "Go back inside," she whispered. "I just—I need a minute alone."

"You could get a minute alone in the bathroom. You're escaping. Running. In high heels, for that matter. You're going to break an ankle, Jenna."

She looked down at her boots as though noticing them for the first time. "So you chased me down the street to make fun of my shoes?"

"No, I chased you down the street because I want to understand what just happened back there."

He watched her throat move as she swallowed, her fingers clenching and unclenching at her sides. "You want answers. So does everyone in that room, Adam. I can't give them to you."

"Running away isn't the answer, Jenna. Hiding isn't going to get you anywhere." He cringed, hating the patronizing tone in his voice. Apparently, so did Jenna.

"So what are you, some sort of expert on coping strategies?"

"Kind of. It's one of my areas of specialty, actually."

She rolled her eyes. "It figures. I'm sure you can plot out my behavior on a chart, figure out why I'm as fucked up as I am. Go ahead, Adam. Judge me. Tell me all the psychological reasons I created this whole mixed-up mess of lies and deceit and cover-ups."

"I'm not judging you, Jenna," he said, forcing himself to keep his voice calm and even. "I just want to know what's going on."

"You want to know why I didn't tell you about the miscarriage."

He raked his fingers through his hair, hating the pain in her eyes. "Look, maybe it's none of my business, but it seems strange, doesn't it? We spent an entire weekend together sharing family stories and intimate details. You know the name of my grandparents' dog and the poem my mother read at my wedding. You didn't think to mention something as major as that?"

"So I owe you the story?"

"I'm not saying you owe me," he said, resisting the urge to shake her. "I'm just saying, I thought we were on the same page. As far as intimacy and truth and sharing and—"

"It's where I met Mia."

"What?"

"In a support group for women who'd had a miscarriage."

The air suddenly felt colder. "Mia had a miscarriage?"

"It happens, Adam. To one in four women. Did you know that?"

"No, I—I mean, I knew it was common, but I didn't know the numbers. I'm sorry, I didn't realize."

Still, something wasn't adding up. He wanted to reach out and touch her, tell her they could get through this. That the half-truths and cover-ups could be over now, and they could start fresh. "So you had a miscarriage. Recently?"

She looked away. "Two years ago. Right after I broke off my engagement to Sean."

"I see," he said, not entirely sure he did.

She looked back at him then, her eyes locked so tightly on his that he couldn't look away, not even if he wanted to. "Sean is sterile, Adam."

All the air left his lungs. "What?"

"You heard me. My fiancé—the man I was supposed to marry—wasn't the man who got me pregnant."

He turned the words over in his head. They didn't make sense, or maybe he just wasn't grasping what she was trying to tell him. "What are you saying?"

Her hands were balled at her sides now, fingers clenched into tight fists. "That I cheated on Sean, okay? That I'm no better than your ex-wife. Isn't that what you've been braced for? To find out my tendency to cover things up, to pretend everything's just peachy keen—that makes me just as untrustworthy as Mia. Congratulations on being right, Adam."

He stood reeling in the torrent of words. He didn't know whether to hug her or push her away or push her for answers, but a tight ball of dread had formed in his gut. She'd lied. Cheated. Hadn't he expected this?

Part of him didn't want to hear another word. Part of him wanted to hear the whole damn story. He took a deep breath. "What happened?"

She shook her head. "Sean and I dated for about three years. We always had this on-again, off-again relationship, but we kept coming back to each other. We talked about getting married, about having three kids and a dog and a house in Lake Oswego."

Adam nodded, trying to take it all in. He didn't know what to say, so he was grateful she kept going with no prompting from him.

"We used to break up for a few weeks or months even. We'd get back together and then break up again. It was a stupid cycle, really hurtful." She took a shaky breath and kept going. "During one of the splits, I reconnected with an old college boyfriend. Technically, Sean and I weren't together anymore, and I was lonely. It was a one-time thing, a stupid, casual fling." She gave a dry little laugh that sounded hollow. "It was the only time in my life I'd ever had a one-night stand."

"Until me."

"Until you," she repeated, her voice shaky. "I was on the pill, but it's only ninety-eight percent effective. I guess I was one of the two percent." She took another breath, looking weary and worn down. "Anyway, Sean and I got back together a few weeks later, and I found out I was pregnant right after that. I didn't know what to do, but I figured odds were still pretty good he was the father. We hadn't been apart that long, right? I was still figuring out how to tell him when he proposed."

"Out of the blue?"

"It wasn't totally out of the blue. Like I said, we'd been talking about it for a while. I knew he wanted kids, and we'd looked at rings before, talked about a future together. It seemed like a sign, you know?"

"So you said yes." His voice sounded flat, but not judgmental. He hoped, anyway.

"I said yes." She sighed. "I was scared, and I didn't know what else to do. I didn't want to marry him. The relationship felt like it was already on its last legs, and part of me knew that. But I didn't think I could say no."

"Did Sean know you were pregnant?"

She shook her head. "No. I was still figuring out what to do, whether to say anything about the hookup with the other guy, or just—"

"Cover it up."

He heard the hollowness in his own voice. The unspoken accusation. The sight of tears welling in her eyes told him she'd heard it, too.

"We started planning our wedding," she said. "He wanted to do it quickly, even went ahead and ordered these stupid invitations without telling me. I was only seven or eight weeks pregnant at that point, and I'd only known for about ten days. But I made up my mind I was going to tell him over dinner."

"Let me guess," Adam said, nodding at the gaudy neon sign behind them. "Rigatelli's?"

She nodded, tears welling in her eyes. "It was our special place. We had our first date here, had our first anniversary celebration. I thought—" she stopped, wiping her eyes on her sleeve. Adam wished he had a tissue to offer, but had nothing. Not even a napkin. "I thought I could just ease into the story, you know? Gauge his response to being a father and go from there."

"How did that work out?"

She shook her head. "The whole thing didn't go like I expected." She closed her eyes as though forcing herself to revisit that night. "As soon as we ordered, he said there was something he needed to tell me. That he felt guilty about hiding the truth for so long, but that he felt like I needed to know. He started talking about adoption, about the US foster-care system and babies overseas, and at first I couldn't figure out what he was saying."

"He was sterile."

Jenna nodded and opened her eyes. "The baby couldn't have been his."

"Jesus."

"So I broke up with him."

Adam blinked, wondering if he'd heard her wrong. "What?"

She closed her eyes again, the guilt etched plainly in her face. "I broke up with him. I said I didn't want to get married and that we needed to call off the engagement. I said it wasn't about having kids or not having kids or anything to do with that. I just knew I didn't want to marry him. I knew it before I said yes, and I knew it beyond a shadow of a doubt right then."

"I see."

"The thing is, it was true. I *didn't* want to marry him. He wasn't the one." She closed her eyes, her face so creased in pain that Adam felt his own throat tightening. "That evening, I went home and started having cramps. I wasn't sure at first—it was so early in the pregnancy, and it can be hard to tell."

"You had a miscarriage that same night?"

She nodded and opened her eyes to look at him. "Part of me wondered if I made it happen. The lying, the cheating, the deceit."

"It couldn't have been your fault," he said, feeling dumb offering such an empty platitude.

She shook her head. "I never told Sean about the pregnancy or the miscarriage. He never knew. Hell, he probably still doesn't. He barely looked up from his phone when Mia said what she did just now."

Adam stared at her, trying to wrap his brain around the magnitude of it all. "Who knows about this?"

"Only your ex-wife," she whispered, shaking her head. "Christ, what a tangled mess. Mia knew about the miscarriage, but Sean didn't. And Mia didn't *know* Sean didn't know, because what kind of woman would hide that from her fiancé?" She choked out a sob, her voice rising higher. "Sean knew I was sneaking off to meet you a few weeks ago, but Mia didn't. Gert knew, too—that you and I were seeing each other. Gert's agent knew I was trying to keep her story suppressed, but Gert didn't. Gert knew I went to Seattle with you, but Mia didn't." She was sobbing in earnest now—big, heaving gasps that made her shoulders shake. "I've spun such a ridiculous web of half-truths and lies and cover-ups that even I don't know what's real anymore."

Adam swallowed, his chest tight with emotion. "And the whole thing blew up in your face tonight."

She nodded, watching his face for a response. Adam didn't have one. He didn't know what to think, what to feel. Tears were streaming down her face, and part of him wanted to put his arms around her and comfort her. Part of him wanted to walk away.

He stood rooted in place, torn in two once again.

Jenna wiped her eyes.

"You should go, Adam."

"What?"

"I can't," she said, sniffling. "I just—I can't. I'm so done."

"Done," he repeated, not sure he understood what she meant. "Done with what?"

"With everything. With this whole tangled-up mess of secrets and betrayals. I'm just done."

Her words sounded brittle, her voice like someone else completely. He nodded numbly, the echo of the word in his brain.

Done.

With him?

The finality in her eyes, the stiffness in her posture, told him the answer.

Maybe it was best. She looked up at him then, tears shimmering in her eyes. Waiting for him to stop her? Or waiting for him to say his goodbyes.

"Adam! Jenna!"

He turned to see Gert bustling out of the restaurant, her hair wild and her coat flying. She spotted them on the street corner and hurried toward them, running damn fast for a seventy-eight-year-old woman. Adam moved toward her, bracing himself to catch her if she tripped.

But she didn't trip, and she waved him away as he approached.

"We have to go to the hospital *now*!" she shouted.

Jenna gasped, drawing a hand to her mouth. "The baby. Mia's having the baby?"

"No," Gert panted, halting on the sidewalk. "No, not the baby."

Jenna moved toward her, reaching out as she drew closer to her aunt. "What is it?"

"It's Mark." Gertie drew a hand to her throat, her eyes wild and fearful. "He's been shot."

Adam blinked, fighting to process the words. "Shot?"

"Shot," Gert repeated, nodding. "By his ex-wife."

$\sim$

Jenna drove in a trance to the hospital with Mia beside her looking pale and stunned. She held her phone in her lap, but she wasn't looking at it. She stared out the window, wordless and stiff, with her red hair falling over her face like a curtain.

"How did it happen?" Jenna asked, braking at a red light she wished she could run right through.

"They don't know. The police are still at the house trying to sort through the details." She fell silent, and for a moment, Jenna thought that's all she intended to offer. Jenna nodded, gripping the steering wheel tightly.

Mia cleared her throat. "Apparently she had a handgun in her purse. She was arguing with him about something and dropped it on the floor, and somehow—"

She broke off sobbing, her face crumpling into a mess of tears and terror. Jenna reached over and touched her arm. "Mia, I'm so sorry. For everything. I don't even know where to begin—"

"Don't," Mia whispered. "Not now. I just want to get to the hospital and see Mark. That's what matters right now."

Jenna nodded, withdrawing her hand. She took a sharp right turn onto the road leading to Belmont, thankful at least that the ambulance had brought Mark to this hospital. She knew the exact location of the ER, the spot in back where she was sure to find parking. "Do you want me to drop you in front or come in with you?"

Mia seemed to hesitate. "Come in with me."

Jenna nodded, not sure whether to take it as a positive sign or a practical one. Did it matter at this point? Mark had been shot. Her best friend's husband—for better or worse, even if they did happen to be experiencing the latter right now. Jesus, what was Mia feeling?

She turned into the parking lot, trying not to picture the look on Mia's face the moment she'd realized Jenna's betrayal. The moment Jenna had stood and fled, leaving her behind without answers or explanations.

She looked at Mia now and her gut twisted. The only thing worse than seeing this much pain on her best friend's face was knowing she was responsible for some of it.

"Here," Jenna said, pulling into a spot tucked off to the side near the ER entrance. Mia had the car door open before Jenna had even pulled her keys out of the ignition, and she was halfway to the hospital door by the time Jenna caught up with her. "Careful, Mia," Jenna cautioned, reaching for her elbow. "The ground gets slick here."

"I know, I'm okay," Mia said, and hurried ahead, one hand on her belly.

The automatic doors whooshed open, and they found themselves blinking in the brightly lit lobby of the ER. A nurse rushed over with a wheelchair. "Ma'am? Let's get you to the birthing center right away."

"No," Mia said, throwing her arm out as though stopping the nurse from forcibly taking her. "I'm not in labor. I'm here to see my husband. Mark Dawson? He's been shot. I'm Mia—Amelia Dawson. Please, someone tell me what's happening."

The nurse's expression changed from all business to sympathy, and Jenna tried not to think the worst.

"Come with me," the nurse said, shoving the wheelchair aside. She looked at Jenna. "Are you a relative?"

"No, I—"

"Family only, you wait here." She pointed to a hard plastic chair in the waiting area, and Jenna sat automatically, too terrified to argue. She watched as the nurse led Mia away, watched the slump of her friend's shoulders and the slow, awkward gait of her movement.

The doors leading outside whooshed open again, and Gertie rushed in with Adam on her heels. Gert looked around, her white hair frizzy and wild as she scanned the waiting area. Spotting Jenna, she hustled over with her handbag banging against her hip.

"What did they say?" Gertie demanded. "How's Mark?"

"I don't know. They whisked Mia away before I could ask anything. I'm not even sure if he's alive or—"

"Don't say that," Gertie said, dropping into a chair beside her. "Do we know where the bullet hit?"

Jenna shook her head as Adam dropped silently into the chair to her left. "I don't know anything. Just that the gun was in Ellen's purse when it went off. They think it was an accident, but no one knows at this point."

"Thank God Katie wasn't there," Gertie said. "That's the first thing Mia said when the police called. I guess the roof repair was taking longer than expected, so Ellen let Katie have one last sleepover at a friend's house before school starts. She didn't see her daddy get shot."

Jenna nodded, grateful at least for that. She looked at Adam. He still hadn't said a word, and his face was stony and pale. She started to reach out and touch his hand, then stopped herself. She kept her hands in her lap, fingers clenched in a sweaty knot.

"Adam? You okay?"

"Yeah." He raked his fingers through his hair, making it stand up on end. "I just can't imagine what she's feeling right now."

He stopped, and Jenna nodded. "I know. I keep seeing the look on her face."

All three of them fell silent, waiting. In the background, machinery beeped and medical staff called out to each other about detox and defibrillators and dinner breaks. The smell of disinfectant floated around them like an angry cloud, mixing with the scent of spilled coffee near a grimy-looking coffee pot on a table beside Adam. In the corner, a woman sat with red-rimmed eyes, knitting something that looked like a scarf.

Gertie reached out and touched Jenna's knee. "It isn't your fault."

"What?"

"I know you. And I know you're sitting there thinking about

how you could have done something different to change this. Maybe if you'd called Mark and told him how upset Mia was about the class, or maybe if you'd taken a right turn instead of a left one on the way to the restaurant. There's nothing you could have done differently, Jenna."

She felt her eyes filling with tears, and she blinked them back. "I could have done a lot of things differently. I could have avoided lying to my best friend. Betraying her. Hurting her on what's obviously turning out to be one of the worst days of her life."

Gertie shook her head. "We all make mistakes, sweetie. You, me, Mark, Mia, Adam. We're all just bumping around together on this planet, trying to do the best we can for ourselves and each other. But there's only so much we can control."

She felt Adam stir beside her, and turned to look at him. His face was creased in shadows, and he looked ten years older than he had on their car ride to Seattle. Jesus, had it only been three days?

Adam looked up, seeming to feel her eyes on him. He stared at her for a moment, then reached over and took her hand. She thought about pulling back. About telling him this was the last thing in the world they should be doing right now.

But his palm was warm and solid, and she felt her lungs expand, then contract and expand again. She couldn't remember the last time she'd taken a deep breath, so she kept her hand in his, savoring the connection and the oxygen. What was it about him that made her breathe easier, feel safe and secure and calm even while everything around them was spinning?

A nurse stepped through a set of double doors from the ER and looked around. Her eyes landed on Jenna, and she walked toward them with purpose, her expression unreadable.

"Ms. McArthur?"

"Yes," Jenna said, letting go of Adam's hand as she stood up. "Mia Dawson asked me to come find you."

"How's Mark? Can I see him? Can I see Mia or—"

"I'm sorry, Ms. McArthur. You're not allowed back there. Family only."

"But what's Mark's condition?"

"As you know, HIPAA allows us to give a one-word condition report."

Jenna froze, recognizing the stilted language she'd used so many times with nosy journalists and visitors. "I—yes, I understand."

"Mr. Dawson is in fair condition."

Jenna nodded, her brain running through the different terms. "Fair" was better than "serious" or "critical," but it wasn't "good." It wasn't "treated and released."

And it wasn't the information Jenna would get if Mia had given her permission to share more. Mia knew hospital rules. All she had to do was sign the form, give the okay to release more detail and let them know what was happening.

Jenna sat down, feeling numb. Adam reached for her hand again. "She probably just didn't have time."

Jenna turned to look at him, barely recognizing his features. "What?"

"To sign the HIPAA forms. That's what you're thinking, right? She's deliberately shutting you out?"

"I don't—"

"We'll wait here," Gertie said, reaching out to take Jenna's other hand. "Until there's more news, we'll be right here."

The nurse nodded. "Okay then. If I'm able to tell you more, I will."

"Thank you," Jenna said.

The nurse vanished the same way she'd come, the double doors making an impersonal *swoosh* as she passed. For a moment, none of them spoke. They sat connected by palms and fingers and breath and bone.

"So we wait," Adam said, the first to break the silence.

"I guess so," Jenna said, and squeezed his hand so tightly it hurt.

Adam wasn't sure who fell asleep first. He woke sometime around seven in the morning, his back stiff and his legs asleep. Jenna's hand was limp in his, and her head lay heavy on his shoulder.

He watched her for a moment, studying the rise and fall of her chest and the way her hair fell over his arm. She was beautiful, even now with tear tracks smudging her cheeks and her hair matted to the side of her face.

She'd taken Gertie home sometime after midnight, insisting someone who'd broken a hip in the last year needed a good night's sleep in a bed instead of a hard plastic chair. Gertie had tried to argue, but Adam had seen the relief in her eyes, the way she winced as she stretched out her sore leg.

Aside from that short run home, Jenna hadn't left her seat all night. Neither had Adam, and his body ached from it.

His heart ached for other reasons.

Trying not to disturb Jenna, he pulled his phone from his pocket. No messages.

What had he expected, really? A text from Mia saying, *Just wanted you to know the guy I left you for is in good condition.*

Still, it would have been nice to hear something. He'd stirred briefly around 3:00 a.m. when there'd been a shift change in the nursing staff, but no one had come to talk to them. Did Mia know they were all out here waiting? Was Mark still in the ER, or had he been moved to surgery?

Adam lingered on that thought for a moment. In the three years since the divorce, he'd had plenty of unkind thoughts about Mark. What kind of man takes another man's wife? What kind of man swoops in when a relationship is in trouble, weaseling his way into the cracks of a broken marriage?

A man with faults. An imperfect man. A man who makes mistakes.

A man not unlike himself.

Part of him would always hate Mark. But right then, he said a small prayer the guy would pull through.

He felt Jenna stir and shoved his phone back in his pocket. She sat up, blinking in the harsh light of the fluorescent bulbs above. She turned to look at him, her eyes still blurry with sleep. "What time is it?"

"A little after seven."

"No word?"

"Nothing. Check your phone though, maybe she messaged you."

Jenna nodded, tucking her hair behind her ears as she bent down to rummage through her purse. She pulled out her phone and sat up, frowning at the screen. He watched her, trying to gauge her expression.

"Anything from Mia?"

"No." Jenna slid a finger across the screen, her frown deepening. "But there's an e-mail from Kendall Freemont in Human Resources."

"This early? What does it say?"

He watched her eyes move as she scanned the words. The color drained slowly from her face, and Adam felt his gut clench. "What is it?" he asked again.

"She's asking me to report to her office at eight-thirty this morning," Jenna said, moving her finger on the screen to scroll down.

"She says it's an urgent meeting regarding Belmont Health System's employee fraternization policy."

A chill snaked down his spine, and Adam forced himself to stay calm. "Is there anything else?"

Jenna nodded, her eyes wide and fearful as they met his. "Yes," she said. "It's addressed to both of us."

Chapter Sixteen

Jenna straightened her skirt, then straightened her spine and took a deep breath. She was five minutes early, but that was better than being on time or late, wasn't it?

She had no idea. She'd rushed home to shower, donning her best power suit and high heels that pinched her toes. That wasn't a bad thing. A little discomfort would keep her tough, make her strong enough to do what she had to do.

Her hand was shaking as she reached for the door of the conference room next to Kendall's office. She willed herself not to cry.

You're the Chief Relations Officer for a major medical center, she told herself. You worked hard to get here. You can handle this.

She took another deep breath and pushed the door open. Her eyes fell first on Kendall, who was seated primly with her hands folded on the desk in front of her. She wore a black jacket and cat-eye glasses that had slipped a little down her nose. Across from her was Adam, looking clean-shaven and stiff in a dark gray suit.

Beside him sat Mia.

She wore a dark blue maternity dress with her red hair pulled back in a severe chignon. She wasn't smiling.

"Mia," Jenna gasped. "What are you—how's Mark?"

Mia rested one hand on her belly and looked up. Her eyes were red, her expression unreadable. "He's going to make it," she said, her voice soft and sandpapery. "The bullet missed a major artery in his leg. He'll need a few months of physical therapy, but it could have been a lot worse."

"Oh, thank God." Jenna felt the tears starting, and willed herself not to let them fall. She'd been here less than ten seconds and she was already crying. Jesus, she'd never make it at this rate.

"Thank you for joining us," Kendall said, nodding from behind her desk. "Could you please close the door, Jenna?"

"Of course."

She pushed it shut, then turned to face the room. An empty chair sat between Adam and Mia, and she started toward it. Then she stopped. Clasping her hands in front of her to keep them from shaking, she forced herself to stand straight and tall.

"There's something I need to say."

Kendall glanced at Mia, then at Adam. "I'm not really sure it's necessary for you to—"

"No, I need to say it. In front of everyone—Mia, Adam, you." She swallowed, surprised to discover her voice was steadier than she expected it to be. She'd spent her whole career perfecting the art of polished presentation, but nothing inside her felt polished anymore. She felt raw and empty and completely unraveled. She took a steadying breath and lifted her chin.

"I'm sorry." She paused, feeling oddly fortified by that word, so she said it again. "I'm really very sorry. I know I've been cavalier with the company's policy on employee fraternization, and I know

I've conducted myself in a manner unbecoming to an executive of this organization. I understand if you need to penalize me for it, and I accept the consequences of my actions. But that's not what I'm most sorry for."

She took another breath and looked at Mia, willing herself not to fall apart. Not until everything was out on the table. "I'm sorry for any pain I caused you, either by dating your ex-husband, or by hiding that from you. I should have had more faith in the strength of our friendship and in your strength as a person."

Mia's eyes held hers, but they'd started to shimmer. It might have been a trick of light, but Jenna didn't think so. Behind the desk, Kendall opened her mouth to speak, but Jenna held up a hand.

"I'm not done. Please, just let me finish. Mia, I should have trusted you to know better than almost anyone that people can't always help who they fall in love with. They can't always control where it happens or whether it's an inconvenient time or an inconvenient person. But that doesn't make the love any less valuable or sacred or real." She cleared her throat, fighting the thickness that made her voice tight and shaky. She stole a glimpse at Adam, steeling herself to say what she needed.

"And the fact of the matter is that I love Adam," she said. "I love him for the man he is now, and I love him for the man he was when he belonged to you. I love him for who he'll become tomorrow, which may be a new variation of the same man. But it's one I'm prepared to appreciate no matter what."

It was getting harder to get the words out, and she was having a tough time seeing through the tears pooling in her eyes, but she commanded herself to turn and look at him. The force of his gaze locking with hers nearly sent her reeling backward, but it also gave her a fresh surge of power. She took another deep breath.

"Adam, I love you. In case I didn't make that clear just now."

He nodded. "I think I got it." He offered a small smile. "I love you, too."

"I'm going to screw up. A lot. I won't always handle things as well as I should, and sometimes I'll use the wrong words or the wrong coping mechanism or the wrong fork at dinner. But my heart's in the right place." She unclasped her hands. "It's with you."

He stood up, pushing the empty chair aside. Jenna didn't need any further encouragement. She stepped into his embrace and felt his arms wrap around her, felt herself sink into his heat and strength and safety. She closed her eyes, hoping like hell this wouldn't mean the end of her career or the end of her friendship.

Hoping, maybe, it could be the beginning of something new.

Behind them, Mia cleared her throat. "I feel like I'm supposed to applaud or something."

Jenna drew back, pushing her hair behind her ears. She smoothed her skirt and looked at Mia. "I'm sorry."

"Stop with the sorry," Mia said, shifting a little in her chair. "That shit gets old in a hurry. Just ask Adam, he'll tell you."

"Yep." Adam nodded and sat back down. "For once, I'll have to agree with my ex-wife."

"I'm making a note of that," Mia said, and picked up a stack of papers on the desk. "So the real reason I asked everyone to meet this morning was that I'm requesting a change to some corporate policy. Namely, the anti-fraternization rule."

Jenna blinked. "You requested a rule change?"

"I was actually planning to be circumspect about the reason for the request." She glanced at Kendall, then back at Jenna. "You kinda fucked that up just now with your little speech. Congratulations, by the way. And you're forgiven. Not that you need my forgiveness or my blessing."

Jenna blinked, too stunned to know how to reply. "I need both, actually."

"Then you've got it. Along with my well wishes for dealing with this bastard. You're going to need it." She smiled for real then, and Adam smiled, too, a private joke between them that somehow didn't leave Jenna feeling left out.

"So," Mia said. "The fraternization rule is bogus, and I'd like to suggest a revision, but since we've already got mountains of more important corporate policy to negotiate with the bargaining team, it seemed silly to bring this to the table. I thought this might be better handled within our core group. A group that already dealt with a personnel matter along the same lines just last week."

Kendall frowned, her cheeks reddening. "How did you know about—"

"Oh, please," Mia said, waving a dismissive hand. "Everyone knows Brett Lombard has been mailing photos of his junk to Susan Schrader for months. It's the worst kept relationship secret in the hospital."

Adam snorted and glanced at Jenna. "There's an honor I'm glad we didn't achieve."

"Nope, you were actually pretty damn good at hiding yours," Mia said, "which is the reason I hope we can make this policy change quietly and with as little fanfare as possible."

Kendall steepled her hands on the desk, and looked down at some papers in front of her. "I've reviewed the amendments you've suggested, Mia. I appreciate that you've taken into consideration our need to address supervisory relationships and situations where a legal conflict of interest might exist, but what you've spelled out here seems like a good starting point."

"Thank you," Mia said. "My stepfather is an attorney. I was on the phone with him at four o'clock this morning quizzing him about anti-harassment regulations and corporate law. It beat the hell out of thinking about gunshot wounds."

"I can imagine," Jenna said, still too stunned to come up with anything smarter. "I don't understand. Mia, you have every right to hate me right now."

"I choose not to exercise that right. Hating someone is kind of a pain in the ass, when you get right down to it."

Adam cocked his head to the side. "You know, all this agreeing with you is starting to freak me out a little."

"Don't get too smug about it, ex-husband of mine. There's actually another ex who gets the credit here."

Jenna winced. "Sean? God, I need to apologize to him."

"You do, and you will, because you're a good person," Mia said. "But I wasn't talking about Sean. I'm talking about Ellen."

"Ellen?" Jenna blinked. "Mark's ex-wife?"

Mia nodded and pressed a hand into her lower back, wincing a little as she rearranged herself on the hard plastic chair. "She brought Katie to the hospital in the middle of the night to see her father. The shooting was an accident. The cops said so, and Mark agreed. Ellen dropped her purse on the floor and forgot the gun was in there and the whole thing was just one of those stupid moments you watch happening in slow motion and wish like hell you could hit rewind and do it all differently." Mia shrugged. "I guess I can relate."

Jenna nodded, feeling the tears prick the backs of her eyes again. "Me, too."

"Anyway, Ellen and I got to talking," Mia said. "About regrets and apologies and hate and love and everything in between. We might have swapped recipes for banana bread—the details are a little hazy. But my point is that we connected. For the first time in three years, we saw each other as human beings instead of 'that bitch.'"

"Wow," Jenna said, reeling too hard to come up with anything beyond a single syllable.

Beside her Adam was shaking his head. "So you thanked her for shooting your husband, and she thanked you for stealing him, and then you hugged and made up?"

Mia choked out a laugh. "Hardly. But we don't hate each other anymore. That's progress. I've gotta say—it's the most free I've felt in a long time."

"Forgiveness will do that," Adam murmured.

Mia smiled. "And once more, the exes agree on something."

Behind her desk, Kendall cleared her throat. "I hate to rain on this lovely parade, but I believe there's still an issue on the table."

Jenna turned to face her and gave a grim nod. "Right. Uh—even if the fraternization rule changes, I assume there will be a penalty for my failure to follow an existing rule?"

Kendall opened her mouth to reply, but before she could say anything, Mia interrupted.

"The lawyer in the room can correct me if I'm wrong here, but if a company fails to enforce a rule with one employee and then punishes another employee for a similar violation, wouldn't that second employee have a valid case for legal recourse?"

Adam blinked. "You're referring to Brett and Susan again?"

"Exactly."

"Legally, yes. That second employee would have a case."

"See?" Mia beamed at Kendall. "Looks like I got something from my years of marriage to a workaholic attorney."

Kendall pressed her lips together. "Perhaps it would be best if we all stop talking about penalties and litigiousness and focus on moving forward in a positive fashion."

"My thoughts exactly." Mia smiled and turned back to Adam and Jenna. "So the policy I'm suggesting is commonly known as a

'Love Contract.' If a couple employed in the same workplace initiates a consensual relationship, they'll be provided with documentation on the company's sexual harassment policy. They'll also be briefed on regulations concerning public displays of affection and retaliation in the event of a terminated relationship. After all the paper shuffling, they'll get a contract to sign indicating they're aware of the rules and promise to abide by them."

Adam leaned forward, adjusting his tie. "I assume they'll have the right to consult with an attorney before signing?"

"Of course," Kendall said. She pushed her glasses up her nose and lifted her chin. "The company I worked for prior to Belmont had an informed consent policy similar to this one. Obviously, this sort of policy requires some very specific language about job performance expectations and the impact of a relationship on the work environment, but I've seen similar systems work quite nicely in a corporate setting."

"Okay then," Mia said, turning back to Adam. "You're a lawyer, and you obviously have a vested interest in creating a positive work environment at Belmont. Do you want to be involved in crafting the new policy?"

He nodded, turning to look at Jenna. She felt a flash of heat arc through her as his eyes held hers.

"I do," he murmured.

"And Jenna," Mia said shifting again in her chair. "Would you be comfortable with this sort of clause in the company's policy? Hypothetically speaking, of course, if Adam were to remain attached to Belmont, do you think you'd be willing to sign a document like this?"

Jenna slid her eyes from Adam's to her best friend's and back again to his. She nodded. "I do."

"Well all-righty then," Mia said, whacking the paperwork on the desk with finality. "By the power vested in me by—well, myself—I now pronounce us a policy revision committee. You may *not* kiss the co-worker. Not now, anyway."

"Of course," Jenna said, her cheeks warming. "Even if PDA weren't a factor, I wouldn't dream of disrespecting you by—"

"No, no—that's not it at all," Mia said, shifting in her seat again. "You can disrespect me all you want. I kinda like it sometimes, especially if there's spanking involved."

Adam grimaced. "That I didn't need to know."

"Whatever, lawyer boy. You're just jealous I never asked you to smack my ass."

Kendall frowned. "Could we please refrain from—"

"I'll tell you what I need everyone to refrain from doing," Mia interrupted, turning to Jenna. "Talking. About anything. Because you know all that shit we were saying about my water breaking at dinner?"

Jenna frowned. "What?"

"I think it just happened. Either that, or I peed myself in the Human Resources office, which wouldn't be the first time, now that I think about it. So can one of you help me get to the Family Birthing Center? I'd rather not have this baby on a conference table."

"She's beautiful," Adam said.

He watched as his ex-wife looked up and smiled, her red hair tangled and lovely as she cradled the infant tightly in her arms. "Thank you."

Beside her, Mark leaned forward in his wheelchair and stroked a finger over the baby's clenched fist. She stirred, offering up a sleepy, sucking noise that made Mark grin and made Adam remember again that he might not hate the guy after all.

"Would you look at that?" Mark murmured. "Knows her daddy already."

"Smart girl," Jenna said, and Adam watched Mia's gaze slide to her best friend's. The two women exchanged some sort of unspoken communication, and Adam held his breath, not wanting to break the connection.

"Smart, and very lucky," Jenna murmured. "To have the two of you as parents. And Katie as a big sister."

"You got that right." Katie grinned and bent down to plant a kiss on the baby's forehead. Then she drew back and looked shyly at Mia. "Want me to run to the cafeteria and grab one of those Snickerdoodles you like?"

Adam watched as Mia's eyes widened a little with surprise and pleasure. Then a smile broke over her face. "That would be amazing. Grab my name badge out of my purse so you can just charge it to my account. Get one for yourself, too."

"Okay." Katie kissed the baby again, then scampered away. "I love you, baby sister," she called. "And daddy. And Mia."

"I love you, too," Mia murmured as Katie bounded out of the room.

Adam slid an arm around Jenna's shoulders, not sure if it was the right thing to do just then, but knowing it felt good. Sometimes, that was enough. She responded by leaning against him, fitting into the curve of his chest like she belonged there. Like she'd always belonged there.

Mia smiled at Mark over the top of the baby's pink knitted cap. "I'm so glad they let you out of the recovery unit for this. It meant a lot having you here for this."

"You kidding me?" Mark smiled. "I could have had bullet holes in both legs and arms and I still would have found a way to crawl down to the birthing center to be here for this. Wouldn't have missed it for the world."

"I'm happy you were able to do it without all the extra bullet holes," Mia said.

Mark nodded, glancing quickly at Adam and Jenna before leaning forward to touch his wife's arm. "Look, Mia—I'm sorry about everything. I know I haven't been there for you like I should be these last couple weeks. I've been torn up thinking about how I let Katie down, how I'm not able to be the father I always thought I'd be. But I need to be a good husband, too. I'm going to do better. For you, for Katie, for little Lola here—for all of us."

"Me, too," Mia whispered, her eyes shimmering. "I'm going to do better, too."

Adam felt Jenna squeeze his hand as Mark leaned forward to kiss his wife.

His wife. Adam repeated the words in his head, and they felt right this time. They fit. He squeezed Jenna's hand in return and leaned down to murmur in her ear. "Think we should give them some time alone?"

"I heard that," Mia said, looking up. "No, I want you two here. I need to say something before Katie comes back or my parents show up and start making a bunch of noise."

Adam quirked an eyebrow. "Is this the season for heartfelt relationship speeches or something?"

"Shut up, Adam," she said, but her voice had no venom. "I just want to say that I'm happy to have you here. Both of you. All of you." She smiled at Mark, then looked back at Adam and Jenna. "I know things have been weird this past month, and I'm not pretending they won't be pretty damn weird in the future."

Jenna nodded, her hair brushing the hollow beneath Adam's chin as she moved. "I think we can pretty much guarantee the weirdness."

"It's the nature of modern relationships," Mia said. "We're all a little fucked up, but there's also a lot of love to go around."

"I think I saw that on a Hallmark card," Adam said, sliding a hand up Jenna's arm.

Mia smiled. "The nurses and administrators and union reps might squabble like siblings, but they'll figure it out. And a few people might balk at the Chief Relations Officer having an erotica-writing aunt, but that's all just noise. It's the stuff that keeps life from getting boring, but it's not the stuff that matters. Not really."

Adam watched his ex-wife's gaze drop to her new daughter's face. She stroked a finger over the baby's cheek, her eyes soft and filled with feeling. She looked lovely and serene and more at peace than Adam had ever seen her.

I never made her look like that, he thought, only this time, it didn't make him bitter.

He pulled Jenna tighter against his chest, and she turned to smile up at him. "What are you thinking?" she whispered.

"About birth. Rebirth. Fresh starts. The chance to get it right on the next go-round."

She grinned, and he was hit by an overwhelming urge to kiss her. "That's pretty deep," she said. "I was just thinking I want a donut."

"I'll get all the donuts you want. Donuts for life." He planted a kiss on her forehead, knowing there'd be plenty of time later to claim her lips and all the rest of her.

A rustling in the hall made them all turn toward the doorway. Aunt Gertie bustled in, her white hair flying as she clasped her hands together and looked down at Mia and the baby.

"Oh my word! What an absolute doll. Isn't she just precious?"

"Thank you," Mia said, beaming. "Her name is Lola Jane. Would you like to hold her?"

"Of course," Gertie said, shuffling into the room as she slung a heavy-looking bag from her shoulder. "Actually, I brought something for her. It's a book I've been working on. I was hoping maybe I could read it to her as her first bedtime story."

Adam felt Jenna stiffen in his arms. He tightened his hold on her hoping she wasn't planning to lunge. "Uh, Gert?" she said. "I'm not sure the *Panty Dropper* series is really the best thing for an infant."

"Oh, pish," Gertie said, waving a hand as she settled into the rocking chair at Mia's bedside. "There's nothing wrong with a little erotica, but that's not what I've been writing. Not this time anyway."

Gert set her bag down and began to rummage through it. Mia peered over the edge of her hospital bed, shifting the baby in her arms. "What is it, Gertie?"

"It's a children's book," Gertie said, straightening up with a square cardboard book in her hands. "It's a story about love and families and how they're all different. Sometimes mommies and daddies live in different places, or sometimes there's more than one mommy or brothers and sisters with different parents. There are all kinds of combinations, and they're all beautiful."

Mark leaned forward, peering at the pages as Gert spread the book open. "Are those spiders?"

"Yes, they are." Gertie grinned. "The book is called *A Lovely Tangled Mess*."

Jenna snuggled back in Adam's arms, and he held her against him, resting his chin on her head. He felt the steady rhythm of her breathing, and matched his own breath with hers as the warmth spread between them.

"I'd love to hear it," Jenna said. "Start at the beginning."

Acknowledgments

I've seen authors use the term "the book of my heart," but didn't fully grasp the meaning of that until I wrote this one. For everyone who made it possible, I owe you endless gratitude, hugs, and awkward butt squeezes.

Big thanks to Michelle Wolfson for believing in me long before you had a good reason to, and for being my friend and safety net well beyond the realm of most literary agents. I can't imagine navigating these waters without you.

Thank you to Helen Cattaneo at Montlake for falling in love with this story before I fully knew where it was headed, and for trusting me to take it the direction it needed to go. I'm also grateful to Krista Stoever for pointing me back on track when I veered off course, and for whipping this bad boy into shape. Kudos as well to Irene Billings for shepherding me to the finish line with enthusiasm, professionalism, and panache. Thanks to Kelli Martin, Anh Schluep, Scott Calamar, and everyone else at Montlake for your amazing work on publicity, cover copy, artwork, and the million other things you do behind the scenes. You guys are rock stars.

As always, my amazing critique partners and beta readers are responsible for reducing the number of readers tempted to hurl my books at the wall. I'm deeply grateful to Bridget McGinn, Minta Powelson, Linda Grimes, Cynthia Reese, and Larie Borden. You bitches rule.

Thank you to Jenna McCarthy, Julie Klingman Rector, and Meah Cukrov for the names, and to Dr. Ashley Hampton for the guns. That sounds like an awesome setup for a bank heist. Endless thanks to Donna "Hot Lips" Libolt for inspiring elements of Aunt Gertie, and to Tamara Zagurski for the beautiful bits and pieces of Shelly. I also lift a big glass of Sangiovese to Margaret Kolata for the job title.

So many friends, colleagues, and family members propped me up and mopped me off during the divorce that would eventually become one of the catalysts for this story, and there aren't enough pages in this book to properly express my appreciation to all of you. Nevertheless, thank you to Lindsay Allen Landgraf, Larie Borden, Aaron Sallee, Linda Brundage, Dan & Gina Streck, Aislin Goldrick, Mary "Harley May" Jones, Jessica Corra Larter, Jeffe Kennedy, Stephanie Anderson Stroup, Claudine Birgy, Adam & Laura Fenske, JJ Shew, Sheri Abbott, Cherri Miller, Cathy Staley, Dianne Capozzola, Diane Kirpach, Karen Tippets, Nancy Zurflu, Katy Elliot, Bethany Powers Flint, Lynnette Braillard, and Valerie Warren. I couldn't have gotten through the muck without you.

Though my parents, Dixie and David Fenske, deserve a starring role in that last paragraph, they kinda require their own paragraph for all the love, support, and cheerleading not only in my darkest times, but in my brightest ones, too. I owe everything to you guys, and I'm so lucky and proud to be your kid.

Thanks also to Aaron and Carlie Fenske for being a kick-ass part of my support system and family.

Cedar and Violet—I never expected my life to include kids without four legs and fur, but thank you for giving me reasons every single day to tell people I won the stepkid lottery. I love you guys.

Most of all, thank you to my husband, Craig Zagurski, for making it possible for me to write a story about finding amazing love in the aftermath of failed relationships. You are my rock, my muse, my daily source of laughter, and the one who makes my heart (and other stuff) throb with joy. Love you, baby.

About the Author

Photo © 2013 Craig Zagurski

Tawna Fenske is a romantic comedy author who writes humorous fiction, risqué romance, and heartwarming love stories with a quirky twist. Her offbeat brand of romance has been praised by Booklist as "A tame Carl Hiaasen on cupid juice," and *RT Book Reviews* nominated her debut novel for contemporary romance of the year. Tawna is a fourth-generation Oregonian who can peel a banana with her toes and who loses an average of twenty pairs of eyeglasses per year. She lives in Bend, Oregon, with her husband, stepkids, and a menagerie of ill-behaved pets.

To learn more about all of Tawna's books, visit www.tawnafenske.com/books